as far as you can go

as far as you can go

LESLEY GLAISTER

BLOOMSBURY

First published in Great Britain in 2004

This paperback edition published 2005

Copyright © 2004 by Lesley Glaister

The moral right of the author has been asserted

Bloomsbury Publishing Plc, 38 Soho Square, London W1D 3HB

A CIP catalogue record for this book
is available from the British Library

ISBN 0 7475 7468 5

10 9 8 7 6 5 4 3 2 1

Typeset by Hewer Text Ltd, Edinburgh
Printed in Great Britain by Clays Ltd, St Ives plc

All papers used by Bloomsbury Publishing are natural,
recyclable products made from wood grown in
well-managed forests. The manufacturing processes conform
to the environmental regulations of the country of origin

www.lesleyglaister.com

For

Hilary Mantel

GREAT OPPORTUNITY FOR THE RIGHT APPLICANTS

Western Australia. Housekeeper/companions required. Would suit young couple. Remote, rural location. Cooking, cleaning, gardening and caring duties. Applicants must be self-sufficient and resourceful. Applications by 3rd August to Mr L. DRAKE c/o Cavendish Hotel, Kensington Rise, LONDON W11 7AX.

One

The lift is lined with mirrors, with many Cassies. She can see a back view of herself, a queue of back views receding deep into the bleary yellow-tinged glass, each one with the same amateurish French pleat. She licks her fingers and tries to smooth the wisps back. She pulls out a lipstick and does her lips. She does want to be *plausible*.

Room 302 is round the corner from the lift. A cart full of folded sheets and towels, sachets of coffee and shampoo waits in the corridor and from the open door of the room next door comes the dreary whine of a vacuum cleaner banging against skirting boards. She knocks on the door, the weak sound of her knuckles disappearing into dark wood. Whoever was vacuuming bursts into 'I Will Survive', triumphantly out of tune.

She waits and knocks again, harder. The numbers 302 are made of some metal, maybe brass, the 2 skew-whiff. The door opens. The man is small with a grey, pointy beard. His wiry eyebrows are winged upwards, maybe that's what makes him seem surprised. He's wearing a black polo-necked sweater and his hair is a luxuriant, not far off bouffant, silver.

'Cassandra? Larry Drake. Delighted to meet you.' His hand as it takes hers is small and soft. He looks behind her.

'Graham wasn't well enough to travel, I'm afraid,' she says. 'Flu. He's really sorry.'

He pauses. 'A shame. No matter. Hold on.' He leans past her to hook a 'Do Not Disturb' notice on the door-handle. 'Come in, shall I order coffee?'

'No, but thanks.'

He gestures her into the room, a room dominated by a huge bed. Wouldn't the lobby have been better? she thinks. Seems very odd to be squeezing round a bed with a complete stranger.

'Please, do sit down.'

Two chairs have been arranged beside the window where the sunlight struggles in through a swathe of net. On the bed, amongst a scatter of papers, she can see her letter of application, written one morning when Graham was still asleep. She'd gone out, got the paper, read it, seen the ad, written the letter, gone out again and posted it. And all before he'd even opened his eyes.

'Can I offer you a drink?' Larry says.

'No thanks.' Or is it rude to refuse? 'Maybe some water,' she says, '*please.*'

He takes a Perrier from the mini-bar and hands it to her with a glass.

'Do you not drink alcohol?'

'Not at eleven in the morning!'

He regards her for a moment. 'Mind if I do?'

She blushes. 'Course not!'

He tips a miniature Scotch into a glass and sits down. They are close, knees only inches apart. There should be a desk or something between them. She feels exposed. Her knees vulnerable in the sheer biscuit-coloured tights. Should have worn trousers. Should have been *herself.*

His nails are sharp and pearly and chink against his glass. He gazes at her for a moment, saying nothing. Cassie makes herself gaze back. His face is carefully shaved, a thin moustache like a strip of pipe cleaner, a little stripe of beard between his lower lip and the grey point on his chin. It must be more trouble than ordinary shaving. Almost like topiary. His eyebrows make him

4

look devilish with the wiry licks at the ends. The skin beside the grey whiskers is tanned like fine leather, lightly creased.

'Well then,' he says at last, 'tell me why you'd like the job. You and Graham.'

Cassie clears her throat. 'Well, we feel – Graham and I – we both feel like we want to do something else.'

He leans back in his chair and crosses his ankles. 'Ah, I see. An adventure?'

'Yes. Sort of. Exactly.'

'Life a bit dull, eh?'

'No, no, we just thought we'd like a change. Patsy, my twin sister, she's had a baby and I want to do something. Before I do. Have a baby, I mean.'

Larry nods. 'Well then, tell me about yourself.'

Cassie takes a breath and goes though the list: school, degree, jobs. He listens politely. 'Thank you,' he says. 'Now tell me about *you*.'

'Me?'

'The *relevant* you.'

'Relevant!' Cassie tries to think of something witty, can't, the wait goes on too long. She blushes again, tries to laugh. 'Not much to say.' So *lame*. The right applicant will not be *lame*. She remembers her water and takes a prickly sip.

He makes a small impatient sound, looks at his watch. That's that then, she thinks.

'For example,' he says, 'what do you like to do?'

'Well, I love gardening. That's actually what caught my eye in your advert. I teach it.'

'Yes?'

'Organic gardening – adult education.'

'Ah.'

'And I thought it might make an interesting module – you know gardening in another climate. What's the climate like in Western Australia?'

'Hot. We're right on the tropic of Capricorn, fringes of the desert.'

'Desert,' she repeats with relish. 'I was reading something about that, about desert reclamation, the use of mulches –'

He laughs. 'Well you'd be very welcome to experiment. I'm sure the garden would flourish.'

'What do you grow?'

'Oh,' he waves his hand, 'tomatoes and so on. Now, what else do you have to recommend you?'

'Just the usual things,' she says, 'cooking I enjoy. Dressmaking and mending things. I really enjoy *decorating*, strange as that may seem.' She pauses, notices a pink smudge of lipstick on the rim of her glass. 'But gardening and cooking are what I like best. Ideally combining the two, growing things and then cooking them –'

'A useful person *indeed*,' he says. 'Now, tell me about Graham.'

She looks down at the bubbles streaming to the surface of her water. 'As I said in my letter, he's a painter.' He waits for more but her mind goes blank. 'He plays the harmonica a bit sometimes, but not in public,' she says.

'You probably have questions,' Larry says, withdrawing himself a little, taking another sip of Scotch. 'The advertisement was anything but explicit. Deliberately so, in order not to – cut off avenues prematurely. You see?'

She wonders how old he is. The white hair made him seem quite old at first but the way he moves is young – the way he speaks – you can't tell. There's something pleasantly reptilian about him, a grain of gold in his skin. If he took off his shirt you wouldn't be surprised to find a pattern there, like lizard skin. She blinks, startled by the thought.

'Well –?'

'What would we actually do?' she says. 'On a daily basis, I mean.'

'What would you expect to do?'

'I'm not sure – housekeeping and so on?'

'Yes. Certainly that. Mara, my wife, she is not – let us say not entirely "well". She needs help with –' the corner of his lip twitches, 'housekeeping, yes, but she also needs companionship. I'm away sometimes, and,' he stretches out his arms, 'as you see, the place we live – Woolagong Station – it's somewhat . . . remote.'

'Station?'

'Was a sheep station, half a million acres, but it's no longer worked.'

'Half a *million* acres?'

'Farms – what you would call farms – are much bigger there. A different scale entirely.'

'How far is Woolagong from – say, Perth?' she asks.

'A long way. What drew me to your application, Cassandra –'

'Most people call me Cassie.'

'Cassie. Charming. Well, do call me Larry. What interested me – us – was that Graham paints. You see Mara – well, she has painted in the past, she was good. I think it would benefit her to have the company of another painter. Would Graham be prepared to encourage her, do you think?'

'Definitely.'

'And is he handy too? There might be some maintenance work involved.'

'Well, I'm "handier" than him actually. He's more the, you know, "artist".'

He raises his flying eyebrows. 'Do you happen to have a photograph of him?'

Cassie takes her purse out of her bag and hands him a photo. Graham on the beach, bare tanned torso, his long black hair tied back from his face, so that it *could* look short. It gives her a pang to see it, him suddenly there in the room, as she lines up her ultimatum. It might be the end of them. She swallows.

Larry glances at the photo, nods and hands it back without comment. 'Are there any medical conditions I should know about? Either of you on any prescription drugs?'

'No.'

'Any psychological problems?'

She frowns.

'You see, Woolagong is quite remote. The couple I appoint, they must be – how shall I say? Quite stable and robust.' Larry laces his fingers together, bends them back till the knuckles click. 'I'd be taking a risk, without meeting Graham. How would you describe him?'

She looks down at the photo. 'He's – it's difficult to describe someone, isn't it? He's artistic, he's not *that* domestic to be honest. He's good company, very you know, *popular*.' She presses her lips together, wondering what sort of popular he's being at this very moment. 'He's robust and –' she crosses her fingers in her lap, 'stable. We both are.'

Larry smiles. 'I must say you sound perfect.'

'Do we?' She feels a little spurt of pride and pleasure.

'If you were to be offered the positions I'd need full medical reports – blood groups and so on.'

'Of course.'

'And when would you be available to begin?'

'Whenever you like.'

'Good, good.' He smiles. 'If we said early October? That would be better for you – spring. You'd acclimatise better. So.' He puts his glass down. 'How does it sound? Housekeeping, gardening, companionship – some artistic input from Graham, who would, of course, be free to pursue his own interests in that direction. In fact, that in itself would be an encouragement for Mara. And the rest of the time your own. Perhaps, with your organic methods, you could reclaim the desert!' His face creases into a full-on smile.

Cassie smiles back. Is he offering them the job? 'I expect you've got others to see?'

'No other *painter* has applied,' he says. 'And you seem very,' he pauses, searching in a leisurely way for the right word, '*suitable*. In every possible way. As for remuneration, I'd pay your expenses – quite considerable, incidentally – and your keep would be, of course, entirely gratis. And if you complete a year with us, that is a full twelve calendar months, you'll receive 25,000 Australian dollars.'

'Twenty-five thousand dollars!'

'*Australian* dollars.'

'That's still good, isn't it?'

'Yes. But I must stress that this is payable only as a whole sum at the end of the twelve months. If one or both of you decide to leave us before the year is up, well, there would be no pro-rata offer. It's all or nothing.'

'Fair enough.'

'Don't decide now. Think it over. Discuss it with Graham.'

'Is this – I mean, are you actually offering us the job?'

He smiles. 'I have prepared a small display, to give you an idea of what to expect. Or perhaps to tempt you.' He indicates a slide projector on the bedside table.

*

Opposite Cassie is a woman, fast asleep, her mouth gaping open to show a full house of dark grey fillings. Cassie looks away and tries to drink her cardboard cup of tea, but it's too scalding hot. She takes out her phone. There's a message from Patsy, of course, asking her how it went. She rings her back.

'So?' Patsy says.

'It all seems great.'

'So you'll go?'

'Don't know.' She looks down at the photo Larry gave her. Low tin-roofed buildings against blue sky, red dirt, hens, wind pump, gum tree, dog slinking away in the distance. The shadow of the photographer sharp in the dirt. Woolagong Station. 'It looks great, *really* great but –'

'Depends on Graham?'

'Mmmm. I don't know *what* he'll say. You just can't tell, with him.'

'A *year*. We've never been apart so long – or so far apart.'

'If only *you* could come.'

'Some hope.' Patsy laughs. Cassie can hear baby Katie grumbling in her arms.

'Hi Katie,' Cassie says. 'Oh, do you *really* think it'll work?'

'Worth a try,' Patsy says. 'Though I still don't get it. *Graham?* When there's so many other – I much preferred Rod.'

'*Don't* Pats. Listen, I'll ring you when I get home.'

Cassie gazes at the photo. After the interview, Larry had drawn the curtains and shone a glorious light-show on them: red rocks and gleaming ice-white trees, vivid green, water so blue it had made her blink, all rumpled against the curtain folds, everything warped and oddly shadowed but still. Weird to be in a darkened room with an almost stranger watching images of a distant land. Maybe a bit foolish. He could have been anyone, done anything. But he was fine, practically, she smiles at the old-fashioned expression that comes to her, a *gentleman*. Still, it had felt oddly intimate, the dimness and the soft hum of the projector, dust specks dancing in the wedge of coloured light.

'You will be welcomed by flowers that time of year,' he'd said and showed her a meadow, you could only call it that: acres of blue, yellow, sparks of red amongst the green. He had told her how the dust comes to life in spring, how magical it is, what a relief to thirsty eyes, the colour and the rising sap. What a miracle in the – almost – desert.

She would love to see it for herself. But it might not happen. Tonight might be the end. She hugs herself miserably. It could all backfire on her. Graham might tell her to get stuffed. But she has to try it. She attempts to drink her tea but the train lurches and it spills, splashes on the photo. She picks it up and shakes the drips away. The woman wakes, closes her mouth, makes a fussy pecking sound.

'How long's the flight?' she'd asked, when the slide-show was finished, the curtains opened.

'About twenty hours.'

'God,' she'd said. 'So *far*.'

'About as far as you can go,' Larry had replied, 'before you come back up the other side.'

Two

Graham yawns, watches Jas grind out the wet end of the spliff. She lies down again. Sunlight through the window scatters glitters on the ceiling, reflecting off the tiny mirrors on her bedspread. Like underwater, he thinks. She nuzzles her head under his chin, spiky hair tickling his nose so he has to smooth it down. He puts his arms round her. Tiny thing, like a fish in his arms, her little bones.

'Nice,' she murmurs into his chest. 'Welcome back.'

He sighs.

'What's up?'

'Nothing.'

She pulls back, squints at him. 'It's Cassie, isn't it? Isn't it?'

He looks at her, puzzled. Of course it's Cassie. What does she think? She glares at him and pulls abruptly away, curls her back against him, the vertebrae standing out like knuckles under her tawny skin. He runs his finger down them.

'Don't.'

He hauls himself up. Sits back against the wall where she's tacked a length of purple velvet. The whole room is mirrors and ethnic stuff, the smell of patchouli and Christ knows.

'Where is she?' Jas's voice is muffled.

'Dunno,' he says, 'London.'

'Why are you here?' Jas demands. She sits up suddenly and

runs her fingers through her hair. Short, sticky, hennaed hair. Tiny tits. Just peaked nipples on her ribcage really. He thinks of Cassie's soft white breasts and shakes his head.

'Well, you'll have to go soon, I'm going out.' She looks at him a minute, as if waiting for him to ask her not to but he says nothing. She gets up. Pulls on a pair of tatty purple knickers, embroidered jeans, a long sweater.

He pulls himself together. The grass has slowed his mind. Shouldn't do it, gives him weird dreams, makes him do weird things. Cassie doesn't smoke and he doesn't much either when with her, she's good for him that way.

'Are you upset?' he says.

She hunches towards a mirror, putting stuff round her eyes.

'I would just like to know what the hell you're playing at. What was that all about?' She gestures at the bed.

He shakes his head and the room sways, a second behind. Sex, of course. What does she thinks it was about? She turns and puts her hands on her hips. One eye darkened, the other not. Her funny squinty brown eyes funnier than ever.

A laugh comes out.

'What are you laughing at?'

He shrugs. 'I dunno, Jas. Cup of tea?'

'Get it yourself. I'm going out.'

'Where?'

'None of your business.' She storms about, collecting things and stuffing them in a bag. He marvels at her energy, she's almost a blur of movement if you half shut your eyes and filter her through your lashes. She gives an exasperated sigh, stops, flumps down on the bed and takes his hand. He looks down at the small brown paw, nails bitten to the quick, silver rings on every finger and thumb. At least one of these he will have given her, way back when they were together. She looks into his eyes again, eyebrows oddly black with her hair so red.

'So, you still serious about her?' She does not look into his eyes.

'Did I ever say I wasn't?'

'So why are you here?'

He frowns. The question tires him.

'Why?' she insists.

'Because I am.'

She snorts, stands up again. 'Sorry, Graham. That's not good enough any more.'

'Because,' his mind scrambles sluggishly. 'Because we're mates – you invited me. What do you mean?'

She gathers up some pencils from the floor.

'What *was* that all about? Kissing me, making love to me –'

'Didn't hear any complaints.'

She presses her lips together, runs her fingers through her hair, making it stick up in crazy spikes. 'No,' she says in a low voice, 'you're very good, I'll give you that. But I sort of thought maybe things weren't going well with Cassie, maybe that's why you were here –'

'No it's fine.'

'So if it's fine –?' She gestures at the bed again. He shrugs again.

'Ha!' She shakes her head in a sort of triumph. 'Do you know, I pity her.'

'*What?*' He starts to feel pressure. Does not need pressure. Can't take it.

'Does she know you're here?'

'What do you think?'

'Do you want her? Do you,' she hesitates, gulps as if swallowing something too big, 'are you still in love with her?'

'Guess so.'

She narrows her eyes at him. 'Then what the – Dickens are you doing here? Get out of my bed.'

He stares up at her. *Dickens?*

'Get out!' She points at the door.

'OK, OK.' He shifts about a bit, glances at the little clock by the bed. The bus doesn't go for a couple of hours.

'I'm going to my studio,' she says, giving up on him. 'When I get back please be gone.' She shrugs on a shaggy purple coat that doubles her size and slings her bag over her shoulder.

'Jas,' he says, as she makes for the door.

She stops, turns. 'What?'

'You've forgotten one of your eyes.'

She snorts, opens her mouth to speak, shuts it again. She grins unwillingly, goes back to the mirror to complete her make-up.

'OK?'

'Fantastic.'

She leaves, slamming the door, making her mobiles rattle.

He listens to her feet clattering down three flights of stairs and the front door banging and then lies down again, stretches between the cooling sheets. *Are you in love with her?* she'd said. And he tests the idea, prodding at it to see if it's alive. Yes, it is, he *is*. He ponders this, watching the mirror reflections on the ceiling, listening to the fidget of the mobiles. Maybe Jas has a point then. Why *is* he here?

Because why not? is the only thing that comes to him. Cassie doesn't like it but she's number one and she knows that. Jas knows that. He hardly ever actually *lies*.

He remembers how, soon as he saw Cassie, he'd had to have her, and how new that had felt. He'd had so many others: one-night stands, holiday flings, a couple of serious lovers, Jas on and off for years since college. He just loved women, talking to them, being among their stuff, getting intimate with them – not necessarily sexually, not always, sometimes it was just good enough to hear their secrets. Sometimes he almost wished he was a woman, though he wouldn't be able to fuck them then so that wouldn't work. But when he first saw Cassie it was different. Something happened. Not in his heart so much as in his guts, his bones. If he hadn't managed to *get* her he would have been changed anyway. Never even thought of settling before. Settling for one person or one life. Why should he? Settle. The word rubs him up the wrong way, makes him itch.

He'd been at college, teaching. An afternoon life-class. Cold afternoon, maybe May. Petals from a flowering cherry had blown and stuck themselves to the wet window. The model was a burly guy, so hairy that some of the efforts were looking like bears. The students had been hard at it, holding up pencils, framing with their angled fingers and thumbs, sketching away. The air had been charged with concentration, the rub of charcoal, breaths held. And she'd come barging though the double doors, looked at the model, flushed, said, 'Whoops!' and disappeared again leaving him with a dazed impression of pink and gold; neat blue denim arse.

He'd shaken his head, made some crack, but after the class he'd packed up quickly, shooing the students out instead of hanging about to gas as usual. He'd gone to the entrance and there she was, talking to someone in a leather jacket and he'd felt something, Christ, he had almost felt *jealous*. He'd approached, heard her laugh and say, 'Next week then.' The guy she'd been talking to walked off. She'd looked at her watch and looped a strand of hair behind her ear. A milky opal stud had gleamed at him from her ear lobe.

'Hi,' he'd said.

She turned. 'Hi? Oh, sorry about that. Was looking for AR2 – but do they have numbers on the doors?' She pulled a face.

'Yes they do,' he said.

'Oh!' She grinned. 'Well I didn't see.' She'd wrinkled her nose and that was when the something happened in his bones. There was a gap between her front teeth that made her look kind of goofy. Her skin was dappled gold, only freckles but they were like sunspots shimmering through clear water. He shook himself.

'No sweat,' he said. 'You teach here?'

'Started today.'

'Art?'

'Organic Gardening. New class – if I can get it off the ground. Ha ha. Hope I didn't embarrass the model!' Her lips were so pink he wanted to ask her, is that real? It looked like the surface of natural skin but very pink. He wanted to put his finger out and touch – see if it smudged.

'I'm Graham,' he said.

'Cassie.'

Cassie. He liked that. Suited her. Maybe it was just the whiteness of her teeth that made her lips look quite so pink. He realised he was staring at her mouth and looked away, down at the swell of breast inside her shirt.

'Well, see you then,' she'd said and grinned, walked off, fringed bag bumping on her hip, blonde hair halfway down her back. Christ. He even liked the way she *walked*. He'd hung about for a minute then followed her out into a scattery rain. But she'd gone. He'd realised he hadn't noticed her eyes. Usually the first thing to get him. But he'd known they would be blue. They must be, to go with that pink and white and gold.

He turns over, rubs his face in Jas's patchouli-smelling pillow. He's never seen her mad before. She's so unlike Cassie. Not beautiful. But very alive and sharp – almost feral with her squinty brown eyes, black eyebrows and sticky reddish hair. She's started looking older, lines round her eyes when she screws them up against the smoke. But looking older suits her. He's known her twenty years, since art school. She knows his parents, he knows hers, been in her childhood bedroom with the old scribble-faced dolls her mum won't throw away. And now she's turned him out. Jas! But she's his *mate*. His oldest mate. And he didn't exactly drag her into bed. He's never pretended anything is any different from how it is.

Cassie said he had to get his act together. *You're thirty-six,* she said. *It's time to grow up*. That was last night and he wonders now if *that* is why he's here. But now Jas is at it too. He groans, hugs a pillow. He ought to leave Cassie. She's so unlike anyone before. She's a proper person with a cottage and a cat. A *routine*. She gardens and cooks and has a more-or-less regular job. And soon, he knows it's looming, soon she'll want a kid. That has never been on his agenda.

Last time she'd said it he'd headed for the hills, or gone off and slept on a few floors anyway, but he couldn't get her out of his mind. Her skin; the way he felt when she took him in her arms; her eyes – He gets up, goes to the window, draws the curtains back, stands, naked, looking at the sunny street, a sycamore tree, leaves just turning yellow; the dusty tops of cars, the crowns of a couple of heads moving below him. A kid. Well, maybe. A little girl like Cassie to ride round on his shoulders. That could be cool.

It had bugged him after their first meeting that he hadn't noticed her eyes. He'd thought about her all that week, deciding what to say. No chat-up lines, no small talk. He planned to go straight up to her and say something like, 'I think you're gorgeous. Are you single? And even if you're not, will you meet me for a drink?' And if she blew him out? It was a risk worth taking. How often does that happen? That certainty, just from the look of a woman, the way she walks, the way she tucks her hair behind her ear.

But she hadn't shown up for the next few weeks. He'd told Jas – they'd split up by then – about her. When he'd described her, Jas had groaned. 'Not long blonde hair? God, Graham, what else? No, let me guess. Legs to here?' she'd pointed to her armpits, 'and eyes like what, like fucking *cornflowers*? Can't you give it a rest? It won't drop off, you know.'

Weeks later when he'd almost got over her, almost convinced himself she couldn't have been as great as all that, she'd walked past the art-room window and mid-sentence he'd dashed out of the room and called, 'Cassie!'

She'd turned, puzzlement on her face giving way to recognition. 'Yeah? Oh hi.'

He'd walked straight up and looked her in the eyes. 'Grey-green,' he'd said, surprised.

'Sorry?'

And that was the start of it. He pads into Jas's shower, tiny cubicle off the bedroom, cluttered with plastic bottles, splashed with henna stains, hairs snarled in the plughole. Cassie would go mental if she could see. Or if her bathroom looked like that. For the first time in his life, he's started cleaning the bath. She does not *know* what a step that is for him. How against the grain it goes for him to lean over with a cloth and scrub the bath. He stands under the spray, soaping the smell of Jas away. He should go back, be there when Cassie gets back. And probably should not do this again.

Three

C assie gets off the bus. Just getting dark, birds fluting in the trees, leaves dripping. She hitches her bag over her shoulder, crosses the road and starts down the lane, straining her eyes to see if there are any lights on in the cottage. If he's there. Her feet are tired in the stupid shoes, the heels give slightly with each step, making her sink as if walking on soft sand. If it wasn't wet she'd take them off and walk barefoot. The lights are all blazing, the curtains undrawn. Her heart thuds warily against her ribs. Best to go straight in and tell him where she's been and what she wants.

She opens the door, kicks off the shoes, sticks her feet into cool friendly clogs. He comes to the door to greet her. 'I've missed you,' he says.

'What!'

He hugs her. He has a clean shirt on, smells clean, though of unfamiliar soap. She pulls away and looks at him. Shiny black hair pulled back in its ponytail, face smoothly shaved.

'What's up?' she says. 'Going somewhere?'

He shakes his head, smiles and, as always, her heart lurches like it's coming unhinged. Long green eyes, black lashes, sexy lines crinkling.

She shoves him away. 'What do you mean you missed me? I've only been gone a day.'

'I've cooked you a meal,' he says, 'been at it hours.'

'Not my birthday, is it?'

She follows him into the kitchen. No smell of cooking, but plenty of peelings and splashes, a sink full of pots. A bottle of red wine open on the table, two glasses.

'Sit down,' he says, pouring.

'No, I need a pee – I'll just change.'

She climbs the stairs, takes off the skirt and tights, pulls on a pair of jeans and some woolly socks. She goes into the bathroom and stares at herself in the mirror, frowning and seeing the lines it makes. Mascara smudged owlishly, a greasy sheen around her nose. She blows her nose to get rid of the black London bogeys.

She hears him shout, 'Shit!' and watches her own face grimace. More lines. She has that fair skin that ages early, like her mum. Patsy's already got tramlines on her forehead, but then she has had a baby. Graham forgot to turn the oven on, she guesses. For a change. She takes the clips out of her hair and shakes it loose – warm waves against her face. This is her home and she loves it. Her bathroom with the fingers of ivy tapping the tiny window. Her garden out there in the darkness. Her bedroom with its low ceiling and view of wooded hills. If he goes it will all still be here. It won't kill her.

She pulls on a sweater and goes down the narrow curve of stair. 'What's up?'

He's rolling a fag on the kitchen table. 'Frigging oven wasn't on, was it? So it'll be a while.'

'What is it?'

'Sort of curry.'

'No, I mean what's all this in aid of?'

'Make a baby with me.'

Her forehead rises into her hair. '*What*?'

He licks his Rizla and gleams at her. 'You heard.'

She gets a sensation like warm sand trickling between her

ribs. If he'd said that years ago. If she could trust him. She suppresses the smile that wants to plump her cheeks, the shred of her that wants to rip both their jeans off and get down to it right now, on the kitchen table.

Instead she picks up her wine glass, twiddles the stem between her fingers. She takes a breath. 'I need to talk to you.'

'*Oh no!*' He lights his fag, leans back and squints through the smoke. 'Where've you been anyway?'

'London, I told you, that's what I want to talk to you about.' On the table there's an envelope he's doodled on: a tree, he usually doodles trees or women's bodies. This tree is sinuous and bare but for one dangling fruit. She puts her glass down and scrunches her hands together till they hurt. He gazes at her, waiting. He looks almost anxious.

She takes a breath. 'I've been for an interview.'

He exhales a long plume of smoke. 'You're not going to work in *London*?'

'It was an interview for a job in Australia – for both of us.'

He laughs as if it's a joke and then stops. His turn to stare. 'A night of surprises, eh?' she says.

The cat flips in through the cat flap and launches himself at her lap, turning, claws prickling through her jeans, till he's comfortable. She strokes his white head as she tells him about Larry, about the job.

'But,' he says into the long silence that follows, 'I never said I wanted to go to Australia.' He sounds wounded.

'No,' she says. 'I know. Graham, how long have we been together?'

He squashes the life out of his dog-end and thinks. 'Two, three years?'

'Nearly four.' She takes another deep breath, feels like she's about to jump from a plane unsure of her parachute. 'You know I do want to have a baby.' She holds up her hand to stop his response. '*Seriously*. I'm thirty-one. I want to have a baby when I'm thirty-two. Before thirty-three anyway.'

'I know. I'd love a kid.'

'Since when?'

'This afternoon.'

'What happened this afternoon?'

'Nothing. Just – came to me. *Shazam*.'

'But – what about last month when you went out for a paper and disappeared for a week? Or July? No – don't. I don't want to hear any excuses or anything. I want you to be here for me. Like a proper partner. A proper *committed* partner. No more flings. No more disappearing off. If you can't do that then –' She slices her hand through the air.

'*Cass!*' His green eyes spark, 'You don't mean that.'

'I do.'

'You don't.' He smiles but she won't let it infect her. Will not let him charm her any more.

'That's what Australia's about.'

A faint smell of curry is beginning to wisp from the oven but her stomach balls up against it.

'If you're serious about me, us, then we go together. Just you and me. No Jas or whoever to run to. Give that poor woman a chance to meet someone else.'

He looks at her suspiciously. 'Have you two been talking?'

'Give *us* time to – just be together – just us. Prove to me that you can do it. You could paint, maybe get back on track that way too. You seem a bit – *aimless*, lately.'

'No way.' He stands up, his chair grating against the floor. His raised voice is so rare that Cat opens his eyes and blinks, lashes the tip of his tail. 'I don't want to go to Australia. No way. No. Sorry. You can't *organise* me like that.'

The cat jumps off Cassie's lap, maybe thinking Graham's going to feed him. He stretches, and arches, white tail quivering.

23

'OK, then,' Cassie says, softly, 'That's it.'

'Don't be so stupid. I love you.'

'You never say it at the right time.' She will not look up. 'I love you too but it's not enough.'

'You want me to leave?'

'Yes.' The word falls like a stone from her mouth and rolls into a corner. He goes as if to speak, changes his mind and leaves the room, the door clicking shut abruptly behind him. She listens to his feet on the stairs, right up to the attic where he has his studio and most of his stuff. She stares for a moment at the door, at his squashed fag-end, at a long splash of yellow sauce on the oven door. Whose soap does he smell of? she wonders. The cat miaows and rubs against her shin. She tops up her wine and reaches for the phone. She'll speak to Patsy.

Four

A bird screeches and Graham tries to peel himself from his
dream, but the sound insists. Where is he? Light all wrong
and hot so hot –

But then he gets it. The other side of the tin wall, someone
moving about. The guy called Larry. The sizzle of something
hitting hot fat. Bacon maybe. His mouth floods, stomach
buckles with a pang of hunger.

He peels himself away from Cassie, the sticky heat between
their chests. She yawns and turns on to her back, stretches,
creaking the bed frame outrageously. He nuzzles her shoulder,
the salty skin.

'Get off. Too hot,' she says. 'And this is only *spring*. He said it
would be cool. If this is *cool*.'

'Yeah.'

They lie for a while, smelling bacon and listening to Larry
whistling something operatic. Graham runs his finger down the
bony plane between Cassie's flattened breasts. Her skin is
cloudy with sweat, almost translucent, a delta of blue veins
beneath.

'Never seen you sweat before,' he says.

'You must have.'

'I'd kill for a shower.'

'I'd kill for a cup of tea.'

'Yeah.'

'A bacon butty.'

'Mmmm.'

But they lie there, sweltering, overcome with lassitude. Graham begins to drift back to sleep, back into the drone of travel noise, the aeroplanes, the long queasy bumping drive.

'I wonder where his wife is?' Cassie whispers.

He starts out of the beginning of a dream. 'What?'

'You'd think we'd have met –'

'Breakfast.' Larry raps at the wall.

'OK,' Graham calls. 'Bloody hell,' he mutters, 'like living in a tin can.'

'Don't you think? But when I said –'

'We were all too wrecked last night.' Graham turns over and the bed groans. Cassie sits up, stretches. He watches the way her breasts tumble back into their birdy shapes. Least in the heat he'll see more of her body. More of her altogether. Well, that's the idea. He shuts his eyes and his stomach growls. And Cassie, of course, is obediently getting up, he can hear the catch of fabric on her skin.

In the end it was Jas who made him agree to come. He'd persuaded her to meet him for coffee and she'd come out of her huff long enough to agree.

'OK, what's up?' she'd said, when they were sitting with their cappuccinos between them. 'You?' She'd pushed her baccy tin towards him and they'd both rolled and lit up a skinny fag before they said any more. She'd breathed out blue smoke, picked a fleck from her lip. 'That's better. Now go on, shoot.'

'Who says something's up?'

She'd narrowed her eyes at him and pursed her lips. He'd laughed and shrugged, enjoying the scrutiny of her bright brown eyes.

'So you're telling me everything's hunky-dory?'

He'd looked down, blown a dent in the foam on his cappuccino. He told her about Cassie's ultimatum. '*Australia*, man!' he'd finished, gulping in smoke.

'Think she means it?'

'Yeah.'

'You could try calling her bluff?'

'Nah, Cass – when she makes up her mind –'

'Oh.' She'd grinned, the funny squinty grin. 'Well, she's got balls, I'll give her that! Fancy giving *you* an ultimatum.' She spooned froth into her mouth. He was tempted to take her hand, little and grubby and lying on the table in easy reach. But it seemed that wasn't on. '*I'd* go,' she said, 'if I was you.'

'You would?'

'What about your painting?'

Graham opened his mouth. But she was right. He was royally stuck. She blew smoke contemptuously, nodded at someone who had come through the door. Not someone he knew. Mimed talking into a phone before switching her attention back to him. 'Maybe a different light is what you need. Yup, I'd go like a shot, me.' She coughed, a husky smoker's cough that seemed to rumble from a bigger chest than hers. 'Think about it,' she said. 'I think –' she paused, 'I think that there comes a moment in your life,' she stubbed out her fag, 'when you have to make a leap. No safety net. You have to take a big risk. If you really love Cassie.' She swallowed, seemed about to continue, closed her mouth. She had a few tiny black hairs at the corners of her lips. He stared at them.

'But I said no. We've split up, kind of.'

'Oh well, that's *that* then,' she said, gathering her fag box and lighter and shoving them into her bag. Her voice rose: 'Doss around here the rest of your life then, forget *painting* – too much like hard work, eh? Do you remember how talented everyone said you were? How *dedicated*. We all thought you'd be *brilliant*. You'd be the one. You used to paint all night. Now what? Stay here, screw around to your heart's content, never make a –' her voice broke on the word, 'commitment to art or anything. Any*one*.'

She got up.

'Don't go,' he'd said reaching out his hand but she'd snatched hers away.

'What have you got to *lose*?' she'd said and gone, out the door, a flash of purple coat and she was out of sight. Not even drunk all her coffee. He finished it before he left. Miserable cold wet day. Might as well be winter. Rain on windows, in gutters. What *had* he got to lose?

He'd looked into the faces of the people in a bus queue. Black or white, it didn't matter, they were grey. The expressions: tense, cold, the shoulder hunch, the leaning forward; the wet ground reflected up into their faces. Slate-coloured, concrete-coloured. He'd strode along, sniffed the grim comforting leak of hot fat frying, a beery gust from the swinging door of a pub, thinking of tea-slops and matted wool, dampness drying on a radiator: England in winter.

'Come *on*.' The sun stings his eyes as Cassie shakes him from his memory. He sighs and pulls himself upright. She hands him his jeans, sits on the bed and watches as he balances on one leg then the other to put them on. He looks down at her. 'What?'

'You OK?'

He pulls on a vest, gets a whiff of his own armpits.

'Not regretting it?' she says.

'Give me a chance!'

She giggles. He reaches for her but she slips out of reach. 'Come on, let's get fed.'

'It's beautiful, man.' Graham stands on the kitchen threshold, bacon sandwich in one hand, mug of tea in the other, gazing out at a distant skin of colour. Flowers everywhere, a fizz of yellow bushes. 'Wattle,' Larry had told them on the journey. 'It's ubiquitous.' In the station wagon Graham had crossed his eyes and mouthed this word at Cassie. She'd looked out of the window, refusing to laugh. As far as you could see, the scattered patches of yellow, pink, white and harebell blue soften the red ground. A stand of gum trees a little way off glitter green and white.

'Heaven, but hot as hell.' Cassie hunkers down beside him, the cup by her feet. 'Honestly, Gray, I don't think I'll be able to stick summer.' She looks up at him, bacon fat gleaming on her chin.

'You will acclimatise,' Larry says, startling them both. He looks clean and dry, miraculously cool. Smells of aftershave. 'Our first few months – they were a trial – but I assure you your constitutions will accommodate. Once you are back in England, you'll see, you'll miss this sun.'

'Hmmm,' Cassie says.

It had been raining the day they left. The taxi calling, just as the sun struggled up, grey rain sliding down the windows, motorway sluices of wet thrown up by lorries, the edges of the road just visible, long green smears. Already it seems hard to believe in such wetness.

'It's like a million springs all happening at once,' Cassie says. She stands up.

'What did I tell you?' He smiles. 'Excuse me a moment.' He goes off round the side of the building.

'When he was showing me the slides,' Cassie explains. Graham looks down at the daisy tattooed on her foot, half obscured by the strap of her new brown sandal.

'Still no mention of Mara,' she says.

He shrugs, stretches his arms above his head.

'This is not the place,' she says, suddenly.

'What?'

'This is not the place on the photo, is it?'

Graham considers. There's no way he can make it be that

place. 'No,' he admits. He tosses the last scrap of his sandwich, crust and fatty bacon rind on to the ground and squats down beside Cassie. 'Don't fret,' he says.

*

His arm across her shoulders is too hot and heavy. There's a headachy edge to the sun. He rubs his face on hers. He needs a shave. Smells of stale smoke and sweat. But so, probably, does she.

'Fancy you,' he says in her ear.

'What, now?'

'Why not?'

'The bed – too creaky. The walls too – He'd hear.'

'So?'

Cassie shrugs Graham's arm off her and stands up. Maybe it's just jet lag making her feel so cranky, that, the glare of the sun and not knowing, quite, what's going on. Feeling out of control. *Her* plan: them here. But it all feels too – tiring.

She wanders away towards the trees. She'd thought no trees anywhere in the world could come close in beauty to English trees, the oaks and beeches in the woods at home, but these gums are exquisite, the skin of them so white, the deep pools of scented shade beneath them. A bird shrieks above her – a parrot! A scarlet parrot! To see a *parrot* loose in a tree! She nearly calls out to Larry who's going back towards the house but sees in the dazzle of green above her that there are more, a flock of them, sitting in pairs on the branches like feathered fruits. And, of course, parrots must be commonplace, here.

There's peace around the trees. She presses her hot brow against the bark of one, soaking in the peace, the eucalyptus smell, until something sets one of the parrots off and, as if the tree is flying apart, the flock of them clatter and screech, flashing red/green, cacophonous and piercing.

It's a true headache now, a tight tin hat squeezing her skull.

She looks back at the hut, long and silver in the sun. Too bright to look at. Stupid to be out without sunglasses. She goes back to get aspirin, find Graham and Larry. By the door a thin line wavers, she thinks it a hair blowing in the dust but it's a column of ants summoned by Graham's sandwich scrap. She steps over them and up into the kitchen.

Graham's resting his bum against the table, back to her, watching Larry hang their mugs back on their rusty hooks. 'When do we get to meet your wife?' he says.

'We'll go this afternoon.' Larry turns and smiles at Cassie. 'Have a morning off. Relax. Why not go for a swim in the gorge? Last chance you'll get for a dip in a while.'

'Go?'

'You didn't think this was Woolagong?' Larry says.

'See,' Cassie says. 'Told you.' She flops down on to a stool. 'God, I need a drink.'

Larry smiles at them. 'You've misunderstood me, the two of you. Possibly I wasn't clear enough. We'll fly to Woolagong this afternoon. I'm taking the car to Kip's – only 50 k – and he'll fly me back, then we'll pick you up. In the meantime the gorge is just half a kilometre away. An easy stroll.'

'Oh.' Cassie sits down. 'Maybe. My head is splitting.'

'Probably just a touch of the sun.' Larry opens his briefcase and takes out a pill-bottle.

'What are they?'

'A good analgesic. You'll feel better in twenty minutes. Right, I'll see you later the two of you. About three. Be ready. Have fun.' He picks up his panama and goes outside. They listen to the station wagon start up and drive away.

Cassie's headache lifts as they trail along the dirt track that winds through the bush, stopping to look at the weirdness: bushes with spines long as darning needles; thick spider webs stretching metres between bushes; blossoms emerging incongruously from the grit. There's the track and even a sign to show them the way – otherwise the bush stretches out for ever, it seems, on all sides, brilliant with the temporary flowers – *exhilarating*. The idea that you could wander free. With nothing. No people, nothing. But still, good that there's a track.

The gorge appears, at last. A crack in the red earth, zigzag-patterned cliffs rearing up to one side, white gums against the blue and red and startling green of the rushy grasses.

Soon as he reaches the water's edge, Graham strips, hopping about as he takes off his sandals. Cassie watches. His skin is white beside the gum bark, dull tender English white. He picks his way along the rocks, looking for a suitable place to enter the water, each step taken a little more awkwardly than the last – must be sharp on his bare foot-soles. On a smooth edge of rock, he pauses, looks back at her.

'Come on. Chicken!'

She lifts her chin, 'I'm not chicken,' she says, but quietly to herself. A lump rises in her throat. He looks so small and naked. *Poor forked beast* floats into her head from somewhere. And it's her fault that he's here. So out of his element. He raises his arms to do a flamboyant dive.

'No!' she yells.

He stops, lowers his arms. 'What's up?'

But there's nothing up, nothing she can say. It's cold water, that's all. They are hot sweaty humans. It is quiet. No one about to see. The echo of her shout is an edge of metal ringing in the air.

He waits. '*What?*'

She shakes her head and walks towards him, careful on the glittering rock, sharp and slippy under her sandals. He turns away, raises his arms again, dives and disappears, the splash a gulp, the water darkly opening and closing its lips around him. Circles like a laugh skim out towards the edges. She holds her breath, stands in the shimmer and the cliff leans into its reflection and the sight of a human swallowed up.

Her heart beats three desolate times. She closes her eyes and as she opens them he pops up a few metres from where she's been looking. He snorts the water from his nose, head sleek, seal-wet, and waves. 'Come on!' He ducks under again and she breathes out. Her heart resumes its normal beat. There's nothing wrong, she tells herself, just a man jumping into water for a dip on a hot day. What could be more normal or pleasant than that? *Her* man, perhaps, jumping into clean fresh water, which is what she should do.

She takes off her hat and sunglasses, everything suddenly several degrees brighter and sharper. She peels off her T-shirt, bra, shorts, sandals. Her skin looks even whiter than his. Dazzling. Her breasts are startled by the sun, which they have scarcely seen before. It almost stings.

'Get 'em off, Gorgeous!' Graham shouts, from way out.

His voice echoes, silly, against the ancient cliff.

She looks around. No one. Of course. She peels off her knickers and goes to the place where his clothes are dumped. Turns to see him on his back, floating, eyes closed, flapping his hands beside his hips like fins. His shrunken penis bobs, wrinkled mauve and comical, breaking through the water's skin.

A smile rises through her. Everything's OK. But she can't plunge straight in like he did. She lets herself down gently, feet and legs in first, goose-pimpling as the cold gradually creeps up and envelops her. The water is stunningly cold. How can it be so icy in this sun? But once she's in and swimming it turns to silk. After the heat and dust and sweat, it is perfect, it is a joy. The clean cold of it licking over her, inside her, everywhere.

Keeping her head up she breaststrokes towards Graham, who floats out of the direct sun in the shadow of the cliff. When she reaches him, she turns on to her back too. They hang together, the cliff reflected like a half-developed photo on their wet skins; deep dark water beneath them and, above, the shock of crazy rearing geometric rock stark against the blue.

Five

The plane – no bigger than a taxi-cab – swoops violently. 'Sit back,' Cassie says, 'it's safer.' She takes Graham's hand and squeezes.

'Safer how?' he mutters. But he sits back, glassy-eyed. She lifts his hand and brushes it with her lips. Larry turns round and raises his eyebrows at her. Cassie glares at the pilot. Surely there's no reason to drop like that and rise again? Close to her face, the nape of his neck is thick red, coarsely grained beneath the leather brim of his hat. Some kind of test, she thinks, an ordeal for the bloody whingeing poms. See how long till they squeal. Well, she, for one, will never squeal.

She keeps hold of Graham's hand, trapping the sweat between them. All the freshness of the gorge evaporated already. His hair drying in long weedy strands. Larry doesn't like the look of Graham – she saw the way his eyes flickered when they met – taking in the tatty jeans, the long hair, the gold ring in his ear. Not what he'd expected at all. In the photo, maybe, the tied-back hair had looked short. He had looked less – himself. Well, that's not *her* fault.

'OK?' she says, rubbing her cheek against Graham's shoulder.

He looks at her as if she's mad. She sighs and leans over, peers down at the bush, the patches of red between the dull greens, the violent yellow froth of wattle. Sometimes the spidering of a dry river bed. But looking forwards or sideways instead of down you get the sense of nothing, nothing but a faint endless undulation of dull greenish grey. You can see the curve of the earth against the sky. It's like nothing so much as looking at the sea. A dry ocean, rippling as far as the eye can bear to see.

At take-off the pilot had looked over his shoulder. 'OK?' he'd said and they were off. No safety procedures, no mention of oxygen masks or checking of belts, just that casual OK and the jerk and grind over dirt and up, tilting till the earth rose sheer beside them.

Larry sits up front beside the pilot. He turns round.

'How far?' Graham asks.

'See that ridge –?' Larry points to a mark becoming visible on the horizon, like a smudge of crimson crayon. 'Just beyond that is Woolagong. Look down.'

Cassie leans to look again. The plane skitters and Graham crushes her hand, eyes straight ahead. Sweat beads on his forehead. 'Not long,' she mouths into his ear. Please don't be sick, she thinks, not in the plane. There are no sick bags that she can see. And she couldn't bear to give the pilot the satisfaction. Although he'd probably have to clear it up. And serve him right.

Stupid that earlier she had been so scared. Of nothing. Of a pool of water – and now dancing above desolation she feels fine, exhilarated, sort of *free*. Here they are, she and Graham. High and free, in an adventure. She looks at him: he's gone putty-coloured, eyes shut.

Below is the straight line of a road, a thin scar leading to an open mess of brown, ochre and rusty red.

'Gold mine,' Larry yells. 'Used to be. See the old town?'

A flock of birds swim under the plane like a shoal of tiddlers, and beneath them Cassie can see nothing but jerky glimpses of a junction, a neat cross, the arms of which give out again into the scrub. And one track threading away, travelling miles to nowhere obvious. Nowhere but the bush.

'Where are the houses?'

'Long gone.' The plane jerks and Graham gulps and nearly breaks her fingers. Cassie scowls at the smug red neck beneath the hat, the oily-looking strands of hair that show beneath. He surely is enjoying himself.

'Steady on, Kip!' Larry says to the pilot. He raises a wiry eyebrow at Cassie. 'All right?' He nods at Graham.

Graham snaps open his eyes. 'I'm fine,' he says.

Cassie's fingers are numb. She disengages her hand and shakes it to get the circulation back, a drip of sweat splashing on her knee. She reaches for her water bottle, swigs, offers it to Graham but he ignores her.

'Just hang on,' she says.

Again the bush has closed below them, featureless but for a rock here, something a bit greener there. The sun is lower in the sky, making the ridge glow, powdering the green with gold, complicating it with shadows.

Cassie leans forward and touches Larry's shoulder. 'It's beautiful,' she says, gesturing at the glorious effect of the light. The aeroplane dips, tilts a wing and her heart soars.

The landing is a bumping roar culminating in a dusty choke of red so that for a moment there is nothing to see but dust. Graham is out, soon as the door opens, just in time, turns away, puking on the ground.

Kip grins. 'Oh dear. Pom got crook, eh?' Cassie flicks him a look and goes to stand by Graham, but she has to dip her head to hide a smile. So they really do talk like that. Or is he having her on?

'Care for a beer?' Larry says.

Kip shakes his head. 'Nah, mate, wanna get back before dark.' He turns back to the plane, unloads the rucksacks and the eskies of food, dumps them in the dirt beside the plane.

Graham straightens up.

'OK now?' Cassie says.

He grins sheepishly, scrubs his mouth with the back of his hand. 'Never better,' he says.

'See yers,' Kip says. 'G'luck.' He jumps back into the plane and it takes off, churning up the dust again. They turn, hands shielding their eyes to watch it rising into a glare of sun, banking and diminishing into a speck of black, mosquito small till it strains their eyes to see. He leaves a hush in which the rhythmic creaking of the pump is the only sound.

'Welcome,' Larry says. 'Welcome at last to Woolagong Station.'

'Ta.' Graham spits and, out of the corner of her eye, Cassie catches Larry's wince.

'I recognise it,' she says, seeing the angle from which the photo was taken. The pump, the giant tree, the buildings, the hens pecking about in the dust. And even the same old piebald dog staggering towards them, wagging a stubby tail.

'Meet Yella,' Larry says.

'Hi Yella.' Cassie pats his head.

'Deaf as a post.'

'Poor thing.'

Larry turns to Graham. 'Recovered now?'

'Fine.' Graham picks up his rucksack and swings it over his shoulder.

'And we'll finally get to meet Mara.' Cassie looks around, surprised that the woman hasn't come running out to meet them. Or at least to welcome Larry home.

'She'll be resting.'

'She must have heard the plane.'

'She is – somewhat shy of strangers on occasion. Come on, I'll show you in and you can unpack,' Larry says. 'Freshen up. I'll sort you out some supper.'

'Thanks,' Cassie says. 'Could you face anything, Gray?'

'Maybe.'

'You'll soon feel better.' Larry hefts an eskie under each arm and leads them across to the sprawling building, past a low shed, up the steps of a veranda where the dog settles down under a table. Larry pushes open a door and they are in the kitchen. A flyscreen bounces tinnily behind them. The room is hot and dim, almost filled with a square table, cluttered with crockery, papers, tools, fruit. A rusty black range with pans and a kettle on top takes up one wall. Despite the screen, flies buzz. A speckled flypaper dangles beside the window, another over the table. A greasy ceiling fan swishes the heat about.

Larry pushes his load on to the table, picks up a paper bag with a note scrawled on it. He reads it, nods, screws it up, opens the door of the range and throws it in. He looks at his watch. 'Just missed Fred,' he says. 'What about a cup of tea before I show you your quarters?' He moves the kettle a few inches and immediately it starts to bubble.

'Fred?'

'Nearest neighbour. I employ him to help out. You'll meet him soon enough.'

At least there are neighbours, Cassie thinks, looking round for any signs of a woman. It is a masculine room. Nothing like a tablecloth or curtains. An oily spanner rests on a plate of wizened oranges.

'Generator,' Larry says. He goes out again.

Graham pulls out his tobacco.

'You could ask if he minds you smoking in the kitchen,' Cassie says.

'He'll say if he does.'

There's a stutter and then a hum. Larry comes back in. 'We use the generator, couple of hours morning and night. Electricity for the fridge and lights. Otherwise we rely on the solar panels. So no wastage, please.'

'Solar power. Good,' Cassie says.

'Glad you approve.' Larry smiles and she flushes, feeling foolish. Larry stows sausages, milk, cheese and bread into a wardrobe-sized fridge. He empties a round brown teapot into a bin, rinses it with water from the kettle, spoons tea leaves inside. 'I think, possibly, that we'll save the introductions for tomorrow,' he says. 'We'll all feel brighter in the morning.'

Before Cassie can react, Larry's eyes are on her. 'Or would you like me to disturb her now?'

'Of course not!' She forces a smile. 'I just thought – well, assumed – that she'd be interested to meet us. We're dying to meet her, aren't we, Gray?'

'Yeah.'

She follows Graham's gaze to a small vivid photo on the wall beside the door.

'All in good time.' Larry pours the tea into tin mugs for them. Cassie takes a sip and burns her lips on the rim. She thinks longingly of thin bone china or even the chunky pottery Graham likes. The sort of thing Jas is prone to giving them for Christmas, a matching pair of ugly mugs. Anything's better than tin though. First trip to town, top of the list: *nice mugs*.

'This is the pantry.' Larry opens a door. More flypapers dangle inside the door of the deep, dark space. The shelves are crammed with cans. He kicks a metal bin. 'Flour,' he says. 'You must always keep the lid on everything. Ants. Or worse. Now,' he says, lacing his fingers together and bending them back till his knuckles pop, 'finish your tea and I'll show you to your new,' he smiles, 'home. Home from home.'

'Aren't we staying here?'

'Thought you'd prefer some privacy. I'll take your bags round.' Larry picks up Cassie's rucksack and goes out, the flyscreen bouncing shut behind him.

Graham goes to take a closer look at the picture – not a photo, a painting, a small square of painted wood, richly coloured like an icon. Cassie peers over his shoulder. It is not any sort of icon but a painting of a woman and two blonde-haired children, photo-sharp, surrounded by a heavenly glow. 'Wonder if that's Mara?'

'Or maybe she did it?'

The door bangs making them both jump. 'Ready?' Larry holds the door open and sweeps his hand in an exaggeratedly polite gesture. They follow him down the steps. Outside, Graham stops to grind his fag out in the dirt and Cassie catches sight of something – some kind of lizard, big as a Jack Russell, gleaming violet-blue, poised as if frozen beneath the steps.

'Look, Gray.'

Larry turns. 'Oh, that's just our old goanna,' he says. 'He lives under the veranda. Won't hurt you. Meant to bring good fortune, I believe.'

She stoops to look closer at the glistening folds of scaly skin, the closed trap of its jaw, the exact cold circles of its eyes.

'Isn't he amazing?' she says, but Larry and Graham have disappeared round the side of the house. She follows them round the back, which is really the front of the house, though it looks like it's never used. She can't see any garden. The steps up to that door are wonky, a rusty old swing-seat on the veranda. They go through a patch of bushes and scrubby trees to a long, corrugated-tin shed.

'Shearers' shed – as was,' Larry says. 'Quite a crowd, the shearers, itinerants. Once a year they'd descend.'

'But no more?' Cassie asks. *Obvious*.

'What is there to shear?' Larry laughs. 'Your own private residence. And conveniences.' He points out the dunny. On one wall of the outside of the shed is a tin sink. 'Your bathroom,' he says, without apparent irony. 'There is usually water but don't drink it. That well is shallow – saline. Warm too – suitable for washing. Drink only the kitchen water.'

'No *proper* bathroom?' Cassie looks dubiously at something

hanging from a hook above the sink that might once have been a flannel, and a lump of dusty hair-encrusted soap.

'We don't extend to modern conveniences, I'm afraid, but you'll soon get used to it.' Larry opens a door on to a dim corridor with six further doors. 'You can take your pick,' he says, 'except this one –' he indicates a door, 'that's Fred's when he stays. But I prepared this one. Only one with a double bed.'

He opens the first door on to a room in which their rucksacks squat like old friends beside a sagging iron-framed bed. The curtains, drawn against the windows, are patterned with the ghosts of unicorns. On the wide, splintery floorboards, like a tan and white butterfly, a whole cowskin. On the box by the bed, a jug and two plastic beakers, and a thick white candle, fresh but warped by the heat, melted on to a jam-jar lid.

'What do you think?' Larry says.

'I love it,' Cassie says, breathing in the dry biscuity smell.

Graham flops down on the bed, grating the rusty springs, causing a patter of rust.

'Rather basic, I'm afraid,' Larry says.

'No, it's lovely.' The look of the bed – it makes Cassie's legs tremble with tiredness.

'You must keep the door shut – and the window,' Larry says. 'Against flies, mosquitoes, spiders, snakes.'

Cassie catches Graham's expression and goes to the window to hide her smile. She lifts the curtain to look out, nothing but scratchy twigs jammed against the glass. 'I wanted to ask you, I was reading about, you know redbacks and funnel-webs.'

'Don't get funnel-webs here.'

Cassie lets the curtain fall back, and turns. 'No, but what do you do in an, um, emergency?'

'We cope.'

'Presumably you radio for help?'

'We don't have a radio here,' Larry says. 'And anyway *I'm* a doctor.'

'*You?*' Cassie stares. 'You never said.'

He shakes his head and tuts. 'You didn't ask!' He smiles. 'So you see, you've nothing to worry about. By the way, do notice the fire sensor.' He indicates a small box attached to the ceiling. 'You'll see we've got them everywhere. Obviously, there's no fire brigade round the corner. But there are extinguishers. Familiarise yourself with their whereabouts, please.'

'But no radio?'

'I think you would do well to unpack. Wash, get settled in. It's getting dark.' Larry flicks a match to the candle. 'You'll need more candles – pantry. There's a lamp in the kitchen you can bring back with you. Top of the the fridge. Electricity doesn't extend over here. Used to –' he indicates a switch by the door, 'but that was in the old days. While this was still a working operation. I'll put your supper on the table. I'll leave you to have it in peace. And see you in the morning. I've got things to do. And, tomorrow you really *will* meet Mara.' He smiles and closes the door behind him.

'Well,' Graham says. 'Here we go then. Operation Cassie.'

'*Don't,*' she says. 'No *radio*?'

'Right now,' Graham stretches and yawns. 'I don't give a shit.'

'No proper bathroom. He never told me that!' She unfastens her rucksack and takes out her washbag. The familiar candy-pink stripes make her want to cry.

Graham touches her on the shoulder. 'Hey?'

'It's OK, isn't it?' She tilts back her head to stop the stupid tears that have risen like hot beads behind her eyes.

'It's cool. More or less our own place.'

'S'pose.' She presses her lips together, waits for the wave of self-pity to subside. Just tiredness. Exhaustion. She sniffs and delves down in her rucksack, pulling out knickers, books, T-shirts, until she finds two small framed photos: one of her parents, arm in arm, taken a year before her dad died; one of

Patsy with baby Katie. She stands them on top of the chest of drawers. She fishes out the mirror that was her gran's. Wrapped up in a fleece and not broken. An oval hand-mirror, black, lacquered with purple pansies. She and Patsy had fought over it for ages when they were children, but she had won. She peers at her tired face for a moment and puts it down. 'There.'

Graham laughs. 'Anything else in there?'

'Just making it more homey.' She bites her tongue. He's allergic to that word. 'At least he's a doctor,' she says. 'That makes me feel safer.' She sits down on the bed. The mattress is soft. She bounces a bit, squealing the springs. 'I do like the room. No electricity though.' She takes off her sandals and lies down beside him. They tumble in towards each other.

'Crap mattress,' he says, enclosing her in his arms.

'We should go and eat.'

'Let's just rest a minute.'

She feels fuzzy, light-headed, the horizontal position claiming her, reminding her body about all the sleep it has missed. They press themselves together. His familiar body feels so right and comforting. In and out in all the right places. His breath is sour but it is still his breath and she holds him tight, her face against his neck, looking over his shoulder at the outline of the window, fast disappearing in the dying light.

'Listen,' Graham murmurs, his breath tickling her ear.

She listens. 'What?'

'Nothing. That's just it. *Fuck all*. Silence.'

She hears it. There *are* sounds – a creaking from the pump, the hum of the generator, but behind all that, silence is happening in a big way. Millions upon millions of square miles of bush and desert crowded out with silence.

'It's never silent,' she says. 'There's always *something*. Listen.'

There is a dry scuttle from somewhere like the rush of a frightened heart. 'It's never silent,' she says again, her voice

43

small. They lie together, hearts beating, breath mingling. It is too hot in the stale trapped air of the room to be so close but too silent not to be. The physical noise of a friendly being pressed up close is the only thing to drown out the silence. She shuts her eyes.

And wakes to him shaking her.

'Hey sleepy, let's go and eat.'

She hauls herself up, a thick furry taste in her mouth, bleary eyes, and allows him to lead her outside. It's now properly dark. He shines a torch on the ground and they pick their way through the bushes. She feels as if she's dreaming, the strange landscape hinting at itself through the dark, a high moon sailing. In the kitchen Larry has laid out hard-boiled eggs, bread, cheese and tomatoes with a couple of bottles of beer. The electric light is dim and there is a constant buzzing: flies, the generator perhaps, a sound that seems to Cassie as if it's emanating from her own ears.

'Well, cheers.' Graham snaps the beer bottles open and hands one to her. The dull light emphasises the blue shadows under his eyes.

'Cheers,' Cassie says, 'to us. To our – adventure.' They chink their bottles and gulp cold beer.

Six

T he sun shines through the thin curtains, and Cassie lies for a few moments looking at the outlines of the unicorns. They are really here! Graham is still asleep, lashes dark against his cheeks, a little trail of drool escaping from his mouth. She climbs out of bed, careful not to jolt him awake. The walls are pale pink, an old pleated lampshade hangs from a bulbless socket. It is a lovely room, square, pleasing, though a little small and she'll have to get rid of the cowskin rug – makes her feel queasy, stepping on it.

She looks at the photo of Patsy. Apart from missing her this is going to be *great*, she thinks. It's so amazing to be somewhere so *other*. You don't realise what a rut you've been in till you climb out of it. She can feel in her bones that this is going to be good.

Graham is looking at her. 'Hi Gorgeous,' he says.

'Gorgeous yourself,' she says. She leans over to kiss him and he tries to pull her down.

'Come on, let's go and get something to eat,' she says, 'I'm *starving*.'

For breakfast they eat oranges and porridge with molasses. Strange breakfast to start a new life on but Larry has made porridge for Mara and extra in case they want some too, and they feel obliged to want it. And though porridge is just about the last thing Cassie could possibly have imagined wanting, she eats greedily till she's scraping the spoon round her bowl. It fills in between her ribs, makes her feel solid, earthed after all the flight and movement of the past few days.

She washes the dishes and Graham feeds the sloppy strips of dead porridge that float off the sides of the pan to Yella, making him stand up on his back legs like a circus dog. Larry sits at the table, flicking through some papers.

'Oh, by the way, what do we do about post?' Cassie asks him.

Larry looks up over his reading specs. 'Writing home already?'

'Well, we need to say we got here safely.'

'Put your letters in that –' he nods towards a cigar box on the side. 'They'll be taken to the roadhouse, though I warn you it won't be often. We have a mailbox there.'

'That's where our post will come to?'

He nods.

'How often?'

'Tends to be a bit sporadic, I'm afraid.'

'Oh. Well, long as it's not too sporadic! I'd love to see the garden,' she says, fishing the last spoon out of the water and drying her hands.

'Of course. After you've met Mara.' Larry folds his glasses into his breast pocket. 'Ready?'

He takes them not further into the house but outside and down the veranda steps to a long low hut opposite. The hut has two blue painted doors – one into each half. 'This houses the generator – at the other end,' Larry jerks his beard towards the far door, 'and Mara stays in here.'

Cassie looks at him. 'She doesn't live in the house?'

'She prefers – well –' Larry seems to struggle for a moment. 'Well, you'll see.'

Cassie looks at the door, the slivers of peeled blue paint

showing up a rusty undercoat. She'd barely noticed the shed last night. Certainly never dreamed that Mara might be inside. Beside the door is a window, the glass dusty like all the glass, like everything, and swathed with a thick curtain.

Larry opens the door into a dark room. They go in. Larry closes the door and the drape that covers the door falls with a muffled gasp.

Cassie grabs Graham's hand, seized by a fierce urge to giggle. Once the door is closed she can see nothing for a moment, eyes full of sun-dazzles – and then the detail creeps back: red Turkish carpet on the walls and floor, cushions, piles of them, long and square and round, all shades of red from black to vermilion. The shadows are solid, beastlike, everywhere, lounging in corners, slumped against the walls. There's a strong smell, female, a thick perfume, a woman's private odour, familiar and shocking.

'Could we –' Cassie begins. Not funny now, she needs the door open, needs to breathe. Feels about to suffocate or faint.

'Wait,' Larry says. 'Mara? They're here.'

'I can see that.' The voice comes from a corner. Despite the stifling heat, Cassie's arms riffle with gooseflesh.

'Perhaps you'd like to greet them?'

The darkness stirs and a jumble of shadows jumps together. A woman becomes visible, struggling up. Short and wide, her eyes gleam in the sparse pinkish light.

'How do you do?' Her voice sounds creaky, as if not lately used.

Cassie takes a deep breath and pulls herself together. She lets go of Graham and shakes the moist, spongy hand held out to her. 'Fine, thanks,' she says. 'And you?'

Mara yawns hugely. Cassie looks away from the gape of her throat. They stand in silence for a moment.

'They've been very keen to meet you. Cassandra and Graham. I told you. Graham is a painter,' Larry says.

Graham holds out his hand. 'Hi.'

'I used to be a painter,' Mara says, taking his hand and frowning down at it before letting go.

'They were beginning to think you didn't exist,' Larry says. 'That you were a figment –'

'I am no *figment*,' she says, her voice rising, panicky.

'Of course you're not.' Larry pats her arm. 'Now I'm going to show them round. And later we'll have lunch together. Get properly acquainted. Eh? I'll come and fetch you in time for lunch.'

'I've not been well,' Mara says, leaning towards Cassie. 'I have these – turns, Fred was here, he helped me.'

'And now Fred's gone and we have Cassandra and Graham.'

'Cassie,' Cassie says.

'Come.' Larry lifts the curtain over the door. Mara turns away but as the door opens, a blade of sunshine flashes across the room, illuminating heavy black hair tied loosely back, a red velvet dressing gown, deep sadness sketched in round a full-lipped mouth.

'See you later, Mara.' Cassie picks up a prickle of the woman's sadness.

Outside, she presses her hands over her eyes, the sun making her reel. Like coming out of a theatre into the brightness of a sunny afternoon. She pulls her sunglasses down from her hair but still it's blindingly bright. Above them the pump creaks, a bird shrieks and far above, deep in the sky, a plane draws a chalky stripe across the blue.

'Fucking –' Graham starts but Larry puts a finger to his lips and leads them away from the door.

'Yes?' He smiles, a curl of eyebrow rising from behind his sunglasses.

'Nothing.'

'Good, and if you don't mind, I'd really rather you didn't swear.' Larry turns and walks away. Are they meant to follow?

Cassie takes Graham's arm. Words have failed him and she doesn't blame them.

The dog comes stiffly down the veranda steps and walks with Larry, nose pressed against his knee. Devoted. Larry walks with his hands clasped behind his back, panama tilted forward, shirt blinding white. He clinks slightly as he walks, a bunch of keys clipped to his belt.

He turns and beckons. 'Ready to see the garden?'

The garden is squashed between the far side of the house and the pump – a steamy rectangle, shadowed by nets to keep the sun from burning the tomatoes, lettuces, peppers, beans. Relieved, Cassie pinches and sniffs the catty reek of a tomato leaf. Small birds with spiky voices hop and cheep amongst the leaves. There are tomatoes begging to be picked, big rough ones, some fat enough to split their skins. She's pleased to see a bushy basil plant growing alongside. If they stay, she'll plant parsley too, chervil, fennel. Companion planting. She can't wait to get at it.

'I'm not much of a gardener, as you see,' Larry says. 'Fred has a go but now that you're here –'

'No, it's *great*,' she says, 'isn't it, Gray? And there's so much more we can do.'

'Well, order any seeds you like. And use the vegetables of course. We find we are almost self-sufficient as far as salad is concerned.'

'You water from the pump?' Cassie asks. There's a lovely refreshing sound, the rhythmic gush of water into a great galvanised tank. Larry shows them the overflow tank, shallow and open to the sky, the water glazed with dust, floating with dead and dying bugs.

'This is a good well,' Larry said. 'Excellent, cold water, not saline. It's never failed us yet. Without it Woolagong Station could not exist. Watering cans.' He points to a couple of big ones along with bags of chemical fertilizer and pesticide (which will have to go), a jumble of forks and trowels and a fearsome-looking rake.

'Splendid. And now,' he says, 'let us take a little walk. I'll show you the glories we have to offer.'

They trudge off again, following Larry away from the house for five minutes or so. The crust on top of the dust is crisp under their feet, their sandalled toes etched red around the nails with dust. Here and there feeble patches of prickly grass push up through the dust, lifting flakes of the crust with it.

Eventually, Larry stops and bends down. 'See?' He cranes his neck round to look at them. He cups his palm open under a blossom, clear crisp white, many-petalled, on a fine green stem. Cassie crouches beside him, marvelling at the frail stalk emerging from the sun-baked dust.

'Beautiful,' Graham says.

'And look.' Larry stands and points to the downward slope before them. They blink and focus on a pale shimmer, like a mist, hovering above the ground.

'Everlastings,' he says. 'Miraculous, aren't they? It's against the law to pick them, but here in this – nowhere – who would miss a few? Mara would love them. A centrepiece at lunch perhaps?'

Cassie wobbles upright and smiles. Sounds like a crossword clue. She tries to think of an answer but it's much too hot to think.

Larry turns to face them, tilts his hat back, removes his sunglasses. He looks into the eyes of each of them for a level moment. 'I do admire your discretion,' he says.

'You what?' Graham says.

'You must be curious about Mara but you have restrained yourself from asking. Mara – you must allow me to explain.' Larry closes his hands as if in prayer, puts his fingers to his lips for a moment in contemplation before he speaks. 'Mara has a *condition* which makes her incompatible, shall we say, with society. But she is a good woman, a fine woman.'

'Um what is it?' Cassie says. 'I mean, is it a physical thing?'

The corner of Larry's mouth twitches. 'You think it is

possible to separate the body from the mind. How much you have to learn!'

Cassie bristles. 'Of *course* not, not always. But there are things – what about tonsillitis? Or flu – are they mental?'

Larry laughs. 'It is nothing like tonsillitis.'

'I didn't mean that I –'

He holds up his hand. 'There is little point in me attempting to explain Mara's – condition – in those terms. You are here now. You'll have ample time to judge for yourself. She has phases –'

'Like the moon?' Graham says.

Larry smiles sadly. 'Phases when she is – out of sorts, shall we say. When she has to take a medication that sedates her. And then she recovers – as now – I think she is recovering from a "phase".' He pauses. 'Fortuitously. You will soon have a chance to make these observations for yourselves.'

He shades his eyes and looks into the distance. He looks so sad that Cassie's crossness melts. Poor man. He does need help. How can one man on his own work and run this place and care for someone who needs – who seems to need – so much looking after? No wonder he is a bit strange. Anyone would be strange. It will be good to help.

'Shall we meet for lunch on the veranda?' Larry says. 'I'll leave you to your own devices. Something light for lunch, a salad perhaps? There is bread but you might like to bake some more? Everything is there. I'll get a little work done and see you later.' He does a sort of salute against his hat brim and walks briskly away, keys clinking, Yella trotting at his heels.

'Well,' Graham says, soon as he's out of earshot. He pokes her in the ribs. 'This is another fine mess you've got us into.'

'*Don't*, Gray,' she says, but she's relieved at the humour in his voice. 'Her in that shed!' She reaches for the giggle she's been suppressing – but it has died away. She hunkers down, sweat squishing in the creases behind her knees, and fingers the papery petals of the flower.

Box 25
Keemarra Roadhouse
(Woolagong Station)
22nd October

Dear Mum,
Well, here we are safely arrived at last. It's hot and really does seem to be miles from anywhere. We've got no proper address even! At least, the post isn't delivered here, it's picked up and delivered from the roadhouse. You'd love the wild flowers, but they'll soon be over apparently. Nice garden, tomatoes, beans etc. Larry and Mara are an unusual couple, but seem very nice. Well, must go now, bread to bake! (I'm trying your failsafe recipe to start with – thanks.)
Love,
Cassie
xxxxxxxxx

Seven

Cassie stands in the hall of the shearers' shed. The floor is made of wide-beamed wood, silky with age, needing a sweep to rid it of the dead bugs, leaves, drifts of dust. The doors stretch either side of her, three each side, a door to the outside at each end. A bit like a railway carriage. Larry said they could look at the other rooms but still her heart beats as if she's doing something wrong. *Snooping*. Dark in the corridor and almost cool. The walls are papered with a design of flowers and vases. Was that appreciated by the shearers? A couple of framed photos on the walls: sweaty men swilling beer down their gullets; a shearer with a sheep struggling between his thighs.

She tries the far door. Narrow bed, khaki blanket, pair of boots, kerosene lamp. Must be whatsisname's – the neighbour. She shuts it. The next is stuffed with junk: broken bed-frame; drawerless chest; bundle of stuff, old covers and curtains. A faded calendar dated 1979: half-naked women on farm machinery, advertising sheep dip. On the opposite side is a room with a sagging single bed, the window patched with a sheet of tin. And there is a room filled with light, bigger than their room, a lovely feel to it. Not that there's anything wrong with theirs but – she steps in.

The floor slopes but still – they could bring the double bed across – the curtains are buttery yellow, the walls dappled with faded roses. A pretty room. Why did Larry give them the other one? White chest of drawers, rag rug. She crouches and examines the bits of different material, just tiny cotton rags individually but gathered into a subtle mottled swirl, like a dust storm. And on the small humped bed a patchwork quilt, fantastic, a pattern she's never seen before, shading from cool blue in one corner, diagonally across to fiery reds and oranges. Cold to hot. Hand-done. She could make a quilt, while she's here. Copying this pattern. She can just see it on her – their? – bed at home. People will say, *How exquisite* and she'll tell them, her *children*, even, she'll tell them about this place, this odd chapter in her life. *My Year in the Outback*. Will Graham be part of her life then? Will he be their father? She sits down on the lumpy bed and sighs.

*

Graham stands by the kitchen window, looking through the smeary glass to Mara's shed outside. The shut blue door. He takes a roll-up from behind his ear and lights it. What *is* that woman doing in that shed? She must have some story to tell. What is *he* doing in this kitchen, in this sheep station, in this *country*, in this *hemisphere*?

Least he's alone. First time in days. The tap drips, the fan squeaks, flies buzz studiously over the table, his jam-smeared plate. He turns the tap and waits for the water that comes cloudy at first, almost as if soapy, and then clears, though it never gets completely cold. He swigs some anyway and goes to look again at the little painting. If *she* did it she's amazing. The brush strokes fine; the finish shiny. Maybe shellac? Good. Not his sort of thing, but pretty good. But then what *is* his thing any more?

He thinks back to college. Hell of a long way back. He knew his parents were disappointed. *Art college* after the packet they spent on school. Couldn't have a kid but they'd adopted him, at four years old, and spoiled him something rotten. He knows he's spoilt – what's he meant to do about it? Nothing he couldn't have – that you could buy. Remembers the piles of presents, the silver-wrapped bike under the Christmas tree; the room full of stuffed tigers and elephants. 'Jungle theme,' his mum would say, showing it off to guests. The computer before everyone had computers. Wanted him to be lawyer like his dad. Sold a pup, weren't they?

He remembers walking into that room for the first time: the frieze of animals stalking, more toys that he'd ever seen outside of a shop. The smell of new paint and plastic toys. Lawyer! But he *could* draw. So, architect they thought, but no. *Not* straight lines but grey skies, sulphur yellow reflected in puddles, oily rainbows on the canal. Got him a first at college. 'Difficult Light,' his dissertation. No difficulty here, the light is all too easy.

'*If I had your talent I wouldn't squander it.*'

'Cheers Jas,' he mutters. What would she say about this set-up? Where his leap has landed him. *Twenty thousand miles away*. She'll be in her studio now – but no, maybe not. What time in England? Eight hours difference one way or the other, can't be arsed to work it out.

He picks three oranges up from the table. Throws one up, another, till he's juggling, each orange landing with a cool thwack in his hand, a smell of citrus rising with the bruising of their peel.

Cassie bursts into the kitchen and he drops an orange. She chucks her sunglasses on the table and, before she speaks, drinks down a glass of water, not even waiting till it clears. Her face is deep pink, the spray of freckles on her nose looks almost green.

'What've you been up to?' he asks, putting the oranges down. One has rolled under the table and he leaves it.

She wipes her lips on the back of her hand, comes over and kisses him, her lips cool and wet. 'Just poking around,' she said. 'Exploring. I found us a new room! Come and look.'

'You've caught the sun.'

She squints at her shrimp-coloured arms. 'Yeah, went for a

walkabout before. Forgot to put more cream on, never mind. Mmmm,' she snuggles her hips against him. His arms go round her like a shot, but she peels herself away.

'Come and look at the room. Larry said we could –'

'Which one?'

'Opposite ours. It's got a much bigger window.'

He hesitates. 'Thought I'd use that. For painting. Better light.'

'Oh – but –' Her mouth turns down. 'I thought you'd be painting outside.'

'Still need a studio.'

'Studio!' she snorts.

'Our room's OK. You said you loved it. Want me to paint, don't you?'

She goes to the fridge. 'Did you find any bread?'

'Not yet.'

She turns. 'I think it's really selfish of you. You could easily paint in the other room.' Sounds like she's about to burst into tears.

'Hey Cass –' He grabs hold of her again. 'You said you liked our room.'

'Before I saw the other one.' She turns her face away. 'Must get the lunch.'

'Premenstrual?'

'Oh fuck off.'

'Tut tut.' Her shoulders are smooth and sun-flushed. He pulls her to him, kisses her hair, snuffles up the salty, sweaty scent.

'Must get the lunch,' she repeats, stiffening.

'No rush is there?'

She pulls right away. 'Why not go and paint or something? Do some sketching. You've got an hour, at least.' She crouches down to peer into the bottom of a cupboard, pulls out a bowl, leaps back with a little cry as something live falls out. 'And we can *talk* later.'

56

The threatened *talk*. He goes quickly out of the kitchen and round to the shearers' shed to get his pencils.

*

Cassie takes a basket round to the garden to pick tomatoes for lunch. *Premenstrual!* But anyway, lovely breathing in the thick green smell, listening to the dull gush of water in the tank, the cheeping of the birds, the rasp of a grasshopper or something like. Something chips at her, like a beak. Maybe this is all a mistake? Herself and Graham? No. Give it a *chance*.

She cups a tomato, still attached to its plant, in her palm. She wonders what variety it is. A hot heavy handful, rough-skinned. Digs her thumbnail in and the skin grins open, revealing an ooze of cloudy flesh. She does feel sexy, could have done it if she hadn't felt so cross, they would have had the time. Why should *he* have the best bloody room all to himself? She licks the juice off her thumb. The taste is warm and sweet, pungent in a way that English tomatoes just aren't. The tomato unclips itself easily from its stalk. She picks three more. So huge that one each will be plenty.

She gathers some runner beans and a warm limp lettuce, cradled between the leaves of which is a yellow caterpillar, thick as a baby's finger. It rears up at her, displaying the black hairs on its concertina-sectioned underside. She flicks it off and watches it wriggle in the dirt. She lifts her foot to squash it. If she doesn't it will turn into a butterfly and lay a million eggs. Most of the lettuce leaves are frilled around their edges with caterpillar-bite shapes. There isn't a thought in its head, it won't suffer – just simply cease to exist. It would hardly even count as a death. Just a patch of dampness on the ground, drying to nothing within half an hour.

She grits her teeth, looks away and does it. Better than using pesticide.

She wipes her sandal-sole in the dust and goes to fill the watering can from the overflow tank. Good to be busy, doing things, enjoying the green and the smell of growing. *Studio!*

Something so self-important about that word. Why not just *room*? He'd better bloody well get painting, then. The earth darkens with the water, the thick tomato stalks slurp it up, the leaves seem to quiver and stiffen as she watches. She will start a compost heap. Today.

Yella comes round into the garden, nudges her leg with his nose.

'Hello, boy.' He cocks his head at the watering can. 'Want a drink?' She remembers that he's deaf and bends to pat him.

'He doesn't want to drink it.' Larry makes her jump.

'Pour some on his back,' he says.

'What?'

'Go on.'

She lifts the watering can and lets the spray run over the dog's back. He arches it, closing his eyes and groaning with comical pleasure. Cassie ducks and laughs as he shakes, a glittering spray speckling her legs. The stupid creature rolls on to his back and wriggles in the dirt. And stands up, bright-eyed, spiky with mud.

'Simple pleasures,' Larry says.

'Well, yes!' Cassie rubs her sprinkled shins. 'Larry?'

Larry squints at something on a tomato leaf. 'These need a squirt.' He indicates a drum of pesticide. 'Yes?'

'Can I ask you a question?'

'Naturally.'

'Why – I mean, I know it's none of my business but why – when Mara's so ill and everything, do you choose to live so far from – well – *civilisation*, without even a radio or anything –'

'If we lived nearer *civilisation*, as you put it,' Larry says, 'it is likely that Mara would be incarcerated in an institution.' He steps closer and smiles. 'Believe me, strange as it may seem, it's the best solution.' His beard is jutted forward, his pale eyes looking down into her own.

'I'm sure,' she says, 'it must be so hard. It's very unselfish of you.'

'Unselfish?'

'To live here – to give up everything and all for Mara. Not everyone would. What about work?'

'I work.'

'What do you do?'

'Oh,' he shakes his head. 'Plenty of time for all that. Now, must get on.'

She picks up her basket of vegetables. 'I'm going to use organic methods,' she says, 'rather than you know, nasty chemicals.'

'Nasty chemicals!' He gazes at her a moment longer, shrugs. 'Up to you entirely. Incidentally, now we're alone, Graham –'

'What?'

'How shall I put it? He's not quite what I was expecting.'

'What did you expect?'

'Someone more,' he says, 'someone more –' but he breaks off, shrugs, gives her a wry smile. 'But I'm sure we'll all rub along. When we get used to each other. Now,' he looks down at his watch, 'I'll be busy until lunch.' He turns and leaves, Yella at his heels.

Cassie takes the salad and beans inside, washes and slices the tomatoes. Someone more what? Polite? Tall? Humble? Efficient? But she knows what he means. She wishes he was someone more ? too. That's why they're here, isn't it? She picks a tiny grub or two out of the flesh and sprinkles the juicy slices with pepper, salt, oil and torn basil leaves. She boils eggs, cuts up the remains of one loaf and locates another – naturally Graham forgot – in the white furry depths of the freezer. Later she'll start a new batch of bread.

She has an uneasy feeling between her shoulder blades as if she's being watched. But there's no one. She opens the pantry and peers in at the tins. Something scuttling away from the light makes her recoil. An old brown smell in there: oilcloth, candle wax, plain ordinary dirtiness. The whole lot'll need clearing out – some of the cans are ancient, rusting round the rims, the labels scarcely legible. It'll be fun, in a way, getting it all in order. She finds a can of tuna, another of anchovies. Salade Niçoise? Though there are no olives that she can see.

She nips and peels the strings from the beans. He's right. They'll get used to each other. In time. It'll all be fine. She carries knives, forks and plates out to the table on the veranda. A big table, the top of it made of a single slab of wood, but like wood magnified, all the grain wide and whorled around a complex knot. Dirty, too – old food, old God-knows-what, candle wax embedded with crumbs – so much to do. She smiles, remembering the look on Graham's face when Larry told him not to swear.

She stands at the top of the steps and looks past the shed, past the wind-pump and down an incline to a stand of gums. Used to be a paddock, Larry told them, a paddock of five thousand acres, there were still relics of the fence here and there if they cared to look. *Five thousand acres*. Ten times bigger than a whole farm back home.

She can see Graham in the distance, sitting with his back against one of the trees, sketch pad on his knees. He's wearing the unravelling straw hat he's picked up. And she softens, glad about his talent. OK, have your *studio* then. If only he would start to paint again, to be serious about *something*. Their cottage is lined with his paintings, strange things, reflections, oily ripples. How can he be so talented and not want to paint? He says he's stuck but – the way he can catch a movement in a single line. He doodles when he's on the phone, one line he does, never lifting the pencil. With his long graceful fingers he'll sketch a girl turning, the swing of her skirt, a bird taking off, a smile *happening* on a face. That last she'd noticed when he was talking to Jas once. A long and mumbled conversation during which she'd felt resentfully obliged to leave the room, though she'd been there first. And when, afterwards, she'd looked at the pad by the phone there was this *smile*, such a smile, amazing being only a line, actually infectious enough for her to catch it, despite herself.

Eight

Graham stops by the veranda steps. Cassie doesn't see him at first, chin cupped between her hands, she gazes at what? The back of her neck gleams under her heavy ponytail. He lifts his own thick hair off his sweaty skin. She's put the flowers in a vase and filled a glass jug with water, floating with lemon. The big tomato slices overlap on a plate, shiny with oil and green fragments of basil. Could be a composition, a painting there for him, not that still life is his thing.

'Penny for them?' he says.

She starts. 'Don't waste your money. How'd you get on?'

He grasps the sketch pad tighter under his arm. Nothing to show, just a few lines, a tree trunk, a horizon, the flick of a lizard's tail. It's too big to paint. He'd gone into his studio first but no good. So he'd wandered outside, sat under a tree, ready, the paper in front of him, the pencil raised – and nothing. The light had danced whorishly in front of him. What is the point of painting, it made him think, the point of making another painting? If you burnt every painting in the world, then – when the fire was out, and it was all a pile of ash – what then? What's the point?

He kisses her. She tastes of tuna fish. 'You were miles away,' he says. 'Where were you?'

'Just waiting.' She goes into the kitchen and comes back with a plate of bread. A fly settles on it as she puts it down and she flaps her hand at it.

'What's up?'

She looks serious. 'Please, Gray, we need to talk.'

'We *will* talk.' His heart sinks.

'We've come all this way to talk.'

'What about?'

'Us, of course. What do you think? The footsie index?'

He takes a breath. 'I'm *here*, aren't I? That's what you wanted –'

She pulls off a corner of bread, and nibbles, flecks of crumb on her lower lip. 'Yes, you are, aren't you?' She smiles.

'How's the garden then?'

'Great. Gray, *please*. Let's just clear the air,' she licks a crumb off her finger, 'about us. Then we can forget it.' She pauses, 'You know that all I want is a proper monogamous relationship.'

He can't prevent a groan.

'*Don't*. What?'

'You *know*. That word. The M-word.'

She bites her lip. He can see the almost invisible peach fuzz on her cheek, lit up by the sun. 'I don't want to go on and on about it,' she says, 'if we can just have *one* proper conversation, get things straight.'

'It's not the actual being –' he searches for a word that he can swallow, '*true*,' he says, surprised by the simplicity. 'It's that *word*. It's like – monotony.'

'It's *not* the actual being true?' She gazes at him. 'What's the problem then?'

'*No* problem,' he says. At this moment that seems true, too. Her irises are crazed with tawny flecks in this light, more grey, less green.

She pushes her hair behind her ears. '*So?*' she says.

'So, I will, from now on, be true,' he says, finding that he likes

62

that word. That single simple syllable. Doesn't *sound* as oner-
ous as monogamy.

'Not much chance of anything else here!' she says. 'Just so we
can be clear, start off with a clean slate, will you tell me the last
person you slept with?'

'Will *you*?'

'You *know* – it was Rod. And I didn't really want to, it was
only because of you. Only because you did. I never really
wanted to. Though I have to admit –' Her eyes go dreamy
and he feels an unexpected kick of jealousy. She shakes her
head. 'Anyway, that was nearly a year ago. You –'

The door of the shed opens and Mara comes out, Larry
behind her. Graham breathes out gratefully. How true is true
exactly? Mara's hair is a fat plait over one bare shoulder.
Wrapped tightly round her breasts and tucked in to make a
kind of sarong, is a thin brown sheet.

'Are we ready?' Larry asks.

'Yes,' Cassie says. 'I'll just fetch –'

'A bottle of wine?' Larry suggests.

'Oh Larry, yes!' Mara claps her hands.

'As a welcome, a celebration of sorts.'

'Yesss.'

'That would be nice.' Cassie goes into the kitchen to fetch the
grub. Graham smiles at her retreating back. She never drinks at
lunchtime. He likes it when she does though. And later, he
flexes his fingers, bed. He takes his tobacco out of his pocket.

'What's for lunch?' Mara walks with some difficulty, because
of the sheet tangling round her feet, up the veranda steps.

'Something with tuna fish, I think.' He can still taste the kiss.
He pulls out a Rizla and rolls up.

'I like tuna fish,' Mara says. She sits down on the nearest
chair and looks into Graham's eyes. Hers are caramel brown,
darkly shadowed underneath. 'What is tuna but a fish?' she
says. 'You don't say sardine fish or trout fish.'

Graham shrugs and speaks with the fag between his lips. 'But you say dogfish.'

'True,' Mara says.

'You have to.' Cassie plonks the salad bowl on the table. 'Otherwise it's just a dog. Maybe you should smoke that *after* lunch?'

'I, for one, would prefer it if you waited,' Larry says. He pours red wine into the glasses Cassie meant for water.

'Fair enough.' Graham removes the cigarette from his mouth and puts it on the table beside his fork. He sniffs and sips his wine. Soft and peppery, the temperature of blood. 'Excellent,' he says. Even a small sip, even the *smell* of it goes right to his sun-baked brains.

'You know about wine?' Larry turns to him.

'I'm no expert,' he says, 'but I do have some idea. My dad was into it in a big way.'

'What do reckon to this – the grape?'

Cassie flicks Graham an amused look. He sniffs again and frowns, having no clue at all, despite Dad and his famous cellar. 'Cabernet Sauvignon?' he tries.

'Shiraz.'

'Oh yeah.'

'Do help yourselves,' Cassie says. 'It's hard in someone else's kitchen till you get used –'

'Don't think of it as someone else's,' Larry says. 'Think of it as yours.' He raises his glass to her.

'Cheers,' she says.

'Well, cheers. Welcome.'

'Welcome,' Mara says.

'Thanks.'

'Yeah. Cheers.' Graham scratches his chin, not shaved for a couple of days and the stubble itches. He eyes the neat little tube of white by his plate, one ginger wisp of baccy trailing out.

Mara eats with hungry delicacy, dabbing her mouth on the corner of her sheet. Larry has a white linen napkin in a bone ring. He fetches it himself and with some flourish pulls it out and tucks it into his shirt. The rest of them do without. Graham's mother always had a thing about napkins, linen. You had to roll them up after the meal, rolls of white. He eyes his fag again and looks away.

On the sheet under Mara's thick brown arms scoops of sweat are spreading. The smell of her – impossible not to notice it. Repulsive or intoxicating, can't make up his mind, but maybe the last is just the wine? Not like male sweat or sharp and salty like Cassie's, which he's getting used to lately. This is musky and cloying, even sweet – but that's probably perfume.

'You paint, Mara?' he says.

'I *can* paint,' she says.

'Mara is a splendid painter.' Larry smiles at them all, his smile lingering on Cassie the longest.

'Went to the Slade,' Mara says.

'Really?' Graham says.

'You sound surprised.'

'Not at all,' he says. Although he is. Hard to imagine Mara at the Slade – where he once spent a term. He'd started an MA but that's when the rot set in. Hard to imagine Mara anywhere for that matter.

'What are these?' Cassie runs her thumbnail along one of the shallow, wavy indentations on the table's surface.

'Termite trails,' Larry says. 'You'll see them everywhere. See –' He indicates the door frame.

'Termites.' Cassie shudders. 'Why does that sound so much worse than ants?'

'A queen termite can be the size of a cucumber,' Mara says. Graham blurts out a laugh but she looks quite serious. 'Have you seen the termite mounds?' she says. 'They are amazing, aren't they, Larry? That would give you something to paint.'

'Where are they?' Graham asks.

'The nearest colony worth seeing is – oh – quite a distance.' Larry drains the last of the wine into Mara's glass and opens another. The cork rolls down the steps.

'When's Fred coming back?' Mara asks, her voice colliding with Graham asking to see her work.

'I don't paint.' Mara looks down and delicately forks together a sliver of tomato, a slice of bean, a flake of fish and puts it in her mouth.

'I'll explain later,' Larry says.

'No, you will not explain.' A piece of bean pops out of her mouth. 'Excuse me. *I* will explain. There is no need to explain. I paint and burn because I can't paint – paint and burn, paint and burn.'

'Calm down Mara,' Larry puts a hand on her arm. 'I had to stop her,' he explains. 'Fire risk.'

Graham swallows. 'That's weird,' he says, putting down his fork. 'This morning *I* was thinking that.'

Cassie looks up. 'Thinking what?'

'After lunch, a nice rest –' Larry almost looks nervous.

'Aborigines eat termites you know,' Mara says, shaking his hand off. 'But never the queen.'

'You *weren't*,' Cassie says.

'The queen is sacred.'

'I *was*.' Graham frowns. 'Well, not exactly,' he says, softening his voice. 'Hard to explain.'

'No need to explain here. There never is, is there, Larry? Let it be a rule.'

'Mara,' Larry leans towards her, 'you're getting overexcited.' He turns to Cassie. 'Shouldn't have let her have the wine really. But special occasion –'

Mara laughs, her lips, despite the constant dabbing with the sheet, glistening with tuna oil.

'Doesn't mix with her medication. *Do* calm down, Mara.'

'That is now a rule. I *am* calm.' She holds up her glass: 'I hereby declare it a rule. Rule number – I don't know – that we never need to explain.'

'Explain what?' says Cassie.

'Anything. No need to explain. It is illegal to explain. Or to ask someone to explain.'

Cassie stares at her for a moment. 'Brilliant!' she says, smiling at Graham. 'Eh, Gray? What a brilliant idea!'

'Yeah,' he says. What a pity she doesn't mean it. He catches Larry staring sharkishly at Cassie. Can't blame him. Beside Mara – not that Mara's ugly or even plain – Mara meets his eyes and he realises he's been staring at the sweaty sheet and the squashed slopes of her breasts above it. Small dark scattering of moles like a constellation. He looks into her heavy-lidded eyes. That plait, it's thick as a rope.

'Would you paint me?' Mara says.

'Don't do portraits as such.'

'As such!'

'Could you pass me the water, please?' Cassie says. She nudges him under the table with her knee. He looks down. Her shorts have ridden up to reveal the very white skin there above the blurry edge of tan. Rightio then, he thinks, after lunch on that old bed.

Larry pushes the jug towards Cassie. She pours water and drinks, eyes closed with the pleasure of it. Graham watches the smooth swallowing motion in her throat.

'What do you do?' Mara says, suddenly jabbing her finger in Cassie's direction. 'He, he is a painter.'

Cassie wipes her mouth. 'I teach part-time, adults. Gardening and stuff.'

'She does all kinds of things,' Graham says. 'Mind if I light up now?' He flicks his lighter and inhales the smoke. 'She's a great cook.' He breathes out smoke. He feels suddenly good. Happy, lazy, half-pissed. In the mood for sex. 'A *great* cook.' Great in bed, he thinks.

'A terrifically useful person.' Larry says.

'Sounds like an obituary!'

'But true,' Graham says, putting his hand on her leg and squeezing. 'A very practical person.'

'And practically pissed too. Shall I make some coffee?' She stands up and staggers a bit, catches her hip on the corner of the table. 'Ouch. *Shouldn't* drink at lunchtime.' She begins to stack the plates.

'Leave it for now,' Larry says. 'Go and lie down. I'm sure you'd like a lie-down.'

'Well,' she grins and holds on to the table as if for balance. 'Yes.'

Larry meets Graham's eyes and smiles.

Nine

G raham follows Larry's eyes following Cassie down the
steps and round the side of the house.

'I wonder what it's like to be blonde,' Mara says. An
iridescent green fly crawls at the corner of her lips. 'I wonder
if you see colour differently through different-coloured eyes?
I've always wondered.'

'There is no way of telling,' Larry says.

'No.'

They sit for a moment, considering this. Flies drag their legs
stickily over the plates, making Graham itch. Rubs his chin.
Must shave. He should have got up when Cassie did. Feels stuck
now. He rolls himself another fag.

'Smoke?' Larry says.

'Sorry, want one?'

'Got some nice grass –'

'Yeah, sure.' He conceals his surprise in a yawn. Cassie will
want to sleep anyway. Maybe after a smoke Larry will mellow.
He slaps away a fly. Doesn't understand how they can be so
indifferent to them – though it's Mara they crawl on, not Larry.
Impossible to imagine flies crawling on him. Mara eventually
lifts her hand and flicks the fly off her lip and into the air where
it buzzes dully and alights on Graham's arm. He shakes it away,
slapping the skin against the crawly sensation of its feet.

'Won't hurt you,' Mara says, smiling at him. 'Just a little fly.'

Larry pinches a line of dried grass on to a brown cigarette-paper. His tongue flickers like a lizard's at the paper.

'Neat?' Graham says.

Larry nods and juts his head forward for a light. Graham flicks at it with his Zippo.

Will he ever get used to it, flies or any of it? He lolls back in his chair, stretches out his legs, looks around him. A couple of lamps and many candles and candle ends are balanced on the wide veranda rail. Rusty wire implements, meant for God knows what – one a trap maybe? – hang from nails.

Mara yawns. 'Sleepy,' she says. She stands up, steadying herself on the table, treading on the hem of her sheet so it tugs down to show the side of a breast.

'Be with you shortly.' Larry looks at his watch.

'He's wonderful to me.' Mara puts a hot and heavy hand on Graham's shoulder. 'Where would I be?' She fills a glass with water, gulps it greedily and fills it again, takes it with her down the steps, holding it with two hands like a child. The back of the sheet is damp where she's been sitting, a butterfly print of buttocks and thighs. She goes inside the shed and closes the door.

'Ta.' Graham takes the skinny spliff, damp from Larry's mouth. He closes his eyes and sucks in a lungful of sweet smoke. Immediately the floor beneath him seems to lurch. 'Jesus,' he says.

Larry throws his head back. 'Nice, eh? There is some advantage in genetic modification!'

Graham squeezes his eyes shut. Can't think. Half-cut, disorientated, jet-lagged, now this blast, which is not what he needs now. Shouldn't smoke, doesn't do his brains any good. Never has. Makes him act up. Makes him paranoid. Inside his eyelids lights fizzle like sparklers. He opens his eyes to see Larry smiling, cool as a bleeding cucumber.

'Interesting. A sensitive constitution,' he observes.

'I'm fine.' Graham takes another shallow puff, holding the smoke in his mouth for a moment before exhaling and handing it back to Larry.

'Nothing to be ashamed of,' Larry says.

Graham gets up to demonstrate his fineness, props himself against the veranda rail, his back to the view.

'Do you have a particular sensitivity to drugs of any kind?'

Graham stares at him. 'What? Why?'

'Cassandra?'

'*Why?*'

'You and Cassandra – how are you, together –' Larry hesitates, 'physically?'

'*Fuck* off,' Graham says, on a whoosh of anger. He shuts his eyes a moment. Squeezes his hands into fists, takes a breath, gets himself under control. 'Sorry.'

Larry shakes his head, and leans towards him. 'Listen, my friend. If you and I are going to get on,' he begins and stops, as if choked. Christ. He's not going to *cry*? Graham turns his back, looks down at the stand of gum trees, tiny from here, sharp against the blue. A parrot hops on to the veranda rail, pink and grey, what seems to be a common type. It tilts its head and eyes him maliciously.

Larry clears his throat. 'Galah,' he says.

'Sorry?'

'Name of the bird.'

Yella heaves himself up, goes over to his water dish and laps. Sits down and scratches his ear, dust puffing from his fur. Cassie will be naked, maybe not asleep, maybe waiting for him in bed. And he thinks of Mara. Waiting for Larry? Hard to picture it. He grins at the picture that does flash into his mind, Larry's spindly white legs between Mara's monumental thighs.

'What about you and Mara, *physically*?'

Larry looks back at him without expression.

'None of my business?' Graham suggests. A parrot screeches behind him, making him start. 'Look,' he says, 'this wasn't my idea, right? Let's get it straight. I came to please Cassie. And I hope to get back into painting. OK?'

Larry's face is bland. 'Absolutely. And I too would prefer not to be here. I stay here only because of Mara.' His expression seems fragile, a thin mask. Bravery? Bravado? Graham feels a spasm of pity. Little jumped-up control freak that he is, Larry is trapped. There must be, somewhere in there, an OK streak. You have to give him that.

He turns, feels as if the world is turning with him. Grasps the veranda rail to hold himself still. Larry offers the spliff but he shakes his head. Larry takes one more puff and grinds it out. 'She takes some looking after,' he says. 'Some patience. Without the medication she's –' he opens his hands. 'And even with it, it's not always possible to keep her stable.'

'Where do you get it?' Graham says. 'The "medication".' A smile worms through him; he imagines ridiculously, a giant bottle and spoon. 'You don't have the "flying doctor".'

'Mara's condition is a bit beyond any "flying doctor", I'm afraid.' Larry stands up, starts stacking plates. 'I'll do these. *This* time, while you're still acclimatising.' He smiles. 'By the way we are both looking forward immensely to seeing your work, seeing you begin to paint. What you make of –' he gestures to the view.

Graham feels something twist in his guts. He is, it comes to him, afraid. He wants to be painting again, didn't realise how much till this moment. How unsatisfied he's been. *Unsatisfied.* That's what's been the matter. For years. It seems so simple. Why has it not come to him like that before?

'You look done in,' Larry says. 'Why don't you go and rest now, with Cassandra.'

'*Cassie.* She hates *Cassandra.*'

Larry nods, sadly? And Graham feels bad again, obscurely guilty. 'I'll go and get some kip, then. If you're sure.'

Graham goes down the steps, looks at the peeling blue door behind which Mara will be awaiting her 'medication'. He almost trips over a hen, scrabbling something out of the ground, surely not a worm in this dryness. It helter-pelters away on its long stringy legs, squawking.

As he walks round the house, he sees the end of a ladder, sticking out from under the veranda. He bends down to look. Can see the frozen shape of the goanna – good fortune, eh? – under there along with Christ knows what else junk. He pulls out the ladder, a tall one, old grey wood, rusty rivets. There's a trick he used to do. Way back when. The ladder sheds bits of web and crud and he drags it away from the veranda, stands it up, balances it, up against nothing. If he can do it, then it'll all work out OK.

He holds the smooth, wide, textured sides and looks up at the narrowing perspective of the rungs as they recede, counts: twelve. He puts one foot on the bottom rung, then the other. The ladder holds. He goes up a rung, then another. Remembers the physical sensation of it. The ladder swaying, you have to oppose the sway, concentrate on the balance, adjusting all the time, a rung at a time, balance, balance, balance and fuck it all, he nearly does it! Gets up more than half the rungs and stands there swaying, high in the blazing afternoon.

*

As she'd sat, wine glass in hand, her eyes had suddenly gone unfocused, tiredness had crashed into her like a car. Jet lag maybe. She'd thought she'd got away lightly. She'd half stag-gered back, went in the dunny, shutting her nose to the smell, her ears to the deep booming of flies beneath her; splashed her face with water and then, at last, got into the shed, into their room, too warm but shadowy at least. Private. More homey now she's brought in another chest and a couple of chairs, swapped the cowskin rug for the rag rug, and borrowed the patchwork quilt.

She'd peeled off her clothes, folded them over a chair and sunk down on to the soft old saggy bed to wait for Graham. Please don't let him annoy Larry. What will they be talking about? But really she's too tired and treacle-brained just now to care. Doesn't feel right, naked and uncovered. That stupid feeling that someone can see. She pulls back the quilt and blanket, covers herself only with the thin pink sheet. Outside, the birds, a kind of budgerigar cheeping, maybe *actual* budgies and something else squawking. So much less sweet than English birds. How long till the foreign bird song starts to sound normal? The pillow is soft and she immediately begins to slide steeply and surely into sleep.

Sometime later and from some echoey cavern she hears Graham come in, hears the clink of his belt as it hits the floor, tips towards his weight as he gets into bed. She catches the sharp tang of coal tar soap and then he is kissing her, his face moist and bristly, breath hot with smoke and wine.

'I climbed a ladder to the sky,' he mumbles drunkenly into her ear.

'What? Leave off.' She tries to push him away.

'Come on Cass –' His hand goes to her breast and squeezes, travels down her belly and, though the advance is crude, his hand stirs her up. He makes a glow where he cups between her legs, like something radioactive. It's time they got round to it, after all. She shifts her legs apart a little, kisses his smoky mouth. He touches her, one hot finger creeping into her folds, rocking back and forward, making her slippery, making her heart beat fast. She grabs his hips and pulls him against her. He pushes inside and she groans and gasps, it's a surprise every time, how good it is, how he fills her till she feels her heart will burst. How good they are, the two of them. How she loves him,

74

how whatever else she feels at other times, her body is in love with his. She digs her heels into his backside, arches up under him.

'I love you,' she says.

'Me too.'

They do it very fast and hard. The kind of sex that leaves her wanting more, but now in this heat she's happy to lie, sticky and pleasantly throbbing, listening to him fall asleep. She kisses him between his shoulder blades where a patch of black hair grows like a crop of silky grass. She's never mentioned the hair to him, wonders if he knows it's there. Hopes not. It's like a secret between her and his body.

After only a moment, his breathing turns to snores. But she can't sleep now. Randy, too hot, squashed. There's no way they can avoid being squashed together on this dipping mattress. She always says 'I love you' first, and he always says, 'me too'. The pedantic streak in her that she tries to suppress, squeaks its objection. He loves himself? That came from her dad, who always twiddled with any word you said. She'd hated it as a child and now she does it too. She turns over crossly. But why can't he just say it first, for no reason. Maybe she should stop saying it and see how long before he notices – if he ever does.

She needs to pee again. But it puts you off, using that horrible dunny. Weird that there's no bathroom in the house. Why haven't they seen the rest of the house? They haven't got past the kitchen. She tries to ignore, to deny, the full prickly feeling in her bladder but it's no good. She heaves herself up and Graham rolls right into the middle, snuffling contentedly in his sleep.

She pulls on her dressing gown and sandals and goes outside. Facing the scrubby bush, small trees with leaves like tooled leather, she opens the dressing gown, holds it wide like wings, feeling the breeze on her body, quite delicious. If this place was near that gorge it would be perfect. A swim every day to keep them fit and clean and cool them down. She wonders how far to the nearest swimming pool. If they could only swim – even once a week.

No one around, no one to see. Some lovely parrots, pink and grey ones, squabble in the trees. The leaves make a silvery shushing, cool-sounding, almost like water. She walks a little way from the shed into the bushes and crouches down. The grass that looks so soft is like spines. She jumps up rubbing her bottom. Maybe that's spinifex – good name for it if it is. Squatting again, feeling like a little girl indulging in an illicit pleasure, she watches the urine pooling between her feet, splashing her sandals, and sinking into the earth. A poor ant struggles up out of it waving a feeler. She goes to the sink, rubs between her legs with a soapy flannel. She rubs a bit harder than she needs to, the soap stinging the tender skin, feels her heart beginning to skip again, catches her breath – stops abruptly. What if someone *could* see? She pulls her dressing gown round her, hurries back inside to bed.

Ten

Graham bends over to study Cassie. Heavily asleep, hair sprayed over the pillow as if she's fallen from a great height. One breast shows above the sheet, flattened by gravity, the nipple smooth, rosy. The same shade of rose as her lips. He puts the mug of tea down on the floor and sits gently on the edge of the bed, leans in close to her face. Her skin gleams, pale eyebrows damp, jaw loose, eyelids like frail veined petals. You can see her as a twelve-year-old, all the tension erased from her skin in that faraway sleepy place. When he kisses her, her eyes flip open and she looks at him without recognition, just for a startled second, before she frowns.

'Hi,' he says.

'Been watching me?'

'Brought you some tea.'

'What's the time?'

She hoists herself up to sitting, and her breasts, hair, everything, tumble into their everyday, wakeful order. She scrubs her eyes. 'Couldn't think where I was.'

He hands her the mug.

'Ta. So, what were you and Larry talking about?'

'We had a smoke.'

'A *smoke*? Larry?' She pulls a face. 'Ouch, hot handles.' She wraps an edge of the sheet round the handle. 'Really?'

77

'Grass. Yes.'

The frown lines between her eyebrows deepen as she gazes at her tea. She blows on the surface of it before she sips. 'Get on OK with him?'

He shrugs.

'Next time we're in town I'll buy some china ones,' she says. *Next time we're in town?* He looks at her. The feathery blonde tips of her lashes in the steam. Is she joking?

She lifts her arm to loop her hair away from her neck. 'Maybe he has it for Mara? The grass. For therapeutic purposes.'

'Nah. She went to bed.'

'I like these siestas. Where's *your* tea?'

'Going to drink it on the veranda. Shady. On the swing-seat.'

'OK.' She draws her legs up, rests the mug on the table of her knees. 'Hey – all that about the rule!' She sips tea through her smile.

He looks at her blankly.

'"It is illegal to explain." All that stuff. Do you think she's putting it on?'

'Not a bad idea,' he says.

'Hmmm. You're not getting out of it that easily! We haven't finished that talk – no, don't look like that –' she smiles. 'I just want us to get straight, get everything straight then we'll start again. Clean slate, sort of. If we're seriously going to give it a go.'

'OK,' he says. 'Fair enough. But later, eh?' He gets up.

'Wearing that sheet!' she says. 'Like some sort of toga!'

'Yeah. Right. See you in a bit.' The door bangs behind him as he leaves. Some of the little trees have things growing out of them, like big candles poking up. A weird type of flower. And wiry stretches of cobweb glinting between them. How do the spiders spin so far, from tree to tree? Assuming they are spiders and not some other Australian peculiarity he's never heard of. His mouth feels like the bottom of a parrot's cage only the parrots aren't in cages, they are loose.

78

The front veranda steps are rotting and what was once the front door is blocked with all kinds of crap. He reaches for his tea and sits down on the swing-seat. It rocks back, creaking, rust flaking from the chains. He looks at the shearers' shed through the bushes, twisted gums behind it, salt-water pump tower, a couple of red hens, a patch of that yellow stuff – what is it again? Looking this way, rather than from the back veranda, the scale is more familiar. And a couple of young gums with their white trunks – they could almost be silver birch. Maybe he could paint this? But what for?

His heart slumps against his ribs. He rolls a fag, closes his eyes. Tired still. Feels like weeks since they left home but it isn't yet a week. He listens to the birds, the creak of the pump. Amazing he can still do that ladder trick though. Nearly. He lights up, leans back, shut his eyes. *If we're seriously going to give it a go. Seriously.* When he looks at her, touches her, when they make love, when he thinks of never seeing her again, it's all clear. But words like *serious* –

Last row he had with his parents; last words his father hurled at him. *Grow up.* They'd been to his degree show. Proud, though it wasn't what they'd chosen for him. But still, he'd done well. *A first, darling!* They'd brought an art dealer friend with them. A lot of talk about pulling strings, all that shit. Pressure. Dinner afterwards in a restaurant, his mother with her hair sprayed into a stiff gold seashell. It was fine but then they had to start, the two of them. Some double act. *Time to buckle down, old chap. Join the real world. We've given you every advantage.* The pleasure of his success had leaked away. He'd thought they'd at least be pleased; that they'd see who he was; that he'd proved he was OK. But it was still the same. Not good enough. Translation: he wasn't really theirs.

They'd drunk champagne to toast him, then wine, then he had ordered more, even after they'd started putting their hands over their glasses. He'd listened as long as he could to them going off on this riff about his future, about being *serious*, about *responsibility* and then he'd stood up and told them to fuck off, knocked his chair down, grabbed the bottle from the table. 'I say,' the art dealer friend had said. 'Fuck responsibility,' he'd shouted again, loud as he could, revelling in the scene. It makes him cringe now. But what can he do? And then he'd walked off. The last thing Dad had said to him: *Grow up*.

He's hardly thought about them for years. Cassie can't understand it. Why not trace your real parents then? she'd asked. But that would just be someone else with expectations he couldn't live up to. So close to her twin, she can't imagine not having family. But family –

A sudden tickle on his thigh and he jumps up, yells, mug flying out of his hand off the veranda, tea arcing into the dirt. A spider, a huge hairy fucker, gone now, somewhere. He scrubs at his leg. Must have come out from under the cushion. Can't see it now. He looks up into the eaves where it is dark and rustling. Feels as if a million tiny eyes are on him, all those spiders who could be gathered there in the deep shadow, taking the piss. He looks thirstily at the cartoonish splash in the dirt.

The door of the shearers' shed bangs and Cassie comes out, twisting her hair up as she walks towards him. She picks her way through the bushes, stands below the veranda looking up at him. 'What's up?' she says.

'Nothing. Spider.'

'Spider?' She looks down at the mug, the splatter of wet in the dirt. She picks the mug up, comes up the steps, her lips twitching.

'It was fucking huge. Right on my leg.'

'Where?'

'Gone.'

'What colour?'

'What difference –? I dunno. Spider-coloured.'

'*Oh*.' She shakes her head, squashing down a smile. She's

wearing the dress he likes, loose, light-blue. 'Let's have a look, then.' She pulls the flat cushion off the swing-seat and there is a spider – smaller surely than *the* spider – crouching there, body suspended between its hairy legs, white eyes in a black head.

'There,' she says, trying to shoo it off the seat. It doesn't scuttle away and hide like any decent British spider but sticks there, gloating. 'Looks pretty harmless to me,' she says. 'I'll ask Larry. Maybe he's got a book we could look it up in.'

Her braless breasts swing like bells against the thin cotton of her dress as she leans over. Larry appears. 'Everything all right?' he says. 'Thought I heard a shout.'

'Yeah, yeah, it's all OK.'

'He saw a spider.' Cassie wrinkles her nose and smiles. Larry's eyes – bloodshot – slide from her smile to her tits.

'Right to be cautious,' he says.

'What is it?'

'Oh, common or garden,' Larry drags his eyes away from Cassie, 'squash it if you want but don't tell Mara. She thinks it brings bad luck. But you make your own luck here in my opinion. In future, before you sit down, do look under cushions and so on.'

He goes down the steps, humming something. From above you can see the gleam of pink scalp through his hair.

'Hey,' Cassie puts her arms round Graham's waist and kisses him, lips moist and slightly open so he can feel the edge of her teeth. He cups her buttocks and squeezes. 'Bet you feel a prat,' she says.

'Did you see him looking at your tits?'

She pulls away from him. 'Yeah. Some men do that, you know, they can't help themselves. They don't even realise they're doing it. It's like – routine – like you might check the year of a car or something.'

'Do I?' Graham says.

She tilts her head, eyes sparkling into his. 'Well, yes, actually.'

She goes off, grinning over her shoulder. 'See you in the kitchen.'

*

Cassie sticks the kettle on and gathers together flour, yeast, a big bowl just like her bread bowl at home, bumpy brown outside, white inside. *Outback Kitchen. Cassie's Outback Kitchen*. She sifts the flour, holding up the sieve to demonstrate to an imaginary TV camera. She grins thinking of Graham and the spider, she'll write about it on her cards to Patsy and Mum – *you should have seen his face!*

The yeast practically jumps out of the packet in this heat, the granules fizzing as they touch the sugared water. No problems with it proving in this climate. The smell of yeast must be somewhere near the smell of heaven; she breathes it in. Delicious, heady, bready, healthy smell. The smell of something coming back to life.

She pours the yeasty froth into the flour, pulls a spoon round the bowl, plunges her hands in to gather the sticky strands into one mass, begins to knead. Imagining the camera focusing in. The dough is warm as flesh, growing buoyant as she squeezes and presses almost like . . . mmm – she sniggers – getting turned on by a lump of dough!

The door opens and she starts a smile, expecting Graham, but it's a stranger: male, short and barrel-chested in a dirty black vest.

He stops, looks startled to see her, as if he's seen a ghost or something, then collects himself. 'Hey Yella.' He scratches the dog behind his ears.

'Hello?' Cassie says.

He blinks at her a moment, shakes his head, smiles. 'Sorry, you look like someone. Took me aback, like. I'm Fred.'

'Hi,' Cassie says. 'Larry mentioned you. I'm Cassie.'

'G'day, *Cassie*. You here alone?'

'With Graham, my boyfriend. He'll be over in a mo.'

Fred nods thoughtfully. 'Larry about?'

'Somewhere – maybe working. I'd make you a cup of tea but –' She splays her fingers and the dough stretches between them like flabby webs.

'No worries.' He dumps the plastic bag on the table. 'Meat,' he says.

'I'll put it in the fridge in a minute. You live nearby?'

He hacks out a laugh and she can see a gold tooth glinting. 'You could say that.' He sits on a stool and watches her. She kneads self-consciously. She can't guess his age, skin brown and creased like an old man's, though his shoulder-length hair is brown, dusty but not a thread of grey. His eyes gleam at her, squinting as if she's in the sun.

'So, how do you like it here?'

'Australia? I love it.'

'But *here*?'

'Well –'

'Takes a bit of getting used to, doesn't it?'

'We've only just got here.'

He opens his mouth to speak but changes his mind. Cassie lifts the dough out, slashes the cushiony mass into three, covers them with a damp cloth. 'Tea then.' As she fills the kettle she hears Larry whistling something operatic. He comes into the kitchen, claps a hand on Fred's shoulder.

'Good man,' he says. 'Heard the ute.' He looks over at Cassie. 'You've had the pleasure, I see.'

'No, mate, but I've met her.' Fred throws his head back and laughs, a sound like an outboard motor starting up. She's been warned about Australian men – especially in the outback. Unreconstructed, is the word. He finishes laughing. 'You didn't say you had people coming.' He looks at Larry and he gazes back, a shiny blank look. 'Can I speak to you outside a minute, mate?'

Larry holds out his hand: 'Our neighbour. All in good time, Fred.'

'Nice to meet you. How far away?' Cassie asks.

'Hundred k. East,' Fred says.

'That's *miles*!'

'And after that, there's no homestead in that direction for what?' Larry says.

Fred shrugs. 'Thousand k or so I reckon. Edge of bloody nowhere here. End of the flaming world.'

'Hmmm.' Cassie feels sure there must be closer things in *other* directions. The way this lot show off about distance. As if there's something clever or macho about being miles from anywhere. She looks at Fred's bare feet on the floor. Stubby feet with childishly neat toes. He must be mad to go barefooted with all the . . . things about. Her eyes get stuck for a minute, fascinated by the loveliness of the feet, leather-soled and some-how innocent.

Graham comes in, blinking with surprise to be faced with so many people. 'Graham, Fred, Fred, Graham,' Larry says.

'Hi.' Graham holds out his hand.

Without getting up Fred extends his and Cassie sees with a pang that he has no thumb on his right hand, sees Graham noticing and flinching in the instant before he grasps the hand.

'Fred's our next-door neighbour,' Cassie says. 'Only 100 kilometres away!'

'Beer anyone?' Larry says. He pulls a pack of beers out of the fridge.

'Meat,' Fred says, nudging the plastic bag, dark and wet inside. A smear of blood has leaked on to the table. 'Roo. Roadkill – but fresh.'

'Beer, Cassandra?' says Larry. She shakes her head, eyeing the meat, hoping she isn't going to be expected to deal with it.

'I'll light the barbie in a tick,' Fred says.

Obviously quite at home.

Graham takes a beer. Fred grasps one to his chest with his thumbless hand, nicks the top off with the other. 'How's Mara doing?' he asks.

'As always.' Larry pours his beer into a glass.

'So, what's your line of work?' Fred swivels round to Graham, swigs from the beaded bottle, belches. 'Sorry, love, better out than in.' He winks at Cassie.

'Graham paints,' Cassie says.

Graham wipes froth off his top lip. 'Sometimes.'

Cassie goes to put the kettle on. She wants tea even if no one else does.

'Fred,' she says, 'do you have family? Children?'

The air seems to condense. Larry winces and looks down.

'No,' Fred says. And there is a long and awkward silence in which the three men audibly swallow their beer and the water in the kettle fidgets towards a boil.

'What do you do out here?' Graham asks.

'I mind me business,' Fred says.

Graham flushes, bends down to stroke the dog.

'No offence, mate.'

'None taken,' Graham says, stiffly.

' 'Spect you're wondering what happened to my thumb?' Fred says, catching Cassie looking at him.

'*No!*' she says, 'I hadn't even –'

'Remarkable lack of curiosity,' Larry says.

'No,' her face goes hot, 'of course I'm interested.'

Fred laughs again, the startling sound. '*Course* you are, love. See.' Fred holds out his two hands, the right one is almost rectangular without the wing of thumb. 'When I was a nipper, 'bout twelve, I was off with me dad in the bush, having a rare old time. And there was this snake, see – well, I didn't see – not till it was too late. Brown Snake, deadly. Well, just come out of the water – having a swim – and this little brown bugger – before I knew it –' He clutches the place where his thumb was.

'There was me dad with his knife, grabbed hold of me and hacked it off.'

Cassie squirms in her seat. 'Cut off your thumb?'

'It was either that or watch me cop it then and there. Once that bugger's venom gets in your bloodstream you're a goner, no two ways about it. Then he dug a hole and buried it.'

'The thumb or the snake?' Cassie grasps her own precious thumbs against her chest.

Fred laughs. 'Me thumb! Didn't take a very big hole.'

'I could *never* do that,' Cassie says. 'Could you, Gray?'

'It was that or curtains,' Fred says.

'One never really knows *what* one would do if one was pushed to the very limits,' Larry says. He smiles at Cassie. 'Does one?'

'Well, no.' She looks down at her knees. If only she could think of something witty. 'Excuse me a minute.' She goes outside and down the veranda steps, a blast of laughter following, not *you* they're laughing at, she tells herself. What *is* up with her?

She stands irresolutely in front of Mara's door. It's not right, not healthy, Mara shut up in there, in all that stuffiness. Maybe she could offer her a cup of tea? She knocks but her knock sounds feeble and there's no reply. The paint has peeled off in map shapes; she picks at a flake, sharp under her fingernail.

She longs to talk to Patsy. If *only* there was phone or email. It had never occurred to her that there would be no phone. The distance makes her giddy suddenly, a rope unfurling from her diaphragm to her sister but it's too far to reach, the connection gone. Not even in the same time zone, can't imagine what she'll be doing. She walks out into the humid, almost solid, afternoon heat. She walks away from the house until it is small behind her.

First, noting the stand of trees on her right, she shuts her eyes and walks as if through a field of hanging sheets, her hands pushed out ahead to part the air. Under her feet the crust of dried dust reminds her for a second of snow, but that memory melts instantly, leaving the sensation of grit on her lips. Hard to make herself walk with her eyes closed, hands pushing forward, hard to trust that there's really nothing to impede her. There *is* nothing.

Small sharp shrubs dried to leather, nothing else for maybe half a mile until the bush thickens. There's nothing and no one. She needs someone to talk to. Someone other than Graham. Mara in that shed, suffocating hot red room, the thought of it makes her gasp for air. She dares herself on, like she and Patsy used to, on the beach, or the playing field. A competition, who dares to keep their eyes shut longest. They'd walked, eyes shut, hands in front like sleepwalkers. One leading the other, step up, step down, stop!

She remembers leading Patsy very near the edge of the canal, Patsy trusting her, just the smallest step out of line, the smallest stumble and she'd have fallen in. The temptation to make her walk right along the very edge, just to see if she might fall. Patsy's blonde ponytail just like hers, the checked school dress, the runkly white socks under her sandal straps. But she didn't fall. Or maybe she was cheating, looking through her lashes, just like Cassie did when it was her turn.

A sharp jab on her shin makes her eyes fly open – a snake! But it's just a thorny plant, a bright bead of blood on her leg. She smears it and licks the dark taste off her finger. And looks round, startled. She's swivelled on her course. The trees are behind now instead of on her right. Yet she didn't turn. She walked straight, she's sure of it.

Feels like someone's watching, stupid, they're all indoors. No one watching. What *is* up with her? But the *feeling* is there – a shadow at the corner of her eye? She whips round. No one. Of course. Idiot. Just the sun playing tricks, eyes playing tricks, imagination playing tricks. She goes back towards the house, forcing herself to walk at a normal pace and not to run.

Dear Patsy,
How are you? Do you realise this is by far the longest
we've ever been out of contact? Of course you do. It's all
pretty weird here. The man, Larry, and G haven't really
hit it off that well, but I think it'll be OK. L _is_ a bit weird
but I like him, he's amazing, giving up everything to live
out here with Mara, his wife, who's really not well. Mental
rather than physical. Not sure yet quite what's wrong but
she wears a sheet and spends most of the time alone in a
shed!

Hope Katie likes the picture of a kangaroo. I really miss
you, Patsy. I'm not used to not being able to tell you
everything – and knowing everything about you. Hope
Al's not being a pain, tell him he'll have me to answer to.
(That'll scare him!)

It is beautiful here though, in a stark sort of way. We're
getting brown. And, G would say, browned off! Though
he's bagged a room (the best) for a studio so I hope he'll
start painting. He's petrified of the spiders! Quite sweet
really. I'll bore you rigid with photos when I get home.
Garden lovely and I've started a compost heap.

Give Katie the biggest hug you can without squashing
her. And stroke Cat for me, give him some extra Munchies. Thanks again for having him.
Lots of love,
Cassie
xxxxx

Eleven

Graham lets his head hang back, stretching his throat. The sky is wrong. The constellations warped and much too fierce.

'That's the Southern Cross,' Larry says. He leans close to Cassie on the log seat beside the barbecue. Graham watches her chin travel up, her eyes follow his finger through the meaty smoke and into space. 'That group of three and –'

'Tucker's about done,' Fred says. 'Where's the plates?'

'Refill?' Larry offers more wine around. Whatever they are likely to go short of here, Graham thinks, at least it won't be booze.

Mara sits beside him, the flesh of her thigh pressing against his, her smell again, maybe just the smell of an older woman, sort of ripe. She's wearing the same old sheet, dark smudgy lipstick. Scarlet parrot-feather earrings tangle with her hair.

'Like your earrings,' Cassie says.

'Fred made them for me.'

'Make you some an' all if you want.'

'Oh thanks!'

'Keep your eyes skinned for a couple of nice feathers.'

'Most intelligent creatures on the planet, parrots,' Mara says. 'Fred said, didn't you Fred?'

'Humans aside, presumably.' Larry eases out another cork.

'Heard it on the radio.' Fred flips the kangaroo steaks over one last time. 'Ready with them plates, Laz?'

Laz? Things are obviously fine between Fred and Larry now but earlier he'd left them in the kitchen to go for a slash and when he'd got back they'd been rowing. Least, he'd heard Fred shout something and, rather than walk into the middle of it, he'd gone away again. But maybe he'd got it wrong.

'Some test they did,' Fred continues, hefting alarming hunks of meat on to the plates, 'whales, dolphins, dogs, parrots, and parrots came out tops, would you believe.'

'Can't imagine *how* you'd test a whale alongside a parrot,' Cassie says.

'Anyway!' Mara is triumphant. 'Parrots won!'

Graham winces at the thought of such intelligent creatures flying free, *thinking* all over the place. Thinking *what*? Doesn't seem right, somehow. Some old aunt or something of his mother's they used to visit when he was small had had a parrot, a stinking grey thing, blind in one eye, that clutched your fingers in its scabby claws if you stuck them through the cage. 'It'll have your finger off,' the old woman used to say but he couldn't resist poking at it, though the smell nearly made him choke. He wonders what *it* thought, if it was so clever.

Larry hands out the loaded plates. In the light from the kerosene lamps the meat looks almost black, covered in ashy flecks. Graham takes a bite of the tough charry meat and chews.

'What do you think of the kangaroo?' he asks Cassie.

'Very nice,' she says through a mouthful, refusing to meet his eye.

Larry sits back down beside her with a contented sigh. 'Fine bread, Cassandra.'

Cassie swallows with difficulty. 'Thanks. *Please* call me Cassie.'

'If that's what you'd prefer. Though it seems a shame to mutilate such a beautiful name,' Larry says.

Fred guffaws. 'Mutilate! Get a hold of yourself, mate!'

'Cassie,' Larry says, tipping his glass to her.

She smiles and sips her wine. Graham stares at her expression, sort of pleased and smug. Is she getting off on these smarmy looks?

'So, you're gonna be painting?' Fred says. 'Used to dabble in that line a bit meself.'

'Yeah?'

'Years back.'

'The painting in the kitchen that caught your eye,' Larry says.

'That's not you?' Graham looks through the smoke at Fred, a shadowy shape but for the lit point of his fag. 'It's beautiful, man. And you don't paint any more?'

'Nah.'

'That's criminal.'

'You can talk,' Cassie says.

'*Criminal*,' Larry repeats, amused.

'What exactly *is* it that *you* do, Larry?' Graham says.

'Research,' Larry replies, shortly.

'On what?'

'Collation of pre-existing data.'

'Into –?' Graham says. He enjoys making Larry squirm. What's the big mystery? And where does he get off, looking at Cassie like that? Prat.

'*Graham*,' Cassie says, giving him a look.

'Good and lean,' Fred smacks his lips.

'There's plenty more,' Larry says, 'do eat your fill.'

'What do *you* do then, Graham?' Larry says. 'I take it you haven't been artistically productive lately.'

'I'm starting a compost heap,' Cassie says.

Fred almost chokes on his food.

'So put all your fruit peels and tea leaves in the bucket by the sink.'

'I can get you a sack of compost, love.'

'No,' Cassie says. She leans towards Fred and begins to explain.

The meat in his mouth, the smell of Mara by his side, remind Graham of something. He strains his mind at the tease of it and remembers the old woman with the parrot again: how once he'd had to stay with her alone, can't remember why, Mum in hospital maybe. She'd called him into her bed in the mornings, for a cuddle. She'd had no children of her own, she'd told him, never even married, but she did like to cuddle a boy, she'd said, and he had submitted, face against the scratchy lace of her nightie, holding his breath against the smell of her. Once she'd said, 'Shut your eyes and stick your pinkies in your ears,' but he'd watched her squat over her chamber pot, her nightdress spread, and heard, despite his fingers, the slow widdly sound, watched how she patted herself dry with her hem before climbing back into bed.

And in her cold kitchen the meat she cooked for the cats. That's it. Something rises in his throat, preventing him from swallowing. She didn't keep a cat because of the parrot but all the strays in the neighbourhood would come every afternoon to her door. Her friend the butcher gave her unsold meat to feed them with and afternoons were the smell of it boiling, the grey liquor she poured down the sink, the knobbles of chewed gristle and yellowish beads of bone the cats left in the yard.

He swigs his wine, empties his glass, the thick purple taste of it washing away the taste of the meat. He hasn't even *thought* about her for years. And now, he almost misses her. Although she must, surely, be dead? And he never knew. Can't even remember her name. Or who she was. He's hardly given his parents a thought for that matter. Never felt the lack. Though it is a lack. Only from this distance can he feel it.

Beside him, Mara chews the meat, he can hear it mashing and catching between her teeth. He focuses his ears away, outward to the noises of the night, scuffles and cries, the generator.

Mara's arm brushes his. Through his sleeve he can feel the cool of her solid flesh. The skin at the tops of her big sheet-flattened breasts is brown, almost sheeny, the line between them fine and black like a brushstroke. He looks away quick. Under the veranda he sees a movement, catches a gleaming eye. Only the lizard thing, the goanna, squatting by the veranda steps.

'I'm whacked,' Cassie says. 'I'll have a cup of tea and go to bed if nobody minds. Anyone else?'

Fred startles everyone with his laugh. 'Tea! Bloody sheilas!' He knocks back his beer and cracks open another bottle.

'Gray?'

'No, ta.'

Cassie carries her plate inside. To chuck her meat away, he guesses, enviously. He's got to a thick bit that may not be cooked right through.

'I'm going in too, Larry,' says Mara.

'I'll get you your pills,' Larry says.

'Don't hurry,' Mara hauls herself up. 'I'll go and talk to Cassie in the kitchen.'

'No,' Larry says. 'You're tired. You should go to bed.'

Mara pauses, opens her mouth, then shrugs. Feeling Graham's eyes on him, Larry turns. 'She mustn't get overtired,' he explains, 'it exacerbates her condition.'

'Hey,' Graham says, a surge of energy, impatience. He puts his plate down. With any luck the dog'll eat his meat. 'Before you go, Mara, I've got a trick, wait –'

He goes to fetch the ladder.

'Shine the torch, Cass.' He points to Fred's big tungsten torch sitting on the veranda rail.

'Why? What are you doing?' Cassie says, but she switches it on. It dazzles him a moment.

He holds his finger up, 'Silence please, ladies and gentlemen,' The ladder rises above him to the stars. He climbs one rung, the next and the next, hearing Mara gasp, smiling as he steps up

93

again, swaying, swaying, he sees the long swaying shadow, maybe too much wine, his foot slips and he has to jump down, just manages to catch the ladder before it crashes on to the barbecue.

Larry gives a slow handclap. 'I'd say, stick with the day job if –'

'Try again,' Mara says.

But Cassie is shaking her head at him. She switches off the torch. The energy has gone. *Prick*. 'Nah, need more practice.' He puts the ladder back, and standing in the dark, looking out into the pitchy nothingness, feels like he could cry.

*

Cassie scrubs her teeth, spitting the froth into the sink. There are still stringy threads of meat between her teeth. Doesn't really like eating meat but at least kangaroo is free-range, about as free-range as you can get. Can't find the floss. Too tired to care. Too tired to care that her skin is clogged with suncream and sweat. Too tired to care about anything but getting her head down. Behind the bedroom door, she lets herself go in a voluptuous yawn and stretch. The candle burns low. She lights another. The light wavery and soothing, kinder to her tired and prickly eyes than electric would have been. She sheds her clothes and staggers into bed, the creak of it carrying her almost immediately into a deep and fur-lined sleep through which she doesn't hear Graham come to bed.

The first she knows is a hard kiss on her mouth, so lacking in tenderness, so *unlike* him, that for a moment she thinks it must be somebody else. But it is his face, the chin bristly, the breath hot with wine and meat.

'Hey,' she grumbles, 'I'm asleep.'

But he doesn't stop kissing and in the candlelight his eyes look blind. He fumbles at her breasts, jams a knee between her legs, forcing them apart.

'Hey?' she says and tries to pull away but finds herself unwillingly turned on. He's never like this, it's weirdly exciting. She puts up a mild struggle but he forces himself inside her, sore and tight. He's hardly in before he finishes, groans and rolls off. And that, it seems, is that.

She lies staring at the ceiling, waiting for him to speak, but he says nothing.

'How was it for you?' she says after a minute.

He mumbles something. Maybe sorry? She gets up, the insides of her thighs warm and tacky.

'You bastard,' she says half-heartedly. She pulls on her dressing gown and goes outside to wash. The sky is sequinned above her, preposterously bright. She stares upwards, all those wonky stars and the cloudy swathe of the Milky Way. When she gets back in he's asleep, lashes casting angelic shadows on his cheeks in the candlelight. She stares at him. Did that really happen? Asleep and breathing evenly, like a child. She thinks to kick him awake, turn him out of bed, make him sleep in his bloody studio.

But it is *Graham*. And she is tired. And doesn't want to be alone. She puffs out the candle, climbs back beside him, rolling unwillingly close against his hot skin. The starlight prickles through the thin curtains. Between her teeth the threads of meat begin to taste of rot.

Dear Mum and Dad,
You'll be surprised to hear from me. I am surprised to be
writing to you. I'm in Western Australia with my girlfriend
on a kind of disused sheep station. I've come here to paint.
I

Twelve

Alone in the kitchen, Cassie slices onions and weeps. Weeping because this morning she broke her mirror. Just knocked it flying. She picked it up but the glass was cracked, still in place but cracked into maybe twenty pieces, curved and geometric shards that reflected her face in bits like something by Picasso. She can get new glass, of course, when she gets home, but it won't be the same glass that reflected her grandma. Cassie remembers Grandma holding it up so that she could check the back of her hair, in her dressing-table mirror. New glass will not be the same. She didn't cry when she smashed it. Maybe the sting of the onions has set her off.

And maybe it is tiredness too. Couldn't sleep last night. Graham's peaceful sleeping breath. She'd lit the candle and watched his cheeks ballooning with air and then his lips opening with a soft *puck* on every exhalation. She'd tried to think about the garden. If they could start a pond and have frogs then the frogs would eat the bugs. She'd wondered if there were any indigenous frogs in this dry place, must ask Larry. She tips the onion skins into the new compost bucket (how will she ever stop it swarming with flies?), pours oil into a pan, slides it on to the hot plate.

She wipes her eyes and turns at the sound of the door opening, hoping it is Graham – he was up and out early this morning so there has been no chance to talk. And he never gets up before her. Up and out early to make damn sure there was no chance to talk. At least he can't escape for long. Not here.

But it's not Graham, it's Mara, stark naked except for a pair of men's boots, laces trailing.

'What's up?' Mara says.

'Nothing.' Cassie wipes the back of her hand across her face, smearing tears with salt sweat. She half smiles, wondering if Mara is aware of her nakedness. She seems completely unabashed. Cassie doesn't know where to look.

'What are you making?' Mara asks.

'I normally start frying onions then I decide.'

'Use up the poor kangaroo?'

'Roo Stew?' Cassie wrinkles her nose. A speciality in *Cassie's Outback Kitchen*?

'Fred adores stews.' Mara pulls up a stool and sits down, her heavy breasts resting on the table like a couple of seal pups. It's hard not to stare. The breasts are fine, at least supported by the table like that, the skin smooth and plump, years younger than that on her neck and face.

'Larry says you haven't been well –'

'Not well! I am a danger to man and beast! What has he said? Larry?' Mara grabs Cassie's hand and pulls her near. 'What has he said about me?'

'Nothing, he only says –' but Cassie's mind has gone blank. She's distracted by Mara's nipples gazing at her like calm brown eyes. The hand squeezes. She can't remember quite what Larry said or implied. 'Something like you needed peace and quiet – that you are –' The word 'delicate' comes to mind but that is the last word for this broad, brown woman in boots. 'That you like your own space,' she tries and Mara releases her hand.

'My own space. Well, that's right.'

'He's obviously devoted to you.'

'We are a devoted couple,' Mara says. But the way she says it – Cassie frowns. 'I'm not stupid you know,' Mara continues, fiercely.

'I can see you're not. Larry says you're brilliant,' she improvises.

'He says that?' Mara's face opens with pleasure. 'Brilliant people – they must be sensitive. The world does hurt so.'

Cassie picks at a speck of something on the table. *The world?*

Mara gives a sudden cavernous yawn, stretching her arms up so that her breasts lift, so that Cassie glimpses the wet red at the back of her throat. She turns away and slides the onion slices into the pan of swimmy golden oil. The sizzle is immediate, electric, sweet.

'Fred now,' Mara says. 'What do you make of Fred?'

'Seems nice enough.'

Cassie gets the remains of the meat out of the refrigerator. She puts it on a wooden board and saws through its sinews with a knife. Blood oozes into the grooves on the wooden board. She holds her breath against the smell and the memory of the thick clump against the bottom of the car as they'd hit a carcass in the road on the way.

'Oh, Fred.' Mara smiles and shakes her head. 'Care for an anchovy?' She goes into the larder. The shape of the chair seat is printed on her wide and dimpled bottom. Her hair is in a thick plait down her back, the tail of it reaching into the groove between her buttocks.

'Not for me.' Cassie hacks the meat into rough chunks, shoves it into the pan and rinses the wooden board and knife under the tap quickly to rid them of the blood. The frying pan makes a deeper sound, the blood instantly killed, turning to sticky brown.

'I adore anchovies,' Mara says. 'But I can't open the flipping tin.'

Cassie takes it and unpeels the top with its fiddly key. Mara sticks her fingers in and lifts out a couple of bristly fillets. Dripping oil, she puts her head back, opens her mouth and pops them in. Cassie smiles, thinking seals again. Mara's eyes close as she relishes them.

'Anything salty,' she says, 'but anchovies especially. Anchovy paste now. That on toast.' She sighs.

'Never tried it,' Cassie says. 'Have we got some?' *A spoonful of anchovy paste adds an intriguing dash of flavour*. A drop of fish-flecked oil slithers into the gully between Mara's breasts.

'Yes. Larry loves Gentleman's Relish. *Peperium*. What a word.'

Cassie hears a noise outside – maybe Graham. She starts: what if he walks in with Mara stark – but it is only the dog nosing his way round the flyscreen.

'Yella,' Mara says and the dog jams its nose into her crutch. Cassie looks away. Graham's bound to come in, sooner or later.

'Mara,' she says, waving her hand vaguely, 'you are –'

'What? Oh, you mean *me*. Get off.' She pushes the dog away and he humphs and curls up under the table. 'Don't believe in clothes,' Mara says. That's why we live here, partly. Heard of naturism? Didn't go down well in Lewes – but here –'

'Naturism? Oh. But Larry –'

Mara holds her belly and bends over in a fit of mirth. 'It's not Larry's . . . cup of tea.' She straightens up. 'Without his clothes he would be . . . insignificant and we can't have that!' Her eyes sparkle with mischief. 'And he makes *me* cover up in company. But you're not company any more, are you? You're part of it and he pays you.'

'Hmmm.'

'Worrying about your man?' Mara laughs and sucks a finger.

'Might make him uneasy though, don't you think?'

'Does it make you uneasy?'

'To tell the truth – well, a bit. We're just not used –'

'But you'll soon *get* used. You could take yours off too.'

Cassie hesitates, then giggles, imagining Graham's face if he was to walk in on the two of them naked in the haze of fried onions.

'The others, they never got used –'

'The others?'

'You look like her.'

'Who?'

'Lucy. Anyway, Larry's not here. Just me. It's only me – and Graham – and he's seen you, hasn't he? He knows you, inside out.'

'Lucy?'

But Mara shakes her head.

Cassie moves the pan away from the heat, the meat is cooking too fast. It will be tough as Mara's old boots. Probably should have marinaded it. 'Anyway, where *is* Larry? Do you think he'd mind if I opened some wine, for the stew?'

'Doubt it. He went off with Fred. Didn't he say? *See*, now you're here, he's got the freedom. To come and go.'

'But where?' Cassie stares at her. 'I'm cooking all this stew.'

Mara shrugs. 'I could eat a horse,' she says. 'Maybe I'll have an egg to be going on with.'

*

Graham's head is thick, brains curdled with sun and dust. The scale is impossible. The light makes no shadows and even where there is shadow there is no *moulding*. It is all too big. He is helpless in it. The ridges of hills they flew over he understands now as like the ripples of sand left on a beach after a choppy tide – but immense, gargantuan. He stands insect-like, a speck under the steady pulse of the sun, lost in the vast spaces between the dry ripples. There is no clear place to start.

He'll head back instead. Face the music. In the early morning, feeling ridiculous, grinning to himself at the absurdity, he had left a trail of objects as he walked out – to guide himself back. But it proves not to be absurd because he sets off back in the wrong direction. There's something that confuses him every time. Maybe the sun's in the wrong place? The other side of the sky? You might think you don't notice where the sun is but if it's on the wrong side, in the wrong hemisphere, it disturbs something in the brain. You are disorientated on some level you didn't know you had.

He walks back, the way that feels the wrong way and finds the first object: a matchbox. He heads off now with confidence, picking up a pencil, a book, toothpaste (that has split its minty chalk into the red dust), and a couple of beer bottles, till he begins to recognise the lie of the land, that stand of gums then the eye-stinging glint of sun on a tin roof. His mouth is dry, head wet under his hat. A crow mocks him with its Siamese cat's cry, hopping and dragging its tail feathers, flapping heavily upwards and landing in the dust beside him as he follows his trail. The bird with its dirty carrion beak and its knowing eye makes him feel sick or maybe it is just the sun.

He's hung over. He wants Cassie, longs with sudden fierceness for her northern arms around him, for the something cool that she retains. But she'll be mad still about last night. It isn't him at all, to act like that. And then to fall straight asleep! He simply, momentarily, wasn't himself. Almost literally. Yet he can imagine what she'd say if offered that as an excuse.

He smells cooking from miles away, approaches, hears women's voices in the kitchen. Something comforting about that. Something ordinary. He pauses outside, takes off his sweaty hat. Inside, it takes a moment for his eyes to focus on Mara's skin. Broad back, swell of hips, sturdy legs in boots. Cassie's eyes meet his over Mara's shoulder.

'Something smells good,' he says, voice coming out a bit high.

'It's me,' Mara says, turning, massive tits shoogling about with laughter.

'Roo stew,' Cassie says.

He goes to the fridge, opens the door and stands with his front in the cold waft of stale air. 'Beer?' he offers.

'Let's all have a beer,' Mara suggests.

'Should you?' Cassie says.

'Yes.'

He sits down, stares at the mess on the table, eggshells, crusts, a sticky anchovy tin with, of course, a fly dragging its legs in the pooled oil. Big nipples, tiny black hairs like spiders' legs –

He opens three bottles and presses the chilled glass of one against his cheek, gulps it down, the beer so cold and prickly it almost hurts. Mara passes him, her breasts swaying inches from his face and sits down. Her skin is every shade of caramel brown. Cassie is watching him so he can't look. Can't think of a thing to say. The ceiling fan turns above, stirring the hot shimmery smell of cooking. He feels that he might choke.

'Where is it?' Mara asks.

'Sorry?'

'What you've done.'

'Not today. You know how it is.'

Mara laughs again, a cascading jiggle of flesh. 'You're embarrassed. By me. It will rub off.'

Graham stands up. He forces himself to look squarely at Mara before he leaves the room. The lines of her. To look at her as a thing, an object in space. Taking in all of her he can see at the table, the overlap of flesh at the seat of the chair, the brown shin with its straight black hairs disappearing into a flap of boot, the shoelace coiled like a query on the floor. He looks up at the large breasts, the kind of breasts you could cast yourself upon and weep. Cassie's eyes are on him, watching him look. He can't look at her.

He goes out. The cold bottle already heating in his hand. He stumbles over hens round to the shearers' shed, runs the tap, sloshes his face with tepid water. He takes off his shirt and splashes his chest and neck. He picks up the soap and tries to make a lather with the briny water, not much of a lather but still it smells childishly of coal tar.

In the hot room, he pulls off his shorts and flops face down on to the bed, grinding his face and hips against the scratchy cotton of the patchwork quilt. Last night rises in him again like a dream. And a jumble of images – dust and meat and naked skin. He groans.

*

Cassie opens a tin of chickpeas, another of tomatoes and adds them to the pan. She crumbles a stock cube and throws in a handful of herbs, her concentration shot, the way Mara is watching her. Makes her clumsy.

'You cook with – what's it? Pizzazz,' Mara says.

'Pizzazz! This kind of thing, it's you know –'

'No?'

'Never the same thing twice. Hey, Mara, it's nice to have someone to talk to. A woman.'

'Shouldn't really.' Mara puts her head on her arms. Her long plait knobbles like a second spine down the centre of her back.

'Shouldn't what?'

'I'm sleepy.'

'Why not go and lie down?' Cassie gives the pot a final stir and puts a lid on it. 'I'll clear up then I might take a break.'

'OK.' Mara's voice comes muffled by the flesh of her arms.

'Will you be all right? When will Larry be back?'

'Maybe tonight, maybe not.'

'All right, well, this'll keep. Might taste better tomorrow. Mature.'

'He was embarrassed,' Mara says, sitting up suddenly, her face red and damp.

'Well, maybe a teeny bit.'

'I call it naturism but really it's – I can't bear a thing about me tight, especially about my waist. It chokes me.' Mara's voice rises to a wail. 'And the *choosing*. One day I woke and knew I couldn't dress or else. Couldn't choose. I can't tell you what the feeling's like – like *graspers*.' Her fists open and close, a look of panic on her face.

'It's OK,' Cassie says. 'Calm down.' She looks at the door, wondering about Mara's medication, if she should be taking something right now. Larry should *not* have gone off like that without a word.

'If Larry hadn't been there. It is why – why everything here – what I did –'

'Yes?' Cassie bites a finger. What to do?

'And here I am free of waistbands and obeying. Free to paint. To not.'

'I see.'

'And Larry he is a saint although . . . he *is* a saint, getting me the drugs I need and deciding everything for me so all I need to do is be. All I need now –' Mara loosens her fists and lays her hands on the table, palms up, the skin fretted with nail marks.

'What?'

Mara shakes her head.

'Anyway, I think I understand,' Cassie says.

Mara searches her face for a moment. 'Yes? I think I must go and lie down.'

Cassie breathes out. 'Yes, yes, that would be best.'

Once Mara's gone she leaves the clearing-up, hurries straight round to find Graham. He's flopped face down in the middle of the bed, wearing only his boxer shorts.

'Hey.' She perches on the bed's edge and takes off her sandals; starts to pull her T-shirt off, changes her mind and smoothes it down again.

Graham turns over. His hair is stuck in wet strands to his forehead. She hesitates and then lies down beside him. 'Move over,' she says. He tries to inch across the hollow mattress, but their bodies tip inwards. His arm comes up, pauses, comes round her shoulders. She sighs and lifts her head to let it.

'So?' she says. His arm is hot and rubbery under her neck.

He puffs a stream of slightly sour breath. 'Sorry, OK? Don't know what got into me. Maybe a bit pissed.'

'You only had to *ask* –'

'Just came over me,' he says, 'like a huge *urge*.'

She giggles warily.

'Won't happen again.'

They lie for a moment in the cube of sweltering air; relax against each other as the tension leaks away.

'I love you, anyway,' she says.

'Me too.'

She turns and kisses the side of his face. 'What about Mara, then?' she says after a moment, lifting herself up on her elbow to see his face. 'You got quite an eyeful there.'

'Nowhere else to look, was there?'

'S'pose not. Did it turn you on?' The question flips out of her mouth before she can stop it.

He breathes in, holds it, replies on his out breath. 'Just taken aback.'

'*Taken aback!* Yeah, me too.'

'What about *Larry* then?' Graham says, narrowing his eyes.

She wets her finger and smoothes down his eyebrows, which are bristly with dust. '*What* about Larry?'

'Fancy him, do you?'

'*Graham!*' Surely he can't think that? She stares at him to see if he's joking but his eyes are shut. She lies down and snuffles up the smell of him: sweat, soap, his own peppery man smell. 'She normally does go naked, she was saying to me. Clothes give her a sort of claustrophobia. Sounds like she has had some kind of breakdown. Larry made her wear the sheet just till we got settled in.'

'We'll have to get used to it then,' he murmurs.

'She got a bit – worked up. She's quite disturbed. We need to know what to do if – if she goes off her rocker or anything. Hey, did Larry tell you he was going away?'

'Don't think so.'

'Not very good, is it? Just pissing off like that without a word.'

'No.'

'What shall we do?'

Graham turns on to his side so they're facing. His long green eyes smile into hers. 'Hmmm?' She catches her breath. He runs a hands down from her shoulder, skimming the side of her breast and brings it to rest on her hip. The tip of his tongue rests on the centre of his lower lip, as he concentrates on her in the way that makes her melt.

'Again?' she says, her voice gone husky, her belly dissolving to syrupy gold.

Thirteen

He wakes to the sensation of her hand stroking softly from his breast bone to his belly, ticklish. He squirms, opens his eyes. His limbs feel like sandbags. He could easily sleep again. He shuts his eyes against her scrutiny.

'Just smoothing down your hairs.' He feels her breath on his chest as she leans close. 'Oh look, you've got a white one.'

His heart goes still under her fingertip.

'I'll get some tea, shall I?' she says. 'Or shall we get up?'

He feels her move away, the bed shift as she leaves it.

'Won't be long.' She pulls a dress over her head, sticks her feet into her sandals and goes out. He listens to the sounds: some cicada thing, birds, a gurgle in his guts. He sits up and looks down at the wings of hair on his chest, and there is one white hair amongst the black ones. Not only that, he sees with horror a kind of softening around his belly. Could be the gut of an older guy. A middle-aged gut. His heart beats dully in his ears. He takes the white hair between his finger and thumb, pinches it between his nails and tugs it out. Sharp nip that brings a sting of tears to his eyes. You settle down, you get old, you die. He holds up the hair. It glistens, a sinuous white pointer to somewhere he doesn't want to go.

He gets up, pulls on his jeans, a vest. Leans forward to see himself in Cassie's cracked mirror. Separate scraps of face.

Lines round the eyes; white hairs along the hairline and when he bares his teeth they look yellowish and uneven. He goes out to the dunny to have a crap. Sitting in his own smell with the rumble of a million flies beneath him, he feels a surge of panic. There is no way out of it. Either you die young or you grow old and die and he's already too old to die tragically young.

He goes out. Must do something, it's rushing past like a film, he's here now, what is he doing here? This is his *life*. He reaches over and puts his hands in the dirt, kicks up, falls down, kicks up again and again until he's balanced on his hands, wrists straining, arms trembling and he takes a step.

*

Cassie comes round the corner: teapot, biscuits, mugs on a tray. She stops and blinks. She'd thought he was going back to sleep and here he is walking on his hands, neck bulging with the effort, hair trailing in the dust. 'Hey!' she says. She feels like that woman from the nursery rhyme, what is it? Old Mother Hubbard. *She went to the baker's to get him some bread, when she got back he was stood on his head.*

He flips his feet back to the ground, stands up, red-faced.

'Coming back in for tea?'

He hesitates, looks past her as if there's somewhere else he'd rather go, then shrugs. 'OK.'

They go in. It's so *hot*. She slips off her dress, sits cross-legged on the bed, naked, pouring tea. He stands by the door as if ready to bolt.

'What's up with you?'

He comes over to the bed and sits down. Reaches for a half-smoked roll-up and lights it.

'If we have a baby together,' she says, '*big* if, I know, you'll give up, won't you?'

'What?' he says, drawing the fag away from his lips and squinting at it.

'Smoking.'

'Give up *smoking*?'

'What was all that about outside?'

He shrugs. 'An impulse.'

'You should have been in a circus, you.' She smiles. 'Have your tea. At least not smoke in the house, then, not around the baby.'

He puts his head back and lips a smoke ring and then another. She watches them rise, swell and disperse. Though the smoke is still there in the air. She's surprised he doesn't set the alarm off. A spasm of irritation tinges the warmth she was feeling.

'You never answered me,' she says.

'It's hypothetical.'

'But that's what this is *about*.' He stares into his tea, picks something out of it, a little fleck or a fly. There's red dust in his hair, getting on the sheet. 'Anyway, I didn't mean that. I meant what we were talking about before.'

He looks at her, a skin of something hazing his eyes. His pupils are huge. Even his long curving lashes have dust on their tips. 'Why do you want to know? You'll only get upset.'

'So we can,' something like fear slides in her stomach, 'so we can start with a clean slate.' It sounds pathetic, even to her. Why does she want to know? He's right. What does it matter?

'This isn't going to work,' he says.

'What?'

'I shouldn't have come.'

She feels winded. She says nothing. The impulse to cry drags her mouth down at the corners so she can't sip her tea.

'I mean, fuck it all!' He gets up. 'A *year*! A year of my life. Stuck *here*. I can't waste a *year*.'

She manages to get her lips under control. He's smoking angrily, shifting about, making the floor creak. 'A year will go past anyway,' she says, 'whether you're here or not.'

He frowns at her, then snorts so that smoke streams from his nostrils.

'Anyway, it's not a waste, is it? Not if you get painting again. Really, in a way,' she treads carefully, 'you could say the *last* few years have been wasted if you look at it like that. And –' She holds out her hand to him and, after a beat, he takes it, 'if we're going to be together. I really do,' she presses his fingers, her lips tremble, 'love you.'

'Yeah. Me too. Maybe I'll go and paint then.' He goes out quickly, leaving her wincing with a spasm of painful love. She looks down at the crumpled dusty sheet; a smear of ash; the place where tan turns to white high on her thighs. At least here he can't run away.

Box 25
Keemarra Roadhouse
For Woolagong Station
16th November

Dear Patsy,

Feels like we've been here yonks already. Sometimes I wonder how we'll stick it for a year. G and I getting on fine, mostly. But we are on top of each other a lot (ha ha). We are, literally. I have never felt so randy in my life. Must be the sun. I've stopped using my diaphragm – can't wash it properly, don't want to catch something amoebic – and Graham says condoms spoil it. (Did I say there's no bathroom? Which is good of course, ecologically speaking, dunny outdoor, far less water wastage, but I must admit I'd love a proper shower and hairwash. My hair looks like shit – can't shampoo it properly, it just goes all sticky with the salt. Goodness knows how Larry always looks so clean.)

So if I fall, I might end up a single mum. Don't care. Anyway it'll probably take months. Took you a few months didn't it? I really really miss you. No one to talk to. We had a row this afternoon. He's gone back to walking on his hands and stuff. Is that a good sign???? Another kid!!!! ??? There's a man called Fred who's nice, very Australian, kind of rough but _normal_ if you know what I mean. Hope Katie likes this koala card. I'll bring her a stuffed one (toy!) when we come back.

Love to her and Al, extra Munchies for Cat.

Miss you _loads_,

Cassie

xxxxxxxxxxxx

PS You'll never guess, he accused me of fancying Larry! What a turn-up for the books! Do you think that's a good sign?
PPS I don't of course, though I admit he has got a certain something . . . Maturity, I guess.

Fourteen

From under the trees, Graham watches the arrival of the ute. Larry and Fred unload boxes and eskies, bags. A silvery chink of bottles travels across the dust and Graham swallows against a sudden thirst. He presses his back on the bark of the tree and swigs tepid water from a bottle as he watches them. Watches tiny Cassie in the blue dress and straw hat go down the veranda steps to meet them. From here she could be almost anybody. *Give up smoking!*

With a surge of energy he lifts his pencil and begins a line, but the energy dies straight away, the line trails off across the page. His wrist tired, sweat on the pencil, time smearing on the page. He must do *something*. This light baffles the hell out of him. Doesn't lift his heart as even the wettest grey/yellow concrete winter city light would. His *home* light. He could paint *that*, why did he let them stop him? But what can he do with this? It is all too stark and open, nothing to reveal. Every mark he's made on paper so far – it's all a load of bollocks.

He swigs more plastic-tasting water, tears off and screws up his sheet of paper, drops it on the pile. He flicks his lighter. The flame's too pale to show. He idly picks up one of his screwed-up pages and sets it alight, holding it between finger and thumb as the flames gnaw along the creases, turning it to ash that holds its shape for just an instant. He drops it when the flames reach his fingers and it collapses to nothing in the dust, nothing but a smudge. Before he gets up to go back and join the others he burns every other page he's wasted, one by one.

*

Candles flicker on the table and the veranda rails. A moth bats against the pale globe of the kerosene lamp suspended over the table. Each pause in the conversation is filled with the dim flutter of flaking velvet wings.

The food is finished, red smears left on plates. Larry fills the wine glasses again. No one refuses, though they have all had far too much. Cassie picks up her glass immediately and sips. It's spicy, dark, she doesn't care what. Perfect with the stew, Larry said. So glad he liked it. So glad when he and Fred came back. Now she needn't worry about Mara. Cigarette smoke rises and gathers under the veranda roof. It's cool enough for even Mara to have a shawl around her shoulders.

It's late. Time to be in bed but first there's the table to clear and all these dishes. She can't summon the energy so she sips her wine instead. Graham and Fred are deep in conversation about some artist.

'Let's have a tune, Fred,' Larry interrupts.

'Yes, yes.' Mara claps her hands.

'Graham, I believe you play the mouth organ,' Larry says.

Graham's hair is loose about his face, hiding his expression. 'Blues harp, yeah, sometimes.'

Fred goes off to fetch the guitar from the shearers' shed and Graham gets up and follows. Cassie clears some of the plates. Larry comes into the kitchen with the salad bowl. 'Everything all right?' he asks. 'I thought you looked a little –' He looks at her intently. 'I hope you're not sad?'

Cassie shakes her head. He looks so awkward, ill at ease with feelings. Nice of him to notice though. Nice of him to care. 'Just a bit homesick, maybe,' she says.

'Well, that's natural.'

'No one to – you know, *talk* to. I miss Patsy.'

'Naturally. I know it's not the same, but you can always talk to me, you know.'

Graham comes in, slapping his harmonica against his palm. 'Some crud in this,' he says, looking in surprise at Larry, who steps back from Cassie as if he'd been too close.

'Poor Cassie, been telling me she's homesick,' he says.

'Oh yeah?'

'Not very,' Cassie says. 'Well, I bet you are a bit.'

'Just a *bit*!' He smiles, meeting her eyes at last; sucks a bendy wail out of the harmonica.

The sound of Fred twanging the guitar into shape floats through. Larry touches her shoulder and goes out.

'What was that about?' Graham says.

'What?'

'You want to watch him, you know.' He backs her against the sink and tries to kiss her.

'You're drunk,' she says, pleased, shoving him away.

'And you're not?'

She pushes him again. 'Moi?' He kisses her, smoky, bristly, deep with a tinny harmonica edge. She loops one of her legs round his. 'Are we OK then?' He kisses her again, but less deeply and pulls away.

A riffle of ragtime comes through to them. Cassie has a sudden urgent hankering for something cool and sweet. 'Hey, imagine ice cream,' she says and shivers.

As she goes back out with the tea, Larry opens yet another bottle, the sound like a finger popping in a cheek. Like Dad did, she thinks, almost shocked by the memory. You could scream at the top of your voice here and no one would hear you. But maybe tomorrow, someone rounding up sheep a thousand miles away would catch the trail of a scream drifting past and pause to wonder. And then forget. *Stupid* thought. She shakes it from her head.

Mara hunches forward, her breasts crushed together, cradled in her arms like a baby. 'His fingers are like fishes when he plays,' she says, and Cassie can see the shoal of them flickering on the strings.

'Tea anyone?' she asks, but no one answers. And she can't even be bothered to pour it for herself. She settles back and, feeling a glow in her belly, puts her hand there. She feels like she did when they were first together and couldn't keep their hands off each other. Graham looks sexy when he plays. She picks up her glass again and Larry leans over and tops her up.

'I must drink water,' she says into his face. 'I made a pot of tea.' Her voice comes out a slur.

'You and your tea!' Larry laughs and touches her shoulder. Through the fleece she feels his fingertip linger.

Graham shakes his harmonica, picks up his fag. He narrows his eyes, looking at her through the smoke.

'Shall I pour you a cup?' Larry asks but she shakes her head.

Fred's fingers dart across the strings, a sudden feeding frenzy. She grins. Larry is still watching her.

'What?' Larry says. 'What's the joke?'

But she can't be bothered to say, doesn't trust her voice. He gazes at her for a moment longer, as if she's worth puzzling over, then he turns away.

'Who'll dance?' Mara says, getting up and jolting the table so everything clatters. A candle topples over, briefly flares and goes out. Cassie stands it up. Something brushes her cheek, something soft, a scrap of fallen moth-wing perhaps. Mara holds up her arms, her red shawl stretched across her back like wings.

'Like the moth,' Cassie says.

'What?'

But she shakes her head and watches Mara throw her head back, eyes closed, and start to sway. Cassie gathers the hot

116

spilled pool of wax into her palm. It almost, but not quite, burns.

'I love to dance,' Mara says.

Larry gets up and leans against the veranda post. Cassie thinks he's going to dance but he just looks at Mara. She can't read his face. Graham watches too, this naked woman moving to the music. Cassie watches for his expression. It strikes her as funny – almost. She brought him here to get him away from other women, and now there's *this*, right in his face. And him going on about Larry! Well, it won't hurt him to wonder.

Fred's eyes are shut, his features crouched intensely as he improvises a riff, humming with it, beating the side of his fist to make an extra element of rhythm. Looks weird, the way he picks and strums with his thumbless hand, but it works. It's brilliant. He is. Shut inside himself, the music pouring out. The wax is hardening in the scoop of Cassie's palm. Mara's body is waxy and luxurious in the unreliable light.

The shawl slides from her shoulders. 'You, dance with me,' she says, pointing to Graham.

'Nah.' He shakes his head.

Cassie looks to Larry, expecting him to stop Mara, say she's overtired, or overexcited or in need of medication. But his eyes fix on Graham. 'Dance,' he says.

'Why not?' Graham gets up. Mara's smile is like a surprised and grateful child's as she reaches up her arms and sways with him, her breasts pressed flat against his vest. Must feel hot like that. Must feel soft. Cassie squeezes the wax and digs her nails in. They turn, the dancers, so Graham's back is to her. He prats about a bit, wiggling his hips, bending Mara down. All he needs is a rose between his teeth. Mara laughs, breathlessly, her hand like a starfish on the small of his back. It's only dancing. The wine has not agreed with Cassie. She needs to drink some water, needs to get out of here and lie down.

Fred plays on, as if oblivious to the dancers. She feels Larry's eyes on her and when she looks up he gives her a slow smile.

'Dance?' he says.

'No,' she says. The wax is hard, she drops it on the table and gets up. 'No, thank you.'

She pushes past Graham and Mara, who do a half-turn to let her pass. Maybe Graham tries to catch her eye, she doesn't look. 'Dishes in the morn,' she says, careful not to slur, catching hold of the rail to stop herself stumbling down the steps. She goes round behind the shearers' shed and out of sight. The stars are up there, wrong in the wrong sky, the moon is full and blank white, a counter stolen from some game. Its light is strong enough for shadows. In the shadow of a tree, she's sick.

Dear Mum and Dad,
My girlfriend and I are in Australia working on an ex-
sheep station. You'd like Cassie, I'm sure. I'm painting. I
know it's a long time since I've written. After my degree
show I, that argument, I ~~didn't mean~~ *I*

Fifteen

An ashy morning. Burnt-down candles, fag-ends stubbed in the remains of stew, food dried on to plates in a scabby crust. Should have finished clearing up last night. Flies crawling, buzzing, rubbing their dirty hands together. Cassie's head aches, the light stabs as she collects the glasses, carries them into the kitchen. Almost all the plates have got dirty, somehow, as if there were twenty people here, not five. It's getting out of control, the kitchen. The sink still full from last night. *Cassie's Outback Kitchen*. Ha! What is up with her? At home she would never let it get in such a state. She has this kind of almost constant *lassitude*. She hasn't done anything much to the garden except keep it tidy, hasn't even started her patchwork. The effort of planning, the effort of *thinking* – well, there will be time.

The range has gone out so no hot water to wash the dishes till she cleans it out and lights it or Graham does. When he wakes up. How everyone sleeps round here, it drives her mad, the sticky snoring. What she would not give for a swim. A plunge into cold, clean water. Something scuttles in the corner as she reaches for the shovel to scrape the cinders out.

It was only polite of Graham to dance with Mara. What if he'd refused? They are being paid to be companionable and companionable was what that was. The sort of thing companions do. Dance. *She* should have danced with Larry. What would Graham have said to that?

There's a filthy taste in her mouth. At least she doesn't smoke. Today she'll get this kitchen clean, get everything sorted. Drink less, get to bed earlier from now on. Get healthy. Get this kitchen straight and bake some bread. Get out there in the garden. It's something she can do, put things in order, something that is satisfying, absorbing, something that makes a difference to her immediate world.

At home it feels almost like a dirty secret the way she loves to clean, make order out of chaos, make the dull things shine. You'd laugh looking at this lot, but it's true. Not something you can say at dinner parties, '*What do you do?*' '*Well, I love to cook and clean.*' But how has it slipped so far? Sometimes she wishes she was her grandmother. That housekeeping was all she had to do and she could be admired, *fulfilled*, simply for doing it well.

She peels an orange from a sack beside the fridge. You can't keep them in a sack like that. She puts some on a plate. A fruit bowl would be useful here, she adds one to her mental list. The pith beneath the oily peel is soft and dense as human skin. The juice is sweet and pippy. Tea will have to wait. Everyone still asleep, the lazy sods. Dance yes. But not *nakedly*. But it's not his fault, is it? The orange tastes clean in her mouth and somehow innocent. They won't get drunk like that again. *She* won't.

She puts in firelighters and papers, strikes a match, checks that the flame has caught and shuts the stove door. She sneezes, a drift of ash caught in her nose. She goes out and piles up the plates, scrapes wax from the wood, brushes and scrubs. She carries in the wine bottles and lines them up beside the sink. Eight bottles they drank last night. *Eight* bottles between five people; well, four, since Fred was drinking beer. And Mara only had a glass. No wonder she feels rough.

Last night when Graham came to bed she hadn't spoken,

pretending to be asleep, watching him through half-shut lashes. No candle, just the strong moon lighting up the unicorn curtains. He'd stumbled, blundered, stripped, fallen on to the bed beside her with a groan. He'd let something in with him, maybe a mosquito, something that whined. She'd covered herself completely in the sheet, listening to him fall asleep as fast as if someone had pushed him, she actually thought she heard him topple before he began to snore.

She'd lain listening, wanting to wake him up and talk to him. But not knowing how to talk to him. How weird it must feel to be pressed up against a naked woman with people looking on so closely, with her *husband* looking on. Did he get an erection?

She'd lain fretting for what seemed like hours. Heard Fred go into his room, the creak of the bed as he lay down, the rumble of *his* snore. Must be all the drink. Graham hardly snores at home but now he's taken it up with a vengeance. Two lots of snoring, one in her ear, one travelling through the walls; maddeningly sometimes in unison, sometimes not, an almost continuous noise as if they were carrying on a nocturnal dialogue. Amazingly, despite all that, she'd drifted off to sleep, though her dreams were as thin and irritating as the mosquito's whine.

She stands in the hall, looking at all the locked doors. Wide, warped floorboards, a strip of dusty carpet. Locked doors. *Why?* She tries a cupboard, which does swing open, letting out a fusty rubbery smell. She sees, amongst the jumble of things, a giant tin of paint. Brilliant white emulsion. Her heart leaps. She knows what she'll do, what will make things better. Like a new start. She'll paint the kitchen. Larry will be pleased, Mara will. Everything will be different when the stains are painted out, the marks of mashed mosquitos covered up.

Fred shambles into the kitchen, squinting at her with his little lapis eyes. She's very glad to see him. To see another – relatively – normal person.

'G'day,' he says.

'Thought no one was ever going to get up.'

'Early bird, love.'

'I wish,' she says, 'I wish, I wish I had a fruit bowl.'

'A fruit bowl.' He mimics her English accent.

'For the oranges, they would look so nice.' For some reason she's on the edge of tears. She blunders on, 'They're never really fresh in England, oranges or lemons either, you don't realise till you've tasted fresh. Would you like an orange? These are really good.'

'Coffee?'

'I'll put the kettle on.'

Fred digs his teeth into the skin of an orange, screwing up his eyes against the spray of oil. He has a glitter of sweat like dew along his hairline. Plentiful soft dull hair. He pulls up a chair, sits down. His legs are thick and hairy and his lovely babyish feet are bare.

'Fred –'

'Mmmm?'

He holds the orange against his chest and digs his fingernails into the top of the peeled orange, pulls it into two. He pulls one segment off and chews, popping a pip out from between his lips.

'Um,' Cassie hesitates, 'I just wanted to ask you about the, you know, set-up here.'

Fred frowns, chewing another segment, deftly spitting out another pip.

'I mean –' she waves her hand about, 'it's a bit –'

'Don't worry about it, love.' He puts a finger to his lips. She frowns. Did he? Or maybe he was wiping away some orange juice.

He gets up and goes to the window, looks out at Mara's shed.

'What were the others like?'

His back freezes. He speaks without turning. 'Look, love, *you're* here now. Just play along.'

'What on *earth* do you mean?'

Fred shakes his head. The silence goes on far too long.

'I like your painting,' she says, to fill it. 'It's tragic that you don't paint any more.' She gets the feeling that she's sinking into some sort of quagmire, but her voice keeps on coming. 'Need some aspirin, I really shouldn't drink so much, I'm going to clean today, and paint – no, not your sort of painting, paint the walls.'

Fred turns.

'Sorry,' she says, 'I always gabble when I'm nervous, not that you make me nervous but –'

'I'll tell you what's tragic,' he says slowly. He sits down, rests his elbows on the table and presses his fingers against his temples. The place where his thumb should be is a soft, shiny depression. 'I was married once,' he says.

Cassie sits beside him, follows his eyes over to the painting. *Of course.*

'We were driving north. Darwin. Lynnie's rellies. A wedding. Never wanted to go. And I lost it. Stress, maybe I'd had a beer or two, one of the kids screaming blue bloody murder in the back. I lost it. Came off the flaming road, didn't I?' He squeezes his eyes shut as if against the memory. She puts her hand on his knee. Poor, poor man. The hairs crinkle under her palm. It doesn't seem quite right, her hand on his bare knee. He picks it up and holds it. Her own feels lost in his great warm palm.

'Lynnette and Sylvie killed right out,' he said, 'Bonnie, she lived a week, and me – got off without a fucking scratch.' He squeezes her hand till the bones might break. They sit in silence. The kettle boils, but she doesn't like to move. A space fans open in her ribs and aches for him.

She tries to swallow, her mouth gone dry. 'How long ago?'

'Twelve years.'

'Twelve years.'

'Said I'd never – never trust myself with another person.' He makes a kind of smile come on to his face, hauling himself back into the daylight of the kitchen. 'And I never have. Which is why I live on me tod. Haven't had the heart for painting since.'

Cassie takes a breath. She must say something, something is required but Larry comes into the kitchen then, rubbing his hands together. Fred lets go her hand.

'Morning.' Larry's clean and sharp in a crisp white shirt, pleased with himself. There's a tang of aftershave or cologne in the air. How does he keep himself so *clean*? And whatever he drinks he's never hung over, not so it shows. The dog follows him in and lies under the table on the dirty floor. Cassie sees rice and dog hairs, a hair clip, all sorts. As if it hasn't been swept for days. Which it surely has.

Larry nods at the fretting kettle. 'Coffee on the go? True confessions, eh?'

Cassie gets up. 'Shall I make one for Mara?'

'She won't wake this morning.'

'She *might*. She might like a chat, I could take it over –'

'She won't.' He switches his attention away. 'You off this morning, Fred?'

'Yeah,' Fred says, 'reckon so.'

'How long will it take you?' Cassie puts Fred's coffee down beside him. She gathers up the orange peel and dumps it in the compost bucket. 'I'm going to clear up today,' she adds to Larry. 'Sorry about the mess. I don't know how –'

'Not to worry.'

'Couple of hours, maybe three,' Fred says.

'A long drive,' Cassie says.

'Long!' Fred throws his head back and laughs, quite back to normal now. She wonders if maybe he's a little mad. From his loss and from being, as he said, mainly on his tod. She wouldn't blame him, 'Couple of hours is nothing,' he says. 'Get the air-con on. Bit of music. Gives a bloke a chance to think.'

'What's it like, where you live?'

Fred's eyes chip across at Larry and away. 'Nice town.'

'We could visit sometime, maybe,' says Cassie, thinking of her list.

'Dying to escape, eh?' Larry says.

'No, just there's some things I need. And I like looking round shops.'

'Flaming sheilas!'

'No,' Cassie says, annoyed. 'I want to go in a bookshop. I want a book about organic gardening in Western Australia.'

Fred shakes his head, pulls a packet of papers from his shorts and rolls himself a fag in a curiously dextrous way that compensates for his missing thumb.

'You can order anything you need,' Larry says, 'I told you. And it will be fetched. Anything you need.'

Yes but I want to go myself.

'We've got some cards –'

'Put them in the box.'

'Has there been any post yet? I'm *sure* my sister will have written.'

Fred closes his eyes and leans back in his chair. 'Nah, not yet but I'll check when I get to Keemarra.'

'I found some paint,' she says, swallowing her disappointment. 'White. Mind if I spruce up the kitchen a bit?'

'Far from it.' Larry looks around and then at her, more, into her. 'You really are a useful soul, aren't you?' he says.

Dear Jas,
Can't believe how far away this is. Amazing, like you said.
A different light OK. How you doing? Getting bored, not
enough pals, not enough doing. Life passing by. Could be
on another planet. Miss you and everyone. Wish you woz
here.
Luv,
Graham

Sixteen

Graham sucks his oily fingers, one by one. Tomatoes warm and oily. New bread. The four of them have eaten their way steadily though a loaf, dunking chunks into tomatoey oil, mopping it off their plates.

'I will have a lesson today,' Mara states, bringing down her water glass with a clack that breaks the spell of lunchtime dreaminess.

'Yeah?' Graham blinks at her.

There is a pause.

'That was, was it not, part of your rubric?' Larry says.

'Yeah, that's cool.' He smiles at Mara. Her chin is shiny with oil. 'When?'

Cassie looks at him quizzically.

'Fantastic bread,' he says.

'Thanks.' She picks a grain of salt off the table with her finger and licks it, smiling straight back into his eyes, dazzling.

'What did it feel like, dancing with Mara?' she'd asked and idiotically he said, 'Well, *she* felt nice,' out of awkwardness, obviously *not* the right thing to say. But what could he have said?

'Her nakedness, it doesn't *mean* anything,' he'd tried, attempting to convince himself. 'It's just how she is. Think of her skin as animal skin.' But with everyone else fully clothed it *is* disconcerting and impossible to get used to. Whatever he says or pretends, it gets to you, having a naked woman around the place, breasts, buttocks, hairy shadows however hard you try not to look. And he gets the – paranoid maybe – sense that Larry is enjoying his unease.

'Gray!' Cassie leans across the table, grinning at him, snapping her fingers.

'So,' Larry says. 'I take it that's all right?'

'Of course.' Graham smiles, suddenly relieved. To concentrate on someone else for a change. Might be just what he needs to break this spell of doldrums. 'Just say the word.'

*

Graham raps at Mara's door. Still can't get over it – that she lives in a shed. The stories they'll have to tell when they get back. He felt cheerful this morning, waking not to the knowledge that *he* should be painting but to the prospect of working with someone else. Perhaps it'll even set him off again, who knows? And he's intrigued to see what Mara can do. To get to know her.

The door opens. Mara takes his hand and draws him in, the sunshine smothered by the swish of the thick door-curtain.

'Ready?' he says into the nearly dark. 'I've put some paints, paper and stuff on the veranda – unless you'd prefer to be somewhere else?'

'Here.' Mara sounds surprised. 'I've got paint here.'

'But we can't paint in *here*. Mara, you need light.' The air is thick with joss-stick smoke, candle wax, the smell of her skin.

'It's more private,' Mara says. She takes his hand. He's glad that she's at least wearing her dressing gown.

'Come on,' he says. 'You can't paint in the dark.'

So hot in the room. It's unbelievable.

'No,' she says. She lets go of his hand, goes behind him to the door, rustles the curtain. He thinks she's about to open the door but she slides the bolt. 'There. Locked.'

'What's that for?' he says. 'I could just unlock it.' He slides his finger in the air.

She laughs. 'Not to keep you in, silly, to keep them out.'

He looks round. His eyes are getting used to the gloom. Velvet everywhere, the red Turkish carpet on the walls. The cloth over the window is embossed with stripes and the sun swelters through it like the orange bars of an electric fire.

'There's no way we can work in here,' he says, quelling a sort of claustrophobic panic that rises in his throat.

'It *is* warm,' she allows. 'You could take your things off. Are you sweating? No, only pigs sweat. Or horses? Are you perspiring? Ladies only glow.' She laughs and stretches open her arms – and the dressing gown. 'I want you to paint me.' With a flap of her arms, the dressing gown falls to the floor.

'I don't do portraits, look, Mara –'

'No.'

'Let's talk about this outside.'

'Look,' she says, '*look*.' She comes close to him. He has to force himself not to back away. She seems so much bigger in this enclosed space and all the light in the room is gathered on her skin. She lifts her breasts to him. 'Look.' He gets an urge to laugh, it's so preposterous. She can't kill him with her breasts.

'*Look*,' she insists. He has no choice but to look and sees then what she is showing him. On her breasts she's painted something smudgy, green and white. 'Lilies,' she says. 'It's hard to paint on yourself. Can you do them right? And I can do you.'

'What?' A startled laugh catches in his throat. A bead of sweat trickles down his cheek. 'Listen.' He rakes in a deep breath. 'I'm gonna – Seriously. I need out –' The room swims, dots before his eyes.

She steps back. 'Go then. Get out.' Angry but he can't help it, he has to breathe.

'Sorry,' he says and struggles his way into the curtain, shoots open the bolt and steps out into the swingeing heat. He leans over, hands pressing his weight into his thighs until the faint-ness passes. *Jesus*. This place is lunatic.

*

Balanced on a stepladder in the kitchen, Cassie rolls white paint on to the ceiling. 'You're not the only one who can paint round here,' she says, her voice strained with reaching up.

'Hey, Cass,' Graham says. She finishes the paint on the roller and it really is brilliant white beside what was there before. She's wearing a white shirt he's never seen, a man's white shirt and, although she must be wearing something underneath, you can't tell, the way her thighs disappear under the cotton.

'What's up?' She frowns, half laughing. 'You should see your face!'

'I want to go,' he says.

'Where?'

'I mean, go. Leave. Now.'

'Don't be *stupid*.'

'This place is nuts. I've had it.'

Larry comes into the kitchen, the screen snapping shut behind him. 'You've upset Mara,' he says. He looks furious.

'*Graham*. What have you done?' Cassie says.

'Christ, man, she's barking. Wanted me to paint her.'

'Yes?'

'So?' Cassie says. 'What are you on about?' She puts the roller in the paint tray and comes down the ladder. On her nose there's a snowy freckle of paint overlapping her own freckles.

'To *paint* her,' Graham says.

'So?'

'Let's have a drink.' Larry says. 'You seem shaken.' He tries to put his hand on Graham's sleeve but he flinches away. 'Lemonade, Cassie?'

She gets a jug out of the fridge while Larry puts three glasses on the table. Cassie made the lemonade, her grandmother's

131

recipe, she says. It's cloudy and floating with bits of pip. Graham takes a sip and it puckers his mouth. 'Sugar,' he says, wincing. She must have got the recipe wrong. It almost hurts the way the saliva pumps inside his cheeks. He sucks them in and squints.

'It's not that bad!' Cassie pushes him the sugar tin. 'Now, what's up with you?' She stirs a spoonful into her own glass.

'Possibly I should have explained a little more comprehensively,' Larry says. He is so cool. You have to give him that. 'You understand very well by now that Mara isn't quite – which is why we live here.'

'What's *wrong* with painting her anyway?' Cassie says.

'Paint *on* her. Her *skin*.'

'*On* her?'

'I can't see that that's so terribly outrageous,' Larry says. 'What harm is there? Body decoration is an ancient form of art. Arguably *the* most ancient. Here, of all places, in this ancient land, is it not natural that an artist should develop such an interest? Wait.'

He goes through the door into the house to fetch a book, puts it on the table in front of Graham.

'Took a look.'

He flips through the lavish coloured pages: paintings, piercings, tattooing from all the tribes of the world, close-ups of black skins smeared ochre and white, white skin intricately tattooed.

'If I had anticipated such a hysterical reaction,' Larry says, 'I would, of course, have primed you first. Mara has, as you know, stopped painting, paper, canvas, I can't prevent her wanting to destroy what she has painted and now she's taken this sudden hankering for painting on skin and I really don't see the harm. Perhaps it might lead her back to a more permanent form of art. Think of it as a kind of therapy if you wish. Art therapy. Cassie, your opinion?'

She shrugs.

'But she wanted *me* to paint her.'

'Just to begin with.'

'But – it felt, it seems, don't you mind me touching, painting, your wife?'

'Good gracious, what a small mind you must think I have!'

'I don't think Cassie'll like it.'

'I don't think *she's* that small-minded.'

'It is a *bit* weird to me,' Cassie says.

'Seems *fucking* weird to me,' Graham says.

'Now, now.' Larry allows a missed beat. 'If you don't want to help Mara, then don't. No one forces anyone to do anything round here.'

Graham stirs another spoonful of sugar into his glass. Doesn't matter how much he puts in, it is still too sour. He gets his tobacco out, hands shaking a bit. He feels a complete fumbling prat as both of them watch him roll a smoke. 'So it would be OK,' he says, facing Larry out, 'if I refused?'

'It would be all right with me,' Larry says, 'though your refusal would disappoint poor Mara and would, if you think about it, rather make your appointment as,' he clears his throat, 'a sort of *artist in residence* seem rather, shall we say, redundant.'

Graham puffs contemptuously. Cassie frowns at him, shakes her head. Larry stands up, puts his empty glass beside the sink. 'It is entirely up to you. Now I, for one, have work to do.' Abruptly, he leaves the room. Down the corridor they can hear him unlocking a door and pulling it shut behind him.

'*Graham*,' Cassie says, crossly.

'Fucking great prat,' Graham says. 'I've had it.'

'You can't give up already! That's *pathetic*.' One strand of her hair is stiff and white. He looks down at her brown thighs under the hem of the white shirt. Feels a stirring in his groin, presses his fist against it.

'Please,' she says, 'just go along with it. A bit longer. For me. *Please*.'

He runs his fingers from his hairline down to the nape of his neck, smoothes his ponytail through his hand. 'Christ,' he says. He sips the lemonade and his mouth puckers again. 'This is too *sour*.'

'Particularly sour lemons.'

'What?'

She shakes her head. There is a long pause, as if she's working herself up to speak. She takes his hand. 'Gray,' she runs her thumb up and down the bumps of his knucklebones, 'you couldn't . . . fancy Mara or anything, could you?'

He snorts. 'We come all this way and you still –'

'No, it's OK.' She smiles, gappy white teeth, white freckles, white quiff of hair. 'Look, why don't you help me paint this kitchen, then? We could get it done today. Oh look!' she points to the ceiling where a creature is flapping, one wing stuck to the paint. 'Poor stupid thing. Can you get it?' The sleeve falls back, light gleams on the blonde hairs on her arm.

'You know something?' he says. 'You look sensational.'

'This?' Cassie tugs the rolled-up sleeve of the shirt. 'Egyptian cotton, Larry's. I said anything *old* but this is beautiful, don't you think?' She gives a twirl, the cotton lifting away from her legs.

'Beautiful,' he says. He climbs up the ladder to try and free the dying bug.

Seventeen

Cassie sits at the veranda table. She feels almost cool; a tall glass of lemonade in front of her. She opens her notebook. Ought to jot down some ideas for her new module. Outback Gardening. Though, she thinks, that might seem rather irrelevant back home. Would anyone sign up? And anyway, there's nothing much to say. She hasn't done anything. She frowns and chews the end of her pencil. What *is* up with her?

Larry comes out. 'Mind if I join you for a moment?'

'Not at all.' She's glad to be distracted. Larry looks tired, drawn around the eyes. 'Can I get you some lemonade? Cup of tea?' she offers.

He shakes his head. 'Kitchen looks splendid. Thank you. Above and beyond –'

'No. I – we – enjoyed it.'

She's pleased with it, with herself. Pleased with the clean white, with the wet inky smell of emulsion paint. It doesn't cover everything, but it nearly does, if you don't look too close.

He brushes the seat of a chair and sits down. 'Hard at work?'

'Well –' She grimaces, shows him the empty notebook.

'How's the gardening? Enjoying yourself?'

'Just keeping it going really, so far. I did ask Fred to bring me some seeds. Want to grow some scented things, alyssum and stuff. To attract bugs.'

'Not enough bugs for you?' He smiles.

'Yeah! But *nectar*-eating insects – they'll prey on the pests. I wonder how I could attract more lizards?'

He regards her for a moment. 'I do admire you,' he says.

'Admire *me*!'

'Your – industriousness.'

'But I haven't been! Usually I'm –'

'No, no. I like the way you get on with it. You cook wonderfully, inventively. You take things – how can I put it? – seriously.'

'Well!' She doesn't know what to say. 'I – I admire *you*,' she says at last. 'Being here with Mara and being, so –' *Patient* she wants to say, patient with Graham. Though that might seem disloyal.

'Being what?' His eyes are warm, the lines around them crinkle gently.

'Well, Graham *can* be a bit – a bit – *difficult*. About painting Mara –'

'Hmmm.' His chair creaks as he leans back. It's late afternoon, the air humid. A crow lands on the veranda rail, hops heavily, launches itself off again on its shadowy wings. The light is deepening and in the distance there are clouds like bundles of dark cloth.

'What were the last people like?' Cassie asks.

He folds his arms. His gold watch catches the light and winks at her. 'The last people?'

'Was she called Lucy?'

The sides of his nose pinch in as he breathes. 'They were very – nice. But they proved unsuitable. Not up to the job, shall we say. What do you know about them?'

'Nothing much. Mara just mentioned Lucy in passing. That I looked like her, or something.'

He nods and purses his lips. Cassie bends over her notebook, scribbles something pretend in the margin. There's a long pause.

'Sure you don't want some tea?'

He clears his throat. 'I hesitate to interfere between two people so clearly in love.'

'Me and Gray?' She blushes hotly. 'Are we?'

'Well, only you can answer that.'

'No I mean are we *clearly*?'

He chuckles. 'Though – am I right in thinking that Graham being here with you is a penance for something? Don't be alarmed, I have a little – gift, shall we say, for reading situations.'

'No! Not a penance!' She tries to laugh.

'Test, then?'

'No! Whatever gave you that idea?'

She stares at him, startled, but he looks back only with kindliness. 'Forgive my clumsiness. Shall we drop the subject?' He looks embarrassed.

'No, it's OK,' she says.

'You're still homesick, aren't you?'

'A bit,' she admits.

'Do you think you might feel better if you had someone to talk to? Confide in?'

'I miss my sister.' She's embarrassed by the threat of tears in her voice. She swallows.

'Now, now.' He reaches over and touches her hand. 'Don't cry.'

'I'm not, it's just –' She blinks and looks away over the veranda rail, past Mara's shed to the stand of gum trees in the distance until the danger has past. 'You're right, I do – I *so* miss having someone to talk to. Patsy and I, we always, *always* tell each other everything. It's like a kind of pain,' she puts her fist against her heart, 'here. That *missing*. And there hasn't even been a letter. She *must* have written.'

He sighs. 'I'll get Fred to double-check. Look, I am sorry you feel like that. And I know I could never be a substitute but I *am* a good listener.'

She looks at him. He seems really concerned. It would seem rude to refuse to talk to him. And, what the hell, she has to talk to *somebody*.

He waits, head tilted to one side.

'Well,' she says, after a moment, '– you're partly right about me and Graham, some of the reason for coming here, as well as wanting a change and everything, *is* about our relationship. I want to, well, settle down. That sounds pathetic doesn't it?'

'Not in the least.'

'Have a baby. Maybe even get married. Anyway, be a proper couple. You know?'

Larry nods.

'You're right, we are in love. Well *I'm* in love with *him* anyway, it's hard to tell with him! But –'

'He's not the settling kind?' Larry offers.

'Well –' She runs her fingers through her sticky, tangled hair.

'What would you like to happen?' Larry says. 'In an ideal world?'

She gazes at him a moment. 'I suppose I'd like him to be more – kind of stable, home-centred. *Faithful*,' she says, looking down at her hands. Dirt under the nails still, splatters of paint, despite a good scrubbing. They're rough as pan scourers. She feels such a *mess*.

Larry makes a sympathetic sound in his throat. 'I hesitate to offer this –'

'What?'

'No, you wouldn't like the idea.'

'*What?*' She half laughs, tantalised.

He folds his arms and puts his head back. She can hear a faint click in the vertebrae of his neck. His beard juts upwards so she can see the neat edge between his whiskers and his throat.

'At least tell me!'

He looks at her. 'Well, all right then. But listen, this is just a very tentative suggestion. Just a way of helping you to get what you want. If you *don't* want, then –'

'*What?*' He's enjoying the tease, she can see. His wiry eyebrows raised, his eyes bright but serious.

'My work,' he says, 'is in pharmaceuticals. Pharmaceutical research, not so much the research itself as a collation of pre-existing data, conclusions and so on, for a drug company. It's one of the few types of work utilising my expertise that I can do in these circumstances.' He pauses.

'I *really* do admire that,' she says, 'that you've given up so much for Mara.'

'It's rather nice,' he looks down at Mara's shed, 'to have the one you want all to yourself, is it not?'

She hesitates. 'Well, only if they *want* to be.'

'*Of course.* Now, this work allows me to lay my hands on a number of drugs – psycho-pharmaceuticals. I am ever hopeful, you see, of a cure for Mara. But there is a drug –' He holds his hand up to stall any possible interruption. 'It's a behaviour alterant.'

'*Behaviour* alterant? What does that mean?'

'It has the very useful effect of making people *settle*, shall we say. People who have that wild streak, exciting yes but – they have within themselves a tendency – think of it as an internal saboteur which prevents them *buckling down*.'

Cassie laughs. 'He'd never take anything like that! Not for *that* effect, anyway! Say *buckle down* to Graham and he'd zoom off into orbit!'

'Quite.' He taps his fingernails on the table.

'You're not suggesting that we drug him!'

He leans forward, eager to explain. 'It doesn't work quite like a conventional drug. That is to say it has an educative rather than a purely palliative effect on the psyche. If he took it for a month of two you would see an immense improvement. A sort of rewiring if you like. He would still be *himself*, you understand, just a bit less, *hot-headed*. More liable to settle down and be faithful. More able to concentrate on work. He would, you might say, grow up.'

'*No!*' She can hardly believe what she's just heard. Drug him when he's perfectly healthy?

'That's fine,' Larry says. '*Laudable* even.' He gets up. 'It's what I expected you to say. But, it's the future, you know.' He presses his hands down on the table and leans towards her. The veins fatten to blue on the backs of his hands. His nails are like perfect shells. How *does* he stay so clean? 'Before long, people will be mending all sorts of minor personality disorders with drugs, with no more thought than you'd give to taking aspirin, say, for a toothache.'

She frowns. 'But – it doesn't seem right to me, trying to make people into what they're not.'

'No?'

She is startled by his implication. 'I'm *not* trying to make him something that he's not!'

Larry smiles, laces his fingers together. 'Come, come, Cassie, I suggested no such thing! Let's forget all about it. It was only a suggestion.' He pauses. 'But perhaps it would be better not to mention this conversation to Graham?' He gets up and leaves her. The sun is thick gold between the shadows of the veranda rails. She should cook something, plenty of eggs, another bloody quiche? *Behaviour alterant*. What an idea!

The crow appears again, cawing as it flaps past, noise like a flying baby. She goes into the kitchen, stands cupping a brown egg in her palm. *Was* it a reasonable idea? If there was something physically wrong with Graham, it would seem reasonable. But there's nothing *wrong* with him. He's just *him*. The conversation has made her feel a little sick. Is she overreacting? It is kind of Larry to want to help, though. He's a kind man. And maybe it is the future? Maybe he's right. If only she could talk to Patsy. She shakes her head, confused, losing her perspective.

Box 25
Keemarra Roadhouse
Woolagong Station
23rd?? November
(losing track!)

Dear Patsy,
Still no letter. After over a <u>month</u>. Hope everything's all right, not like you not to write. Nothing from Mum either but that's less of a surprise. Sure you got the address right? Full address on envelope. Check again.

   Working really hard, lots of cooking – well, I like that but it's too hot really. Gardening. Compost – though someone threw meat in and I had to fish it out. Maggots, <u>disgusting</u>. I even painted the kitchen. G's painting I think, don't like to ask, and he helps out a bit but you know him.

   Still haven't got through to Mara. Need some female company but she's on medication for some mental thing, not sure what but surely it'd be better to talk? Like <u>counselling</u> talk, rather than be on her own all the time. Will have a go at Larry but he is so protective. He's into pharmacuteicals (or however you spell it) in a big way.

   I wish ~~I could~~

   Had a strange talk with Larry today. Have to talk to <u>someone</u>. What do you think of this, giving someone a drug to try and change their behaviour? He says it's the future. Would you?

   Remember that thing that Dad wrote in our autograph books when we were little? Be careful what you wish for. Remember? I still miss him, don't you? Still feel Mum shouldn't have sent us off to school straight after he died. Oh I know, change the record! Too much time to think here, that's the trouble, too much thinking not enough doing. I just feel kind of – lazy and detached. Not me at all.

Must be the heat. It reminds me of boarding school actually. Nothing like it really but – just that feeling of being cut off from everything. What's going on in the big wide world???

Give my favourite (only) niece lots of kisses, missing her – can she walk yet? I'm so sad to miss that.

Miss you, <u>please</u>, <u>please</u>, <u>please</u> write soon. Stroke Cat. Cassie xxxxxxx00000000xxxxxxx

Eighteen

Graham pauses on the veranda and stretches, breathes in, right to the bottom of his smoky lungs. It's early. Up before Cassie for once. Good to have a sense of purpose. This must be what it's like to go to work. Nah. He remembers the one time he did have a 'proper' job, a 9–5 job. Shipping office, paperclips, forms, a collar and tie! What kind of life is that: a noose round your neck every morning? He'd gone out for a sandwich one lunchtime, ripped off his tie, and never returned. Stick that where the sun don't shine.

He hoists himself up on to the veranda rail and balances. A white bird flaps by, high and loose against the blue. Gets a sniff of freedom, almost. He jumps down and goes into the kitchen. Larry's already there, the air full of his poxy cologne, coffee, toast. He spoons a boiled egg from a pan.

'Ah. Good morning,' he says. 'Want one?'

'No ta.'

'I've poured you some coffee. Milk?' he says.

Graham looks at the scummy jug of reconstituted milk and shakes his head.

Larry spreads his own slice of crustless toast with Vegemite, cuts it into strips, *soldiers*. The egg sits in a blue and white striped egg cup. With the edge of a spoon, he slices off the top. Yellow bleeds down the shell, drips on to the plate. He dips a piece of toast into the yolk, sprinkles it with salt and takes a neat bite. His eyes come close to twinkling as he chews. 'Small pleasures, eh Graham? Small pleasures. You surely cannot beat them.'

Graham's belly rebels against the bitter coffee, the viscous sheen of yolk on Larry's teeth. 'Yeah. Mara up?'

'Once I've finished, I'll take her an egg. To go to work on!'

Graham takes a deep breath. 'Listen, man,' he says. 'She wants us to work in her sh – her room – but it's too hot and nowhere near light enough. Tell you the truth I get a bit claustrophobic. Maybe you could –'

Larry does not look up from negotiations with his egg. 'Oh no. Could not presume to interfere in decisions of such an artistic nature.'

'But –' Graham gives up. Impossible to tell, sometimes, whether Larry is taking the piss or if he really is a world-class prat. He gets up and fills a glass with water.

'But?' Larry holds the eggshell between finger and thumb and scoops out a cusp of slightly jellied white.

Graham swigs the water, sloshing it round his mouth to rinse away the sensation of coffee grounds against his teeth. 'Nothing. But you know how hard she is to – to reason with.'

Larry blinks. 'You're asking *me* that?'

Graham cuts a slice of bread. Can't be bothered to toast it. Decides to take tea out to Cassie. The kettle is hot enough, he makes a pot.

'How's our Cassie this morning?'

'Still asleep.'

Larry nods, dabs the corners of his mouth with his napkin.

'Sure I can't interest you in an egg?'

'No.'

With a spoon Larry lowers an egg for Mara into the bubbling water and turns the timer over. 'Don't you think this is the most ingenious invention? So simple. And really rather beautiful.' He holds it up to the light, eyes on the trickling sand.

'Yeah, whatever.' Graham puts his bread, the pot and two mugs on a tray.

'About an hour, then?' Larry says. 'Mara will be ready and waiting.'

Cassie is asleep until he bangs the tray down on the floor beside the bed. The room smells stale and fusty. She always wakes first. Usually. But everyone seems drowsy here – except Larry.

'God, you're up!' she says, reaching for her tea. Her face is printed with rumple marks and her eyes look tiny. She yawns hugely, and Graham looks away from her fillings and the furry whiteness at the back of her tongue. 'Maybe we'll get some post today,' she says. 'I bet there'll be piles. Gray –' she reaches for his hand. 'I love you, you know, as you are.'

He pulls a face. 'How *else* would you?'

'Yes. This is stupid,' she says, 'but it niggles me you know, that we never finished that talk. The clean-sheet talk.' She smiles. There are crumbs of sleep in the corners of her eyes. He notices for the first time her moist pink tear ducts.

Something whooshes hotly through his veins. '*OK*,' he says, 'Christ's sake! OK, last person I fucked. You really want to know? Jas.'

She stares at him blankly for a moment. A twig squeaks against the window. '*Jas*,' she whispers, a line of white, like a drawstring, tightening across her upper lip. She clears her throat. 'But whenever I – You always say you're just friends.'

'We are.'

'That's not what *just friends* do.'

He shrugs.

'When?'

'Why do you want to torture yourself?'

'*When.*'

'OK. That day you went to London to arrange this magical mystery tour.' He sees her flinch. 'Right. I'm off.' He gets up.

'See you later.' But when he gets to the door he turns. Can't leave her looking so wounded. Even if it is self-inflicted.

'Look, that *was* before we said –'

She nods. Eyes down, staring at her mug of tea. 'Yes,' she says quietly.

'I won't –' he hesitates. 'I will, I am *trying*,' he says.

'You certainly are!' Her eyes when they look up have a glitter to them. 'Not that there's much chance of anything else here. Anyway –' she hitches her mouth into a half-smile, looks at the door. 'See you later.'

He goes out. Feeling dismissed. And does a backflip in the dirt.

*

But for the electric bars across the window showing that the sun is up, it could be the middle of the night. Holding his breath for a moment against the smell, perfumed with joss sticks but still like an animal's den, a female animal's, he waits for his eyes to adjust. He makes out Mara, slumped on the cushions. She is naked. Down boy, he thinks, though she's not his type, no way.

'Ready?'

'Yeah.' She sounds tired or dispirited.

'Maybe not up to it today?'

'I *am*.'

'OK, then. Let's go and sit on the the veranda. Or my studio – nice in there.'

The stuffiness getting to him already. All this for Cassie with the sleep in her eyes, the drawstring round her mouth. Is this some kind of test? Maybe cooked up with Larry? He shakes his head at himself. *Get a grip, Graham.* Talk about getting paranoid!

'It's important we stay in here,' Mara says.

'But – the light –'

'Here are the paints,' she gestures to a low table, 'all laid out.'

'Yeah. What do you *want*, Mara?'

'You *know*.'

'But *you* should be painting. We could go out and –'

'*No!* Her voice rises. 'Larry says you –'

'OK, OK.' He lets out a long stream of breath. Could kill for a smoke now. A nice quiet smoke out in the fresh air. 'Are they body paints?'

'Yes, Larry got them from a theatre shop in Perth. I like Cassie's daisy. What about a daisy? A daisy, here.' She holds out her arm and points to the skin above the elbow.

'Why don't *you* have a tattoo?'

Mara snorts and a bubble comes from her nose; she wipes with the back of her hand, then wipes her hand on the cushion beside her. 'Tattoos don't come off! If I had a tattoo how would I get rid of it? Cut off my arm?'

Graham resigns himself. Soonest done, soonest over. And the sooner she'll get fed up with this daft idea.

As well as paint, there's water, brushes, a palate, paper towels. All very organised. *Thank you, Larry*. Graham lowers himself down beside Mara. He crosses his legs, takes her heavy arm in one hand and prods the skin above the elbow. 'Here?'

Surprisingly cool flesh. He selects a fine brush. Thinking of the delicate branching bones in Cassie's foot, the daisy on the dry skin, he starts, a pointed brush, thick white pigment. Remembers when he first saw the daisy, how he'd longed to take her foot in his hand, to kiss it. Her cool, white foot. How it had seemed perfect and unattainable – but it wasn't. Only a few nights later he had pressed his lips against the daisy and had caught the slight ordinary whiff of her foot.

Mara wriggles as he sketches in the petals. He grips her tightly round the wrist. Can feel the blood throbbing through her veins. Has to lean close to see, and breathes in her smell: sweat and heated skin, the sebaceous smell of hair, some sweet oil – coconut? Her stomach is rounded, a deep crease at the top of each thigh, can't see beneath the curve of her belly from this angle. Focusing on the daisy, he loses himself for seconds at a time. He holds his breath with concentration and sweat trickles down the side of his face.

He mixes grey to shadow the petals, makes a yellow centre and a branching stem. Skin is an interesting surface, the fine greasy grain of it. He could paint on Cassie's skin, that would be different, drier skin, almost blue-white in the places never exposed to the sun. On her breasts where the veins branch he could make river deltas, he could make her pale nipples a dark and luscious red. Mara's nipples are dark, down-pointed, the bump in the centre of each big as a berry. Imagine that between your teeth, the rubbery nub of it.

'There.' He gives a final flourish of green to suggest a pair of leaves and moves back. 'Don't touch it now, let it dry.'

'Spray,' Mara says.

'What?'

'There.' She indicates an aerosol of fixative, SkinFix. A picture on the tin of an arm wreathed in snakes and roses. 'Then it won't rub off so quick.'

He sprays the skin and the smell of it in the thick still air makes the room swim. Christ. He puts his head down between his knees for a moment, blood singing in his ears. Mara's hand touches the back of his neck. 'You are sensitive.' Her voice is a croon. 'More than Cassie. She is a tough cookie.'

'Just need air.' He stumbles up, away from the touch of her hand and the stirring in his body – only a reflex – and to the door, opens it with a gasp of relief, lifts the curtain aside to let in light and air.

Mara stays where she is, down on the cushions, which the sun shows up as stained and worn. She twists her arm to see the daisy. Her body lit up as if in a spotlight, the deep shadows of her, the solid mass.

'Nice,' she says. 'Thank you. Now –'

'That's all for today,' Graham says. Two galahs hop amongst the hens. Squawking like hens too, the clowns. He inhales deeply and the day comes back into focus.

'Oh but –'

'Not so bad then?' Larry startles him.

'Look at my daisy. But I want –'

'Don't be greedy, Mara. Don't push him too far all at once.' Graham darts a look at Larry.

'But more another time, eh? Tomorrow, Mara? Would that please you?'

'Something more,' she says.

'All right with you, Graham? That wasn't so bad, was it?' Larry makes as if to pat his arm, but Graham side-steps.

'Fine,' he says, over his shoulder, walking off towards the shearers' shed.

Box 25
Keemarra Roadhouse
Woolagong Station
30th November (ish)

Dear Patsy,

You must be getting fed up with my letters now, if you're getting them, well you'll get lots of them all at once, this one will go in the post with the last one. I suppose I'm writing instead of phoning. It's driving me mad not being able to talk to you, not knowing how you are. You'll never guess what: Graham is now alone in the shed with Mara, painting on her, I think! On her skin. Talk about mad! It's OK, though pretty weird. And sort of ironic when you think about it . . .

We had that talk and guess what? Turns out that he was sleeping with <u>Jas</u> all along. Can you believe it? All that stuff about them being friends. Load of bollox. I never thought he'd actually <u>lie</u>. I asked him so many times. We even had Jas round to eat a few times – you met her at the goodbye party, remember? Dyed red hair, loud voice, smokes a lot. Flat chest. She was wearing something torn. <u>So</u> I'm not really talking to him. How can I ever trust him again? But there's no one else to talk to. Fred's not here. Well there's Larry, I can talk to him a bit. He's nice, kind, just a bit – a bit <u>strange</u> but then being stuck out here . . . I think <u>I'll</u> go strange after too much longer. Are you picking up my strangeness? Sometimes I wonder if we're actually going to stick it a year. Hope so. It'd be embarrassing coming straight back after that big send-off! Though I so miss you.

Oh no, thinking of coming home has made me want to cry. Please please please please PLEASE write, soon as you can. Kiss Katie, stroke Cat.

Love, Cassie xxxxxxxxxxxxxxxxxxxxxxxxxxx

Nineteen

Not so bad going in again. He feels docile, like a sort of pet. The heat, the naked woman. You can get used to anything. And it will be over soon. This is only a scene played out between tiny people in the middle of nowhere. It will affect nothing. The birds will pass unstartled. He will do the painting and make Mara happy, the best he can do for now.

Last night in bed beside Cassie he'd thought about Jas. Kind of defiance maybe. Also he misses her. She understands him in a way that Cass really doesn't. Why isn't he with her then? As Cass would no doubt say. Jas probably would, if he asked. Be *with* him. But she's not that exciting to him. That's the stupid thing. She really *is* a friend, best mate. Or was. Why did he have to go and do that and then, worse, spill the beans? They *say* they want the truth and then what happens? He gets a fierce pang of longing for Jas, just to watch her scrubby fingers with their bitten nails rolling a fag, see her squint through the smoke at him and laugh her throaty laugh. And that's *all*.

His head is buzzing from Larry's industrial-strength brew. He sits down beside Mara on the cushions. The paints are laid out ready. Her face eager, expectant, like a little kid's before a party. At least he's pleasing someone round here.

He kneels beside the colours, the palate, sighs. 'What can I do you for, then?'

'Flowers and flowers and vines. Are you cross?'

The daisy has gone from her arm.

'I washed it off. Wanted to be clean to start again.'

Graham wets his brush and wipes it across the green. Feels kind of detached. Here but not here in this hot mad shed with a hot mad naked woman. Sort of thing you dream. He paints green vines on her arms, twining round her shoulders. Paints roots on her feet, holding them still as she squirms against the tickle of the brush. Paints quickly, carelessly, what does it matter, it's not for keeps. He traces the veins up her leg, thick greenish skeins, dark buds and flowers, a freedom in it, enjoying a joke of bees swarming, something to be said for the temporariness of this, it'll wash off, he can be free. It reminds him that it can be free like this, painting. The way he used to paint on walls, his parents' horror when he made his room into a forest, sunset bleeding through the trees. Soon had *that* papered over in Sandersons. But it was *his* room. No *real* child of theirs, etc., etc.

Tendrils of vine crawl up above her knees and he doesn't know how to stop, where to stop, how to look at the insides of the thighs, the shadowy junction, the cleft visible through the hairs, the woman smell so heavy and strong, humming in the darkly scented air. He gets hard, who fucking wouldn't, uncomfortable, needs to shift it but can't with her so close and it is only a reflex, even Cassie would realise that, pulls his eyes away, turns to take a swig of juice. Sickly sweet. Keep your mind on something else.

Looks at the belly. How to illustrate that generous space? Takes purple on his brush and follows the curve, paints something, a sea creature curled on the convexity, frond-like fingers. Mara lies back as he paints, open to him, her skin soft, relaxed. But her stomach muscles clench as she sits abruptly up.

'Cramp –' she starts, blinking like someone waking up. She looks down, exclaiming at her legs. She looks more dressed than he's ever seen her, as if she is wearing coloured stockings and sleeves, her naked breasts seem more than naked. He's amazed at how much he's done, no idea how long he's been absorbed but absorbed is what he's been, enjoying the freedom, the freeing-up of this painting, the flow of colour, and seeing that this is what he has to do and only this, loosen up and maybe it will all come back. And what an idea: not to paint Australia, not to try and catch *this* light but paint England again from memory, the different intensity of it, the green, rain and traffic lights, a sycamore leaf stuck on wet glass.

Mara looking down begins to moan. 'Oh, you've painted me a baby,' she says, her hand ruining the paint.

Graham squints. 'Not a baby,' he says, 'it's a kind of creature – a sea thing – curled up in its shell, look, look here's the shell.' But when he looks he sees a baby too.

Tears are running down Mara's cheeks, the biggest tears he's ever seen, like summer raindrops, and scattering on her breasts. One long tear snaking in between.

'Hey, don't cry,' he says, awkwardly. Where to look? 'What's up? Shall I get Larry?'

'No, not him.'

'Cassie?'

Mara puts her hands round her knees, smudging and ruining the paint. She sobs and rocks. 'No.' She looks up, painty-faced. 'I had a baby once, did you know that?'

'You had a baby?' He stares at her hunched form, understanding now the texture of her stomach, the lines, silvery stretch marks which he has veined with emerald and sapphire.

'The baby – a girl – she died,' she says, through her tears, her mouth pulled down, 'she was purple like that blue-purple and very slippery and she slipped away and died and I – that's when I – it is when everything went to soup – to grey.'

Christ. Graham puts his arm around her. What can he say?

'Larry was my doctor. Larry saved me.'

'Yes.' The feel of Mara against him makes him breathless, the stickiness of paint on heated skin, the heavy mass of her in his arms. His heart thumps. She weeps like a child and he holds her, the paint smearing on his shirt, poor woman, the smell of her grief, her tears, is overwhelming, the feel of her in his arms, he grows hard again, the softness of her breasts, impossible not to, doesn't mean a thing but her face is so close and there is no clear difference between holding and kissing to comfort this poor woman in his arms and the rush of hardness, her hand tangled in his hair, the opening of her underneath him; suddenly she's underneath him and his clothes are open too and he's in her, smeared with paint the both of them, paint and tears and sweat and there is no difference between being in her and just being in her room, it's hot and deep and an overwhelming plunge through rolls of soaking velvet and he comes so hard and suddenly that it hurts.

He lies there only a minute before it becomes clear what he has done. He's drenched and dripping with her, reeking. He gets up so fast it makes him reel.

'Don't go away from me.'

He flinches from her reaching hand and zips his jeans. *Christ.* 'Mara that never happened.' His voice sounds thin. He is ashamed but very clear. 'Mara, please – I'm so sorry. I have to go.'

Her wet face looks up at him and down his body. She throws her head back and laughs. A crazy laugh breaking out of nowhere. Well, she is crazy, he has fucked a crazy woman, that is a crazy thing to do, that is what happens when you get too close to crazy people. It leaks right out of them and into you. He looks down at the colours smeared on his skin, shirt, the front of his faded jeans.

'Mara, I have to go right now.'

She says nothing. He can't read her crazy face, the sweat and tears, the sort of *grin.* He closes the door quietly behind him and gasps in a lungful of the dry hot air. Without looking left or right he walks round to the shearers' shed to strip and wash. He closes his mind to the possibility of the shape of Larry at the corner of his eye, keeps his head down, praying for Cassie not to be about, almost trips over a fucking stupid hen. Hard to stop himself from running.

Dear Mum and Dad,
I'm in the desert in Western Australia with my girlfriend
Cassie. A kind of artist in residence, I guess. Long time
hey? I've been thinking, stuck out here, about the past.
Who was the old woman I used to stay with? Don't even
know her name. Was she some kind of relation? I've been
thinking of contacti

Twenty

It's ludicrous, that's what it is. Lunchtime. Mara sitting at the table on the veranda, munching through her sardines on toast like a great beaming child, smudged all over with sticky colours. On her arms you can make out leaves and stuff but the rest of her is like some enormous bruise. And paint all over her thighs and belly and even down into the hairs.

'Delicious,' Larry says, reaching for another piece of toast. Maybe sarcastic – it's hardly a gourmet feast, she'd thought of but rejected the idea of a sardine soufflé – but no, he smiles. The bad feeling between Graham and Larry seems to have vanished now that Mara's OK. That is obviously the key: keep Mara sweet and everything else will be. All Larry wants is for Mara to be happy. Well, that's easy enough, her tastes are simple. There's nothing that Cassie's provided so far that she hasn't gobbled up. When she's conscious.

It's got muddled up inside her. Graham with Jas, Graham in the hot, hot shed with Mara. Stupid, stupid. Here everything is so far from what she imagined that it could almost make her laugh. Taking Graham away from Jas – her heart scrunches at that name – from temptation, well it turns out more than just *temptation*, into a ludicrous, sticky, sweaty proximity with Mara.

He's looking pretty glum though. Guilt. Probably regretting that he told her now. Won't even meet her eyes. 'Gray, you've hardly eaten.' She pushes the plate of fishy triangles towards him. Under the tanned surface of his skin he looks pale.

'Not hungry,' he says.

'*Should* be hungry,' Mara murmurs.

'Look at that,' Larry stands suddenly, jolting the table, and points to the horizon where the clouds are massing once again, 'and feel that –' He holds his hand up. There is a breeze. 'Nor-easterly,' he says. 'We may see rain.'

'Thank Christ,' Graham says to his plate.

'And –' Larry listens, stands up, strains his eyes. 'Yes. I think maybe it's Fred.'

'Yeah?' Cassie's shoulders lift in anticipation. Fred. Thank God. Someone *else*. His little eyes and sweet bare toes. Someone *straightforward*. And the post! *Surely* he'll have the post. The thought of all the news from home makes relief spread through her. And the shopping: fruit, milk, meat, fresh things. Her mouth waters at the thought. Though she can't actually see what they're all looking at. Maybe a distant puff of red rising from the ground which is shifting anyway in the growing wind.

'Can't see a thing,' Graham says.

'The practised eye,' Larry says.

'Maybe we should go in?' Cassie starts gathering the plates. 'Gray?'

Larry helps Mara stand, and they look out over the land-scape, both shielding their eyes. 'Where, Larry?' Mara says. The wind is really blowing up fast and dust shimmers in the air as it moves through the light.

'Think I'll make some bread.' Cassie's mind moves on to tonight's meal. Would pizza be all right? Just make more dough, there are tins of anchovies, if Fred's brought cheese – and it would be another use for the tomatoes. Mara and Larry look so comical standing there, Mara's big creased bottom, the smudges of paint almost like handprints on her skin, her wild puff of hair, and Larry beside her, dapper in his neat grey trousers and spotless grey shoes, his shirt gleaming, staying close but fastidiously not touching – wouldn't want to spoil the shirt.

Graham catches her eye and half grins at her, raising his eyebrows. Sheepishly. Probably thinking he's forgiven. But *Jas*. He picks up the jug and a couple of glasses. 'Come on, Cass, let's get these washed up,' he says, darting her a green glance that makes her heart lurch. His hair is loose, must have stuck his head under the tap before lunch, and it has dried shiny and sleek. She loves him, she does, despite all and everything. She can't help it. There's a sensation like an old bed-spring pinging inside her ribs. That's love.

*

Graham shuts his studio door. Thank Christ for a bit of privacy. His head's going round and round – *Mara, Jas, Mara, Jas, Mara, Jas*. And he never asked for any of it. He sits at the table in the yellow glow that diffuses through the curtains, listening to the wind bullying the fabric of the building, lifting a section of roof so that it bangs and jounces sending a metallic shiver through him. Dust on his teeth and under his nails, red, everything fucking red. He rolls a fag and draws in the smoke. Mara. *Christ*. It's like a bad dream, you just have to forget it. You just have to wipe it out of your mind. Mara is crazy. It wasn't real in the usual sense. It was crazy.

Oh *Christ*. What has he done?

He closes his eyes and forces his mind to travel far away, to hilly fields, the way the lines criss-cross, shades of green graduated and punctuated suddenly with a blaze of yellow rape, the shadows of dry-stone walls, the shades of grey. The cigarette burns down forgotten in the jam-jar lid as the sketch grows under his hands, his heart beating, the watercolours lovely on the white paper, *motionless* white paper no blood beating beneath, no hairs, hardly a smell at all just dry, clean, virgin paper. His breath is shallow with concentration, the sweetness of the colours – the sky a wash, almost clear water, graduating to a deeper rim in the dip between the hills a deeper rim of almost blue. You can smell the rain when you paint the wet on dry paper, like rain on sun-warmed stone.

He's tired but it is great. To concentrate. On something *good*. It removes him almost completely from himself though the crash of the corrugated roof brings him back to a realisation of how totally shagged out he is – ha ha – *knackered* – will lie down on the soft bed and close his eyes and have a kip. Shut it out, shut out the – everything.

But before he gets up there's a tap on the door, a smart, ratchety scrim of fingernails and Larry opens it, juts his beard round.

'Ah,' he says, coming in, door closing behind him. He has, Graham's pleased to see, creases of red dust on his white shirt and a smudge of purple paint. Graham looks back at his sketch, which he has a sudden impulse to shield with his arm like a child. He forces himself to sit stiffly, almost flinching against the feeling of Larry standing behind him.

'Well, well,' Larry says. '*At last*. Perhaps you've found your muse.'

'Isn't that for poetry?' Graham twists his neck up to see the sharp glint of tooth just visible at the corner of Larry's mouth where his lips don't quite meet. He looks down at his drawing. Can see where the final line should go, diagonal.

Larry chuckles dryly. 'As you will. You've found inspiration, then. And, I gather, a source of mutual satisfaction?'

Graham rolls a pencil between his fingers, reading as it goes round, 3B, 3B, 3B. He takes a deep breath. 'Fred here yet?'

'No, my mistake it seems. Cassie will be delighted that you've found yourself inspired. But will she be so pleased with *how*?'

The roof lifts and clangs. Graham can hear the metallic sound in the fillings at the back of his mouth.

'I mean, of course, you and Mara.'

Graham coughs, a laugh like a splinter catching in his throat.

'Me and *Mara*? Are you *serious*?' His voice rises as the wind woo-hoos.

'Gracious me,' Larry says, 'we are in for a storm.'

'I did what you asked.'

'A bit more than that I believe. I think, in actual fact, you rather took advantage of the situation and forced yourself upon her when she was upset.'

'You *what*?'

'I wonder what Cassie will think?'

The pencil snaps between Graham's fingers. Tiny dot of graphite like the shrunken pupil of an eye. 'She wouldn't believe such crap.'

'It's what Mara says.'

'Oh, get fucked. Do you think Cassie would believe *Mara* before she believed me?'

'Well.' Larry leans forward, his voice too close to Graham's ear. 'All the same, it would be better not to mention it – just in case Cassie's faith in your, er, capacity for the truth is not as touchingly solid as you seem to believe.'

'Oh, you think you know her better than me, do you?' Graham gets up, deliberately knocking the chair over behind him. His knuckles itch to grind themselves in Larry's face.

Larry steps back. 'So,' he says. 'We'll say not a word and tomorrow you'll paint Mara.'

'No.'

'You'll paint Mara and if she wants any other attentions from you you'll provide them.' Again the roof clangs. 'Must get that fixed.'

A trickle of sweat creeps down the side of Graham's face. His heart thumps. 'You've changed your tune,' he says.

'Sorry?' Larry takes a step towards the door.

'I thought I "forced myself upon her"?'

'There's always another point of view, don't you find?'

'What are you saying?'

'All I'm saying is that you ought to do anything you can to please her. Poor Mara. She is, her *happiness* is, my *raison d'être*. The reason for this whole establishment. And Cassie need never know.'

'You want me to fuck your wife? What's the matter, can't get it up?'

A muscle twitches in Larry's jaw. Ha. A *reaction*. But he doesn't speak.

'So, what, you're pimping for her now? Listen, we want to leave. OK? You're *sick*.'

Larry steps towards him, eyes narrowed. He lifts his finger, about to speak but Graham cannot stop it, anger rushes from his gut along his arm into his fist and smashes into Larry's face. Blood bursts from his nose. His hands fly to cup it, he brings them away, looks at the shiny red dripping through his fingers and back at Graham.

*

The wind gets into the kitchen, gusting grit and rubbish about on the floor, making the fly screen rattle. Fred didn't come and she could cry with the disappointment. No post and no cheese. She hates the wind. How can you make a decent pizza without cheese? But it's too late now, dough made and rolled out.

The door opens and Larry comes in, bleeding from his nose, splash of red on the front of his shirt.

'Oh my *God*!' she says. 'What happened? Sit down –' She fetches the first-aid box and pulls out a wad of cotton wool. 'Here. What happened?' The way he looks at her, her heart sinks. *Please* let it not be Graham.

'Well,' he says, dabbing at his nose, his voice thickened as if he's got a cold. 'Your boyfriend has certainly got some temper.'

'Oh no. He *didn't*? *Why*?'

His nostrils bubble thin blood, his moustache pinks.

'Have some more cotton wool. Oh God, It's not broken, is it? *Why* did he hit you?'

He shakes his head. 'I don't understand it. I merely enquired about his session with Mara this morning and he –' He makes a hopeless gesture. He's lost his usual poise, looks quite upset.

'Shall I make you some tea, or –? Oh God.' Cassie sits down, hides her face in her hands for a moment. She looks up. 'What's he doing now?'

'Cooling off, I hope.'

'I'm *really* sorry. I know he's a bit – a bit *wild* sometimes, but he hasn't had a fight for I don't know *how* long. Not since I've known him.'

'You did say he wouldn't harm a fly.'

'No, well, he wouldn't! That's the stupid thing, he wouldn't deliberately hurt anyone, it's just if he loses it.'

'Loses control?'

'Yes, sort of.'

'He seems to do so with remarkable facility.'

'No, not usually,' she says. 'Something must have made him mad –'

Larry shakes his head. 'I don't know what I could have said.'

'I'm *so* sorry,' she says, wringing her hands. 'I don't know what else to say. He *is* very uptight just now. We had a bit of a – Look, what about a brandy or something? There's some in the pantry?'

He dabs at his nose again and winces. 'Good idea. If you'll join me.'

'Well –' Last thing she wants is a brandy, but what the hell.

She pours it into a couple of glasses. Is about to say cheers but it doesn't quite seem appropriate. The hot gold makes her cough.

'I suppose that's it then,' she says. 'I mean – you'll want us to leave.'

He sips his brandy, pinches the bridge of his nose, gazes at her for a moment. 'What do *you* want?'

'Well –' She bites her thumbnail, a little wad of raw dough gets in her mouth, she pinches it between her teeth and swallows it. 'Maybe we *should*.'

'Give up?' He looks disappointed in her. 'And you were doing so well. You'll have lasted even less long than the others.'

'Oh,' she says, not wanting *that*. She finds that she feels oddly competitive with these strangers. 'But surely *you* won't want us to stay, now?'

He gazes at her. His eyes are kind, sad, grey eyes, lines of experience and even suffering around them. 'What was your aim, in coming here?' he says.

'You *know*. I told you.'

'Have you reached a conclusion? About you and –' It's as if he can't bear to say the name. He dabs at his swelling nose.

'Not really,' she says, and sighs. The brandy has burnt a trail from her tongue to the pit of her stomach. She feels the muscles in her shoulders give a little. Larry is not angry, not with her at least. 'I think, maybe after a few more weeks we might – well, I feel maybe we were *getting* somewhere. He'd told me the truth about something I needed to know and horrible though it is I feel better about it. It's always better to know the worst, isn't it?'

He coughs out a small laugh. 'Is it?'

'And – I *think* he's getting into some painting.'

'He was painting just now.'

'Was he?'

'So. Would you like to stay?'

'Don't think *he* will!'

'But you?'

She looks away. His eyes are almost too intense. The thought of home, Patsy, her own bed, her garden, almost makes her giddy with longing. But she does *hate* to give up and Larry would be disappointed in her. She doesn't want him to be disappointed. 'I don't know,' she says. 'I – I suppose I *would* prefer to give it a bit longer.'

'He could go and you could stay?' Larry suggests.

'*No*, no, if he wants to go, I'll have to go with him.'

'Well, perhaps he'll stay. We'll have to see, won't we? Mara would be sad to see you go – and so would I.' He reaches out his hand and takes hers for a moment.

'Would you?' She blushes violently and pulls her hand away.

'You know, the substance I mentioned earlier –' he says, 'this is precisely the sort of thing it might prevent. It might settle him down.'

She bites her lip. 'No –'

He leans forward. 'There are no side effects,' he says, 'if that's what's worrying you. That's the wonder of this new generation of pharmaceuticals, they are precisely targeted. Smart-Ceut will be the brand name. No side effects. A subtle behavioural enhancement, a calming effect – we're on the brink of a revolution. In ten years' time, you won't think twice.'

'But he'd *never* take it.'

'You could administer it yourself. Put it this way, I think probably it's the only way to get what you want. If you want to stay –'

'I do want us to stay, at least for a while.'

'Then it might prevent,' he indicates his nose, and half smiles, 'further incident.'

She stares at him. 'Is this some sort of *condition* – for us staying?'

'Good gracious no! What do you take me for?'

'Sorry, I didn't really think that, I –'

'I'm simply trying to help you to get what you want.'

The circles of dough on the table are rising flabbily, cracking at their edges.

'I couldn't do that though.'

'Here,' he reaches into his trouser pocket and brings out a small phial of white pills. 'Easily soluble,' he says.

She takes them, rolls the phial, looking at the contents tumble inside.

'No,' she says, 'I *couldn't*.' She tries to hand them back but

Larry's hands are behind his back. The blood is drying on his moustache.

'Hang on to them, for now.' He smiles. 'In case you change your mind.'

'Well, OK.' She takes them and puts them in her pocket. Later she'll go out and chuck them in the dunny.

*

'What on *earth* is the matter with you?' She finds Graham lying face down on the bed. She slams the door but not in time to stop a rush of dust blowing in, lifting the rug from the floor. Rogue gusts penetrate the room, the roof lifts and bangs back down. 'I can't *believe* you punched Larry! *Why?*'

He rolls over on to his side. 'Because he gets on my fucking tits,' he says.

'But what did he do? What did he say?'

He looks at her mutinously.

'You're nearly forty, Graham!'

'I am *not* nearly forty,' he says.

'Thirty-seven next year. Near as damn it. When are you going to act it?'

He seems to contract into himself as she watches. He sits up, cups his hurt hand in the other. 'I suppose he came squealing to you?'

She sits down on the bed, sighing. 'Let me see.' He lets her take his hand. The knuckles are reddened and swelling. 'You're hopeless,' she says, anger fizzling out. 'Do you want to leave?'

'Course I fucking do.'

'*Gray.*'

'Don't you?'

'Dunno.'

'Thought you were homesick?'

'I am but – Oh God, you're hopeless.' She strokes his long fingers, the little black hairs on the backs of each, on the back of his hands that have always turned her on. The circlet of black hairs round his wrists, the beautiful hairs on his arms that feel so good around her. 'I only started on pizzas because Larry said Fred was coming. They'll be horrid without cheese,' she says miserably.

'You want to *stay*?'

'A bit longer? Just till Christmas maybe. See how we feel then?'

'Dunno.' He grabs her thumb and squeezes.

'I love you,' she says. 'Why don't you ever say it to me?'

'I wouldn't be here, would I?'

He pulls her down. She lets herself be pulled, a twinge in her belly, as he strokes his index finger across her lips, forces it into her mouth. His finger tastes gritty, grit is everywhere, the window rattles. He kisses her. 'You're *gorgeous*,' he breathes, feathering the tip of his tongue against her upper lip. She kisses him, hijacked by desire. She puts her legs round his thigh and presses herself against him. But he stops and sits up.

'What?'

'Thirty-six is a lot different from forty,' he says, reaching for his tobacco tin.

'Sorry,' she says.

They sit in silence while he makes a roll-up against his knee.

'I did a painting today. Sketch for,' he says, flicking his lighter.

'Yes?'

'England. Derbyshire. Hills and walls. Wanna go back, Cass.'

She takes hold of his hand again, grit between their skins. Tries to read his face, his eyes. He won't look straight into hers. Her heart sags. She drops his hand. 'It's Jas, isn't it? You want to see her.'

'*No*.' He sighs out smoke. 'How many more times? It's *you* Cassie, *you*. With Jas I didn't – it didn't mean anything. It just happened.'

She gazes at him until he looks down and flushes. 'The sad thing is,' she says, 'that I believe you. Poor Jas.'

He shrugs.

'Is it, is it likely to happen again?' She tries to make her voice brisk.

He shakes his head. 'It was a mistake. I was being a prat. Not thinking. I'm sorry.'

'You never do think though, do you?'

He does look more sorry than she's ever seen him. His eyes have a shine as if he might be close to tears.

She takes a deep breath. 'So you will, you will be – your word – true?'

He nods, looking at her with a spark of hope.

'And we'll stay?' she says.

'Do we have to?' He smiles at her, the sort of smile that could charm a door open but she hardens her heart.

'Larry's going to give us one more chance. He's being really decent about it.'

Graham snorts.

'What?'

But he shakes his head.

'If you want,' she pauses and takes a deep breath, '*us*, then I think we should take it.' She picks up his hand again, strokes his fingers. Raises his hand to her mouth and sucks the end of his middle finger. Taste of salt and paint and skin. The sexy feeling rises up inside her again like a tide.

'Eh?' she says. She stands up and takes off her shorts and knickers – slight rattle of pills from the pocket. He watches her, eyes hazed. 'Eh?' she says again.

'Yeah,' he breathes.

'Take off your jeans,' she says. She watches him kick out of them and and sit back on the bed, puffing at his fag. His beautiful cock rises as she leans over and puts her lips to it but he smells wrong. Not suckable today. Instead she sits astride him, takes his fag away and puts it on the jar-lid ashtray. She pulls her T-shirt over her head. Given up wearing a bra in this heat. A gritty trail between her breasts. She cups them in her hands and lifts them towards his face. He blinks, long dusty lashes, eyes darkening.

'Fuck me then,' she says.

'Is that an order?' His voice is husky but he looks *sad* almost. He lifts a hand and touches each of her breasts, gently, reverently almost, stroking as if he's never seen them before.

'Your skin is amazingly fine,' he says.

'Come on.' She gets off him and lies down. She unbuttons his shirt, kisses the skin on his neck and chest, the familiar taste, the vibration that passes between them still there, stunning. More passionate than for ages; he sinks his teeth into her shoulder and sucks on her neck so there will be blossoms there tomorrow for everyone to see but that's OK, why shouldn't they make love and why shouldn't they have love bites? She bites him back, bites and sucks at his throat as he jerks, shuddering and groaning into her, then his hand comes down and he touches her until she rises up under his hand and as she comes the roof crashes down, crashes and reverberates. She lies in a soft, dazed trance, then giggles.

'I think the earth just moved.'

'I love you,' he says.

She breathes in sharply. 'Me too,' she says, smiling into his precious peppery skin. A faint foreign oily smell from Mara's shed. But this is *it*. She simply cannot lose him.

She can almost hear Patsy's voice. 'What is it about *him*? There are so many other lovely guys. Lovely *grown-up* guys.' More or less what everyone has said. But lying here beside him she knows why. Because she will *never* fancy anyone the way she fancies Graham; because she will *never* find a better lover than him; because she really *likes* him (most of the time) and because when she imagines the children she wants to have, they are *his*.

It's not a choice. That's simply how it is.

Twenty-one

His knuckles smart. He's drained, feels like some kind of husk. What is going on? Cassie's gone to cook the pizzas, he should follow her but he'll just have another smoke first. How's he going to face them? He rolls another cigarette, clicks the lighter and holds it in his palm, sees his tiny bleared reflection. His mind goes back to when Jas gave it to him. It was his birthday, she'd said nothing about it. No big deal, he assumed she'd forgotten. Fair do's. He never remembered hers. They were in the pub. She'd lit his fag with it. 'That's nice,' he'd said, taking it from her. A chunky chrome Zippo, heavy in his hand. 'Oh, have it,' she'd said and then laughed. 'Happy Birthday, you prat. Bought it for you, didn't I? Don't lose it.' And amazingly he hasn't.

He pulls on his jeans, a clean T-shirt. His other one, screwed in a ball on the floor, is covered in body paint. He kicks it into a corner. What's he meant to do? Waltz over? Oh yeah, shag the wife, deck the husband and then sit down and have dinner with them. What a situation. Could sound funny. When he tells it. When he gets back. If he tells it. But this is *now*. His stomach growls. He *is* starving. He hears a car drive up. Fred maybe. Thank Christ for that. That'll help. Maybe a bit. He puts his hair back with a rubber band, sticks his feet into his sandals and goes.

The wind blows dust in his eyes and he puts a hand up to shield them, dust drying his mouth. Fred's there in the kitchen when he gets in, bags of stuff on the table, salad, a warm smell of pizza, bottles of red wine.

'You're in the nick of time,' Cassie's saying to Fred. 'If I get them out I can shove some cheese on and shove them back for five minutes. Hi, Gray.' She smiles at him, her sexy, gappy, gut-scrunching smile. He's almost floored by a surge of guilt, goes over to kiss her or touch her or something but she shakes him off. 'Want to clear the table and set it?'

'All right, mate?' Graham says to Fred.

'Yeah. Hear you've been having a punch-up! Good on ya!' He roars out a laugh, gold back tooth catching the light. Graham looks at him with surprise.

'I've poured you some wine,' Cassie says, bringing him the glass. 'You look like you could do with a drink.' She watches him drink it, her face anxious. He glugs it back. Good stuff.

'Got the post?' Cassie says, handing Fred a beer.

He shakes his head.

'*Why?*' Cassie almost wails, her face crumpling.

'Some sort of mix-up,' Fred mumbles. He looks down. 'I'm sorry, love. Next time, hey?'

'Mix-up?' Cassie says. 'What kind of mix-up?'

'Sorry, love,' Fred says again. 'Where's Mara?' He nicks the top of his beer and takes a swig.

Cassie sighs. 'Oh, apparently she's indisposed again.'

Thank Christ for that and all. Graham breathes out, knocks back the rest of the glass.

Larry comes in. Clean white shirt, swollen nose. 'Fred,' he says curtly, ignoring Graham.

'Nearly ready.' Cassie looks between Larry and Graham. Pulls a face at Fred. 'Fred arrived in the nick with the cheese.'

Graham lifts stuff from the table. Puts down knives and forks. He pours wine into some glasses.

'I take it,' Larry says, sitting down at the head of the table and unfurling his napkin, 'that after today's debacle you're thinking about resigning?' His voice is stuffy and thick.

Resigning? Graham thinks. *The ponce.*

'We've been talking about it –' Cassie begins.

'Yes?' Larry looks at the stove. 'Shall we eat?'

Cassie picks up the oven gloves. 'Can you help me, Gray?'

He touches her arm as they stoop down to get the oozy pizzas out. 'Hey,' he whispers, 'anyone ever tell you, you are *gorgeous*.' She smiles and blinks at him. Her face is still flushed from before, or maybe just the oven's heat, and her hair is all wispy, slipping out of its ponytail. She looks perfect to him, perfect. Ten out of fucking ten. He puts his hand on her arm to say something, what? But she shakes him off.

'Come *on*.' They get the two big pizzas on to the table. 'Dig in then everyone,' she says, sitting down. He sits opposite her, slides his foot across to nudge hers under the table, and takes a long slug of wine.

'I have a proposal,' Larry says. 'But first,' he holds up his glass, 'a toast to our cook.'

Cassie laughs, her foot slips away from Graham's. 'It's not much!'

'Pizza and a half, love, by the look of it,' Fred says.

Graham can't bring himself to look at Larry. Sitting there kind of triumphant and wounded. He takes a mouthful of pizza. It's hot, great, bits of anchovy and chilli. Sees Cassie giving him a look, should have waited.

'Proposal?' she says to Larry.

'Perhaps if you had a break, the two of you, a trip away, a night or two?' Larry says. 'See how you felt then?'

'Really!' Cassie's eyes brighten. 'That would be *fantastic*, wouldn't it, Gray?'

No two ways about that. He nods. Last thing he expected.

'That's settled then,' Larry unfurls his napkin. 'Fred, you'll take them?'

'Where?' Cassie says. 'Perth?'

Fred shrugs, stuffs his face with pizza.

'When?' Graham asks.

Larry touches the end of his nose and winces. 'Day after tomorrow suit you?'

'Where?' Cassie asks again.

'The mountains?' Larry says.

'I'd like to go to *town*.'

'We'll discuss the finer details later,' Larry says. 'Graham?'

'Yeah, that'd be – cool.'

'*Cool*,' Larry repeats, his eyes lingering on Graham. He holds up his empty glass. Graham refills his own then leans over to top up Larry's. Cassie has hardly touched hers. Stuffy in the kitchen, flies snarling, but the idea of somewhere else, a *pub* maybe, pint of beer, new faces –

'Couldn't we go tomorrow?' Cassie says.

'Mara's expecting a session with Graham in the morning,' Larry says. 'Can't disappoint her, eh Graham?'

Graham chews too hard and bites his tongue. Behind his eyes goes red. Taste of blood mixing with anchovy and cheese. Can't look anywhere but his plate.

Fred snaps open another bottle of beer. 'Couldn't see a flaming thing driving here, dust storm. Have to wash the bloody ute tomorrow,' he says, nervously.

There is a silence. Graham looks up and meets Cassie's eyes. She's lost her flush, looks at him apprehensively, eyes wide. He shoves a wad of pizza into his bleeding mouth though his gut is clenched up like a fist.

'Very nice, Cassie,' Larry says. 'Afraid it hurts to eat though. Been in the wars, as you see, Fred! I'm going to go and see to Mara if nobody minds.'

He goes to the door. 'Wind's dropped,' he says as he goes out.

'Thank the flaming crows,' Fred mutters.

*

Cassie stands in the kitchen. No one up yet. Least, Larry's been up, his napkin is on the table. She put it away last night. White roll of linen in a bone ring. On washdays there is so much white: his shirts; towels; face cloths; napkins; his underwear, old-fashioned white Y-fronts. Seven pairs a week. Much as she can do to get Graham to change his twice a week. Tomorrow would be washday but they're going. She hopes they can go to a town, shops, a chemist, cafés, maybe even a garden centre. Normal everyday things. And she'll be able to phone Patsy, hear her voice. Her heart lifts. And then they'll come back refreshed. Make another go of it.

She stands crunching into a bit of cold pizza, wondering what to do. The washing? She could, she supposes, make a start. Might as well. Graham's waiting for a cup of tea. She'll have to prise him out of bed for Mara's lesson. She spoons tea into the pot. Gets a couple of biscuits from the tin. Puts two mugs on a tray. All the time something pressing against her hip-bone. Something in her pocket. No side effects. If all it does is make him *calmer*, more *reliable*. What could be the harm in that? She gets the pills out; opens the lid. *Easily soluble*. She tips one into her palm.

She feels a twinge, like a string tugging in her belly. So *randy*. What's up with her? Rather nice though. She'll take the tea and go back to bed with him. Just for a quickie. It's like she's on heat. Must *be* the heat. And now they've got all that Jas stuff out of the way. Worry about washing later. A green mug, a blue mug. Rough pottery that Fred bought when she said she hated the tin mugs. The pill falls off her palm into the blue mug. She pours the tea. Adds powdered milk and stirs. White scum in both. She picks up the tea-tray and goes out of the door.

*

He wakes again as Cassie pushes open the door. 'It's a scorcha!' she says.

'For a change. Tea, ta.' He hoists himself up on his elbow. His hand feels stiff. Oh yeah.

She sits on the edge of the bed. 'Just think,' she says, 'tomorrow – won't it be *wonderful*. Wonder where we'll go? We'll be able to phone people. Maybe there'll even be a cyber café, we can email everyone. And then when we come back we'll feel better. Ready to start again.'

Her hair is down. He puts his hand up to touch it. The ends are crisped almost to white, the roots their usual corn-gold.

'Yeah. Listen. I was thinking, we could not come back.' His heart beats with excitement at the thought.

'What?' She hands him his mug of tea. Too hot. He puts it on the box beside the bed.

'When we go off tomorrow, take our stuff and just piss off out of it. Wherever Fred takes us, just tell him we've decided – He's a good bloke, he'll be OK.'

'Hmmm,' she says, wrinkling her nose. 'We *couldn't* – could we? He'd know, wouldn't he – Larry – if we took all our stuff?'

'Not take much then,' he says. 'Money, passports, the other stuff doesn't matter much.'

She looks round. 'No, I suppose not. But –'

'What?'

'Oh – nothing. It's just that it feels like giving up. I don't like giving up on things.'

'*We'd* still be together,' Graham says. 'I want to be with you. I want to be. We can have a baby.'

'Yes?' She gives him a searching look.

'Yeah. Why not?' He reaches for his tea.

'Wait,' she puts her hand on his arm, 'don't drink that yet.'

'Why?'

'I dunno. Hey, I'm feeling really randy –'

'Not again!'

She runs her hand up his leg under the sheet, cups his balls, rubs him, till the sheet starts to rise up like a tent though his heart sinks.

'You're gonna wear me out. Let me drink my tea.' He takes a sip.

'No!' she yells suddenly and knocks the mug from his hand so the tea splashes and soaks hotly through the sheet.

He jumps up, scalded. 'Ow, what the *hell*?'

'God, I'm sorry, are you all right? Come here.' She picks up the jug from beside the bed and splashes cool water over his front, his scalded belly and thigh. Not too bad, but it smarts like buggery. And the bed a swamp.

'What did you do *that* for?'

'I thought I saw a – a thing.'

'A *thing*?'

He stares at her, red in the face, hair all over the place. Has she completely lost it?

'Sorry,' she says again. She bites her lip. 'Look, you drink mine.' She thrusts the other mug at him.

'No, it's OK. Think I'll get up now,' he says. 'Sooner we get away from here the better, eh?'

Her shorts are wet. She peels them off, stands in her black knickers, she looks good in knickers. Couldn't spend his life with a woman who didn't. The thought startles him. *Spend his life*. Did he think that?

'Yes,' she says. 'You're right.'

Dear Patsy,
This might be my last letter. In fact you might not get this
till after we're back. (And I'll certainly have talked to you
on the phone.) It's just all too weird. It all came to a head
yesterday, when G punched Larry. Yes! Terrible. Blood
everywhere. Terrible atmosphere. But the funny thing is,
things feel a bit better between us, don't know why. I think
there's a chance. I did fall in love with him warts and all,
didn't I? He wouldn't be the most stable dad but I think
he'd be fun, don't you? I'll just have to be the stable one. I
found some letters he'd started in the back of his sketch
pad, to his parents. That's progress isn't it? He calls me his
girlfriend in them which must mean <u>something</u>. They're
not finished letters, but – somehow they give me hope . . .

I'll be posting this myself, the luxury of a postbox!
Graham's gagging for a pub. Well, me too. Home soon!!!!
Kiss Katie, stroke Cat, say hi to Al.
Cassie xxxxxxxxxxxxxxx

Twenty-two

Graham stands on the veranda looking at Mara's door. The flaking blue. What he *wants* to do is paint. He was intrigued by what was coming yesterday: the wetness of England, lush green, slate grey, quartz glitter, smooth bulge of water before it breaks over rock, before it falls. But anyway, he shakes his head, what he *should* do is help Cassie with the washing. However, this is what he *must* do. To keep Larry sweet, as Cassie says. Just this once more.

He bangs on the door with his left hand. No answer. OK then. Larry said she was waiting but maybe she's gone back to sleep. Fine. He knocks again, softly, and is about to slope off to his studio when he hears her voice:

'Come in.'

He swallows and pushes, the door opens, sticking against the curtain behind it. He pushes through into the orange gloom, thick sickly-sweet smell. Mara crouching on the floor. What to say? He says nothing. He sits down on a cushion as far away from her as he can. She's wearing the dressing gown, hair is over her face. They sit for a moment. Sweat seeps from his pores, trickles from his brow to his ear, his jaw, down his neck, his armpits, to his side. Feels like he's melting.

He clears his throat. 'Mara?'

She whispers something.

'Sorry?'

She mumbles through her hair. Embarrassed maybe. Something about a baby?

'I can't hear.'

She lifts her face, hair swings back like curtains opening. 'I thought you would give me a baby. Now he says you don't like me.'

He opens his mouth and it fills with the hot stink of joss sticks. 'A *baby*?' He gives a shivery laugh. '*Sorry*.' They sit a while longer. His belly, still smarting from the hot tea, prickles with sweat. Her face is glazed with it.

'Do you want to go out and we can do some drawing?'

'Don't feel well.'

'OK. Shall I leave you alone? His eyes go to the slit of light showing beside the door where the curtain is rucked aside.

'No,' she says.

He looks round hopelessly, cushions, rugs, curtains, everything soft and red. Strong scent of coconut from her hair or skin. Her big toes are warped by bunions. Can't believe what happened yesterday but at the same time, some unwilling, blind part of him could do it again. It's horrible, that animal reflex. His eyes are held by the smooth thighs gleaming in the gap of the dressing gown.

'Do you want to *talk*?' he says desperately. 'Why do you stay in here?'

'It's my own,' she says.

'But where do you wash and everything?'

'I don't wash, I *oil*.' She holds out her hands as if to show him. In the dim light it's hard to see.

'I thought your skin was –' he stops, can't say greasy, 'soft,' he says.

She smiles. Her smile always a surprise in her heavy face, like an unexpected lamp switching on.

'How long have you been here?' he says.

She puts her head on one side, twists her fingers in her hair. 'I don't know.'

She laughs at his expression. 'Really don't know.'

'What –' he says, 'what's the matter with you?'

'Hold me,' she says.

'I don't think so.' He looks at the light again. The thighs. The door. Sweat stings in his eye.

'Only hold. What does it matter? After yesterday. I don't bite.'

He sighs and edges towards her. Puts one arm round her shoulder, her hair a tangled bush. 'Shall I brush your hair?' he says.

'Oh *yes*.' He finds a brush, snarled up with hairs, kneels behind her and drags it through.

'I am sorry about yesterday,' he says, pulling with the brush, lifting the thick, wiry hair, black threaded with grey. Strong reek of coconut. With each stroke she makes a throaty, satisfied sound. Like a wood pigeon. Some strands of hair, charged with static, rise up to meet the brush.

'Fred does my hair like that,' she says. 'Fred is lovely.'

He swallows. 'Mara,' he says, 'will you promise me something?'

'Mmmm?'

'Don't tell Cassie about – about what we – about what happened. *Please*.'

'Of *course* I won't.' She moves her hand across her chest. 'Cross my heart and hope to die. Anyway, why would I?'

Graham puts the brush down and smoothes the hair with his hands. Closes his eyes a minute, feels something inside him give with the relief. 'Thank you.'

She chuckles sadly. 'You're welcome.'

'I am sorry – I don't know – I just got carried away.'

'Mmmmm.'

He smoothes and smoothes, then separates the hair into three and starts to plait it.

'You still think about having a baby?' he says.

'If I had a baby I think I would get better. Losing my baby made me ill. Having another would make me better, don't you think?'

'How would you look after a kid in here?'

'I would come out of course!'

He shudders, imagining Mara and Larry bringing up a kid. Poor little non-existent bastard.

'Why doesn't *Larry* give you a baby?' he says.

'Doesn't fancy me any more. Only fancies blonde girls like Lucy.' She stops.

'Lucy?'

'No, no.' She starts to cry. No. Not going that way again but he does hold her. Fingers on the red velvety stuff of her dressing gown, eyes averted from her thighs, nose full of the voluptuous smell of her. His mother must have tried to have a baby of her own before they adopted him. He tries to see her as a young woman, a sad young babyless woman. Without that stiffly lacquered hair. When they adopted him she was probably the age he is now. That thought threatens to engulf him. Holding this big sad woman, her sobs trembling her flesh, makes tears come into his own eyes, a lump to his throat. Christ, it could almost make *him* cry.

*

Cassie stuffs white things in the washing machine. Twin tub. Whites first. She'd only ever used an automatic before coming here. And only ever will when they get home. And this will be the last time she does the washing here. When they get back they can get their heads straight. Get their lives back. It *is* best they go. So they've given up, so what? She frightened herself this morning. What she nearly did.

Soon as Graham had gone to see Mara she'd taken the phial of pills to the dunny, unscrewed the lid, intending to tip them into the shit pit. But something like a hand on her arm had stopped her and she'd gone back and hidden them in the bottom of her rucksack instead. What she nearly did, though! This *place*. What it does to your mind.

It's quiet but for the water gurgling into the machine through its special hooked hose. Larry in his study. Graham with Mara. She frowns, turns off the water, pours in some washing powder, it's only for today, white flecked with blue. Nice smell as it churns up a reddish scum. Fred outside washing dust off the car. *Tomorrow*. Her shoulders lift in anticipation but in her belly there's a little squirt of fear.

When she'd come back into the kitchen earlier, Fred and Larry had been drinking coffee. '. . . expedite matters,' Larry had been saying, but broke off as she came in. 'Expedite! Speak flaming English, mate,' Fred had said, winking at her.

She prods at the clothes with some wooden tongs. A wet white shirt arm, flecked with detergent, fat with air, rises. She squashes the air out, watches the tangle of writhing cloth and suds. Expedite what? Who cares. This is the last time she'll do the washing here. The last morning in this kitchen. She looks round it. The white walls, stains already looming through. She does hate to be letting Larry down. And poor Mara. Should maybe cook something special tonight. Something nice for everyone. A private celebration and farewell dinner. Everyone'll eat it but they won't know it's a celebration and a farewell, only she and Graham will. She rests against the juddering machine, mmm, pleasant vibration against her pubic bone –

Larry comes in and she steps back flushing. What *is* up with her? He puts a leather overnight bag on the table.

'Mara's not well at all,' he says. 'About due for another "episode" and I find I've run low on her medication. I'm going to have to drive to Kip's, get him to fly me to Perth. Leave Fred in charge. So you see –'

'But Graham's out there!'

'Is he? It's all right. She's well sedated. I'll go and get him now. I'm afraid this means we'll have to postpone your trip.'

'Oh *no* but you *promised*!'

He shrugs his shoulders, spreads out his palms in a helpless gesture. 'I'm sorry. What can I do?'

She sits down too hard, painfully on the edge of the chair. Rubs her bum. She could cry.

'Graham'll go *mental*. Hey, couldn't we come with you? I'd love to go to Perth.'

Larry shakes his head.

'Fred can take care of Mara.'

'Fred will be gone before I get back. As I say, I am sorry. When I return – next time Fred's here – we'll rearrange it. A trip to Perth then, if that's what you really want. A whole week, nice hotel, the lot.' She looks up at him, sore swollen nose, fleck of dried blood snagged on his moustache. 'Now I really must go. Fred will care for Mara while I'm gone.' He nods towards some pill bottles on the side. 'He knows the ropes. I'll go and,' he pauses, 'extract Graham for you, shall I?'

'How long will you be?' she asks miserably.

'Two or three days.'

'But what about Mara if Fred's going?'

'There's enough medication to last. Fred'll tell you what to do.' He puts on his panama, picks up his bag. 'Sorry, Cassie.'

And he goes out. Just like that.

She flops down, puts her head on her hands and lets tears come out of her eyes. She can hear Larry speaking, then Graham's voice. She winces, expecting a shout as Graham decks him. She sits up and scrubs the tears away. Graham comes in. He's red in the face from the heat but looks quite cheerful. 'What's up?' he says.

'Aren't you mad?'

He holds his finger up. They hear Larry's voice, the car door slam, the station wagon drive away. 'Only be a few more days,'

Graham says, 'then *Perth*. It's *better*, we can get to the airport, and vroom, vroom, next flight home.'

'I suppose that is better,' she says. But she feels a great sag of disappointment inside her, like a deflating balloon. Now they're definitely going she just wants to get on with it and *go*. She looks over to the machine. 'You can help me peg that out in a mo.'

'Don't look so fed up.' He kneads her shoulders. 'God, you're tense.' He kisses the top of her head.

'So how *was* Mara?' she asks.

'I'm dry,' he says. 'Any lemonade?'

'Sweeter this time,' she says. 'I was worried about you in there.' Graham pauses at the fridge door.

'Why?' he says, his back to her. His hair, she notices, has grown down past his shoulder blades.

'Larry said she was about to have an episode. I wonder how he knows?'

Graham takes the jug of lemonade from the fridge. 'She seemed –' He pours some out. 'She was OK, a bit drowsy I guess. Want some?'

She nods.

'Here. I'm going to go and paint for a bit, what I was doing yesterday, it –'

She sips the lemonade. Maybe too sweet this time. 'What about the washing?' she says, but he is halfway to the door. 'Oh, never mind. I've nothing else to do.'

'Sure?'

She shakes her head at him. He grins, does a silly salute and goes out. The screen crashes shut. The floor is awash with red, the machine leaking into the dust that blew in last night. He's right. Just a few days more. And then Perth. Airport. Home. Patsy, Mum, friends, the garden, little Katie, Cat. Christmas decorations will be up by now. Weird thought. She remembers them rattling in the wind last year, the red, yellow, green lights, tall tree in the city centre swaying. And there might be snow! The thought of it is almost ridiculous. Something so pure and cold. Hasn't been so much as a spot of *rain* since they've been here.

The machine stops churning and with the wooden tongs she hefts the clean wet clothes into the spin-dryer; turns it on; bloody thing leaps about the floor like something demented, as usual. Fred comes in behind her, doesn't hear him, till he taps her shoulder and she jumps. 'Hey!'

'Want me to hold it?' He leans on it till it finishes.

'Damn near shook me teeth out,' he says into the sudden silence.

'Lemonade? Then I'll hang it out. Put the next lot in.'

He picks up a carrier from the table. 'Brought you a present,' he says. He looks almost bashful.

She takes the bag. Inside, a wooden fruit bowl. An irregular lip of polished jarrah, like a glossy wave curved up, the knots in the dense wood gleaming. 'It's beautiful,' she says and he blushes. *Fred* blushing!

'Where'd you get it?'

'I made it.'

'You made it?' She has to breathe hard to stop tears coming back into her eyes. He made it for her because she'd said there should be a fruit bowl. And now there is. She puts it in the centre of the table and fills it with oranges and lemons.

'There,' she says. 'I'll take it with me when we leave.' *And you don't know how soon that'll be*. She imagines it on the table at home. The one souvenir of – this. Never got past cutting up stuff for the quilt; did no more than maintain the garden. Gave up on her bush-gardening module idea. They'll be going back empty-handed, tails between their legs, after only a couple of months.

Except *maybe* it will be OK with Graham. And that *was* the main point. She'll miss Fred. Everyone else so weird – even she's going a bit weird – but Fred, though maybe full of bluff and terrible sexist stuff, is straightforward.

'You must be hacked off,' he says, 'about your trip.'

'Yeah, well, in a few days.'

She dumps the coloured things in the machine. All her knickers; the pink sheet; a painty T-shirt. She sprinkles powder on top. It gets up her nose and makes her sneeze. 'I quite like washing,' she says. 'Getting rid of all the grot.'

She waits till it's going, then turns. 'Fred,' she says.

'What?' He's getting bread and cheese out of the fridge. A wheel of cool white cheese, a quarter eaten already. Her mouth waters at its nippy smell.

'Want some?' he says.

'Yeah, why not. Fred,' she says. 'This will probably sound *really* stupid.'

He looks round. His eyebrows comic tufts above his eyes. She looks down at his lovely toes.

'I was wondering about Mara, whether she might have – you know, not being in her right mind and all, what she might have done for Larry to need to bring her all the way out here. I mean, might she have, you know,' she makes a stupid bleating sound, 'done something violent. Even *killed* someone.'

He pushes the tip of the knife into the cheese. His eyes flick to the picture of his wife and daughters.

'God, *sorry*,' she says.

'What?' He frowns and follows her eyes. 'Oh. Nah. No worries.' He gazes at the picture for a long moment, shakes his head, turns back to her. He holds a piece of white cheese on his broad red palm, looks down at it. 'Mara do someone in? Never. She's harmless.'

'Why does he sedate her then? Why are they here? I was thinking, it's almost like they're in hiding or something. This would be a good place to hide.'

He shakes his head, puts the cheese in his mouth, chews and swallows. His eyes rest on Cassie's face till she starts to fidget. 'Laz is an oddball,' he says at last, 'or, to put it another way, he's out of his flaming tree –' He grins, specks of spitty cheese visible on his tongue. 'But you know what he says, if not for him she'd be in some loony bin somewhere –'

'Ye-es,' Cassie says, 'but if she's harmless, then *why*?'

Fred looks up the ceiling. She looks up too. Nothing, just the useless fan; the fire-sensor thing; a flies' graveyard in the white china light-fitting.

'What?' she says.

'You take my advice,' he says quietly. 'Go along with him. You'll be OK if you don't cross him.'

'But Graham's already crossed him!'

'Yeah, well.'

'But, Fred, *why*?'

He shakes his head.

'You're scaring me! What's going on?'

His eyes seem to skin over, but he smiles. 'Nothing to be scared of,' he says. 'Time I saw to Mara.' He turns away towards the pill bottles, rattles out a couple of capsules and some pills, shoves them in his pocket. She could scream with frustration. Too many questions at once. Must slow down. The washing machine churns wearily on, she prods at the wet pink sheet.

*

The chilled soup, made from courgettes and stuff, has a bitter taste. Cold soup seems to go against nature, far as Graham's concerned. And the bread's rock-hard round the edges, takes a bit of getting through. In the breeze, the lamp above the table swings, gutters, releases a smell of kerosene.

'Hey mate,' Fred says, through a mouthful, 'what do you reckon to a trip then? There's some Abo cave-paintings couple of hours north. We could go and take a look if you like.'

Graham looks at Cassie, viciously grinding pepper into her soup. It would be amazing to get away. See something, somewhere, different. Ought to see some native stuff while he's here.

Maybe stop off in a pub and have a beer. He almost aches for a pint. *Paradise.*

'Nah, can't,' he says.

Cassie looks up, face shadowy.

'I suppose he wouldn't know the difference, would he?' She speaks not to him but to Fred.

'Spot on there, love. Set off first thing, back in time for cocoa. No harm done, eh?'

'Maybe,' Graham says, keeping his expression neutral, taking another spoonful of the ghastly soup. The washing, which no one's bothered to get in, sways in the darkness like a dance of ghosts.

Fred lifts himself up from his seat and farts. ''Scuse me, love. Back in two shakes.' He goes down from the veranda, farting with every step. Cassie splutters a mouthful of soup.

'Sign of appreciation somewhere or other,' Graham says.

'Somewhere *else*.'

'Cassie?'

'Not very tasty, is it?' she says. 'Don't know what's up with me.'

'It's OK,' he says. He puts his spoon down, twists a crust of bread between his fingers. 'What do you think then?'

'Won't try it with courgettes again.'

'*No*, what do you think about me going off with Fred?'

There is a long pause and a far-off kookaburra cackles.

'Hear that?' Her smile is wistful. He wants to kiss her. 'I think it'd do you good,' she says. 'You lucky sod.'

His heart lollops against his ribs. 'Maybe you could come too?'

'No. I don't know.' She bites her thumb. 'I wonder? If we gave Mara enough to keep her asleep all day?' She wrinkles her nose. 'Nah, shouldn't leave her alone. What if someone comes?'

'What, like the Jehovah's Witnesses?'

'Yeah.' She trails her fingers through a spilt splash of soup, making a wavy line. 'Funny. I'd love to see some Jehovah's Witnesses now. Or a double-glazing salesman. *Anybody*.'

The kookaburra is nearer, the crazy crazy sound, the sky in hysterics.

'Imagine an ice-cream van,' she says.

'What?'

'Oh nothing.'

She stands up. 'I'll get some cheese, shall I? This is inedible.' She stands behind him, brushes her lips against the top of his head. 'I think *you* should go though.'

A door swings open in his mind. He doesn't trust his voice.

'But you don't think it might interrupt your painting?' she says. 'Now you're getting into it?'

'No,' he says quickly. 'Only if you're sure, Cass. He reaches up and catches her hand. 'I wouldn't go if Larry was here.'

She pulls her hand away and starts to stack the dishes. 'What do you mean?'

He pours himself another glass of wine.

'*Why?* Don't you trust me with Larry or something?'

'Course.'

'What did you mean then?'

'Well, he obviously fancies the arse off you.'

'Honestly! Anyway, it takes two, you know.'

He gets up, turns and holds her, buries his face in her hair. She smells of cooking. He looks past her at the dreary sway of washing. 'Shouldn't really go.'

'*I* think you should. I'll be fine. It's only for a few hours, isn't it? Fred can tell me what to give Mara and when and stuff. Will you phone Patsy for me? Just make sure everything's OK. Tell her we're coming home. Will you?' She pulls herself free of him.

'Course I will,' he says.

She smiles. 'Well, tell you the truth, I wouldn't mind a day to myself. And – I can give you a list. Case you go to a shop. You lucky, *lucky* bastard.'

Twenty-three

Cassie rolls over, stretches out her hand to the space where Graham should be. Was, till first light when Fred banged on the door. Before he'd got up, Graham had held her tight, erection pressing against her hip. She'd smiled in her half-sleep, stroked her hands down to cup his buttocks but he'd murmured, 'Seeya tonight.' She'd felt the mattress tilt, heard him zip his jeans, the door open and click shut and she'd slid back, sunk straight back into a dream, not even heard the ute drive away. What was the dream? She screws her mind back to remember – something about water, swimming, lovely, somewhere like that deep blue gorge, cliffs red against the sky. The freshness of it. Today she'll wash her hair.

She rolls on to her back and spreads her limbs, one towards each corner of the bed, stretches till her shoulders click. She smiles. It *will* be OK with Graham, she can feel it in her clicky bones. He's being so nice. And if not, well – don't think. This time next year, maybe, there'll be a *baby*. She presses her hand where she thinks her womb must be and her heart does a little skip.

It feels different. Kind of free. Like a holiday. No men about. No one to cook for – even Mara won't need anything except drugs and Complan. Last night Fred showed her how to crush the pills and mix them with the drink, since her throat muscles might be too loose to swallow properly and she could choke.

On the kitchen table, two half-mugs of cold coffee. The butts of two roll-ups squashed in a saucer. How can they bear to smoke first thing?

She washes the mugs and clumsy, still half-suspended in her dream, drops one on to the row of pill bottles. They roll off the counter all over the floor. Kneeling down to retrieve them, she sees close up how dusty and dog-hairy it is, although she sweeps it nearly every day. Dust that got wet from the washing machine has dried in swirls, maps and footprints. Quite arty. But sticky red dust everywhere, the windows, floor, her hair. Her spirits threaten to sink. But no. Keep light. A whole day to herself, privacy to get the tub out and have a proper bath, shampoo her hair. No one to have to speak to, do a thing for.

Suddenly seems a lonely idea, a yawn of space.

'Pathetic,' she says aloud. 'What a wimp, Cassandra.' Yella cocks his head at her and makes a doggy moan. She scratches him between his ears. Saying her name out loud like that, saying 'Cassandra' into the empty kitchen made her shiver. Why did she say Cassandra instead of Cassie? No one calls her Cassandra any more. Even Larry's dropped it. That's just how they used to say it at school. *Cassandra*, as if it were a curse. It used to make her feel so alone. They were Cassandra and Patricia, separate classes, separate dorms. As if being a twin was a bad habit that must be broken. She feels herself sliding into a trough of old resentments and pulls herself back. *Mustn't* waste this day. This, kind of, holiday.

She puts the kettle on, rattles some biscuits into Yella's dish on the veranda, goes down to feed the hens. They cluck and scutter like a stupid mob, the necks, the rumps of two of them pecked raw and bleeding. A cockerel struts, military style, his feathery trousers gleaming. She makes sure some of the lesser hens get grain, which isn't easy – wherever she throws it the cockerel and the dominant ones barge them aside and stab them with their beaks. She finds only two eggs in the boxes, warm and shit-smeared. Too hot for much of a lay.

She notices transparent things wriggling in their drinking water – creatures made of water, only a membrane between them and the stuff they swim in. She empties and refills it. Can't be good for the hens to swallow the writhing things. Or maybe it is. Maybe it's protein? Who knows?

She prepares Mara's Complan, strawberry flavour, sorts out the pills. Two blue, one white, one yellow. Was that it? The jars are muddled up now. Fred left them together, the morning five, the different six for evenings. She tips some out – more turquoise than blue. But don't split hairs, Cassie. She nips open the capsules, grinds the pills, mixes the powder in with the sickly pink mess.

'Seems immoral, drugging someone like this,' she'd said and Fred hadn't disagreed; had merely shrugged and sighed, said, 'That's the way it is, love.'

'Mara,' she calls, opening the door and poking her head nervously into the gloomy shed. Sweet, rank, intimate stink. She hasn't been in for ages. Her nostrils flutter in protest. Mara's lying on the cushions, fast asleep, her breathing throaty, almost a snore. How can anyone breathe in this? 'Mara?' Mara grunts and Cassie kneels down with the mug of Complan, glass of water, wet flannel for Mara's face and hands.

'Morning,' she says.

The door swings open, nudged by Yella. Mara winces, the light stinging her face. 'Hey,' she says, croakily. 'Thought it would be Fred.'

'Fred and Graham have gone on a trip.'

'A trip?' She blinks at Cassie. 'No, that can't be. Larry's gone, hasn't he?' She grimaces, hand cupping down between her thighs. 'Oh, need to pee.'

'OK. Just a little trip. Back tonight.'

Mara hauls herself up. 'He said he'd be back later.'

'Who?'

Mara sways. 'They can't all have gone away.'

'I'm still here. Let me help.' Cassie holds her breath as she takes Mara's arm and steadies her as she squats over a plastic bucket; she tries not to hear the heavy splatter of urine. She takes the bucket out, gasping in the fresh air outside, and tips the scummy yellow down the drain. Goes back and waits as Mara sips the Complan. It seems wrong to loom over her. She sits beside her on a cushion.

Mara pulls a face. 'This is shit. Don't we have the chocolate kind?'

'I'll see.'

'Does he think I'm ill again?'

'I dunno,' Cassie says uneasily. Seems almost a shame to keep Mara sedated now there's just the two of them. She could do with some company. Maybe it would help Mara to talk and then Larry would be pleased. She considers taking the mug away. But what if Mara really is a danger, if she has an episode? How would she cope with that? She doesn't look violent – but then what does *violent* look like? The big breasts bulge against her solid thighs. Graham has *painted* this skin, got this close to these nipples, this – *stop it, stop it.*

Mara finishes and passes her the mug. She wipes her mouth on the back of her hand.

'When will Fred be back?' she says. Her voice is like a child's on a long journey. *Are we nearly there yet?*

'Soon.' Cassie suddenly feels overwhelmed, suffocated. They're leaving. It's not her problem. 'Must get on,' she says, sickened by the sticky Complan smeared on Mara's face, the stale old joss stick, coconutty, dirty-laundry smell.

In the kitchen she throws away the flypapers, stuck all over with bodies, some of them quite brilliant, one still feebly struggling. She wipes the table, sweeps the floor, makes herself some tea, hacks a piece of bread off a stale loaf, cuts a wedge of cheese. It's so *quiet*. No quieter than usual. Only that today she knows for a fact no one will come.

Nothing to stop a little exploration. She goes through the door she's hardly ever been through, into the high, dim hall. Apart from the front door and the cupboard, all the doors are locked. Very cagey, Larry. But that is the word for him. What other words, she wonders, grasping the flowered china knob of the front room and pushing with all her strength. Suave. Dapper. Enigmatic. Inscrutable. Bloody *weird*. But – kind. *Kind?* Yes. Kind to Mara. Understanding. Amazingly good about Graham hitting him. Suggesting a holiday for them. You can forgive a person a lot if they are kind.

She goes back into the kitchen. What to do? If there was only a phone or a computer. She aches to talk to Patsy. She could write another card, but no point since they're leaving. *No* letters back in all this time, nearly *two months*. Somewhere in Australia there must be a pile of letters addressed to them. Anything could have happened out there in the real world. Must be something wrong, address wrong? Unless Larry brings them, all the letters will arrive after they've left now. Because Patsy *will* have written. She couldn't *not*. She picks up a book but her eyes won't stick to the words. Not in the mood for anything. Tips her tea away undrunk and makes a cup of coffee. Eats a bit more cheese.

Might as well have a clean-up. She goes to get some bleach out from the cupboard under the sink. Such a mess in there: things toppled over, defunct cardboard tubes of cleaning stuff. She'll sort it out. That would be something constructive, at least. She likes sorting. She kneels down and pulls everything out: Flash; a scrubbing brush all nested up with pearly spiders' eggs; some filthy cloths; Duraglit; a can of something – she reaches deep into the cupboard but can't quite get it, it rolls down a gap between the back of the shelf and the wall. She withdraws from the cupboard, sweaty and cross. It'll just have to stay there. But – she frowns, something snagging oddly at her mind – the sound. The sound when it fell was not just like a tin falling on its side. There was a rattly chink like money or something. It fell *on to* something. Maybe a stash of coins? Maybe that is Larry's secret. The place is stuffed with gold.

Ha ha ha. But still, she feels stupidly excited as she pulls everything else out of the cupboard, filthy, sticky load of crap. Peculiar that Larry is so clean yet can bear to live with such squalor around him. Long as he doesn't have to touch it. Long as he has his white napkins, shirts, his clean white towels. She sits back on her heels, picks something off her hair, a furry bit of cobweb. She takes a breath, leans in and reaches down, pushes the tin aside. She puts one knee into the cupboard, stretches further, holding her breath till her fingertips just reach and manage to pick up not money but a set of keys.

*

Miles away and it's still all the same. Cool at least in the noisy air-con. Hard to believe it's really as hot as it is outside, though the road ahead and behind them dissolves into a shimmer. The highway almost empty but for the occasional hurtling monster road train: four, five carriages, great fancy cabs, glinting chrome, funnels smoking. Can't see the truckers only the sheen of light on the windscreens.

Fred drives slowly. Lets everything that wants to overtake him overtake. He doesn't talk much, sticks in another country tape when one finishes, till Graham is sick of prisons, trailer parks and doomy love.

'Poor bloody joey,' Fred nods towards maybe the hundredth carcass today, this one a baby, paws curled up to its chest. 'Follow their mums across the road and don't make it,' he says. 'Roll us another fag, mate.'

Graham rolls a fag each, takes a swig of water. They go over a bump and his stomach dips. Cassie and Mara back there, together and alone. But Mara will be asleep. And, anyway, she wouldn't say. She promised and he believes her. He feels bad leaving Cassie but – it is *great* to be away. Like some poxy great rucksack lifted off his shoulders. He looks down at his bruised fist and smiles.

'How do *you* stick Larry?' he says.

Fred doesn't answer. Acts like he hasn't heard. Graham looks out of the window. The landscape's changed a bit at last. After the interminable, rolling, desert scrub the trees are bigger, writhing limbs of gum. A bridge spans an almost dried-up creek, a ruby trickle snaking through cracked mud, the odd green stem jutting upwards, gigantic seedlings. Seems to make a nonsense of the flood warnings – *Water reaches this level* – showing a metre and a half. 'Don't you believe it,' Fred says. 'Can't depend on a road round here, come the rainy season. Hey,' he nods at a sign. 'Wagammara, 16 km – fancy a trip into town?'

'Town? But I thought –' *Town*, he thinks, *pub*, he thinks, *beer*. 'Yeah, sure. If we've got time.'

'All the time in the world, mate.'

Graham looks at his watch. Not noon yet. Yes, plenty of time. They'd promised Cassie they'd be back by dark.

Fred turns left down the road, the metalling giving out after a couple of hundred metres. Spiky bushes each side of the road, the grass looks so soft but he knows it would cut like little blades. Must be water hereabouts for all this sudden green. His parched eyes drink it in. An emu, or maybe it's an ostrich, a giant anyway, poses between the bushes, round eye glinting.

'Is it big, this town?' It looks to Graham as if there're getting further from civilisation rather than nearer. No other vehicles. The road so badly pitted it looks as if it's been deliberately hacked up.

Fred laughs. 'Wait and see, mate.'

He sticks on another tape. Graham grits his teeth against the twang of a banjo, the slither of a Hawaiian guitar. This guy has some sad taste in music. Still. The prospect of a pint or two. And he said he'd ring Patsy if they get near a phone. But it suddenly dawns on him: he has no money.

'You won't believe this,' he says, patting the pockets of his shorts. 'Haven't got any bloody cash! Would you believe it, I'd *forgotten* about money!'

'No worries, mate,' Fred says, grinning to himself about something.

'I'll pay you back.'

'Sure.'

He stops the ute. Ejects the tape. And sits, squinting through the windscreen. Beside them is an abandoned car, door hanging open, headlights smashed. In front, a ripple of red hills, fresh with the green and white of young gums.

'What?' Graham says.

'Look.' Fred indicates a signpost.

'What about it?'

'Get out and take a look.'

Graham opens the door. The heat hits him like a wall. The heat and the quiet. Very, very quiet. Silent? No bird sound at all. He walks towards the sign, feet scrunching on the dusty road. The sign says 2nd Avenue. He frowns, glances around. And after a moment sees.

More abandoned cars. A gate to nowhere, fixed to gateposts, padlocked – but there is no fence. Bits of broken stuff that might be kerb stones. Trees and shrubs that look cultivated. As if they were once cultivated. A chimney lying on its side.

He returns to the ute. 'This is Wagammara?' he says. Hoping for a laugh, the thirst growing panicky in his throat.

Fred slaps his thigh, delighted with his joke. 'Yup.'

'But. What happened?'

'Asbestos, mate. Mining town, see. Blue asbestos. Look

down.' Graham looks down at the road, the fine glittering dust. 'Surfaced the roads with it, trash from mines – till they realised it was a killer. The silly buggers. Mine shut down. No mine, no town. Used to be the biggest town for a thousand k each way.'

'But where's it gone? Where have the houses, everything, gone?'

'Took them with 'em, built them elsewhere. Nothing wasted.'

Graham climbs back into the ute. Afraid of the poison dust that glitters everywhere. 'So, no town. No pub.'

'Never said there was a pub, did I? My mate Ziggy lives here,' he says.

'Someone lives here?' Graham gazes out. The sign, 2nd Avenue. The car with its door lolling open. The gate leading nowhere.

Fred drives down an impossible road, so broken and stone-strewn it could be a dried-up river bed. Dust rises in a cloud behind them as they head downwards through a tunnel of trees and out into a clearing; looks like an abandoned car park, with the wreck of an old bus. And there's water. A deep ripply blue lake. Willowy gums, dappled shadows and, on the water, silhouetted against the light so that they look black, a pair of swans.

Graham's eyes drink it in. 'Might have a swim,' he says, thinking of Cassie, how she's been on about swimming. But she wouldn't want him not to swim.

'Go ahead.'

'Where's your mate live then?'

Fred points a stubby finger at the bus. 'Chez Ziggy,' he says and throws his head back. 'Better come and say g'day.'

The slamming car doors echo across the water and against the bluish shine of the cliffs, causing almost visible sound waves in the still air. The tyres of the bus look as if they've melted, the chassis slumped low and leaning, gaudy red and yellow painted, stuff strewn all around. PERTH it says on the front.

Fred bangs on the side of the bus. 'Zig? Ziggy?'

There's no reply. Graham looks back at the water. Blue, like the blue of an eye he can't read.

'May as well get your dip,' Fred says. He walks across the broken ground to a turtle-shaped rock under a tree. He pisses against the tree, then sits in the shade, rolls himself a fag. Graham looks at the water. Why is it rippled when there's no breeze? He walks a few metres away, shucks his clothes, lifts his arms and dives, slices through the surface, rises with a gasp. Though blood temperature on top it quickly graduates to bollock-shrivelling icy cold, black and dark beneath him. How deep? But the shock is a charge and after a moment it is great, his body immersed, the sky above a skin of white and the swans – from which he keeps his distance – are actually black, not just seeming to be. The cliff is rippled with gleaming blue, not a natural cliff he realises but the exposed side of a quarry. He crawls fast up and down a few times before he scrambles out. Stretches his wet body up to the sun before he pulls his boxers back on.

When he looks round he sees Fred over by the bus. The door's open and a yellow-haired guy is standing on the step. The two of them are looking across at him. He waves and they lift their hands. He puts on his jeans, sticks his feet in his sandals. Water runs from his hair down his face and neck.

'Nice to meet you, Graham.' Ziggy's voice is cultured, very English. He's coffee-coloured, fat-bellied and skinny-legged with a yellow fuzz of hair and beard and large eyes, pale as mist. Hair froths through the mesh of his stained string vest and Y-front pants. He holds out his hand, horny as hell, calloused all over, huge.

'Yeah,' Graham says.

'Hear you're in the art line yourself?' Ziggy says.

'Sort of, well, yes. You?'

Ziggy's laugh is a high and breathy surprise. Every other one of his teeth is missing. 'You haven't *seen*?'

'Open your bleeding eyes, mate!' Fred shakes his head and the two of them laugh.

Graham flushes. He looks back towards the water and then he does see. The rock that looks like a turtle has been carved. He walks back to look at the patterns on the shell, intricate, vaguely aboriginal-looking shapes, spirals, tiny representations of stick men and beasts. And he sees that the stump of a tree is carved into a woman's form, squat, heavy-bellied, an open crack between her legs, like a fertility symbol. Reminds him horribly of Mara. He looks away, back to the pair of swans. They have still not moved. They are carved out of something black, keeping their place in the water. It is only the way it laps against them that makes them seem to move. How did he not see that?

He goes back, sheepish, grinning. 'It's great.'

'The more you look, the more you see,' says Ziggy.

'You had me going with those swans. How –'

'Ah ha! Do come in,' Ziggy says. 'Coffee?' He leads them up the steps. Following him up, Graham sees a Grand Prix's worth of skid marks on the back of his pants. He'd like to see Cassie's face. The inside of the bus is chaos and it stinks. A greasy sleeping bag on a bed made of several bus seats, a narrow passage to a table, stacks of things, almost impenetrable, mostly junk, some of it stuck together in bizarre combinations: bottles, dolls' heads, heaps of magazines, a split-open tennis ball with a doll's hand sticking out; an animal skull – kangaroo? – painted pink; a coat hanger hung with bottle tops and birds' wings.

'Brought anything?' Ziggy says. He puts a kettle on a tiny Calor stove.

Fred goes out. Graham tries to look out of the window, but it's thickly dusted with bluish white. Sees an old-fashioned telephone, a blonde pigtail trailing from the mouthpiece.

'It's quite –' Has to say something. 'Ingenious,' he says. Ziggy snorts. He wipes a cup on a bit of dirty-looking rag. 'Hope you take it black.'

'Yeah. Actually don't bother about the coffee.'

Ziggy shrugs and turns the gas off. 'Smoke then?' He sits down at his table, the top of which is a car door, and rolls a big, pure grass, joint.

'Yeah.' Last thing Graham wants is a smoke. *Just say no then*, Cassie would say.

'Where you off to?' Ziggy asks.

'Heading north to see some indigenous cave-painting,' he says, thinking maybe he shouldn't say Abo. Confused.

'This lot not indigenous enough for you?'

'I mean –'

Fred comes clumping back in with a box of stuff. 'Not winding him up already, mate? You watch him, Graham. Wind-up merchant extraordinaire.'

Ziggy shrugs theatrically at Graham and hands him the joint. 'After you,' he says, rubbing his hands together. 'Now, what have we here?' He unpacks the tins of tuna and beans, cartons of long-life orange and tomato juice, vodka, Lee and Perrin's sauce. 'Ha! The makings of a Bloody Mary. Do the honours, old chap.'

Graham laughs. There's other stuff in the box too, bottles and things – and the frame of Cassie's broken mirror. He lights the joint and sucks in the smoke.

Fred sees him notice the black oval with its design of faded pansies. 'Yeah,' he says, little eyes shifty. 'Thought Ziggy could use it.'

'But it's Cassie's, man.'

'She wouldn't mind, would she, mate?'

Yes, he should say, *she would mind*. But he says nothing, holds in a mouthful of smoke. 'What do you live on, stuck out here?' he asks, exhaling.

'Friends drop by – generous friends – and I sell my stuff. My "art".'

'Yeah?'

When Ziggy grins, the black spaces between his teeth turn him into a pumpkin lantern. 'No, not this. I do aboriginal stuff, tourist trade. He pulls a box out from under the table. 'Take something for your girlfriend if you like.'

Fred rubs his fingers together, looking at the joint. Graham fills his lungs again and passes it over. He hunkers dizzily down beside the box: painted pebbles and pieces of wood shaped into rough toucans, parrots, crocodiles. He chooses a stone painted with a complex maze-like spiral in ochre, yellow and white that nearly makes his eyes cross, trying to follow it.

'What is it?' he asks. 'I mean, some kind of symbolic –'

'Symbolic, my arse,' Ziggy laughs. 'It's tourist tat. Pretty good quality though, if I'm allowed to say. But it might just *about* qualify as urban aboriginal art.'

'Yeah?'

Ziggy sways in the smoke. 'Uses images from the quotidian rather than symbolic representations.' He draws apostrophes in the air and waggles his head self-mockingly.

'What is it?'

'It's the bus, see.' Graham squints at it for a moment, trouble focusing, then does see. The tiny dots describe four wheels, like a bus ironed flat, each wheel a spiral, and the steering wheel.

'Ta.' He puts it in the pocket of his jeans. 'She'll like that.'

'But I've got another one here, if you like. The real thing. Look at this.' He rummages about on the sill of the bus, amongst envelopes and fruit rinds, and brings out a pebble, hands it to Graham. This one is not painted, but seems to have a map engraved on it, ridges of blue, white, grey and all shades of red and rust.

Graham rubs his thumbnail over the ridges.

'It's natural,' Ziggy says. 'Amazing, eh? I think you appreciate the natural, eh?'

Graham stares at the pebble. Likes the feel of it, friendly in his hand. 'Thanks.' He closes his palm around it. Gets a pang, thinking about Cassie. 'How long have we got?' he says to Fred.

'Long as you like. Seen enough art?' He grins over at Ziggy. 'Maybe we'll just stay here, instead, eh?'

'Don't rush off,' Ziggy says, 'now you're here. In fact, you must stay to lunch.'

Graham glances at his watch. Still not noon, incredibly. Well, time plays tricks. He relaxes. 'Why not? Thanks.' The joint comes back to him. 'Nice grass,' he says, relieved. He feels OK with it. None of the heebies. Feels pretty laid-back.

'Home-grown, my dear chap.' Ziggy stretches, revealing great mops of sopping yellow armpit hair.

It's sweltering in the bus; Graham's T-shirt sticks to his back. Could sit outside. But outside there is the poison sparkle of the dust. He looks through the filthy window at a blur of foliage, settles back, a feeling of – almost – peace. He blows out a fan of smoke. If they're going no further north they've got a couple of hours to spare before going back. Might even get another swim.

Twenty-four

Cassie sits back on her heels, holding the keys. Three of them, Yale-type keys, one bronze, two dull silver on a ring with a chewed-up leather fob. How on earth did they get down there? Her heart throbs painfully. They might be ages old, might not fit any keyhole here – but still. They *might*. She may as well try and see. No one will be any the wiser. She won't touch anything at all. Just *look*. What could be the harm?

She rinses the dust and cobwebs off the keys and goes back into the hall. Four locked doors but only three keys. One door she notices straightaway has a mortice lock. One of the front rooms. Larry's office or study or whatever it is. The other three locks are Yale. She takes a deep breath. Approaches the other front room. Bedroom maybe? The first key won't even fit, the second slides in but doesn't turn. Must be the third. She takes a breath, slides it in – but it won't go. Tries to force it, but it is no good. Doesn't fit. She kicks the bloody stupid door. The clean keys glint at her in the dimness. They are not keys for here after all, somebody else's old keys dropped and forgotten years ago. She stubs her toe on the door. *Ow*. Stupid bloody thing. Almost weeping with frustration she tries another door but, of course, it's the same. The keys are nothing to do with here at all. What could be more *useless* than a wrong key?

Disappointment swamps her. Waste of time and energy. The

day stretches ahead, now dull and pointless. What to do? A walk, maybe; perhaps Yella will come. Before it gets too bloody hot. The doors are blank faces in the gloom. It is *already* too bloody hot. It always bloody is. She stops outside the last door. Tries the bronze key. And it works.

She blinks, startled by the easy turn and click. It really works. Stands looking at the key diagonally in the lock, almost scared to open the door. It feels wrong but not quite wrong enough to stop. She takes a deep breath and turns the handle, pushes open the door.

It is a *bathroom*. A proper plumbed-in bathroom. She doesn't understand, blinks as if it might evaporate in front of her eyes. A *bathroom*. But there *is* no bathroom. She literally cannot believe her eyes. A wonderful *bathroom*. It might as well be heaven. A deep white bath on clawed bronze feet, a toilet, a basin all clean and gleaming white – even a bidet. The floor and walls are tiled in cool white marble, on the far wall a long mirror in which her own face gawps round the open door.

She steps inside, heart thudding. It smells of Larry. All this time he has had a bathroom to himself. Why did he not say? No *wonder* he is always so clean. On a shelf is a pile of French sandalwood soaps in fluted brown paper wrappings. Also a wooden dish of shaving soap, brush, razor, tweezers, a funny little thing – she picks it up wondering, realises it's a device for trimming nostril hair and quickly puts it down. Cinnamint toothpaste, face cloths and towels, a deep stack of the fluffy white ones she washes every week.

Why has he lied? It's like, it makes her feel a bit sick to think it, like he's been taking the piss, seeing them so hot and sweaty, pretending there is no bathroom, that he washes in bowls of water in his room. She should have guessed. She feels almost *hurt*. He seemed so friendly. Why *lie*? It seems mad. Or pathologically selfish, at least. *Cruel*.

She looks down at the bath. As she looks, a silver trickle of water escapes from the one of the taps on to the side like an idea. Why not? Why the hell not? Why shouldn't she? Camomile shampoo. Oh to properly wash her hair, to soap herself all over with that soap and wrap herself in a soft white towel. What harm would that do? What possible harm? And by the time Larry gets back the towel will be washed and dried, the bath cleaned. He'll never know the difference. It would do her so much good and cause no harm at all. There really is no question. She puts the plug in and turns on both the taps.

She takes off her vest and shorts, watching herself in the mirror. She stands sideways. Her belly sticks out more than it did. Not surprising – more eating, less exercise – and her breasts are bigger too, startlingly pale against the brown of her arms and shoulders, face and legs. She twists her head to see her bum, a bit wobbly-looking, a spot or two. But generally she looks OK. She cups her hands under her breasts and pouts, poses like some stupid centrefold. Looks at Larry's razor. Should go and get her own but she can't resist it. She lathers her legs and armpits with the tickly tuft of brush, a bit like Larry's beard she thinks, shuddering, and shaves with his razor. Rinses it carefully under the tap, replaces the wooden lid of the shaving soap, rinses the brush and stands it upright to dry, rinses the traces of scum and hair from the sink.

She turns off the taps and steps in – aaah – the joy, better even than sex it feels right now, *miles* better, to let herself sink into it. The bath is big enough to float in. She puts her head right under and the water snakes in her ear canals, she hears her stomach gurgle, amplified. Will she say anything to Larry? What could she say? She wonders if Mara knows about the bathroom, if Fred does. She should confront Larry but – They are leaving. What would be the point?

She tries to forget about Larry, to let herself relax into the glorious sensation of the water. The shampoo is fragrant, silky lather against her skull. She relaxes back, swishes her head about. When she sits up and runs her fingers through her hair it squeaks, properly clean *at last*. She lies back blinking through wet lashes and notices that one end of the bathroom is a floor-to-ceiling cupboard. Metal, with a lock. She frowns. Gets out, dries her hands, picks up the keys. The second key fits the lock. Might as well look.

Inside are neat shelves of drugs. Like a pharmacy. All for Mara? Packets of disposable syringes. Pills and phials of stuff, all sorts of things. Like the ones she has in her rucksack. She closes and re-locks the cupboard and frowns. Well, there's his research and he is a doctor after all. Needs to care for Mara, be prepared for emergencies, snake or scorpion bites for instance.

She steps back into the bath, the water cooler and scummy now with shampoo and floating hairs, but still, lovely. If they could have used the bathroom, even only once or twice a week, the whole thing would have been so much *easier*. Maybe it's not so ecological as a scrub with a flannel outside but it sure is more luxurious. She picks up the soap and is rubbing it between her hands, thinking that she'll never, for the rest of her life, be able to smell sandalwood without thinking of this stolen moment, or of Larry for that matter – when she hears something. The bounce of the kitchen flyscreen. She freezes, hands a slither of scented bubbles. Someone in the kitchen, definitely someone in the kitchen. The bubbles web her fingers, popping as she watches. She lowers them silently into the water.

She holds her breath, heart beating visibly under her wet skin. Who? Larry. No no no no. Just Yella? But no, it's definitely a person in there, a person moving about in the kitchen. A pipe clanks, someone turning on the tap. Giddily she realises she hasn't breathed, forces a breath into her constricted lungs, stands up, steps out, wincing at the slosh of water, dabs herself with a towel, pulls on her clothes, the fabric of her shorts sticking on her damp legs. Her face in the steamy mirror a pale blur between hanks of wet hair, eyes black spaces. She shivers in the heat. She looks round, no time to clean the bath, wet footprints on the floor, but no time. She picks up the keys, goes to the door.

She opens it quietly, steps out into the hall and with trembling fingers manages to lock the door behind her. She pushes the keys into her pocket. Now all she has to do is go back into the kitchen. And face whatever. It takes a moment to gather the will, but it is quiet there now. Maybe whoever it was has gone? Maybe, just *maybe*, it was imagination. But no. No, there *was* a definite noise. The turning-on of a tap. She is not *mad*.

She takes a deep breath and dares herself to open the door. And there, sitting at the table, is Mara.

'Mara!' Her voice comes out as a high wobble. She goes weak with relief. Sinks down on the nearest chair. 'Thought you were asleep.'

Mara looks far from sleepy, her eyes bright, her cheeks almost rosy. Her breasts loll on the table in front of her. 'Woke up!' Mara says. 'You been in the bath?'

Cassie opens her mouth but nothing happens. 'You know about the bathroom then?' she says at last, feeling foolish as she says it. Obviously Mara knows. 'Why,' she stammers, 'why does he pretend there isn't one?'

'Likes to keep it to himself,' Mara says, as if that's sufficient explanation.

Cassie stares at her. 'Well, I hope *you* don't mind,' she says, at last. 'Me – bathing.'

'*I* don't mind,' Mara snorts. 'But Larry –'

Cassie hesitates. Can she ask Mara not to mention it?

'Maybe I'd better go and clean it?' she says.

Mara nods. Cassie goes back and wipes the bath absolutely clean, dries the soap, wipes every drop from the floor, removes the damp towel and leaves a fresh one folded ready. No way he could tell it had been used. No way.

She locks the door and goes back to Mara, who sits peacefully twisting her fingers in her hair.

'I won't tell,' Mara says.

'Won't you?'

'Why would I?'

Cassie smiles at her. 'Thank you. It's nice that you're awake.' Her eyes travel to the pills. 'I was feeling a bit – kind of lonely. With everyone gone off.'

'Larry went off years ago.' Mara gives her a mischievous look.

'Mara!'

'Shall we eat something?' Mara says. 'I could eat a horse.'

'Mmm,' Cassie says, looking at her with curiosity. 'I'll cook us something, shall I? Some brunch?' Water trickles down between her shoulder blades as she fetches ham and eggs from the fridge. She looks back at Mara. She seems so *different*. 'I was thinking maybe French toast?'

'Pancakes?' Mara suggests. 'With maple syrup?'

'Don't know if – hang on.' Cassie drags over a stool, climbs up and reaches into the back of the top shelf of the fridge. And there is a sticky bottle half-full of maple syrup.

Maybe she gave her the wrong drugs? Or not enough? Or maybe Mara spat the Complan out without her seeing?

'Are you feeling OK?' She certainly looks OK, not crazy or violent. Apart from her nakedness she seems perfectly normal. And even the nakedness has come to seem almost normal. It would be weirder if she put on a dress. Was that a sort of *joke* about Larry?

'Coffee?'

'I'll do it.'

'No, no.' All the same, best keep her away from boiling water. The fan swishes, a faint squeak. Three or four flies dance in the air below it. Another crawls on Mara's gleamy shoulder.

Cassie breaks eggs, beats them together with powdered milk, water and flour. *Cassie's Outback Kitchen. Pancakes, a good staple from store-cupboard ingredients.*

'You do look so like Lucy,' Mara says.

'Lucy and Ben, you mean.' Cassie keeps her voice level. Not too interested. 'No one ever seems to mention them. How long ago did they leave?'

Mara shakes her head. 'Don't know. Lost track.'

'Do you know why they went?'

'One day they were gone, that's all.'

'Oh?'

'You wouldn't do that, would you? Go without saying.'

Cassie shakes her head, a shadow settling in her chest. Should she tell Mara? Could she expect her to keep that quiet? *No*. She lifts the whisk and watches a long yellow gloop of batter drool back into the bowl. Questions boil up quietly in her head. She moves over to the stove, pours water on to coffee grounds, moves the frying pan on to the centre of the heat. Mara is quiet – maybe she's falling asleep, the drugs working after all, having a delayed effect?

'He's so mysterious, Larry, isn't he?' Cassie tries. 'Enigmatic. I mean, I know he is a doctor but –'

'No,' Mara says. Then she looks scared.

'No?' Cassie pours a pool of batter into the pan, swills it around, watches the surface glaze and pock.

'Shouldn't say. My mind is clear. Funny. Like someone took the lid off, type of thing. Like looking through fog, normally. And then I don't care about anything, you know? Don't care.'

'Sounds horrible.'

'Then all I want is sleep.'

Cassie turns to look at her. 'Poor you.' Mara's eyes are large and bright brown. Cassie has never really noticed how lovely they are. She looks younger too.

'Like a dream,' Mara continues, twisting a finger in her hair, 'life, can't tell which part is real and which a dream. Like there are no proper edges. Do you get that?'

'Not – no, not usually,' Cassie says carefully, 'but I think I know what you mean.'

'Though now –' Mara holds a hand out, swivels it on her wrist, 'I *feel* awake. Am I? Do you want to pinch me?'

Cassie smiles, 'Of course you're awake. Mara, why – why do you stay in the shed?'

'Not *shed*! Studio.'

'Sorry.'

'Always wanted my own studio. Like Larry has his own bathroom.' She laughs again, a kind of mockery in the laugh.

'*Why* does he need his own bathroom?'

Mara shrugs and shakes her head. Cassie eases the spatula under the pancake, she daren't flip it. It sticks and tears. 'So, Larry isn't a doctor,' she tries.

Mara huddles into herself, fingers digging into the flesh of her upper arms, breasts and hair all squashed together. 'Shouldn't have said.' She buries her face in her hands. 'Don't tell him I said –'

'Don't worry, Mara. I won't say a thing.'

Mara peeps through her fingers. 'Won't you?'

'Promise.'

'Larry says I mustn't tell anyone ever, otherwise –'

'Just a mo.' Cassie turns the pancake. 'Otherwise?'

'It'll all go wrong again.'

The pancake is a disaster. 'How do you mean?' Cassie says. 'Do you want this one? It's a mess.'

'Don't care.'

'What do you mean, *again*?' Cassie carries the frying pan across the kitchen, and slides the messed-up lump of a pancake on to her plate. Mara slathers it in maple syrup, rolls it up and stuffs half of it in her mouth.

'But sometimes it's good to talk.' Cassie winces at herself. Mara fills her mouth again, chews stolidly. Boiling over with questions, Cassie wants to shake Mara, shake it all out of her.

But must be patient. She pours in another pool of creamy batter, tips the pan to fill the bottom. This time the pan is hot enough and it will work.

'When he was a kid,' Mara says at last, mouth full. 'Mmm, *lovely*. See, he wanted to be a doctor but he wasn't good enough at school. His brother, his little brother, he *was* a doctor –' She swallows the last mouthful and wipes her sticky lips. 'We could have lemon and sugar next?'

Cassie takes a deep breath. She digs amongst the oranges in the bowl and finds a lemon. Bit wizened but still. She slices it in half, the sharp sting of its juice making her mouth flood with spit. 'And?'

'Wasn't fair.' Mara licks her fingers and looks at the pan.

'Coming up.' Cassie turns it over: better, lovely brown frizzy edges. 'What wasn't fair?'

'*Larry* was the one who was always experimenting with frogs and things but then his brother – he gets to be a doctor. Larry was a pharmacist. Always second best.'

'So,' Cassie keeps her voice light. 'He's never really been a doctor.'

'Oh yes, well, he's *been* a doctor.'

Cassie slides another pancake on to Mara's plate. She waits agonising moments while Mara concentrates on spooning a line of sugar down its centre, squeezing lemon till the sugar goes translucent, rolling it and taking a bite. *The perfect brunch. Oh shut up.*

'Mmmmmm.' Mara chews with her eyes shut for a moment, the gritty sound of sugar between her teeth. She swallows and opens her eyes. 'Aren't you having one?'

'Maybe when you've finished. There's loads of batter. You might as well tell me now,' Cassie says, 'you've told me the rest. And honestly, Mara, I can keep a secret.'

Mara pauses, cheek bulging. 'If you tell Larry I told you, I'll tell him about your bath.'

'I wouldn't anyway.'

Mara swallows her mouthful. 'This is what he told me anyway – I think. Sometimes I forget things . . .' She tails off, her eyes focused somewhere in the distance.

'*Yes?*'

'They were the dead spit, Larry and his younger brother, practically like twins. Larry went to visit him when he'd just moved to a new town, new practice and his brother died, suddenly, a heart attack, nothing Larry could do, then – and Larry didn't plan this, funny things do happen, don't they?'

'Well, yes.'

'Someone phoned him – an emergency, took him for the doctor, and he went to help and then, well, then he swapped places with his brother. His brother was buried as him.'

'*No!* Did it work? What about his family?'

'Dad dead, mum gaga. Kept away from family friends and so on. And they *were* peas in a pod.' Mara hesitates. 'Didn't know him then. Wasn't really wrong, was it?'

'We-ll.'

'He worked there for a while and he managed all right. I was a patient, that's how I met him.' She stops, a cloud darkening her face.

'Yes,' Cassie waits. 'You lost a baby, didn't you? Graham told me. I'm sorry.'

'Larry says I mustn't tell anyone ever, otherwise I'll be put in prison, I'll be locked away. Larry takes care of me. Have to do what he says. Or else.'

'I –' Cassie flounders, startled by the sudden change in Mara, her whole shape and voice have altered. Perhaps she really is mad. About to go berserk. 'Sorry, I shouldn't have asked. Another pancake?'

But Mara keeps talking. Cassie slides the pan off the heat and sits down. 'When the baby died I – went off my head type of thing – and Larry and me, well we – we had an affair – sort of – well, we got together. Started with him helping me and then one night – don't remember this but he told me – I went mad, completely off my head and –' she whispers, 'killed my husband.'

'You killed your husband? *How?*' Cassie says. '*Why?*'

'Don't remember. He was ill anyway. Larry was treating him. But *violence*. I was off my head. Larry covered it up somehow. *See*, if he hadn't brought me here and hidden me then, then I would be in prison or in some mad house. Mad and dangerous.' She pauses. 'Mad and dangerous. Don't remember what I do. Sometimes don't know what I do. Some things I do that I don't want to do I do for Larry. Sorry. Sorry.'

What? Cassie can't think of anything that Mara does. 'But,' she says, her mouth dry, 'you don't *seem* dangerous.'

Mara gets up and, involuntarily, Cassie flinches. Mara laughs. 'No? Need a drink of water. Room for one more pancake.'

'Sure, sit down.' Cassie fills a glass for her and pushes the pan back on the heat.

Mara drinks. 'Not dangerous *now*,' she says. 'Right now I feel fine. Sort of clear-headed. But shouldn't have told you. Larry says, he says if I ever tell anyone I'll be sorry.'

'You've never told anyone?'

'Fred knows everything. Fred's my friend.'

'Fred's lovely,' Cassie agrees.

'Don't tell anyone this,' Mara leans towards her and whispers loudly, 'but I love Fred and he loves me. If we could be together we would. One day . . .' She sits back and smiles.

Cassie sits down. Too much to take in. She finds herself wavering, losing faith. Fantasy, like Larry said?

'Do you want coffee now?' she says.

'Fred and me, we – we understand each other.' Mara gets up suddenly, juddering the table. 'Be careful, won't you?' she says.

'Careful?'

'You looked just like her when you came out of the bathroom.

Made me start. Wait.' She goes out. Chair marks printed on her buttocks. The screen clatters. Cassie's heart skitters. A fly lands on the corner of her mouth and as she slaps it her fingernail snags her lip. She follows Mara out of the door and waits. Mara emerges from her shed with something in her hand, a bit of paper, no a snapshot. She comes up the steps. 'See,' she says.

'Lucy?' Lucy is blonde, medium build and height. Her hair hangs over her chest in two long plaits, raggy ribbons at the ends.

'See what I mean?'

Cassie frowns. 'A bit similar maybe, longer hair.'

Mara starts to speak, stops, lifts up her hand. There is the sound of a vehicle approaching. 'Larry,' she says, peering into the distance.

Cassie shades her eyes and squints. 'But he said a few days,' she says. 'Could be the others coming back for some reason.' *Please, please let it be them.* Not yet possible to tell what is inside the approaching cloud of dust.

'Shouldn't you maybe go and lie down?' she says, 'he might be –' But Mara doesn't move. Stands so close to Cassie that her breast presses coolly against her bare arm.

'Why be careful?' Cassie says. 'What did you mean?' She runs her fingers through her hair, nearly dry now, but getting sticky already with sweat and she never even brushed it smooth. A sickly weight settles in her stomach as she sees the glimpse of white that means it is Larry's car.

'Don't ever say anything I told you,' Mara whispers, urgently. '*Promise.*'

'Course not.'

'Cross your heart and hope to die?'

'Cross my heart and hope to die,' she repeats. And shivers. 'Really, maybe you should go and lie down.'

But there is no time for that.

Twenty-five

The car draws up. Larry gets out and slams the door. Yella goes out to greet him, wagging his half-mast tail. Larry greets her with a tight smile on his face. He looks flushed, even a little dusty. He will want a bath.

'Mara awake!' he says. 'I'm surprised. Are you all right?' He looks darkly at Cassie. 'There are some things in the car, could you possibly?'

'Oh no!' Smelling burning she darts back into the kitchen and pulls the pan off the heat; the pancake is black, the kitchen hazed with smoke and stink. She avoids Larry's eyes as she goes out again. The stupid hens scutter squawkily up to her, expecting food again. Never thought she'd be the sort of person to want to kick a hen. On the floor inside the car is an eskie and some carrier bags of food. The smell of bruised apples. She loops a carrier over each wrist and holds the eskie in front of her. When she gets back, the kitchen is empty but for the smoke. She begins to unpack food into the fridge. Butter, milk, bacon, mince. No sign of any post. When she turns her head, Larry's there.

'Where's Mara?'

'Back in her room.'

'But she was –' *Fine*, she wants to say, *absolutely fine*.

'How little you understand,' Larry says. He shakes his head

216

at her. 'Now, more to the point, where are the others?' He waits, gives a little bark of a laugh. 'Surely not abandoned you?

'No, no, they went to see some cave art. Just a little trip.'

He looks puzzled. 'I don't remember being consulted.'

'Well –'

'What the eye don't see, eh?'

'But everything's *fine*. And they'll be back tonight. Maybe late afternoon. I said I didn't mind.'

'Everything's fine?' Larry repeats. '*Everything's fine?* This!' He waves his hand through the haze of smoke. 'And Mara overstimulated, on the verge, I would say, of a psychotic episode. Always heralded by lying. Has she been lying?'

'No, I don't think so. No. We were just – chatting.'

'What were you *chatting* about?'

'Not anything really. Food. Pancakes.'

Larry looks into her eyes for a moment and she flushes, looks down at her feet, her smoothly shaved legs.

'And did Fred give Mara her medication before they set off on their *jaunt*?'

'He told me exactly what to give her.'

'What was it?'

'Well –' Cassie swallows. 'See, I knocked the bottles over,' she says. 'He'd left them in the right order. It wasn't his fault. A yellow, was it, a white, three blues –'

'Show me.'

Her hands shake so that she can hardly unscrew the lid.

'Fortunate I came back when I did,' Larry says. 'Most fortunate they *didn't* trigger a psychosis. *These* are *blue*.' For Larry, he has almost lost his cool, his breath coming hard behind his words. He tips some capsules into his palm, a different colour, yes, she can see now.

'Sorry.'

Larry returns the pills, screws on the lid. 'Not your fault,' he says. 'Don't get upset. But I will have a word with Fred.' He puts a finger under her chin and tips her hot face up. She has no choice but to look into his eyes.

They are calm, almost kind again. 'No harm done,' he says. 'No need for the long face, eh? I'm sorry, I got a bit agitated there. Tired, you know. Tell you what, I'll go and freshen up, why not make another batch of pancakes, eh? With bacon. I've quite an appetite, suddenly.'

He wipes his finger on his sleeve, goes out of the door into the hall, the eskie under his arm. Drugs? Did she lock the cupboard again? Yes, she did, she *did*. She looks at the back door. If she could run. But it is *OK*. It will all be OK. How could he know she's been in the bathroom? He can't know.

She takes bacon out of its paper bag, peels the gummy strips apart. But the door opens again and he comes in. She lays the bacon slices in a pan. She squats down to check the fire in the belly of the stove. His eyes burn into her back.

'Enjoy your bath?' His voice is level, grating gently with disappointment. With her thumbnail she picks at a blister of pocked enamel on the stove door. 'Straighten up, Cassandra, don't be stupid. I never thought that you were stupid.'

'All right,' she says. She stands up, wobbles a bit. Hands greasy with bacon fat.

He has a hair stretched out between his fingers like an invisible garrotte. 'Yours, I believe.' He holds the hair up between a finger and thumb, squints at it, before letting it fall, rubbing his fingers fastidiously together as if to rid them of the sensation. 'How did you get in?'

'Keys.' She fumbles them out of her pocket.

'And where?' Larry indicates the table with his head.

She puts them down. 'There. Behind the cupboard under the sink.'

'*Behind* the cupboard *under* the sink.' He snorts. 'And what on earth were you doing *behind* the cupboard *under* the sink?'

'Cleaning,' she says.

Larry laughs. He slaps his thigh. 'Oh my my.' He comes across and grips the tops of her arms. A shiver runs through her at the touch of his hands. He looks closely into her face. His breath smells of Cinnamint. The whites of his eyes are faintly pink.

'I don't like anyone in my bathroom.'

'Sorry.'

'And one thing I loathe above all other things is a snoop.'

'Sorry.'

'Perhaps you think it strange?'

'No!' she says, flushing. 'It's *your* house.'

'Indeed.' He runs his tongue over his front teeth and then he lets her go. 'Let's have breakfast then,' he says.

*

Fred's out of it, flat on his back on the bus-seat bed, snoring till the windows rattle. Ziggy's moving about, what's he doing? Something was said about food. How long ago was that? Graham looks at his watch again. Still not noon. *Some* grass. But *still* not noon?

'Watch stopped?' Ziggy looms above him. 'Crackers?' He brandishes a crackly orange pack of Jacob's.

'Yeah.'

'Another Bloody Mary?'

'Nah.' He swallows, thick taste of tomato juice cloying on his tongue. He scrunches his eyes at his watch, trying to catch the second hand, a fly's leg that should be jerking round. As he frowns at it, it does a feeble kick and trembles without moving forward. He giggles.

'Magnetic field.' Ziggy wrenches open a can of sardines. 'It's a bugger round here.'

'So what time is it?'

Ziggy looks down at the mash of little fish. 'Lunchtime, I'd say,' and though it's not funny they crack up. Graham clutches his stomach, the laughter jerking out of him till it almost hurts. Hasn't laughed like this since Christ knows.

'No, really,' Ziggy says, when he can speak again, 'I do rely on the old tum to tell me the time.'

Fred sits up, his bloodshot blue eyes blinking wildly till he works out where the hell he is, and then he grins.

'Going for a slash,' he says.

'Don't you want to eat, old chap?' Ziggy says.

'Give a bloke a minute, mate. Nature calls, old bean, tally-ho or whatever.'

'Toodle-pip,' Ziggy shouts after him. 'Have I taught you nothing?' Graham chokes on a laugh, coughs till his eyes stream. Ziggy clouts him between the shoulder blades and he eventually gets himself back under control. Takes a long swallow of lukewarm water. Pours himself a shot of vodka. Better without the tomato and stuff. Clean, carves a hot tube down his throat, so he can breathe.

'You're from England, right?' he says when he can speak.

'How on earth can you tell?' Ziggy grins; it is so huge, that grin, you could get lost in it, the expanse of cracked lip-skin, the dance of teeth, the slice-of-melon size of it. 'Mum an Abo – that's where I get my looks.' He frames his face with his hands and shouts a laugh. 'Dad a travel writer. Yeah! Wrote a famous book about Aboriginal art. *Stepping into Dreamtime*. Read it? Course it's been superseded now but it was a classic of its day. Fuck off, old chap.' He bats his hand through the air at a fly crawling on the sardine tin. 'Good for you, sardines, if you eat the bones. Calcium.' He crunches. 'They went to England, I was born, Mum couldn't hack it – the weather, the prejudice, the philistine way of treating the land – came back, but Dad persuaded her to leave me there for my education. Winchester, the lot! But –' He shrugs.

'Man.' Graham's mouth is dry, nearly stuck together with cracker crumbs. He knocks back the vodka. 'Do you see her much? Your mum.'

Ziggy shakes his head. 'I've seen her. Didn't – didn't work out. She's living on the Kallikurri reservation. New family. Very resentful, unfortunately. I think she's decided to edit the episode that includes me out of her life.' He brings the wide tip of his index finger down and squashes the fly dead against the oily tin, sucks the oil off his finger, wipes it on his vest. 'But – well, that's her prerogative, isn't it? Don't blame her actually.'

'And you just live here alone, all the time, don't you get – you know – lonely?'

Ziggy sticks his fingers in the jar of pickled cucumbers. The vinegary scent is sharp. Graham reaches his own fingers in. *Fork, Graham,* Cassie would say. First time he's been out of her sight, practically, for a couple of *months*. He catches a cucumber and pulls it out, vinegar running down his wrist.

'My choice. Tried marriage,' Ziggy said. 'Delia, English woman. Got a kid actually, up in Cairns.' He lurches up and fumbles through a pile of papers till he finds a photo, a boy in shorts, pale-brown skin, knock-knees, yellow hair that looks like it's been ironed flat against his head. 'Billy. Nice lad. I catch up with him sometimes.'

Graham savours the vinegary nip, the dill-flavoured scrunch of the pickle.

'Thing is,' Ziggy says, 'he can just about get away with being white, what with his mum. But if I turn up –'

'Hey!' Fred blunders back in. 'Let's have some tucker, mate. Or have you scoffed the lot?

The light has changed. First Graham thinks it's his eyes, the dope and drink, the suffocation, the sweltering heat. He goes out to have a piss. Walks back to the water, darker now, rippling steadily against the bank. Notices another carving on a tree. A fish, its bones and innards showing, a maze-like map of a fish. The more you look, the more you see. The swans obviously fake swans, not *fake*, they're art.

He frowns at the distinction, can't think straight, pulls off his

T-shirt, thinking to jump in again, wash the sweat away, clear his head. But the light changes as he hesitates on the edge; the sun casts a hard bright fan of beams and then slips down behind the quarry side, leaving him dazzled, leaving the car park in shade. He shivers. Too quiet. And why the ripples, when the air is still? A face painted on a rock catches his eye, or its eyes catch him and won't let go. A primitive face, mouth open, eyes cornered in white against dark-blue stone. He puts his T-shirt on again and walks towards the bus, feeling the eyes on him, fake eyes that's all, not eyes at all, daubs of pigment but still he's glad to get back in the bus.

'Getting dark,' he says.

'Eh?' Fred doesn't turn his head. He's looking at a magazine, where a blonde girl with her tongue stuck out spreads her legs, shaved cunt gleaming like a freshly opened whelk, a staple right there painful at her centre.

Graham winces and looks away. 'Shouldn't we be making a move?'

'Can't drive now,' Fred says. 'Oh dear, we'll just have to stay.' He flips the page, the same girl kneeling, arse in the air, from the back. Tattoo of a rose right in the middle of one buttock.

'You're most welcome,' Ziggy says.

'Open the Scotch?' Fred says. 'Let's get settled in.'

'In fact, I insist you stay. Where are my manners?'

'Cassie'll go ape-shit,' Graham says.

'Nah, she'll be fine. Tonight, tomorrow, what's the difference?'

'You reckon?'

But there is no choice. Not up to driving himself even if he had a licence. Why didn't he think? He can just hear Cassie saying that. You never *think*. Consequences, all that shit, responsibility. Fuck it. He reaches for the vodka bottle and tips his head back for the dregs.

Twenty-six

It's dark. They won't be back now. Cassie's ears ache from straining all afternoon to hear, sure several times she could hear an engine approaching but no; nothing. Just aeroplanes dragging trails across the sky, birds cackling. No sign or sound from Mara. Larry in his study, working. Stiff and polite when their paths have crossed, though she's avoided him as much as possible, spent much of the day in the garden.

Standing there under the shady nets she'd wished she'd made more of an effort. She turns the compost, amazed to find the centre of the heap already decomposing, dark and crumbly. The magic – eggshells, tea leaves, orange peels, turning into such lovely, sweet-smelling stuff – has happened ten times faster in this heat than at home. She hopes they'll keep it up. Maybe she'll pin some instructions up for whoever's next. But apart from the compost heap she's left nothing to show for herself. She feels a pang of guilt, thinking of Mara. But she *can't* tell her. As if to try and make up for their imminent departure, she's spent ages weeding, watering, tidying before picking the salad stuff for dinner. She'd thought they would all be there and made a huge pan of Bolognese, rich with her own sun-dried tomatoes, but now it looks like it'll be just the two of them.

It might be peculiar of him, keeping his precious bathroom secret, it might be selfish but, she sighs, staring at herself in the mirror, that's his business and they are out of it anyway. She smoothes moisturiser into her face and decides, for once, to make an effort. If she dresses up to please him – maybe he will forgive her. Not that she's anything to dress up in, but she changes out of her grubby shorts and puts on her clean blue dress. Brushes her hair, puts some eyeliner on, a bit of lip gloss.

She tries to keep her mind off Graham but still, something keeps trying to force itself into her notice. Some hard feeling – you can see why they're called hard feelings – of anger or disappointment, or both. But still, she doesn't *know*. Maybe there's a good explanation. Wait till he gets back and hear it. Give him a chance before she goes off at him. She leans in to the mirror to pluck her eyebrows. Too dim, she lights a candle. Still can't see but plucks by guesswork, each sharp sting of extraction threatening to bring tears to her eye. The ends of her hair shrivel away from the candle flame, a sharp stink of singeing.

She flumps down on the bed, pulls her hand through the burnt hair, ripping off the brittle ends. The stench has filled the room. She could easily cry but won't. Lies down on the bed, staring up at the ceiling, the old red lampshade, the fire sensor – the only modern thing in the room. The candle shadows waver, on the walls, the curtains. She is aware of the space beside her where Graham isn't.

So, just herself and Larry then. Will they drink wine? Better not, though she couldn't half do with a drink. She squints at her watch. Time crawls by. Not light enough to read. If only there was a telly, or a phone. She looks at the photos of Patsy and Kate, Cat – and remembers the one Mara gave her. She gets up and finds it in the pocket of her discarded shorts. It's bent now from the shape of her backside. She holds it close to the candle, stares at the fair-haired young woman with the uncertain smile.

She starts at the sudden deafening onset of a noise, like wet chips lowered into fat amplified a million times. She goes to the window and pulls back the curtain to see rain sluicing down the glass. Of course! Rain on the tin roof. Wonderful! The refreshing scent of it creeps into her nostrils, cool and fragrant. But *Graham* should be here with her to share it.

She waits a long time for it to stop or slacken off, but it doesn't and in the end, holding a T-shirt over her head, she goes out in the downpour. The sky is dark-green, a strange light shining up from the ground that seems to be rising in pale strands around her. Tepid water washes over her feet, between her toes, flattening her dress to her body. The T-shirt is useless, she's instantly drenched. Can just hear the hens scandalising in their coop but mainly the sound is of a giant streaming, a deluge of wetness, sky collapsing on to hard-baked earth.

Larry laughs at her when she walks into the kitchen. And she looks down at herself and smiles too, red dust splashed up her legs, dress a clinging blue skin. Her hair runs rivulets into her eyes and down between her shoulder blades.

'You'll have to change out of that,' he says. 'Wait.' He brings her a towel and the white shirt – the same one she used for painting the kitchen. 'Don't worry, I'll leave you to it. That's your wine.' He pushes a glass towards her and goes out into the hall. The kitchen is loud with the rain on the roof, warm with the homey smell of meat sauce. She sloshes some wine from the open bottle into the Bolognese before she strips off her dress. Even her knickers are damp but she leaves them on, rubs dry her skin and pulls on the soft cotton shirt. Still a splash of white paint dried stiffly on the sleeve.

She remembers herself up that ladder, so long ago it seems, though only a few weeks really. She wraps the towel turban-like around her head, takes a sip from the full glass, just the thing, a tough red wine, scrumptious, warming. She feels cheered as she fills a pan with water, two fat handfuls of spaghetti, a salad of basil and tomatoes runny with oil, gritty with salt and black pepper. *Perfect comfort food. Ideal on a wet night in Cassie's Outback Kitchen.*

Larry knocks on the door. 'Decent?'

'Yeah.'

He comes in, nods approvingly. 'That's better. Don't want you getting chilled.'

He sits down at the table and sips his wine. She feels his eyes follow her round the kitchen; the shirt is long enough, quite decent, but still, she does feel his eyes. Nothing wrong about it. Is it her fault that Graham isn't here?

'Do you think it's the the rain that's held them up?' she asks.

'Oh, probably,' Larry says, as if the question bores him.

'They definitely said they'd be back tonight. I made plenty.' She stirs the wooden spoon in the pot.

'Fred's easily led astray.'

'What do you *mean*?' She turns, slopping a streak of sauce down the side of the pan.

'Nothing!' He holds his hands up in mock surrender.

'You mean you think Graham's led him astray?'

Larry examines his nails. 'I don't know. I wouldn't blame him, would you? First time away from here in the fleshpots!'

'What fleshpots?'

He laughs. Files at one thumbnail with the other. 'It has been known for rain to wash the road away between here and Keemarra.'

'You think that's it? Is it *dangerous*?'

'Fred knows what he's doing. Might hold them up for a day or two. Depends when it stops. They won't be back tonight now.'

'A *day* or two!'

'If it doesn't stop tonight.' Larry holds out his hand as if testing the air. 'But I think it will.'

'*Hope* so.'

'You miss him so much after just one day? Less than a day?'

Cassie unwinds the turban from her head, hangs the towel on the rail beside the range and runs her fingers through her hair. 'It's not that. I'd be OK if I knew he was OK.'

'And maybe you're a little irritated?'

She scrapes the wooden spoon across the bottom of the pan. Starting to stick. She fishes a strand of spaghetti from the pot, dangles it from a fork and tests it between her teeth.

'This is ready.'

'He is "OK",' Larry says. 'Don't you worry.'

How do you know? But he'll be safe. Of course he will, knowing him. Probably juggling oranges in some roadhouse by now. Or flirting with a barmaid in some pub. Having a whale of a time. He will *never* change.

Larry pours wine into her glass while she dishes up mounds of spaghetti, and heaps them with sauce. She feels strange and woozy, but what the hell. Larry seems to have forgiven her for using his bathroom. The food smells delicious. The wine's good. May as well enjoy herself, Graham certainly will be. There's a kind of relief from the rain. Easier to move somehow, as if the air itself is lubricated.

Cassie has two bowls of spaghetti and loses count of how often her glass is filled; another bottle is uncorked somewhere along the line. Larry apologises for earlier, that kind of tension, he tells her, often happens before a storm. Is this a storm? she wonders and as she wonders, hears the first crumbling of thunder. The light flickers. Larry goes to switch off the generator in case it gets struck. They light a wobble of candles and kerosene lamps. Cassie's fingers feel fat and sweaty as sausages.

When she's finished eating, he leans towards her, takes her hand. His is no bigger than hers, the nails considerably neater. How does he keep them so neat and clean? Cooler than hers. Why are her palms so clammy?

He clears his throat. 'I realise I have been, perhaps, unnecessarily, *cagey* shall we say. About the bathroom and well, everything. I can see that you're a naturally inquisitive person, indeed, that's part of your charm.'

Charm, the word is warm the way he says it, a kind of caress. She can imagine Graham snorting, but she snuggles into it. *Charm*. No one has ever said she has *charm* before. That appreciation, it makes her swell a little, her shoulders soften.

'I'm sorry,' she says, 'I shouldn't have snooped around. And I certainly shouldn't –'

But he puts his finger up to silence her. 'I'll tell you what, I'll show you round, shall I? It's been unpardonably rude of me not to have done so before.' He shakes his head, looks so sad suddenly, the candlelight starry in his eyes. 'We do get . . . odd . . . living here. You must think us so very odd!'

'No,' Cassie says, 'not at all. It's OK, really.'

He gives her hand another squeeze. 'You are kind. Look, the fire in the sitting room is lit, why not come through now?'

She feels a little buzz of excitement. And she's touched. 'I'd *love* to. If you're sure.'

'To put your mind at rest.' He chuckles. 'No doubt Mara passed some alarming fantasy on to you? It's fascinating really – the way she develops the most elaborate fantasies. If she wrote them down she'd make a fortune! But they do run away with her and she gets –'

'I'm sorry,' Cassie says, 'I think you do wonderfully.' She hesitates, her head almost too fuzzy to think. 'But honestly, she didn't say anything much. Except how if not for you she'd be in a loony bin. That's all she said.'

Larry nods, gazes into her face till her cheeks flush hot.

'Come on then, leave the washing-up tonight. Won't hurt for once. Might even tackle it myself.'

They carry a lamp each. A little procession; she follows him, and Yella follows her, claws ticking against the floorboards. Their shadows sway, huge in the lamplight on the walls of the dark hall. Larry unlocks the left-hand door and swings it open. 'After you,' he says.

It's just a big sitting room. A sofa, a fireplace with a flickering log fire, bookshelves. An ordinary room, big and despite the fire, cool. She doesn't know what she expected. Above the sofa hangs a massive chandelier, no light coming from it, but some of the glass pieces catch the firelight and the candle-light, reflect them back, a cold splintered fire. She feels weird, sort of crawly and detached. She shivers.

'Chilly?'

'A little.'

'We can't have that,' he says. 'Wait a moment.' On the arm of the sofa, neatly folded, is a cardigan. He hands it to her. 'Try this.' It's soft and white, maybe even cashmere. She pulls it on over the shirt. It smells faintly of what? She wrinkles her nose into it. Anais Anais?

'Better?'

'Thanks, it's lovely.' She fingers the mother-of-pearl buttons. 'Mara's?' Although it would be too small for Mara, even if she were ever to wear such a thing.

'Come and sit by the fire.'

She hesitates. If she sits on the sofa he'll sit beside her, the two of them in the darkish room by a fire, maybe too close, together, her bare legs, this dangerous fuzziness around her edges – though Larry is surely honourable enough he *is* drunker than her, he must be. He thinks she's *charming*. It tickles her. That old-fashioned word.

'She holds the sleeve of the cardigan against her face. So soft. The scent *is* Anais Anais. Maybe Lucy's. 'Why did Lucy and Ben leave?'

Larry turns from the fire. The shadow of his beard juts sharply on the wall and darts away.

'Why do you ask?'

'Just wondered – you never mention – just seems funny.'

He sits back down on the sofa, pats the seat beside him. 'Come on. I won't bite. I hardly mention your . . . predecessors because there's no need. And I am – conscious of your feelings. Perhaps it would seem slightly rude – like a twice-married man constantly referring to his previous wife.'

'But –' She frowns. 'It's not at all like that.'

'Why the sudden interest?

'I'm not *that* interested. Just wondered.'

'What has Mara been saying?'

'Nothing. Honestly. She never – Just me, I'm – you know.' She tries to touch her nose and her finger misses. She giggles. 'Nosey.' No more wine tonight, that's for sure.

'Come on.' He pats the sofa again. She gives in and sits down. Either that or fall. The sofa is velvet, old and balding, feels dampish under the backs of her thighs. 'Let's have another bottle,' Larry says.

'Not me. Maybe some tea?'

'You and your tea! We didn't see eye to eye. That's all. No mystery. Just a taste, Cassie – there's something I particularly want you to try.'

He goes off into the kitchen, the door clicking shut behind him. The fire snickers at something in the wood, the dog groans. Shadows jitter on the ceiling and floor. She could fall asleep, easy as anything. Bloody Graham, she might have known, let him out of her sight and – Through the wall she hears a funny sound. Hard to hear with the noise of the fire, the rain. Maybe it was the fire. Only it sounded like a crackle, static, like a radio.

Larry comes back with two glasses, hands one to her.

'Shouldn't.'

'No?' Larry sits down beside her, presses the glass into her hand. 'Just taste it anyway. I'm interested to know what you think.'

'I thought I heard something like –' But she gives up, the fire is crackling away on the gummy log, a burnt menthol scent.

Cassie blinks hard, her eyes almost crossing, she has not had *that* much. She takes a tiny sip and is surprised. 'Mmmm!' She has another taste. 'This is good!' She wakes up a bit. 'I really like it,' she says. 'Very, what's the word, quaffable.' She hears her own voice as if from a distance.

'I'll get a couple of cases.'

'What for me! I don't know a good wine from my elbow.' Words slur, embarrassing. *Shut up, Cassie, go to bed*. But she can't move.

His voice travels smoothly down a tunnel. 'As you say, refreshing – young, but sometimes that's not a bad thing. You're – developing – quite a palate.'

She lays her head back against the sofa, the room going round, cool wet pooling on her lap. The glass is taken from her hand. And dimly, as if through a thick quilt, she hears and feels a growl and smack of thunder, a green smell, an electric taste in her mouth. Her eyes won't open. Her legs are lifted, her head slips as she's gently lowered down.

*

Fred hardly opens his eyes to drive. The road is red mud, slithery, deep puddles scummy and steaming, the sky innocent blue, sun reflecting blades from the wet.

'Stop at Keemarra for a coffee, mate?' Fred says.

'Won't take us out of our way?'

'Nah, not far. Need gas anyhow.'

Graham's head throbs and his eyes sting. Too much last night – drink, smoke, heat, talk. Ziggy, once he got going, surely could talk. 'What's the strangest thing you've ever seen?' he'd asked Graham, last thing he remembers before passing out. Time had melted in that bus, syrup sticking down between everything, in their eyes and mouths, smoke and syrup.

'Dunno,' he'd said. 'You?'

It had seemed like hours before Ziggy replied. 'The strangest thing I've ever seen,' he said, 'is a herd of cows. Couple of hundred k northeast. Came across them during a journey. Picture this: maybe twenty cows crowding round a water tank, right?' Graham had nodded, eyes closed, thinking nothing very strange in that. 'But all these cows, when I got close, I saw that they were dead. Dead on their feet and shrunk, mummified by the wind and the dry sand, skin peeling off, some of them only bones, some withered flesh. A herd of dead cows crowded round a dry water tank.'

Could that be true? he wonders now. Seems both too strange and too ordinary to be invented.

This morning, at first light, he'd got out of the bus, staggered across and launched himself into the water to wake himself up, swam a few strokes against the fast cold ripples. Mad how scared he was last night – not scared, just dope playing its old tricks with his brain – though even in the morning light he wouldn't say he felt easy. Weird vibrations, that's for sure.

But anyway, coffee in a roadhouse, maybe something to eat, his stomach growls at the thought. Then back and what will Cassie say and how will she be? Answer: monumentally pissed off. But long as Mara hasn't said, it'll be OK. He can smoothe it. Mara wouldn't say. Anyway, she'll be flat out. Medicated. Doesn't even seem true from here. The hot – no, won't think, won't go there again. He's cheered by the civilised metalled surface of the road as they turn on to the main highway.

Inside the roadhouse it is fantastically normal. A glass counter with pies and sandwiches; a smell of frying; illuminated signs with pictures of steak and chops and burgers. A cooler full of chocolate, Coke, juice, milk, cartons of iced chocolate and coffee. Sachets of sauce. Plastic pots of strawberry jam and honey. All the things to choose from, the ordinary things, practically bring tears to his eyes. But he has no cash and, like a kid, has to wait for Fred, outside filling up with gas. He goes out to the bog while he's waiting, proper flush toilet, white washbasin – well, white underneath the scum anyway – hot water, liquid soap. He washes his face, new lines round his eyes? He wishes he could shave.

Fred buys him pie and chips and iced coffee and stops to flirt with the woman who serves them while Graham carries his plate across to the window. The woman is young, tiny, bird-boned with black arse-length hair. Graham grins, chewing the greasy pastry, the scalding hot centre of the microwaved pie.

A coach stops outside and old people in voluminous shorts and baseball caps spill out in twos and threes, gabbling. A moment later they come through the door and the place fills with strident voices chattering, laughing, squabbling about who's going to pay. He shrinks into himself. Forgotten how to deal with crowds.

Fred sits down, stuffs a wad of chips in his mouth.

Graham grins, raises his eyebrows, nods in the woman's direction.

Fred snorts half a chip across the table. 'Yeah. Wouldn't touch her with a bloody bargepole, mate, not unless you want your balls torn off, deep-fried and served with barbie sauce.'

Graham laughs. 'Any chance of borrowing a few dollars?'

Fred puts his hand in his pocket, scatters coins on the table. 'Present for Luce?'

'Luce?'

Fred starts at himself, shakes his head. 'Call 'em all Sheila, mate. Best way.' He looks away, does a thumbs-up to the birdy woman.

Graham finishes his coffee and goes to look at a rack of postcards while Fred rolls a fag, puts his feet up on a chair and takes his time over his coffee. He chooses a few cards for himself and Cassie. Sees a phone. Must phone Patsy. And why not Jas? What a sense of freedom. 'Know the code for the UK?' he asks the birdy woman. She rattles it off through small white teeth. *Deep-fried.* He grins as he puts a dollar in the slot and dials Jas's number. Hears the ring. Incredible, thousands of miles away. Another hemisphere. Pictures her red phone on the floor by her bed. Pictures the watery reflections on the ceiling.

'Yeah?' Her voice bleary.

'Hi Jas, it's me, Graham!'

'It's the middle of the frigging –!' There's a pause. 'Graham? Where are you?'

'Keemarra Roadhouse, just thought I'd ring.'

'Ta. It's three in the frigging morning. Keemarra?'

'Sorry. Get my postcards?'

'*No.* Hey,' sounds like she's waking up, voice clearing, 'nice to hear you. Sound's like you're just down the road.'

'Weird, eh?'

'How are you? Missed you. How's it going?'

'Pretty bloody strange,' he says.

'Cassie?'

He starts to reply but is cut off. Stands looking at the phone. Hearing the trace of her voice in his ear. An old woman waiting behind him so he leaves it. Shouldn't ring Patsy in the middle of the night, anyway. A lurch in his guts of *wanting*: to see Jas, everyone, the real world. It rises over him like a wave, all those streets and faces, *friends*, none of it in the same universe even as Mara. He finds he's clenching his fists, heart hammering, almost like panic, an old man in a baseball cap staring at him, concerned. He forces a smile. Revolves the postcard rack. It is homesickness, that's all it is and that is normal. And soon he'll be back.

He wanders out of the human babble and across to an aviary: budgies, finches, a couple of galahs sitting like a pair of jugs on a shelf. And in a pen beside the aviary, a depressed-looking kangaroo, glowering at him from under its long lashes. SHEILA, the sign says. DO NOT FEED. *Call 'em all Sheila, mate.* The coach driver is leaning against the side of the coach, smoking.

A road train roars in and stops, sides shuddering. It towers, hot engine smell, three carriages behind it. A guy, green bandanna round his head, jumps down. He puts his hands up and stretches. Graham hears the clicks in his back.

'G'day, mate,' he says. He's got a toothpick pinched in the corner of his mouth, spits words out of the other corner.

'Hi,' Graham says.

'Pom, eh?'

'How can you tell?'

'Sixth sense, mate!' He puts a finger to the side of his nose and taps. He goes off into the roadhouse. Graham walks round the huge vehicle. Sees his own warped face in the gleaming chrome of the fender. Amazing that one guy can control such a monster. The driver comes out a few minutes later, couple of cartons of juice and a sandwich.

'Wanna look?' he says.

'Yeah.'

He hoists himself up, opens the door and Graham goes up behind him. Like a living room in there. A hammock; blankets over the seats; a flowery cushion; a kettle; photos – a wife and kids; a shelf with a couple of books. Birds, wild flowers. He sees Graham looking.

'See all sorts on me travels,' he says. 'Might as well know what they're called. Where you from?'

'Near Sheffield,' Graham says.

'Steel, eh?'

'Used to be.'

'Got a sister in Leeds.'

'Yeah? Been?'

'Next year, me and the missus and kiddies.'

'Where you heading?'

'Perth. Want a ride? Tell you the truth I could do with some company.'

Graham swallows. Looks out of the window. No sign of Fred.

'Make up your mind, mate. Got to get moving.'

'OK, yeah. Thanks.' Mouth dry, he settles in the passenger seat. Deep seat. The door slams. Engine roars to life. A deep rumble, the books slide on the shelf. Graham notices curtains – yellow flowers, pegged back. Made by his wife? Just the sort of ridiculous thing Cassie would do. They roll past the roadhouse as Fred comes out. Stands looking round, shading his eyes.

'From Adelaide, me,' the guy says. 'Frank.'

'Graham.'

They roll over the gritty forecourt, about to join the highway. 'I knew a bloke called –'

'Stop,' Graham says.

'What's up?'

'I can't – got a mate back there –'

Frank stops the truck, whinny of brakes. Turns. 'Why didn't you say?'

Graham grimaces. 'Sorry, I –' He shrugs. 'Thanks anyway.'

Frank looks at him like he's barking. 'Suit yourself.'

Graham opens the door and jumps down. The truck drives away, huge carriages, blast of hot exhaust mixed up with dust. Fred comes out of the toilets, wiping his hands on his shorts.

'You ready?'

They get back in the ute and drive in silence for a while. Another road train smashes past, sending up sheets of water, red as blood.

Fred switches on the wipers. 'You fucked Mara yet?' he says.

Graham nearly chokes on his own spit.

Fred throws his head back, but mirthlessly, bangs his fist down on the steering wheel. 'Don't look so shocked, mate. Bloody poms!'

'Have you?'

Fred looks grim. He slams on some music. They plunge onwards. The steaming road shimmers and gleams ahead, and behind in the mirror. They come to the bridge and underneath a river flows where yesterday there was nothing but a feeble vein of mud; it's like an artery has burst, pumping and pulsing the low branches of the trees. Should have been with Cassie when it started to rain.

'Hope they're OK,' he says. 'With the storm, I mean.'

'No worries. Larry'll see they're OK.'

'But Larry's not there.' There is a pause. Maybe a flicker passing across Fred's face. 'Larry's not there,' Graham repeats. No expression. 'Is he?'

'He might have gone back last night.'

'But there was no way he'd be back. You said –'

'No, well, probably not, mate, no worries. You've gone white as a flaming sheet.'

Graham gives a puff of breath, an attempt at a laugh but there is something wrong. It grabs him round the ribs and squeezes.

'Listen,' Fred says. 'I'm going to say this once and then I'm going to shut me gob. Get the hell out of there.'

The road glimmers under the wheels.

'What?'

'Spare keys to Larry's car on a shelf above the pantry door.'

'*What?*' Graham turns. A shiver in the icy air-con. 'What are you saying?'

But Fred doesn't speak again. He changes the tape, turns the volume up and scowls out at the road.

Twenty-seven

S omething is pulling her head down. Something pressing on her eyes. There is light but which way up and where? She struggles her eyes open, nothing there, just the weight of her own eyelids. And nothing to hold her head down except its own weight. And the light is coming through a crack in some brown curtains and her throat is so dry she can hardly bear to breathe. She sits up and the walls billow. She holds her head still and blinks and blinks to get the room to settle into a kind of focus.

A dead fire, grey ash feathers. Larry. Oh yes, they came in here last night although she'd thought it was a dream. Has the quality and taste of a dream. There's a blanket fallen on the floor, a glass of water. She reaches for it and takes a long swallow, feeling the dry passage of her throat open. She tries to gather the scattered pieces of her mind. Puts her hands to her face, rubbery and warm.

Why not in bed? Can't remember the end of last night. Maybe she passed out? Gets up, steadies herself on the arm of the sofa. The room in her dream was cosy with the fire, wasn't it? But this is a shabby room, fireplace big and black, iron maybe, the throat of the chimney furred black, the logs all burnt away, a gentle mound of grey that seems to stir as she watches it. On the hearth a bit of rubbish, wrapper of something that missed the fire and hasn't burnt. She leans over to retrieve it, rush of nausea up her throat. *MediSwab*. What? Her face goes hot.

Must leave this room, go and wash. Get properly dressed. *Decently* dressed. Bare legs under the shirt, stained with wine and crumpled from her drunken sleep. But *nothing* under the shirt, surely she had something under the shirt, she can't get it straight, she was so wet – with the rain, that's right. Thunder. She goes to the window and pulls back one of the curtains. Through filthy glass sun glitters out there, like smashed glass. Graham will be back. And then what? *MediSwab?*

She leaves the room, goes back through the kitchen. She picks up her blue dress, hanging on the back of a chair. No Larry, though there's a smell of coffee. The washing-up has been done, a pair of surgical gloves balled up on the table. She feels ashamed, creeping about in the soiled shirt. Leak of wet on her thigh. Shutting the fly screen slowly behind her so as not to make a clatter, she goes out into the brilliance of the day. Into a fresh steam of evaporating rain. The chickens rush to greet her but she stumbles past them. They'll have to bloody wait.

*

'Ah, Graham. Welcome back. Cassie's resting, I believe.' Graham catches a look passing between Larry and Fred, sure, slick and smug, a confirmation. 'One too many last night, I'm afraid,' Larry adds.

Graham presses his lips together, gets a mug of water, makes himself swallow it down before trusting his voice. Like swallowing stones.

'Thought you were away for a couple of days.'

'Which meant you could take advantage? Set off on a jaunt. I'm surprised at you. And you.' He looks at Fred, who blinks and bats away a fly.

'Yeah, well, no harm done. I'll just have a bite to eat and off. All right, mate?'

'Minor glitch with the generator, Fred,' Larry says. 'Would you come and look before you go –'

Fred raises his eyebrows at Graham before he and Larry go out. The kitchen is the same but different. Seems different. Flies in a buzzing column over the table as ever. Wine bottles. Three. Dishes left to drain by the sink, two dishes, two wine glasses upside down. *Three bottles?*

In the shearers' shed, Cassie is curled on top of the bed, hair like a swirl of ice cream above her head, face flushed and damp. Fallen from her sleeping hand is a photograph. Graham puts the tray down quietly. Picks up the photo. A blonde who could almost be Cassie, here, in the bleaching sun. The blurred shape of a chicken in the foreground and the shadow of the photographer slanting towards her.

Cassie wakes as he sits down, blinks at him as if she can't believe he's real. 'Graham!' She flings her arms round him, squeezing his ribs, speaking into his stomach. 'What happened?'

'Sorry,' he says, stroking her hair. 'We stopped off – a mate of Fred's – then got held up – the rain.'

She pulls away. 'You *promised* you'd be back.'

'Couldn't help it.

'Did you at least phone Patsy?'

He swallows. 'I'm sorry.'

'You are *useless*.' Tears sparkle in her eyes. 'Sod off.'

'Believe me, Cassie –'

'The *one* time!' She flinches away from him and hugs her arms round her knees. '*Believe* you! It's what you always do. You're just *useless*. That time you went to get a paper –' She puts her face against her knees.

'That was years ago,' he mutters. 'Look, I've brought you some tea.'

She sniffs.

'I see Larry came back. When?' he asks. 'What happened?'

'Nothing *happened*.' What he can see of her face is red, her voice is muffled against her own skin. 'He came back not long after you'd gone – Oh God –'

'What?

She looks up, opens her mouth, then shakes her head.

'*What?*'

She tells him that there is a bathroom and that she went in it and had a bath. Her hair is clean, he notices, a shade lighter, almost white at the ends. A bathroom. He keeps himself from speaking, listens, noticing how she, mostly, avoids his eyes.

'Where was Mara in all of this?'

'That's weird too, she woke up and she told me all sorts of things – she was really *lucid*.'

A hand seems to reach into his gut and squeeze. He holds his breath, waiting.

'She said Larry wasn't a doctor – told me the story but – but – then Larry said part of her illness is fantasising.'

'Yes?' he says, maybe too eagerly, and she frowns at him.

'But anyway, what she said was, his brother was a doctor and he died and Larry impersonated him – do you believe it?' She tells him the stuff that Mara said, probably lies. Nothing about himself. He starts to breathe again.

'Part of her illness is fantasising?'

'A rich fantasy world, he said, and look –' She scrabbles around on the sheet and picks up the photo. 'Mara said, she said I looked like her. Do you think so?'

He looks at it again.

'A bit, don't you think? Except the pigtails, and she's maybe smaller.'

Graham's hands are wet. Doesn't want to get sweat on the photograph. Acid wells in the back of his throat. Last night catching him up, along with a greasy taste of this morning's pie. He thinks of Ziggy's sculpture, could you even call it that? The telephone receiver, a long blonde plait. But blonde hair is common, every other girl and woman in Australia has fair hair, long hair, always cutting it, hairdressers, not hard to find a long blonde plait if you wanted one. If it was even real, it was probably false anyway, the more he thinks about it the more fake that hair looked, a nylon glisten.

'And look,' she flops over and reaches across for a cardigan. 'Isn't it nice? Think it *may* have been hers. Larry gave it to me. Fancy leaving without it.'

'You and Larry –' He notices a white shirt crumpled on the chair.

'What?' Now she does meet his eyes. Bold. Green-flecked grey. A tiny snaky vein marring the white.

'Have a nice time last night?'

She shakes her head, looks down at her tea. 'OK. Bit boring. I made loads of Spag Bol thinking you'd be back, starving hungry. We'll finish it later. I was *really worried*, Gray.'

'*He* said you had one too many.'

She shrugs. 'Bet *you* had a drink.'

'Well, yeah. But *three* bottles?'

'He must have carried on after I went to bed.'

He gazes at her until she looks down. His fists clench till the nails bite the skin of his palms. He forces a breath into his constricted lungs. 'We have to leave,' he says, keeping his voice even.

She nods her head. 'I feel a bit –' He watches as she gets unsteadily off the bed and picks up a pair of knickers. As she puts them on he sees the long fuzzy smile between her legs. He looks at the shirt. 'What's with that? Is it his?'

'I borrowed it.' She shoves her feet, after a couple of misses, into her sandals.

'Why?' His heart thuds.

'Oh later, Gray.'

He speaks quietly though the words want to shout themselves. 'Did Larry – did he try anything?'

242

'*You ask me* that!' She slams out of the door. He stares at it for a moment, gets up and kicks it. Bangs his forehead against it and stands there a moment, forehead resting against the wood. Heart hammering. Must keep cool. Must think. He must get them out of here and safely. He picks up the shirt and holds it to his face. Smells of Cassie. Smells of Larry's poxy cologne. He screws it up and flings it at the wall. His bag is on the floor. He picks it up and takes out Cassie's mirror frame. The broken glass gone now. He looks into the empty black oval a minute then shoves it in her rucksack. He picks up the shirt, examines it. Wine-stained, crumpled. *No*. He can't bear it. *No*. Hears a car start and drive away. Fred leaving. They have to go. Tonight.

*

Cassie goes to the dunny, holds her breath. She can't get her head straight. What happened with Larry? Can't think. Don't think. The flies, there must be millions down there, booming vibration, millions of maggots. Feels she could be sick and what a headache, hangover, how much did she drink? Worse than a hangover, kind of dullness, numbness of mind.

She comes out, looks back at the door of the shed, would love to lie down but can't face Graham. She washes her hands, lathers and lathers, coal-tar bubbles, and walks out, away from the house, over to the trees. There's a rock there, good rock for sitting, under the trees, her head bangs with the rhythm of her feet.

She sits for a while, eyes open but unfocused. Parrots shriek. A red feather stuck to a white streak of bird shit. A lizard motionless, as if glued to the rock. Tiny splayed grip of its fingers. She puts her hand under her dress and feels her warm wetness. Sticky tangle. Needs another bath. Not Larry, no. Don't think about it. Must just – she frowns, trying to wind her messed-up mind back. Can't remember. How it ended. Like a

243

bad taste in her mouth from something she can't remember eating. The swab: what was that about? Fragments coming back. Like the radio, if there even was a radio, and something else. The wine. A wet cold something – a chilly sofa underneath – They must leave. How can they?

She closes her eyes, hangs her head back, so heavy, stretching her neck. Birds shriek from a long way off and then a touch. She jumps. It's only Graham. He hands her a bottle of water. She swigs greedily, then feels sick.

'What are you doing out here?' he asks.

'Why did you have to go off?' Her mouth bends down to cry but suddenly she's angry. Sparks of energy in her arms and legs. 'What were you doing?'

'I'll tell you about it,' he says, 'but listen. Tonight we go. OK? I know where the spare car keys are. We get the hell out.'

'*How?*' He looks so serious. Four parallel lines across his forehead. Are they new?

'We play along today then we'll leave. But don't *say*, don't show *any sign*. OK?' He looks so unlike himself, so focused. She stares at him. He's serious. He's *never* serious. White hairs threaded through his hair line. More surely than before? The lines round his eyes, the pores round his nose emphasised by dust. A couple of white bristles amongst the black stubble. Soon he could grow one of those badger beards. She sighs and shuts her eyes.

Twenty-eight

Cassie curls round herself in the bed. Is he asleep? He's quiet, breathing softly. She squeezes her arms round herself, excitement, fear and a kind of cringe thinking of the terrible meal. The terrible fist she'd made of pretending everything was normal. Yesterday's Bolognese burnt and served up with stale bread and a salad with too much onion. Larry had looked at her quizzically but made no comment. He'd seemed so normal she'd almost started to wonder if she had dreamed last night. Maybe it *was* as simple as her getting drunk and passing out? How could he be so cool otherwise?

They'd sat on the veranda by the dull light of a smoked-up kerosene lamp with its corona of suicidal moths and bugs. The onions in the salad were wincingly strong, making their noses run. For once there was no wine. The atmosphere had been almost unbearable, contrived attempts at conversation.

'Mara not well?' she'd tried in the end. She could not bring herself to meet Larry's eyes.

'She's recovering.'

'Larry,' she'd said, 'you've got a radio, haven't you? I *heard* it.'

He gazed at her, didn't deny it.

'Why didn't you say?'

He sighed, disappointed, and spoke the way you might speak

245

to a tiresome child. 'It's essential to Mara's – peace of mind – shall we say, to believe we're entirely isolated. But I need a radio, *of course* I do, to contact Kip for instance, do you think it coincidental that he arrives when he's needed? Fred too.'

'Why lie about it though?'

'Mara doesn't know. It would seem . . . inappropriate for visitors to know things that the lady of the house doesn't know.' *The lady of the house.* 'It was the whitest possible *lie*. Now we've got that cleared up,' Larry dabbed his mouth with his napkin, furled it into its ring of bone, 'I've been rather expecting an announcement.'

He looked from one of them to the other. 'No? Correct me if I'm wrong but I've had the feeling that perhaps you feel that this – experiment – is over. In other words, that you would probably like to leave.'

'Experiment?' Graham said.

'Cassie's experiment, to see how you –'

'Not an *experiment*,' she said, face burning. The *stirrer*.

A great beetly thing, big as a wren, batted itself against the lamp and tumbled on to the table, on to its back, legs waving. Graham tried to right it with his fork but the stupid thing wouldn't turn over, rocking on the table like a boat, motor buzzing. He brushed it from the table with his hand but it came back, idiotically battering itself against the flickering globe.

'And when would you like to leave?'

'Soon as we can,' she said, pressing her foot against Graham's.

'Let's see.' Larry put his hands together as if in prayer, placed the points of his fingers under his beard: 'You want to give formal notice.'

She sensed Graham practically imploding beside her but he managed to keep his mouth shut and she squeezed his leg gratefully.

'Well – if that's what we need to do.'

'You realise, of course, that you'll forgo the agreed sum of money.'

'*Yes.*'

'You realise that you'll also be letting me down, not to mention Mara. You have no qualms about that, apparently?'

'Yes.' Her voice was almost a whisper. She made herself look up into his eyes. 'We do have qualms but –'

'Your minds are made up?' He shook his head, laced his fingers together, made the knuckles snap. 'Very well. I accept. The period of notice I require is two weeks. Now if you'll excuse me.' Larry got up from the table and went through the door into the house, leaving them silenced.

'Two weeks,' she said. 'Can we stand two weeks?'

'No way. No fucking way.' Graham turned to her, frowning. 'What experiment?'

'Oh nothing.'

'What?'

She took a breath. 'Just us, whether it could work. You *know*.'

'Didn't realise you confided in him.'

She shook her head.

'Has it?'

She was surprised by the harshness of his voice. 'What?'

'Worked?'

She'd pressed her fingertips into her eye sockets. Feeling better but still spaced out. Distanced from him. They were just such different people. 'Dunno,' she'd said. 'What do you think?'

He'd got up and stalked off.

There's a thin shimmer of moonlight leaking though the curtains. Is he asleep? If they could just stick two weeks, then they could leave properly, pack everything, finish off. It seems more sensible. But he wants to go tonight. Typical Graham. Dashing off into the night when they could wait two weeks and do the thing properly. *Is* he asleep? Doesn't sound like it, too quiet. More like pretending to be asleep. *Two weeks*, it's not much. But he is determined. Maybe she should let *him* go. But then she'd be more or less alone with Larry. *No, no, no.* She tucks her hand protectively between her legs. Maybe nothing happened. No, something did. And she wants to go home. They might make it for Christmas. She wants Patsy. Wants home.

'Gray,' she whispers.

'What?' He's as wide awake as she is. Lying there thinking what?

'OK then.'

He sits up abruptly. Gets off the bed. She sees the small flicker of illumination as he presses the light on his watch.

'Two-twenty,' he says. 'Come on then.'

'Were you just lying there waiting for me to say that?'

He strikes a match and lights the candle. 'I know where the car key is. We'll drive.'

'But you haven't got a licence.'

'You have. And I can drive. Come on.' She stares as he starts to pull things from the drawers. 'Come on.'

She gets out of bed. Shivery. 'Really? But what if he catches us?'

He stops. Meets her eyes with a flinch. 'He'll go totally fucking ballistic.'

'What could he do?'

Graham pulls his jeans on. 'Come on.'

'Maybe we should just be patient?'

'Come *on*.' He goes back to stuffing things into his rucksack. His shadowy face looks serious and scared. He's never scared. It frightens her.

'It can't be that simple,' she says, pulling on her knickers. 'Can it?'

'Won't know till we've tried.'

They haven't got much stuff. It's soon packed into their rucksacks. Graham gets his paintings and art things from his studio, moving about with a sort of exaggerated tiptoe like a stage villain. She finds herself giggling, flopping back on the bed. She could get hysterical, can feel the fizziness like someone's dropped an Alka-Seltzer in her blood. She pulls herself together, goes through the drawers, checking.

Graham's already got the passports, tickets, money. Amazingly organised for him. They need water – they can fill a couple of gallon water bottles from the pump. As she wraps her precious photos in a sweater and stows them in her pack her mind leaps ahead: surely they'll be able to change the tickets at the airport and if not they'll just have to buy more on Visa. OK, so they're losing a few thousand pounds. They can do without. They did without before. Even if they have to sell the car and live on lentil stew for months to catch up – lentil stew by the fire in their own home. Sounds like heaven.

'What if you can't find the keys?' she says.

'I know where they are. If not I'll hotwire it.'

'*Gray!* Can you do that?'

'Ready?'

She takes a deep breath, hoicks her rucksack over one shoulder and takes a last look round the room – unicorn curtains, raggy rug, *some* things she'll miss – before she blows out the candle and follows him outside. This doesn't feel real. So underhanded. Almost criminal sneaking off – but they're not stealing anything (only borrowing the car) and they *are* free. There's nothing criminal about it she tells herself, picking through the scrub. A breeze has sprung up. The sky is almost clear, bristling with stars, just a dirty smear of cloud to smudge the waning moon. The pump creaks but otherwise it's oddly quiet, as if the night birds and creatures are holding their breaths.

They walk round to the pump and fill the water bottles. Then they stand by the car. Waiting there like an invitation. Graham opens the back door and they put their stuff on the back seat.

Cassie stands up, looks at the house for a sign of movement. Thanks God that Yella is deaf. And Mara, presumably, medicated to oblivion. She feels terrible leaving her without a word, just like the others did. She will feel so let down. *Sorry*, Cassie whispers to her shed door.

'The keys are in the pantry,' Graham says. 'Shelf above the door.' He goes towards the steps.

'No I'll get them,' she says, knowing she'll be the quieter.

'But what if –'

'I'll say I need a cup of tea – couldn't sleep or something.'

'But you're dressed.'

'I'll think of something.'

She goes up the steps quiet as she can. Yella is asleep by the door and groans as she pushes him out of the way. Very dark. The fridge hums. She feels around the wall and the table's edge towards the pantry door. Her fingers meet the fruit bowl – would love to take it but just puts a couple of oranges into her bag. The darkness is absolute, can't find the door – ridiculous – her hand touches something made of cloth and she jumps, thinks it's a sleeve, what if Larry – but it's only a tea towel on the back of a chair. Outside an owl cries and she has to smother a shriek. She steadies herself on the table. Takes a deep breath. Pictures herself going from the table to the pantry, to get some flour say. About three steps and she finds the latch, fumbles, hand sweaty, how would she explain if Larry came in, *sleep walking*?

She opens the pantry door. Steps inside, the door swings towards her, creak of hinges, she sticks her foot out to stop it closing. Her heart hammers in her ears. Familiar smell of flour and damp and flypapers. She reaches her hand up, locates the shelf. It's greasy, dusty, things on it, she can't see what, feel like dead things, something like a mouse falls down. She yelps, presses the back of her hand against her mouth. *Pull yourself together*.

Eventually her fingers meet the keys and she can breathe. Now just get back out. She feels her way, carefully, mustn't trip now, make a noise. She goes though the door, quietly, quietly with the flyscreen and out. Seems bright out there. Graham silhouetted against the stars.

'Here we go,' she says, holding up the keys.

'I'll drive till we get to the road,' he says. 'Remember the way from yesterday.'

They both hesitate a moment, looking at each other's shadowy outlines over the car's roof, and get in, gently shutting the doors. A very long time since she's been in a vehicle. The pine nip of air-freshener. They sit there a moment.

'Go *on* then,' she says.

'You realise, if it doesn't start first time we're totally fucked?'

'I know.' She stretches open her mouth, jaw aching with tension. '*Go on.*'

He looks sideways at her as he turns the key. The engine surges, he moves the gear-lever to *Drive* and the car slides off. Cassie breathes out. Not too noisy. Though surely noisy enough. With no lights, Graham steers unsteadily out across the land towards the track, cricking, cracking sounds of things driven over, the scrabbling of bushes, a harsher crack as he hits a stump. But is is OK. Behind them, the kitchen light comes on, the door opens, a figure appears. But they are *off*. Cassie feels a sudden thrill.

'You may as well put the lights on,' she says. '*We're off!*'

Graham puts on the lights and yellow floods the grey-looking pocked land, the dark bushes ahead.

*

At least it's an automatic, easy to drive. Hasn't driven for ages – never did pass his test but when he was younger he didn't let that bit of red tape stop him. He frowns at the land in front, not the track, a patch of scrubby bushes; go much further like this and they'll blow a tyre. The scrub tugs and hisses against the underside of the chassis. Surely it wasn't this far to the track? *Must* get this right. But there are no pointers, no landmarks – though there are the ghosty gums glowing palely to his right as they should be, must be nearly on the track. Won't breathe properly till they are on that track. Talk about *responsibility*.

Cassie shrieks, 'Look out!' as a kangaroo leaps from nowhere through the lights, white haunches a sudden shock.

Graham squints ahead. A stand of bigger trees. Does he recognise them? Everything different in the dark. He negotiates some looming things, rocks, knows where he is then, just about, and then at last, the car lurches up over a lip on to the track. He stops the car a minute, wipes the cold sweat from his forehead.

'Good,' he says. 'We should be OK now.'

'I never do stuff like this!' Cassie says and grins at him. He sighs and rubs his stiff neck before driving off, easier now, down the track and on to the dirt road. Remembers Fred turned right here, so does the same.

'An hour or so and we'll hit the highway I reckon,' he says. His heart sinks as he notices the petrol gauge. Empty it says, but they are going along, aren't they? It could be shot. If there's just enough to get them to the road then they can stick their thumbs out.

They drive in silence for a while. He searches his memory for details of the drive. Why didn't he pay more attention? But he does remember before the turning on to the road a wind-pump surrounded by trees. Won't be visible till they reach it, not in the dark but when he sees that looming shape he'll know they're right. Longs for that sensation of smooth metalled road beneath the tyres – then even if something went wrong they'd be OK. Got thumbs, can hitch. His eyes scour the dark, the splay of scrub lit by the headlights, for clues.

'What *did* you do?' Cassie says.

He frowns at her.

'When you went off.'

He tells her about Ziggy, the bus, the lake. She laughs when he describes Ziggy's dress sense. 'I really *wanted* to get back, Cass,' he says. 'I had no control.'

'Hmmm,' she says and then goes so quiet he wonders if she's fallen asleep. He glances at her, pale hair, smooth cheek, in the darkness. Will not ask about Larry, not now, he grits his teeth, his jaw aches with it. Will not ask now, maybe not ever. He forces his mind away from that. Tries to calculate how many days, if all goes well, till they'll be home. Maybe three? And what will he do then? The painting he started, that idea. It comes to him that it is crap. Couldn't show that to Jas or to anyone. Come all this bleeding way for nothing then. Pissing away his talent, Jas would say. Knob. And even Cassie – maybe he's not up to it. Up to the responsibility. That *word*. Maybe he would always let her down. Let everyone down. He thinks with a pang of his mum and dad. That old aunt, whatever her name was, she'll be dead by now, for sure. The car slides – loose surface.

Cassie leans over and squints at the clock on the dashboard. He keeps his eyes away, doesn't want to know – but surely they should have hit the junction on to the road by now? Time does play tricks though. He concentrates on driving slowly and as smoothly as possible on the rutted track.

'When we get to the road, how long?' Cassie asks.

'Told you, a couple of hours.'

'We'll be there by five. Hope they're open.'

'Yeah.'

'There's *no way* he could catch up with us, is there?' Cassie says. 'I mean, he hasn't got a car now and even if he *has* got a radio they wouldn't get us before we got to the roadhouse and even if they did they couldn't force us to go back.'

'No.' Another kangaroo appears in the headlights, this time trailed by a joey. Graham decelerates almost to a stop, watching their fantastic elastic bounce.

'Don't you feel like we're in a film or something?' Cassie says. 'You were right. About leaving.' She puts her hand lightly on his thigh. 'Wait till we tell everyone –'

'Wait,' Graham says, feeling she might jinx them with this premature crowing, 'wait till we're at the roadhouse. Till we hit civilisation.'

'*Civilisation!* I'm going to have bacon, eggs, hash browns and iced coffee.'

'Yeah.'

'What's the first thing you'll do when we get home?'

'Go down the pub and have a pint.'

'You'll go *out*?'

'Why, what will you do?'

'Go round the house I think, just *touching* everything. Then I'll get my hair cut.'

They drive on in silence for a while. No stand of trees, no wind-pump, no junction. Feels like he's driving down a tunnel, just can't *see*. It just goes on and on.

'Do you really know how to hotwire a car?' she asks.

'Reckon so.'

She gives him a look that's almost admiring: 'England's going to feel so small and safe, isn't it?'

'Yeah.' They go quiet. Thinking. The track is going downhill. He doesn't remember any downhill. Wonders whether to switch off the engine to save fuel. But surely there was no downhill? There was more a sense of *rising* he remembers. And it's looping to the right, is that it? Doesn't remember any looping to the right. A patch of ghost gums floats above the ground, strange lit-up hieroglyphic shapes. The bush getting denser. Must be a watercourse somewhere near. And the track is deteriorating. Two deep channels and looser sand. It's hard not to get bogged, the loose sand slewing the steering. Hard graft just keeping it straight. A tight ache starts between his shoulders.

'Or maybe a milkshake,' Cassie says, suddenly. 'Want me to drive for a bit?'

Graham shakes his head. If they can just get past this difficult bit. This track must lead somewhere. Will probably meet the road a bit further along, that's all. They're going in the right direction, he's almost sure. Probably driving parallel to the highway.

He yawns and lets in a wave of weariness. Should have got a bit of shut-eye but he'd lain there, feeling Cassie fidgeting beside him. If he'd allowed himself to sleep he might not have woken up and they'd have been stuck there another day and he could not trust himself near Larry another minute. Past the trees now and the track's smoothed out. No more trees, low ground. At least there's a chance he will be able to see. Maybe the lights of a road train will show them where the highway is. He thinks of the cosy cab of Frank's truck. That hammock.

'Oi!' Cassie prods him.

He starts. 'What?'

'You were falling asleep.'

'No,' he says, blinking at the bleached track unravelling in the light.

*

But he *was* half-asleep. They should stop but she doesn't want to stop. Not till they're safe. She glances at his profile, hunched forward over the steering wheel, fingers gripping. If he'd only let her drive. She wants to say *relax* but thinks that might bug him. Not as if she's relaxed, anyway. And she's seen the petrol gauge, the red 'empty' sign lit up. He must have seen it too. Her stomach is a solid, aching ball. She shuts her eyes against the dizzying grey on grey on grey, the speckled ground that seems to have gone black now. They should be on the road. It's way past an hour.

She sways her body slightly as if this will keep them going.

Can't wait to talk to another person, another ordinary person, can't wait to see something – a traffic jam or Boots the Chemist or a postbox – normal. *Focus on home.* If, *when*, they'll ring from the roadhouse, yes, talk to Patsy and maybe Mum, buy something for Katie at the airport – a cuddly koala.

'Do you realise, we haven't seen a single koala bear,' she says. 'Ooooh,' as they jolt over a bump. 'Need to pee. Sorry.'

'OK.' Graham stops, bows his head forward and leans his forehead on the steering wheel.

'You OK?'

'Just knackered.'

'I'll drive.'

He shakes his head.

She gets out and takes a few steps into the dark. Cold. A charry smell. The ground black, must have been a bush fire. Things give under her feet, tiny snappings, bits of twig or bone or God knows. It's cold and clear, faint moonlight on the stubbly charcoal. She pulls down her jeans and squats. She can hear echoes, of what, she doesn't know, a throb of something, like a heartbeat almost. Like the heartbeat of the earth. *Only the blood in your own ears, idiot.*

She stands and pulls up her jeans, damp now. She tilts her head back and looks up into the ache of space above her. The sky is a bright whirl, curdled by the Milky Way and underneath it all she feels dizzied. Minute, insignificant to the point of vanishing. She gets back into the car quick.

*

Cassie takes a few steps away and bobs down, white cardigan disappearing from view. He bites the skin beside his thumbnail. He has to face it: he's cocked up. Been going far, far too long and the terrain's all wrong. Gas can't hold out much longer. Should have turned back when he first suspected. Stupid, stupid. Can't be far wrong though. He turned right, didn't

Fred turn right? And there haven't been any other choices. Any other junctions. Have there? He hasn't seen any other junctions but then he can see nothing really, just the lit-up bit in front of the car. Maybe there was a choice and without even knowing he chose wrong.

'Brrrr.' Cassie slams the door and rubs her hands up and down her arms.

'OK?'

'Yup.'

They drive on. The track ruttier, stuff strewn about, burnt stuff. Graham stops and peers forward. The skeleton of a burnt tree right in front of them. They are no longer on a track at all. He turns the key and everything goes quiet.

'What's up?'

'Is there a torch?' He gestures at the glove compartment. Cassie opens it and rifles through.

'All sorts in here – peppermints and, yes, a torch. She clicks it. "Doesn't work though." She shakes it and a dull gleam appears though it doesn't extend much further than the tiny bulb. He takes the torch and gets out.

'Gray?'

He walks about waving the useless smudge of light ahead of him. Why didn't he think to bring a torch? A loud flap makes him jump and yell, some big bird startled: a kookaburra, mad cackle of loony-toons laughter. That cry had made them laugh when they first arrived but no one's laughing now. He grits his teeth. He's only lost the track, hasn't he? Walks round behind the car. Can see nothing much beyond the red glow of the rear lights but from what he can see he surmises that they've been off the track for a while. How did he manage that? Can't believe it. They will have to go back. No point in panicking. It's quite simple. Just turn the car round and drive back the opposite way.

He gets back in.

'We're lost, aren't we?' Cassie says.

'Just gone off the track a bit.'

'You sure?'

'I'm sure. OK?'

'We don't want to go getting lost.'

He bangs his hand on the steering wheel. 'Fuck's sake, Cassie. Just feel free to state the bleeding obvious, why don't you? Right,' he says, making his voice level. 'We just want to go back the way we've come. Just a short way.' He reverses and moves the car round. That was a full 360 degrees, wasn't it? They approached the burnt tree from that way so – but. How to know which way? He stops.

Cassie keeps her mouth shut this time, he can hear the effort it takes her. He gets out again, slamming the door, smacking the torch against his hand to try and make more light. He crouches down and shines it at the ground. If he could just see the tyre tracks he'd know which direction they'd come from and follow back. Should have made some marker. *Wanker*. It's tiredness, that's what it is, he is so knackered he can't think straight. The monotony of driving, the adrenaline that had kept him going is trickling away now, he can feel it running out through the soles of his feet. The scorched smell is sickening. And then he does see what looks like the track, definitely a rut, a flaky charcoal tyre-print. He lifts his head. *Thank you, mate*, he mutters at the sky.

Twenty-nine

'Right we are.' He jumps back into the car. 'Found the track.'

'Good.' Her voice is small.

'Oh come *on*, Cass.'

She turns. Pushes her hair back from her face. 'Yeah. OK, let's go.' She squeezes his knee. 'Have a peppermint.' She opens the tin. 'Curiously Strong,' she says.

They jolt along for a bit. It is definitely a track. Cassie is just starting to say something when there's a bang and she chokes on her mint. He switches off the engine quick.

'Dunno,' he says before she can say a thing. He jumps out, praying for it not to be a tyre. But it is. The back left-hand tyre, a broken bottle, jag of glass embedded in the rubber. He rocks back on his heels and puts his head back. The Milky Way is a great sticky net slung across the sky.

*

She waits for a moment. Can't see him. She's reluctant to leave the safe little room of the car, to step out into that emptiness. She opens the glove compartment. Nothing else of much use – some paper sachets – she shudders. MediSwabs. She tears open one and the smell makes her stomach buck. She opens the door, almost afraid she's going to throw up but it subsides. The medicated smell, her body remembers; she can feel a cold wipe, a thin chilly sensation when all else was a blur. She bites the end of one thumb, jams the other hand between her legs.

Graham calls her.

She bites again, inhales. *Forget it*. 'What?'

'Flat.'

'A puncture? Is there a spare?' She gets out. He's hunkered down by the wheel. He points out the broken glass that's done the damage.

'Part of a whisky bottle.' She picks a piece up, recognising the label. 'Red Label.'

'*Very* interesting.'

'No, I mean if someone's been here drinking we can't be too far from anywhere, can we? We can't really be in the wilderness.' Why did she have to say that? *Wilderness*.

Graham opens the back of the car. 'Good news is,' he says, 'a spare. And a jack.'

'Good old Larry.'

'Ha ha.'

'Can I help?' Her legs are suddenly tired, knees watery weak.

'Nah, you get back in.'

She stands a minute watching as he gathers the tools and hefts the spare tyre out. Feels a surge of love for him standing in the middle of nowhere being brave. She wonders if he's ever changed a tyre before. She hasn't. Wouldn't know where to start.

'I could shine the torch for you.'

'Wouldn't make much difference.' He sounds pretty cheerful. He kneels down by the wheel again. Some creature, maybe a dingo, howls, a curl of cold sound. She shivers.

'Get back in,' he says, 'no point us both getting cold.'

A beetly thing flickers across the ground between her feet. She gets back inside the car and shuts the door, pops another peppermint in her mouth. She puts her head back and lets her eyes shut as another wave of tiredness washes over her. Not *washed*. The horrible sensation of a swab, that smell. But she can't remember. It is all a mess in her mind, that night. Just forget it. *Whatever happened it's not my fault.* She imagines the tiredness like a vine, green shoots curling round and up until –

The door slams and she wakes with a start, a crawl of minty drool down her cheek. 'Is it done?'

He doesn't answer immediately. Then sighs heavily. 'Sorry. No.' Clearly an effort to keep his voice under control. 'Can't undo the poxy nuts, can I? Jammed on. Can't get a grip.'

'You can't get the wheel off?'

'No. And I've cut my finger.'

His index finger glistens darkly.

'I'll clean that. Look,' her voice wobbles as she retrieves the MediSwab, 'good old Larry again.' She pulls the damp gauzy stuff from its pouch and, holding her breath against its smell, wipes away the blood. A dark smear has somehow got on her cardigan sleeve. She tries to rub it away but it only spreads the stain. She stuffs the wipe down beside the seat.

They sit a minute, wordlessly.

'Couldn't you change the tyre without taking the wheel off?' she suggests.

He gives her a look, then goes back to staring at the steering wheel.

'Couldn't we drive – slowly – on the flat?' she says. Blood trickles down his finger. 'You need a plaster on that. Might have one. Hang on.' And she does have a few plasters in the bottom of her bag. She peels off the backing and wraps it tight around. 'That'll keep it clean, at least.'

'I reckon we *could* drive on a bit,' he says. 'Get nearer the road at least.'

'How far do you think?'

'Not too far.'

He jerks the car into drive again and they nose off, a slow

261

bumpy trundle. It is looking more like a definite track, that's something. If only that smell would go away. She doesn't want to state the obvious again but it has to be said: 'Aren't we going back the way we came?'

'We're going back to find where we went wrong. Must have been a fork we missed. Keep looking.'

'But I can't *see*.' She screws her eyes up and peers forward but the headlights make a diffuse cone of light only in front of them, the edges going off into gloom between bushes, and every couple of metres are places that might be forks in the track but probably aren't.

'Why don't we stop?' she says.

He looks at her.

'Wait till it's light. It's impossible to see and we're tired – *you* must be totally knackered. We're far enough away to be safe.' She pauses. 'Get a bit of kip and wait for sunrise?'

Graham drives for a few moments more then sighs, stops the engine and switches off the lights. At once it is easier to see the blackened bush, to see the pallid moonlight bleaching the twigs and scrubby half-burnt trees.

Wilderness.

He smiles wanly at her. 'Let's get a bit of shut-eye then.' He simply drops his head back against the seat.

'Put your arm round me,' Cassie says. She snuggles up to him, head against his neck. He smells sourly of sweat and she is uncomfortable, her neck crooked awkwardly, but he goes to sleep at once and she doesn't want to wake him. At least he is warm and she can feel his heartbeat against her cheek. She shuts her eyes against what is outside the windows, and though she doesn't think she will, she also falls asleep.

*

Graham wakes to see a sky streaked lemon and pearly green. He eases a dead arm out from under Cassie, flexes his fist, wincing at the prickly pulse of blood. She mumbles in her sleep and wriggles herself into another position. He opens the door and steps out. There are high, clear bird sounds though he can't see any birds. They are in the middle of an expanse of burnt bush that stretches on every side of them as far as he can see. In the very distance is a ridge of hills. The same hills you can see from Woolagong, he thinks, the same ridge. If they drove towards that with Fred – then can this be right? Or are they *further* away? He turns again and realises that there is another ridge in the opposite direction, just a low ripple of red caught up in the early light over the black land. Which is the right range?

He pisses on the ground, bubbles floating with particles of charcoal. The remains of the bushes are blistery spikes. There's another broken bottle – which might suggest, as Cassie said, that they're not too far from civilisation. But the label is burnt off. Could have been dropped last week or a hundred years ago.

Cassie gets out of the car, stretches and winces. 'Oooo – ouch – crick in my neck.'

'At least we slept. Good call, Cass.'

'Can you see where we are?'

'Sort of.' He reaches into the car for the water and glugs some down.

'Looks like hell, doesn't it?' She stands twisting and rubbing her neck, gazing around at the charred bush. 'Hey, just *look* at that sky.' She smiles up into it, the pastel colours run like watercolours on her face. It's not too hot yet, the temperature of a perfect English summer morning, the kind you get maybe twice a year. There's even a bit of breeze. 'Want an orange?' she says.

'Didn't know we had oranges.'

She fetches two from the car and chucks him one. He winces as it hits his bad finger.

'Sorry.'

They stand together, backs against the filthy bonnet of the car, peeling the oranges and munching the sweet flesh, juice running down their chins, spitting pips out. He drops his peel on the ground.

'Hey,' she says, 'don't drop litter. Orange peel takes *years* to decompose in the open, you know.'

He looks at her in disbelief. She has her peel scrunched in her hand. He shakes his head and laughs. It's a good feeling after the night they've had – the day they might be about to have. He grabs her and gives her a gentle orangey kiss.

'That's nice,' she whispers.

'Yeah.'

They lean into each other, a moment's peace. But even as he holds her he feels a sting on the back of his neck as the sun begins to strengthen. Time to hit the track. If there's just enough petrol to get them to the road, he plans, they'll leave the car and hitch.

*

The car won't start. Maybe it's just cold. Graham turns the key again and again but there's nothing. Completely dead. He stops trying and puts his head against the steering wheel. He gets out and opens the bonnet. After a numb moment, Cassie gets out too and they stand staring at the engine which, she knows, is nearly as much of a mystery to him as it is to her.

'Would it be the spark plugs, do you think?' She searches her mind for the sorts of things it could be.

'*Shit shit shit shit shit.*' He slams the lid down, kicks the side of the car and walks off. She stares at the dusty metal, smudged and streaked with fingermarks and trails. An orange pip. She flicks it off. She looks around. It's worse in the light – you can see just how much nothing there really is. She gets back into the car and waits. The windows are fuzzed with dust and specks of cinder, the sun beginning to sizzle through.

He comes back, opens the door and leans in. 'We'll have to walk,' he says.

'Wouldn't it be safer to stay with the car? We might get lost.'

'Nah. We just follow this branch of the track to where we went wrong. Then walk up the main track to the road. Something might pick us up on the way.'

She considers. 'Did you see anything when you were with Fred?'

He looks away. 'Yeah. A car or two. A cattle truck.'

He is a rotten liar.

'Don't fret,' he says. 'We've got water. That's the main thing. We'll have to leave our stuff. Just carry what we need. The minimum for –' He stops.

Survival she finishes for him in her head.

'We'll claim it all on insurance,' she says, quickly to stop the thought. 'This is just the sort of thing insurance is for.' She's reluctant to leave the womb-like space of the car. At least it is walls, windows, a roof. Something to be *in*. But she gets out, rubs her stiff neck, looks at him. 'I don't know –'

'Even if we had to walk a couple of hours,' he says, 'it wouldn't kill us. We'll get to the road. But if we stay put, we might still be here tonight minus the water. Or else Larry might find a way –'

Of course he's right. Ridiculous to sit by a broken-down car all day when the road is just a walk away. And maybe they could send for their stuff, if Larry manages to get the car back. Maybe he'd send it if they reimbursed postage? 'I'll change my shoes,' she says. They both change out of sandals into socks and trainers. They slather themselves in suncream, put on hats and shades. She ties the white cardigan, filthy now, around her waist.

'It's ruined,' she says, looking at the dust and charcoal and blood on the flimsy white wool.

'I'll buy you one just the same, for Christmas,' Graham says.

She smiles at him, a wormy curl of love in her belly. Could it work? Could it? His face is greasy with cream, dark bristles poking through.

She puts her little tapestry bag over her shoulder. 'Do you want to put the passports and stuff in here,' she says, patting it. 'Or are you taking your jacket with pockets?'

'What?'

'I'll put them in here.'

'*I* haven't got them.'

'What? *Don't*, Gray –'

'I'm not joking.'

They stare at each other.

'I thought you had them,' she says, mouth gone dry. She unzips the bag and rifles through, *please, please, please*, though she knows she doesn't have them. Remembers the empty interior of the drawer.

'In your backpack?' he says.

'No,' she says dully. 'They're not there.'

She knows just where they will be. At Woolagong Station, probably locked away in the study. For safe keeping, Larry would no doubt say, smoothly and plausibly. Could he have *known* they might take off?

Graham crashes his foot, his fist against the car. 'The fucking fucker,' he says, 'the *bastard*! I'll fucking *kill* the fucking fucker!' Numbly, she watches him. He jumps up on to the roof of the car and jumps, denting it with his weight. 'What the *fuck* are we going to do?'

*

'No point being negative,' Cassie says.

He looks at her. *No point being negative?* He slumps against the car, foot hurting, fist that was just recovering throbbing again. He rubs the stinging knuckles against his mouth. 'No,' he says. 'You're right.'

An aeroplane trawls past, high overhead. They watch it, longingly, until all that is left is a faint scratch on the surface of the sky.

266

'When we reach the roadhouse we'll explain,' Cassie says. 'We'll phone the British Embassy. They'll fly us home. It's what they're *for*, after all. Travellers in difficulty. And that's what we are, I suppose. Travellers in difficulty.'

'Guess so.'

'So,' she says, 'water, suncream, peppermints – wish we'd rationed the oranges –'

He can just see her as the bossy little badge-winning Girl Guide she used to be. A picture she showed him once, her and Patsy in their uniforms, socks held up with elastic, proud smiles under the daft hats.

'Which way?' she says.

He points the way he thinks and they begin to walk. The way they've come. No point in saying he's not sure. He's pretty sure. They need to head north. The sun has risen in the east – or *does* it rise in the east in the southern hemisphere? For a moment he's confused. But of course it does!

'What are you grinning about?' she asks. He shakes his head.

'This water weighs a ton,' she says after a while. 'It's hurting my shoulder. Let's drink some.'

'I'm not thirsty yet.'

'But if we drink it it'll be inside us. We'll be hydrated so we won't get thirsty. I bet it's better not to get thirsty than to wait till you are.'

'But then we'll sweat it out and then it's gone.'

'But if we drink it it'll be less heavy and we might sweat less.'

He stops, shrugs. Who the hell knows. 'But not too much,' he says.

She unscrews the top of her carrier, tilts it back and drinks. Some of it spills down her chest, sticking her white T-shirt to her skin.

'Don't waste it.' He has a drink from his bottle, tepid and tasting of polythene.

'You shouldn't really drink from plastic containers,' she says, 'it could affect your sperm.'

He splutters a laugh, water running down his own chin.

They walk on in silence for a while, single file between the deeply channelled ruts. 'If you had a million quid,' she says, 'what would you do?'

'Cass!'

'Just trying to pass the time.'

'Save your breath,' he says.

*

Cassie gives up trying to talk. She watches the toes of her trainers swapping places, over and over, becoming quickly caked with red and black. Better than looking into the distance. Graham walks ahead, head down, water container bumping on his hip. She can hear the water sloshing with each step.

It makes your eyes go funny if you do look into the distance, everything swimmy and uncertain in the rising heat. There is still the sound in her ears, like a sort of echo of a heartbeat. Not sure if she can hear it with her ears or with some other sense. Oh, think about something else. If only they could get out of the blackness, the burning smell. Incredible that underneath there are charred seeds waiting to unfurl, that in a few months' time it will all be green and filled with flowers, carpets of them, like the pictures.

She remembers a darkened hotel room, a slide show. Australia's famous flora. Tries to remember the names: banksia, boronia, everlastings – of course – kangaroo paw, parakeelya, desert pea. No. Think about English flowers, soon snowdrops then crocuses daffodils and those tulips, red with black middles. In the earth in her own garden the bulbs would be coming back to life, poking up through the heavy soil. Dizzying thought, so far away, new life starting obedient as clockwork.

What if we don't make it? Of course we will, of course we will. She stumbles over a rock. *But if we don't?*

Graham stops and looks back. 'OK?'

'Fine.'

'Look –'

She catches him up and sees that they're approaching a kind of crossroads, or at least a couple of exits from the main track. There's even the stump of what might have once been a signpost. If only it still was.

'This must be where we went wrong,' he says. He takes off his hat and scratches his head. 'Fred must have turned off – come to think of it there was a turning –'

'But that must have been miles back!'

'No.'

It must have been, she thinks.

He walks round the signpost, lifting his hand and squinting each way. A kangaroo comes inquisitively close and bounds off again.

'Which way did he turn then?'

She could cry, so obvious from his face that he doesn't know. And nor does she. He looks baffled, but chippy, a false, confident little jerk to his chin, as he turns this way and that. *You haven't got a clue* she thinks. She looks herself, always terrible with directions, always thought it a laugh before, almost a lovable weakness. But it has never been life or death before. *A life-or-death situation.* Funny how even that can be a cliché. *English Couple Perish in Outback.* She can see it in the *Observer*, spread out on a duvet on a Sunday morning, smeared with butter, sprinkled with croissant crumbs. *Poor things*, some other woman will say and yawn and turn the page.

'This way,' he says, pointing.

'Yeah?'

'I know we turned right once – remember him swinging out. But then we turned right last time, so I think it's left here. That'll take us north.'

Cassie pauses, 'Sure you're not thinking of the way back?'

'What?'

'Well, if he'd turned right on the way back then it would be left now.'

He bites his lip. Red dust has stuck to his suncream so he looks like he's made of bronze. She takes off her sunglasses and wipes them on her T-shirt.

'The sun's there, east, so that is north,' he says. 'We're heading north to the highway so it must be this way.'

'Oh – yes.'

'Listen!' He holds up a finger and she listens. She can't hear anything at first then maybe a low moan.

'What?'

'I thought I heard a road train. Gone now. But keep listening.'

'OK.' They drink some water and trudge off down the chosen track.

Thirty

They walk on. The sun creeps across the sky until it's overhead. Every now and then they stop and sip some water. Cassie squats down to pee.

Out of the corner of his eye he watches her, wondering if it will make her dehydrate quicker. *Don't*, he wants to say but doesn't. They don't talk much. Not a lot to say. Or not a lot there's any point in saying. His feet ache and a blister smarts on his heel. He tries to concentrate on other parts of his body to keep his mind off it. His stomach growls, affronted noises, not used to going without its breakfast. Not far off lunchtime now.

At last they come to an end to the blackness. Been walking hours, covered a fair few miles – must have been some conflagration. They walk across a strip of bare red. Absolutely bare and flat with creamy rocks rising from it, rounded like giant pebbles. A couple of dwarfish thorny trees. Something different to look at at least. Sometimes a bird passes. An aeroplane high, high overhead. People sipping drinks, scoffing peanuts, watching a movie. Or maybe looking down and marvelling at the nothingness. A flock of small green parrots creak and squawk past low.

'Shall we sit down?' Cassie catches him up, points to a stone beneath which is a lip of shadow.

'Shouldn't stop.'

'Gray, I've *got* to sit down.'

They take off their shoes and sweaty socks, pour some water – just a drop – over their aching feet. They drink, scrunched into the shade of the stone. It's a strange shape, globular like a gigantic melted drip of stone. He rolls a fag, breathes in, savouring the bite of the smoke right to the bottom of his lungs.

'Remember these rocks?' she says.

'Yeah,' he lies. 'Not long now.' Truth is he remembers nothing. The truth is that with every step he takes, he gets less sure where they're heading. The track, hard to discern any more in the flat land, must be swerving round, the outlook changing till it seems they must be going back on themselves. If they only had a compass.

'Got another plaster?' he asks.

She rummages in her bag and helps stick it on the raw oval on the back of his heel where the blister has burst. They put their socks in the sun to dry and close their eyes. It would be too easy to drop off. The stone has a hot salty smell. He forces his lids up to meet the eyes of a small lizard, egg-yolk bright. Eyelids so heavy, head throbs, stomach growls. Should not have stopped. How is he ever going to start again?

He puts his hand in his pocket and meets the two pebbles from Ziggy. 'Hey,' he says, giving her the painted one. 'I forgot. This is for you.'

She takes it. Looks puzzled. 'Funny time to give me a present.'

'It's a bus,' he says, points out the wheels, steering wheel, windows.

'Wish it *was* a bus. Ta.'

She looks at it a minute and puts it in her bag. He holds the other pebble in his palm. Warm, smooth, ridged. Friendly. He rubs the ball of his thumb over the ridges, shuts his eyes.

'I was thinking about Mara,' Cassie says. 'What she said, I mean it's pretty weird – Graham?'

He doesn't reply, breathes heavily as if he's dozing, not far off

272

dozing but mustn't. Mustn't doze, mustn't think, not about Mara, not about anything. He hears Cassie moving, through his lashes sees her putting on her shoes and socks, getting up, vanishing from view.

After a few minutes she calls him from a little way away. 'Hey, come and look.'

Reluctantly he eases his feet back into sun-crisped socks and shoes, wipes his shades and puts them on – heavy and achy on his nose and ears – and stands up, steadying himself against the stone. On the other side the glare of sun almost blinds him.

'Look.' She points out a white painting, stick figures, arrows, a commotion of scratches. 'Looks like a battle, doesn't it? And look, here's a funny hedgehog thing.' Despite everything he finds a small spurt of energy for interest. They wander amongst the rocks a bit, discovering more painting.

'Hey.' Cassie looks round nervously. 'Suppose there are Aborigines about?' This might be a reservation for all we know. We might be trespassing. They might be watching us.'

'Nah,' Graham says, looking over his shoulder. 'Anyway, that would be good. They'd point us the right way.'

A beat is missed at this acknowledgement that they are lost. She turns away from him, looks into the distance, then turns back. 'Isn't *that* amazing!' She points to a frieze of men and beasts – a desperate kind of smile on her face.

'Better get moving.'

'Can't be far now,' she says. 'Here,' she says, 'have a peppermint.'

They drag on. Sweat soaks Graham's T-shirt, would take it off but then he'd fry. The sun booms, slams down, the heat actually a weight. So hot and bright, hard to look anywhere but down, but seeing the dusty blur of his moving feet makes him giddy. Walks along with closed eyes to rest them. Foot after foot after foot, throb after throb after throb of his head. His tongue feels thick and harsh in his mouth, like a doormat.

'Look!' Cassie says. He jolts himself out of some dream. '*People!*' She catches hold of his arm. He follows her finger with his eyes. And it seems there are people, a crowd of them – how distant? – spaced out and moving towards them. Small people, a scattered crowd advancing. They reach for each other's hand. *People?*

'They've stopped,' she whispers, shrinking behind him. She's right. They are not moving. They are strange, strange figures. Not Aborigines – what are –?

'Hey!' he laughs suddenly, realisation hitting him. 'They're not *people*.'

'*What* – oh!' She grins at him, a sudden gappy grin under the speckled shadow of her hat.

He says, 'Remember Mara mentioning these?' They drop hands and, laughing with relief, walk towards the scatter of termite mounds, which is like a field of statues.

'Hope it doesn't mean we're walking back,' Cassie says.

He doesn't answer for a moment. The plaster has rubbed off his heel, skin too wet to stick, he can feel it scrunched up in his sock. His mouth is dry, head pounding with each step. A buzz of flies follows them, one buzzes against his eardrum and he thumps his own face trying to drive it off.

'She said they were miles away,' he says. 'Remember? Don't suppose you've got any aspirin or anything?'

'Yeah. Headache? I took some a while back.' She is amazing, burrowing her hand efficiently into her bag. She will be a brilliant mother, he can see that. She should have that. He must get her back safely so she can, one day, have that. She presses a couple of pills out of a blister pack and he swallows them, huge lumps scraping down his throat.

The termite mounds are the strangest thing he's ever seen; if he was ever to see Ziggy again he'd tell him that. He thinks of those cows, parched, mummified round a dry pump. He can believe it. He stares round at the formations, like figures, stalagmites, stumpy vegetal forms, some nearly as tall as Cassie, the same burning reds and ochres as the earth, splattered with white streaks of bird shit. If things were different he would like to draw them. A flock of black cockatoos hop about, suddenly scuttering upwards, flashing scarlet underwings. The mounds cast shadows, the sun has moved, Graham scrabbles his mind to try and work out what that means and draws a blank. Shadows stretch towards them like a hundred fingers pointing back the way they've come. But they can't go back.

'There must be trillions of ants in these,' she says, 'or termites. Or whatever they are.'

But he has to face it sometime. He faces it with the termite mounds looming round him: they are lost. No sign of a track now for who knows how long. They might be going to die. That's what happens to stupid British people blundering about in the bush. They die.

'Come on,' Cassie says.

They walk until the termite mounds are too far behind them to see. They come to a place with withered grey bushes, thorns sharp as darning needles, the leaves like flecks of asbestos. There are bristly clumps of razor-sharp grass and more life, lizards, beetles, birds, a small brown snake printing S shapes in the dirt. A couple of emus stand poised against the light watching them pass, and once they've passed they throw up their feathers, shriek and lollop away. What do emus eat and drink?

He doesn't look at the time. What difference does it make? The sun will go down in the end, whether he knows what hour it is or not – and then what? And so what? A couple of eagles are mauling and scrapping over a kangaroo carcass. He's never seen an eagle before, always wanted to – as a boy it was one of his ambitions. But these are not like the golden eagles of his dreams, these are thuggish things, dirty feathers billowing round their legs as their talons and beaks rip into the meat. They aren't cowed by the watching humans, carry on their dirty business unconcerned.

The light starts to deepen to mid-afternoon and a breeze springs up. They are walking straight into the sun which must mean they're walking west – but what does that mean? – the dry cogs in his head grind – is that right? Can't remember which way it was they had to go. His feet lift and fall and every time his right foot falls it's like a cheese grater against this heel and he forgets for a few steps at a time what he's walking towards or why. Cassie speaks and he's surprised, remembering she's there too.

'What do you think this is?' she says. He turns, can't see properly, the sun dazzles making after-images in his eyes. Limps back a bit, doesn't want to walk back, only forwards. She's got her hand on a post, a bit of rusty wire trailing from it. 'There's another,' she points, 'we've walked past quite a few. A fence?'

A fence – and he walked straight past and didn't see. What sort of a state is that to get in? He tries to pull himself together. And now he looks there is something to the far right of them. Could have *missed* it. Distant, miles away still maybe, hard to tell, something that could be buildings, trees. Little water left in his bottle now but he takes a sip. Maybe a station? Maybe a place of safety, water, food and bed.

'You thinking what I'm thinking?' Cassie says. Sounds like she's got a sore throat. He puts his arms round her and they hug weakly. She pulls away. 'Let's have a mint to celebrate.'

They walk towards the huddle with slightly renewed vigour. The sweet leaks sugar into Graham's blood. If only his foot didn't sting like buggery, but soon he'll be soaking it in a bowl of water. A kind woman will bring him a cold beer. They can shower, or maybe there'll even be a pool. And then later food, roast meat or stew. Gallons of icy beer. A soft cool bed.

They walk side by side now, speaking little, searching as they approach. A pump comes into view beside a stand of trees. 'Gray.' Cassie stops. 'You don't think –'

'What?'

'It's not Woolagong, is it?'

'Nah.' His heart gives a sickly beat in his throat. 'Course not.'

They proceed a bit more slowly. It *can't* be Woolagong, there should be two pumps – but which direction would they be coming from? If it was, he couldn't bear the look of pure ecstatic smarm on Larry's face. *Can't* be. But at least there would be a bed to lie on, fresh water, beer and grub. He grits his teeth against the pain in his heel, scrambles his brain trying to work something out from the sun's direction. But it's no good, that part of his head is burnt out.

'What would we do?' she says.

'It's *not*.'

'But if? I know,' she grabs his arm, 'we could creep back to our bed and rest. He wouldn't know – and then –' she trails off.

'It's not!' he says, shaking off her arm. He can see it now, the whole layout is wrong, the whole lie of the land, type of bush, it's smaller altogether, not the same place at all, nothing like. Her hand flies to her heart. Under the sunburn and dust and freckles she looks pale.

'Drink some water,' he says.

'What shall we say when we get there?' She swigs. 'Nearly gone, still it's OK now, isn't it?' She finishes it and wipes her mouth, her lips pink and wet where the dust's washed off. Looks at her watch. 'Five past four,' she says. 'Just in time for tea!'

'Come on.' He limps off towards the station. More signs of civilisation – posts, rusty bits of machinery, a broken-down shed. The deafening drone of flies. But no livestock in sight, no cars, voices. There is movement, he sees, the pump turning. But his optimism wanes the closer they get, visions of kind women and cold beer evaporating. It is a ruin. The wreck of a station. Some trees – the most beautiful gums, startling white and green, alive with birds, a fantastic freshness for the eyes – but otherwise nothing. No house, no people, just piles of old sun-silvered timber, corrugated iron, a couple of wrecked utes.

But there is something. As they walk amongst the wreckage they hear, smell, see it together, a splash of water – water spouting intermittently into an overflow tank open to the sky, as the breeze drives round the pump. They hurry over: the galvanised tank is deep with greenish water, floating with small dead things.

'Think it's OK to drink?' Cassie says.

'No choice.' Graham dips his finger in the tepid water and licks. 'Not salty, anyway.'

'If we catch the next gush,' she says, unscrewing her water bottle. 'That'll be OK.'

He eases the bloodstained sock off his foot, tiny fibres of cotton sticking on the raw place.

'*Ouch.*' Cassie winces for him.

He strips, gets hold of the edge of the tank, hauls himself up and drops in. It is lukewarm, thickish and mushy at the bottom. But still, the sensation of water all over his body. Just don't look too hard.

'Come on,' he says, 'it'll do you good.'

'But –' She frowns at the bobbing mass of insects, feathers, slime and God knows what else. 'I'll just sit on the edge and wash.' She strips off her clothes, climbs up, lets her feet dangle into the water. The middle part of her is blinding white, almost blue against the tan of her legs and arms and face; her nipples a couple of soft pink flowers. She reaches down and scoops water, rubs it under her arms.

Graham dips his head under to get rid of the cloud of flies, then comes up bubbling, tugs her foot and she slips in and right under, her hair streaming out, releasing a fuzz of bubbles.

'You pig!' she splutters. She grabs the side and hauls herself up. She starts to laugh then screams looking at his arm, 'there's something on you! Get out,' she says, more calmly. 'It's a leech.'

They scramble awkwardly out of the tank and land on the red dirt. It's clinging to his arm above the elbow. A slimy bluish sausage skin swelling as they watch. He chops at it with the side of his hand, but it just goes on getting bigger. Its mouth grips like a metal clip. He feels faint.

'Hold on –' she reaches for her bag and pulls out a box of matches, lights one but it goes out, lights another and holds it against the leech until it jerks and falls off, releasing a bright trickle of blood.

He leans giddily against the tank a minute. Then laughs. 'Thank God for the Girl Guides.'

'What?' She looks at him crossly. 'Oh, ha ha.'

He swallows. It looks like a bloody old condom twitching in the dust.

'Get your shoes on,' Cassie says. 'Ants, everywhere.' They are already swarming towards his drying blood. They pull their sweaty clothes on over damp skins. She finds him another plaster for his heel and he puts his trainers on, undone, minus the socks. They wait beside the tank for a few minutes or so, till there's a gust of breeze strong enough to turn the pump. Flies buzz deafeningly, batting softly against their faces. The pump creaks and Cassie manages to catch maybe a pint of clean water. They take a swig each. It is warm but clean, tastes of clay.

'At least we won't dehydrate,' she says.

He looks at her and shakes his head. 'How *did* you know what to do about the leech?' he asks.

'Obvious, isn't it?' she says. 'These *bloody* flies.' She flaps her hand, jams her hat down as far over her face as she can.

A big white cockatoo lands on the edge of the water tank. Stiff white quiff like a frosted Elvis.

'Hello,' Cassie says in a stupid voice.

'*Cockie, cockie,*' it replies, in a creaking voice. '*Good boy Cockie.*'

She laughs. 'Cockie?'

'*Cockie, cockie.*'

'Poor thing. Must have belonged to whoever –'

'But this place must have been derelict for *years*.'

'Maybe things rot quicker in this climate? Anyway parrots live ages.' She slaps her calf to get rid of the ants climbing her leg. 'Let's get away from here.'

They go across to a pile of sun-bleached, splintery timber and sit down. The late afternoon light is shading to a syrupy gold. No proper breakfast, no lunch, and soon no supper. Graham manages, between the awkward planks, to wangle himself a place to stretch out. He smokes a fag, flies crawling on his fingers, the fag, the corner of his mouth. Above him the sky is still blue though the quality of the light is changing; what is it that's different about afternoon light than morning? The breeze rustling the leaves of the trees sounds like the sea. Imagine the cold North Sea. His stomach moans.

'Yeah,' Cassie agrees, batting the flies away. 'If we only had some food we'd be OK.'

He shuts his eyes. Obviously they'll stay here tonight. And then? Shuts his mind to the question. Too tired, too hungry. The wood is warm to lie on. He's starting to melt towards sleep when Cassie says:

'Get up!'

The tone of her voice makes him obey and it is not until he is standing on the ground that he sees the snake, a skinny, black and red thing, deadly-looking, rearing up, flickering its tongue. They back away. The snake holds its pose for a moment and then flows away under the woodpile.

'*Exactly* the sort of place for snakes and all sorts,' she says. 'We should have thought.'

'Yeah.' Graham looks forlornly at the comfortable plank.

'We'd better look for something to eat,' she says. 'There must be something.'

He limps, bad heel squashing down the back of his trainer, behind her through the heaps of debris. They find a patch of melons the size of tennis balls. He splits one open but it is dry inside, thready and bitter. Inedible.

'We could dig up grubs,' Graham says. 'They're meant to be nutritious.' He means it as a tease but Cassie looks at him quite seriously.

'Only if the worst comes to the worst,' she says.

'Or I could *kill* something,' he suggests, looking at the white cockatoo, which is getting on his tits, hopping round with them, congratulating itself. *Good boy Cockie.*

'Anyway, it won't hurt us not to eat for one day. Think of it as a detox. We've still got a couple of peppermints. Want yours now or save it?'

Graham holds his hand out. Puts it in his mouth and tries not to crunch. His jaw aches to chew something. What about tomorrow? But can't face the question now. If he can't eat he must at least get horizontal. But where? The place is heaving with bugs, snakes, there's a great tough spider's web stretched between two bushes, thick as fuse wire. Imagine the bugger that spun that.

'If you could have anything to eat, anything in the world, what would you have?' Cassie says. He looks at her in disbelief. She closes her eyes and smiles. 'I'd have a glass of lemonade – with ice – and a huge slice of Victoria sponge. With strawberry jam and fresh cream. Thick, cool, white –'

'*Shut up.*'

'Don't –' she begins then stops. 'Hey?' She holds up her hand. 'Hey, *listen.*'

'What?' A gust of breeze fluttering the leaves, a creak of the pump, the poxy parrot squawking, a gush of missed fresh water. Should have rigged something up to catch it –

'*Listen.*'

He strains his ears. She's right, there is something. An engine sound. He shuts his eyes to listen better. The noise quickly gets louder. A plane! It is a plane! They go out into the open, search the sky till it appears, a small plane, flying low enough, surely, to spot them.

Graham takes off his T-shirt, waves it, Cassie waves her hat, jumping as the plane comes low. '*Here, here, here,*' she shrieks. The plane dips a wing and circles low and then away again.

'It must have seen us,' she wails.

He waits, watches. 'It's coming back.'

'Oh thank God, thank you, God. Oh no –'

It seems to be leaving but it is only banking into a turn.

'Working out where to land,' Graham says. The blood roars in his head, he feels he might pass right out with the relief. He pulls his T-shirt back on. *Oh thank you*, he looks back at the sky, at whatever, *thank you*. He pulls Cassie towards him, holding her tightly, she is alive, he is alive, it is all OK. They stand waiting. Holding hands like a couple of kids until the plane finally does touch down and bumps towards them, sending up a storm of dust. The cockatoo croaks and flaps away.

They grin at each other, walk towards the plane and – at the same instant – stop.

Thirty-one

Out of the dust walks Larry, adjusting his panama. 'Well, well, well, what have we here?'

Graham blinks. Scratch of dust in his eye. Cassie's nails dig into his hand.

'Thought you'd take a little stroll, eh?' Larry says. 'Can we offer you a lift or would you rather walk back?'

Graham looks at Cassie but her head is down, hair sticking to her face, hat scrunched in her hand. He looks round at the ruined place. The pump turns, slosh of water. The trees swish. The birds, which had risen in fright, settle back amongst the leaves. There's nothing for it but to follow Larry to the plane.

'G'day.' A smile crawls across Kip's face. Blank shine in his eyes. They do up the belts. Larry slams shut the door. Cassie looks away, out of the window. He sees her throat contract as she swallows, the white line above her upper lip. But no tears. He reaches for her hand. The plane roars into life, bumps across the ground and lifts, leaving his stomach behind. He sees a startled kangaroo and joey bounding away and then they tilt and he can see nothing but sky.

His guts lurch as the plane lifts and banks. Nothing in his stomach to be sick with, only water. Cassie's grip on his hand tightens. A pool of sweat between their palms. The back of Larry's head is in his face, bouffant grey hair exposing the thinness underneath; pink skin, yellow bone, what kind of sick brain?

Graham swallows down a surge of nausea. Forces himself to look out again, down at the land below, patterned with a trace of road, stippled bush, crawly shapes of dried watercourses. Shadows are scrawled huge by the low sun. The mountain ridges have gone purple in the granular orange light. He leans back, closes his eyes – and something strikes him that he missed before. Thinks of the pebble. Slides his free hand into his pocket. Too giddy to look but he knows the look of it. The angular lines, the shades of red and blue. Burnt colours. A weird geometry of lines, angles. He looks out again. From above, it makes sense, this land makes sense. You can understand the scale from above. The relationship between the immensity and this tiny pebble pattern. Like macro and micro. If not so nauseous he'd be excited. The pebble as a kind of key. A way in.

In a humiliatingly short time, they land. All night they drove, all day they walked and, in a few minutes, they are back. The tin roof ridged deeply golden by the setting sun.

The car is there. Parked in its usual place. No sign of its adventure, except a dent in the roof. How has he got it back? They get out and stand and watch till the plane is nothing but a speck in their eyes against the burning tangerine sky.

'I've put your belongings back in your room and I've pre-pared supper,' Larry says. 'I expect you're hungry?'

'We found some melon things and tried them –' Cassie says.

'Paddy melons!' Larry shakes his head. 'You must have been desperate.'

Cassie laughs suddenly, sounding harsh and mad. 'God, we must seem like a pair of idiots!'

'We-ll.' Larry gazes at her and she smiles, almost *coy*, looking down. But when Larry turns his back she gives Graham a meaningful look. Christ knows what it means, but something.

They sit down at the kitchen table. There is wine but Cassie doesn't touch it. Larry urges her several times during the meal. 'It's the one you particularly liked,' he says, eyes flicking down her neck. She smiles but puts her hand over her glass. But Graham gulps it down. Two bottles on the table, one their side, one his. It's light, cool, refreshing. 'Just the thing, I thought,' Larry says, 'after a day in the sun. Quaffable was how you put it, didn't you, Cassie?'

Graham's grits his teeth. Larry is asking for it, asking for it, asking for it. His fist throbs in time with the blood beating in his head, thudding like footsteps over and over.

'Water would be better, Gray,' Cassie says but he doesn't look at her. She nudges his knee under the table with her own and he shifts away.

The food is a slimy mess of potatoes, bacon, peas. Dull and filling. Eggs in there somewhere, a bit runny. Graham shovels it down mechanically. Sits back and watches the food disappearing down his own maw, the wine swilling after it. Bad idea to drink though, the realisation hits him. Cassie right as usual. Sticking to water which she fetches herself from the tap.

'Eat up,' Larry says, leaning towards her, 'I know it's not up to your standard.'

'Bit sun-struck – not hungry after all,' Cassie says. 'Not that it's not nice,' she adds quickly. 'Delicious. Just the thing.'

*

Cassie's dream is of walking, her own two feet plodding and plodding, endlessly plodding over crumbling ground and then there's a tearing noise, a jerk, the ground splits and she wakes to hear Graham vomiting.

It's pitch dark. She fumbles for the torch and shines the puny beam on him. He's kneeling on the floor by the door. She gets up, goes over, careful not to step in anything. She puts her hand on his shoulder, the skin cold and clammy. The stench of vomit fills the air. He heaves again and half sobs. 'Sorry, was trying to get out.'

'Don't be daft. Have you finished?'

'Think so.'

'Back into bed then.'

She pulls on her dress, pushes her feet into her sandals. The shrinking moon raggy tonight under a tat of cloud. Outside the kitchen door the goanna sits, like something carved in stone. Its eyes swivel at her and then it moves like a clockwork toy out of her way. She drinks some water then takes a cloth and bucket, detergent, fresh water for Graham. The bloody idiot. What does he expect, gulping wine as if there's no such thing as tomorrow after a day in the sun? And his sick makes her feel sick too. She picks her way back to the stinking shed, lights a candle and tries not to breathe in as she crouches down to clear it up.

Graham mumbles sorry every now and then, but she can't find it in herself to say, it's OK. If you're going to get pissed you could at least clear up after yourself, she thinks as she scrubs at the floor.

When she's cleaned up as best she can, she goes out to wash the smell from her hands. The clouds are pearl and silver, beautiful she supposes though she can't *feel* their beauty, feels nothing but nausea. Actually – her hand goes to her stomach – actually, she has been feeling a bit – No. It will just be sunstroke. But her nipples prickle and her mouth tastes as if she's been sucking a penny. Patsy said she *knew* the moment she conceived. From these same symptoms. From the moment I conceived, she said. Didn't need even to miss a period to know. Or it *could* just be sunstroke. Could be.

Every hour or so all through the night Graham vomits into the bucket by the bed and every time she hauls herself out of sleep, takes it out, tips it out into the dunny, washes her hands. Notices the gradual adjustment of the moon across the sky until at last the sky lightens and the cockerel begins his ignorant racket. And Graham keeps vomiting. By the morning he can't even sip water without bringing up a stream of bile.

'I should get Larry,' Cassie says, as he sinks back, clammy and grey.

'No.'

'I know but he *is* a doctor. Sort of.'

'No.'

And she does put it off, until he's so sick he doesn't care any more. Until there's no choice.

Larry doesn't say much or seem surprised. 'Sunstroke,' he says. Goes over to the shearers' shed and injects Graham with an anti-emetic and when that seems to have worked, gives Cassie some pills to help him rest and recover. He's actually pretty decent about it considering the trouble they've caused. Actually very kind. She is so confused she gives up trying to think at all.

It's mid-afternoon before she can even bring herself to consider food. The routine has been shot to bits. Such a blow of homesickness when she thinks about home. *Needs, aches* to talk to her sister. She sets herself the task of weeding, taking some comfort from the greenery, the cheeping birds, glad of something mindless and time-consuming to do. Larry keeps out of the way. It's way after lunchtime when he comes out and reminds her, quite gently, that she *is* still the cook.

In the kitchen she breaks eggs into a bowl, her stomach rising to her throat as the thick yellow slime of the yolks streaks into the mucousy white. She tries to fork out the bloodspots, which are the dividing cells maybe dividing still as they are beaten and seasoned and poured into the pan, ceasing only when the temperature is hot enough to stop them. Four less chickens in the world. So what?

Just enough for her and Larry. They sit in the kitchen. She

doesn't want to eat it herself, does no more than nibble a crispy edge. If she could *only* remember that night, if she could only *remember*.

'How's Mara?' she says.

'A little under the weather. She was upset by your – what shall we call it?' Larry pauses. 'Unexpected escapade. But she'll be pleased to see you back.'

'Sorry,' Cassie says.

'You surprised me, the two of you. Still, all right now. And that was *magnifique*.' He dabs his lips with his napkin.

'Just an ordinary omelette.' She puts down her fork. 'Larry, listen, the other night –'

'Which particular night?'

'You know. When Graham and Fred –'

'*That* delightful evening.'

'It sounds ridiculous, I know,' she bleats out a sort of laugh, 'but – I can't remember quite what happened.'

'No?' He spreads his immaculate hands. The nails so shiny she wonders if it could be lacquer. Does he sit there, in the depths of his house, manicuring his nails?

'Did you –' The words fail in her mouth.

'Did I –?'

'Did *we*, I mean. Or did you take advantage of me sort of thing – when I was –'

'Indisposed?'

His devilish eyebrows twitch. His smile is slow, the tooth at the corner just glinting between his lips.

'Did you?'

He suddenly puts both hands on the table and pushes himself up. 'Tell you what. You wait there, put the kettle on perhaps. I've something to show you. Something I, for one, am rather pleased with.'

He goes off, humming, beard jerking forward. Cassie scrapes her omelette into the bin and fills the kettle. A brown thing scuttles across the floor. She watches, detached, as it disappears under the sink.

Larry returns with an envelope from which he takes some prints. 'Ready?' He spreads them out on the table.

Gravity forces her down on to a chair and she is hardly even surprised at what she sees. There she is, white shirt pulled up, head thrown back, posed on the sofa, eyes shut as if in pleasure or anticipation.

'You bastard,' she says quietly, her heart beating thickly in her throat.

'And how could anyone possibly refuse such an invitation?'

'I was out cold.'

'Not *so* cold.'

'You must have given me something,' she says. 'Did you? Like that,' she swallows, 'that date-rape drug.'

He makes a steeple of his hands and rests them on his lips, gazes at her for a minute. There she is on the table, images and images, everything showing. Everything. She tears her eyes away. 'The MediSwab –'

'In the interests of hygiene.'

'*Hygiene!*' She gets up, jerking the table. 'I'm telling Graham.' Not sure if she means it but she has to say something, can't bear the sticky miasma of *collusion* that is gathering around the table. 'Do you know,' she says, her voice grating, 'I actually thought you were OK. I thought you were *nice*. Graham said you were a sleaze-bag but I – you really took me in.'

'*Sleaze-bag*,' he repeats, with a trace of amusement. 'Just consider for a minute, before you run off, how this is going to look.'

'He'll believe me.'

'Despite the evidence? Are you sure?' He gathers up the photos and returns them to their envelope. 'Just consider for a moment. If you were to see a picture of him, say, *copulating* with another woman. What would you think?'

Copulating. She shudders.

'If the evidence was there before your eyes?'

Her mouth opens and closes.

'Well, in any case,' he says, 'give it a bit of thought. Now. Must get on.'

'To do what? File your nails?' comes out of her mouth and then she wants to sink to the floor at the childishness, the petulance, the ridiculous *irrelevance.* But naturally it only makes him smile.

*

Graham hears the door open. The light makes a sugary halo round her head. She closes the door quickly, comes across to him. She smells of sweat, cattish, almost feral.

'OK?' he says. He hardly dares to look into her eyes. What does she know?

'What about you?'

He props himself up on his elbow and the room doesn't swing around him any more, like a jolted lampshade. That's *something.* He looks at her profile, the peachy down on the slope of her cheek, it doesn't tell him a thing.

'He told me to give you some more pills but – listen, I don't think we should eat or drink anything unless we get it ourselves.'

He watches her expression.

'I just think –'

He lies back.

'I mean I didn't drink last night – it was probably only the sun that made you ill and all that wine but –'

'You're getting paranoid,' he says.

'OK then,' she says. 'Take them.' She tips two pills out of the bottle and transfers them to his hand.

He holds them in his palm. Two snowy torpedoes. She smiles at last, her freckles scrunching. 'Maybe I *am* getting paranoid but – look, I do want to leave. Soon as we can.'

'Yeah.' He waits. 'Is – is everything else all right?' He dares to look into her face. Something odd going on there. She's not being straight with him, but would surely be far, far angrier if she knew about Mara. 'Could you bring me something to eat? Just dry toast or something.'

'Good,' she kisses his forehead. 'Maybe a cup of tea?'

She goes out. He waits a few moments and then swings himself round to a sitting position. It's OK. From under his pillow slide four pills. The last two doses. The same thought. The same conclusion arrived at independently. Only he'd had a worse thought – a nightmarish thought – that Cassie was in on it. That *she* was drugging him. *Cassie?* Is he going off his head?

He opens the door and stands outside. The sun casts rosy streamers of light from low on the horizon, the shadows of the trees stretch a hundred times their height. Washing still hangs stiff and sun-baked on the line, casting its own complex shadow. Seems like weeks ago that Cassie did that. Larry's shirts, a sheet, Cassie's knickers. Mara's shed door shut.

He goes up the veranda steps and puts his hand on the screen. And stops. They are in there talking, Cassie and Larry, he can see through the gap of the open door. Her profile, hair tied back, but wisps stand out whitely like strands of light. Can't see Larry from this angle. But he can hear his voice.

'Now, what shall we do with our evening?'

'I'm tired. Think I'll have an early night.'

'That's a little dull,' Larry says. Graham sees a shadow flit. Slaps his arm, feeling the hot prickle of a bug bite.

'Really, I'm tired, and Graham's all alone.'

'He will be asleep.'

'How can you know?'

'The pills, sleep is nature's great healer, you must know that. The pills will speed his recovery by ensuring a deep and sound sleep.'

Quiet.

'Let's go through into the sitting room again, shall we,' Larry says. 'Relax a bit before dinner.'

'You must be *joking*!'

Graham barges into the kitchen. Larry looks up, surprised. 'Well, well, I assumed you'd be asleep.'

'*Bet* you did. Thought you were meant to be bringing me some tea,' he says to Cassie.

She gets up, flustered. 'I was just –' She gestures towards the kettle.

'Perhaps you should start the meal?' Larry says. He doesn't take his eyes off Graham's. 'Maybe we should get Mara up?'

'You're not hungry *again*?' Cassie says, looking at the un-washed plates still on the table.

'I'll help you,' Graham says.

'No, no,' Larry says, 'sit down.'

Cassie stands looking at the two of them, until Larry switches his attention to her. 'Perhaps you could give us a minute?' he says.

She looks terrified. 'I need to er –' She tails off, throws Graham a strange pleading look and goes out.

He sits down. Legs weak. 'What's going on?' he says.

'Tell you what,' Larry says, 'why not come through into the sitting room? Sit down comfortably. I've got something to show you. Could you stomach a beer?'

'No.'

'You'll excuse me if I –' As he passes, Graham gets a whiff of the sickly cologne. Saliva floods his mouth as if he's about to spew again. Larry opens a beer, the neat knob of his Adam's apple slides as he takes a swallow, wipes his mouth on the back of his hand. 'Come on.'

Graham pushes himself up and follows him into the hall. Larry unclips the keys from his waist and unlocks a door into a big dim room. Just as Cassie described. Only no fire.

His eyes go to the sofa. Brown velvet worn bare in patches

like the hide of an old bear. He looks away, notices a painting above the fireplace, glass so grimy you can just make out a watercolour of the bush, a black figure with a stick on a rise. Red hills rippling behind him.

'Came with the house,' Larry says. 'Worth a bob or two. However, that's not what I wanted to show you.' He puts down one envelope that he'd been clutching and picks up another from the mantelpiece. He slides a photo out of it. He hands it to Graham and goes over to the window, pulls the curtains back to let in the last of the light. Graham sits down on the sofa. Dim blurry print, digital. It is of a couple having sex. His arse is small and pale between her dark, sturdy, paint-smeared thighs. Her face is swoony with pleasure. And it is Mara. His face is hidden, but there is no doubt that it is himself.

'I warn you, any violence and Cassie will immediately become familiar with these.'

He can hear Cassie, back in the kitchen again, the regular chop, chop, chop of knife against wooden board.

'What do you think?' Larry walks over to him. Stands above. Graham will not look up. Larrys voice is filled with glee. 'What is that absurd expression? Gobsmacked,' he says. 'Don't think I've ever seen anyone look *gobsmacked* before.' He waits, his legs twitching in their pale pressed trousers. Graham squeezes his eyes tightly shut and sees red. Energy pumps through his arms, he stands up but Larry has backed off. Is over by the door before he can take a swing at him.

Larry tuts, hand on the door handle. 'Now, now,' he says. 'Can't we talk like civilised people? Won't beat about the bush. You behave or I show Cassie this rather splendid image. Deal?'

'*Behave?*' Graham goes over to the grate and flicks his lighter at the print. It's not readily flammable and takes several flicks until it catches, the image shrivelling away to ash. He drops it in the grate.

'Plenty more where that came from,' Larry observes. He's

half out the door. Something in Graham could almost laugh. 'Now, I'd like you to spend another morning with Mara. Tomorrow, shall we say?'

Graham pauses. 'How did you take it?'

'Trade secret. Now come on, let's see how Cassie's doing in the kitchen.'

Graham shakes his head, stands up, then goes for him. Larry's out the door, tries to slam it but he's misjudged Graham's speed and he gets through after him. Chases Larry through into the kitchen, gets him smash on his jaw and he falls backwards, just goes down; crash of his head against the stove, spray of blood sizzling on to the hot plate where the kettle is rising to a boil, immediate sausagey smell of cooked blood, bubbles rising and charring black. Larry slumps down beside the stove, blood coming from his head, eyes shut.

Graham goes back into the sitting room, takes both envelopes from the mantelpiece, brings them through and stuffs them into the flames inside the stove. The flyscreen bangs and he jumps up. Cassie stands in the doorway, open-mouthed, arms full of white washing.

'Graham!' she wails. Drops the washing. 'Oh my –' She drops to her knees beside Larry.

Graham's legs give way. He gets on to a chair, puts his face in his hands. Maybe passes out for a second. Deafening fizz in his ears. Fist burning *again*, skin split. Stink of burnt blood.

'Gotta get out,' he says. Goes out the door, looks back, Larry slumped, Cassie kneeling, white clothes on the floor. Steam from the kettle. He walks away from the house and into the dark. Air is warm around his feet and legs; cooler, higher. Maybe his fist is bust. Takes a breath. A couple of stars have come out. The moon gleams like a dead old tooth.

Thirty-two

The kettle hisses. Cassie gets up and moves it off the hot centre. Black-flaked bubbles. The smell mixing with the chopped onions on the side. Larry is unconscious but not dead. She takes his limp hand, tries to pull him into a more comfortable position. She gathers up some of the shirts and bundles them under his head for a pillow. At least they're clean, like dressings. Dark blood soaks into them. They'll be ruined. Yella pushes in through the screen. He comes across to Larry, whines, sniff, licks his face.

She doesn't know what to do. What do you do? You phone someone, an ambulance, but there is no phone. She thinks of the radio. The keys are clipped to his belt. For his own good she should go through. Radio and bathroom – get some stuff for his head. For his own good. Antiseptic or something? The wound is underneath, can't bring herself to turn him. She's ashamed. Just leave it. Head wounds bleed a lot, she remembers that from somewhere. They look much worse than they are.

'Larry?' she tries – not a flicker. His face is grey, but he's breathing quite steadily, she watches the rise and fall of his ribs. His eyelashes are stubby and grey. He's bitten his lip, fleck of blood, shiny swelling. She unclips the keys from his belt. A heavy bunch. She stands up, giddy from crouching. She goes to the door and looks out. Almost dark. A clear evening, moon up.

The sound of an owl. Mara's door shut. Should she take her anything? Should she *tell* her? She squints across towards the trees and sees movement.

'Graham,' she calls, not too loud. She beckons him. He walks towards her, feet dragging like an old man's. He says nothing, goes into the kitchen, stops and stares at Larry. He sits at the table. He looks so unlike himself. So pale.

'You still haven't eaten anything,' she says.

He shakes his head. Looks at her as if she's mad. Half his hair has come out of its rubber band and hangs beside his face. His fist, lying on the table, is bruised. Flies buzz over the table, over Larry.

'We should see if we can radio for help,' she says. She holds up the keys. He nods weakly. 'Look,' she says, 'you *must* eat something.' She opens the biscuit tin. 'Have a flapjack,' she says.

'Couldn't.'

'Eat it.' She puts it on the table in front of him with a glass of water. Stands by him while he chews and swallows. 'OK?'

'Yeah.' He looks at Larry again. 'Christ,' he says. 'He slipped – I didn't mean *this*.'

'Shhhh. Come on. Oh, we'd better take a light.' She lifts the globe of a kerosene lamp and lights it. Not quite dark yet. The wick smokes and the flame flutters till it settles, throwing a soft yellow glow.

They go into the hall. She fumbles about with the keys until she's able to unlock the study door. A clustery, sick excitement rises inside her. First thing they see in the lamplight is a picture of the two of them, pinned on the wall. A black and white print. It is themselves, naked, making love. Taken in their room, on their bed. Not very clear but it is definitely them. Cassie's eyes are closed, her mouth open in a smiling grimace, as if she is in agony.

The blood drains from Cassie's face. 'The *pervert. How?*' In the shadows thrown by the lamp Graham's face scares her. She looks round. There is a radio; a computer; shelves of audio tapes; files. It's so neat, she's never seen anything so neat. Everything labelled, dated in black ink, his minute, cramped but *oh so neat* handwriting. She props the door open so they can hear – just in case.

'Can you work the radio?' she says.

He tears his eyes away from the picture. 'Dunno.' He leans over. 'What will we say?'

'There's been a fight, that's all.'

Box files marked with dates. Photographs. She shudders. One marked CORRESPONDENCE. She takes it off the shelf and opens it. Sees at once her own writing. A card to Patsy. *Miss you so much. Why don't you write?* 'My God,' she says, '*Graham*, these are our letters and stuff.'

He makes the radio hiss. 'Mayday, Mayday,' he says, pressing something.

'Stop pratting about. *Look* – he never posted anything!' She sees her own words: *Graham and me – why don't you write – it's all so strange.* She shuts the lid, opens another file. More cards and letters. She picks one out. The same parrot postcard she'd sent – thought she'd sent – herself.

Darling Mum and Dad,
Mum, you would die at the dirt! Could you send me some more T-shirts – very cool ones and that old broderie anglaise dress? I asked Larry, Dad, no he doesn't play golf! Think time's going to go pretty slowly. Keeping up my French. Will write more later. Miss you tons. Lots of love, Lucy. (And Ben) [added in another hand].

Cassie fights to keep her voice level, 'The others. What do you think happened to them?'

'Can't work this bloody thing.'

297

She looks round. Fear prickles like sharp fur down her back.

'He can't hurt us now,' Graham says, touching her hand.

'Let's see what we can find out. *Now*, while he's out of it, quick, just see if we can find out what the hell's going on. Keep trying the radio.'

She pulls one of the cassettes off the shelf. '*26th October: location 1.*' She shoves it in the machine. Sits down in an office chair that swivels under her weight. Presses 'Play'. A long silence, a hiss of noise, a clunk: something dropped. A voice says *Shit! Graham, what you doing? Taste this, salty enough?* The voice is tinny and odd but still hers. Sound of hissing, clattery movement. *Great*, Graham's voice. Her laughter. *Your face!* She switches if off.

'The sensors,' Graham says.

'What?'

'In the rooms.'

'What?'

'We've been bugged. The *fire sensors*.'

The breath catches in Cassie's throat. The fire sensors? Surely not, he wouldn't do *that* – but all the times he seemed to know things he couldn't know. His little talent for reading situations. Her hair almost seems to lift from her head. Maybe. *Yes*.

Graham switches on the computer. 'Don't,' she says, stomach clutching up with fear, 'Let's not look, there might be things –' But the computer starts up, goes through its codes, files appear on the screen. He opens a document file, closes it, opens another. It is called Spycam.

'Oh yeah,' Graham breathes. 'Here we go.'

On the screen is an outline plan of the buildings, a blinking light to indicate the sites of camera and recording equipment. He clicks on the kitchen and there it is, seen from a high, oblique angle: a button invites him to 'take'. He clicks again on the shearers' shed and there is their empty bed, covers all messed up just as he'd left it, seen from above. Cassie hugs her arms and shudders. Neither speak as Graham switches locations. They see Mara slumbering, oddly lit, grainy like a film of nocturnal creatures on the telly – infrared?

'So that means he could sit in here watching us –'

'Too right he could. The fucking perv. The *weirdo*.'

She puts her hand on his shoulder. 'Don't look any more, Gray.'

'Hang on.' Graham closes Spycam but clicks on another file marked 'Data'. He stops, lifts his hand to his mouth, leaving a sweaty film on the mouse. 'Christ.'

Cassie leans over to see.

25.10 Subjects 3 and 4. Approximately 500 mg XX32. Prolonged sexual activity.
26.10. S3. Complained of moderate headache.
30.10. S4. Withdrawn.

A list of such entries, dated from shortly after their arrival at Woolagong.

'What?' Cassie says. She doesn't get it. Graham scrolls so fast the screen's a blur.

15.11 S4 1000 mg XX12. First usage. Usual dose, behaviour consistent with previous experiments. Repeated invitations to S4.

Graham starts to speak but they both freeze as they become aware of a sound in the kitchen. Of footsteps coming down the hall. Nothing they can do. Slow footsteps followed by the clicking of the dog's claws.

*

He stands in the door frame behind them and they turn. Graham swivels the chair round and stands up. Cassie edges towards him and reaches for his hand. Larry takes a step into the room. His neck, shoulder and all down one side of his shirt are dark with blood. The dog follows him, sits down and scratches, thumping its leg against the floor and groaning with pleasure.

Cassie swallows. 'Are you . . . all right?' she says. 'We were trying to radio for help.'

'A touch concussed.' Larry's eyes flick round, taking in what they've seen. 'That was unfortunate, was it not?' He looks at Graham.

'You should lie down,' Cassie says. She forces herself to look into Larry's face. Sharper even than usual, pale, shadowed beneath the eyes. One side of his lip swollen where his tooth went in.

'What – what's this all about?' she manages to say.

Larry frowns. Runs his hand back over his hair, spreading blood. Looks at his hand with distaste, wipes it on his trousers.

'You've been bugging us! *Spying!*' Her voice rises.

'Clever system, don't you think? Modelled on a security system. With the addition of audio, of course.' Larry glances at the pinned-up print. Cassie's nails serrate her palms.

'You've been *drugging* us, man,' Graham says.

'Is *that* why –' Cassie stops.

They both look at her.

'Yes?' Larry says.

'What?' Graham says.

'Why I've been feeling so –' She looks down.

'Amorous?' Larry supplies.

'You've been *experimenting* on me. On *us*!'

Larry picks up a silver pen and clicks the propelling mechanism up and down.

'Why?' Graham says. His mouth sounds dry. She swallows, dry too, desperate for water.

'These are important experiments,' Larry says. 'I have Mara, of course, but obviously I require an interaction of subjects. I like to observe.' He clicks and clicks the pen. There is a long pause.

'So,' Graham says at last. 'What now?'

'Well, of course, it's over,' Larry says. 'Once subjects are aware of their experimental status – a shame you have to be so curious. Why are subjects so curious? If you could just accept the status of subject, just *be*, then all would be well. As it is –' He spreads his hands as if helpless in the matter.

'You're *mad*!' Cassie says.

'I suggest you get on with things now,' Larry says. 'As normal, as it were. Fred will be here soon, and I've a funny feeling –' he lifts one of his winged eyebrows, 'that Mara will be hungry.'

'What was the experiment about?' Cassie asks.

Larry lean himself against the desk. 'No harm now, I suppose. In layman's terms, the effects of chemical alteration on psychosexual behaviour and pair bonding. Subject 4 has provided fascinating data. And Subject 3 has shown an interest in pharmaceuticals herself.' Larry smiles at Cassie. 'Haven't you?'

Graham frowns between her and Larry. '*What?*'

Larry steps towards the door but Cassie is there before him. She blocks his way and pushes the door so it shuts behind her. Larry's hand goes to his head. 'I rather think I do need to sit down,' he says, face grey, bubble of spit in the corner of his mouth. He lurches towards her and with all the strength of her fear and revulsion she shoves him, two hands hard against his chest. His pale eyes meet hers for a moment and then he falls, Graham could have caught him but he steps aside and Larry falls back, crunching his head against the corner of the desk.

Graham stares at her, at Larry, back at her. Cassie's hand rises to her open mouth. Larry lies still a moment, eyes empty. Yella licks his face, sniffs at the pooling blood. Larry hauls himself up and sits down heavily on the chair. His hair flops over his eyes in a stiff plume, exposing the carefully hidden bald spot. The chair swivels away from them, exposing the caved in skull. He makes a gurgling noise in his throat as if about to speak, then exhales, falls forward, head bumping on to the desk. The dog whimpers. The pen that was still clutched in Larry's hand drops to the floor and rolls across the wooden boards.

Thirty-three

They sit in the kitchen. Dim bulb casting grubby shadows. More flies than usual. A tall dance of them, complex column, dark sickly buzz. In the corner, a pile of bloody shirts.

'We've killed someone,' Graham says. He's said it many times. Always with the same wondering inflection.

'It was an accident,' Cassie says, again.

'Was it?'

'It was,' she says firmly. 'A fight and then an accident.'

They've been round it and round it and done nothing. Presumably Larry will still be lolling forward on the chair, the same expression on his face, the stuff still coming out of his head – or maybe stopped now.

'The wounds are in the back of his head,' Graham says, his voice thick. 'That looks like murder.'

'*Accident.*'

'We've killed someone.'

'We should go.'

'How?'

'Car.'

'We can't just leave Mara.'

'No.'

The time passes and the conversation circles round like the flies. 'Perhaps we should put him somewhere cool,' Cassie says.

'Where?'

'Dunno.'

'Tomorrow.'

'What about *rigor mortis*?' She whispers the words and gets a terrible urge to giggle.

Graham gets up to fetch the Scotch from the pantry. Jerks the bottle towards Cassie but she shakes her head. Just the thought of it makes her want to heave.

'Getting drunk's not going to help.'

'Say something obvious, won't you?'

'Don't get at *me*.'

She swallows down a sick feeling, remembers with a lurch of shock the life that may be starting up in there. The little bloodspot of dividing cells. That must be protected.

He takes a slug of whisky. Rolls himself a fag.

'Cassie, we've *killed* someone.'

'It was him or us,' she presses her palm against her flat stomach, 'maybe. What do you think happened to the others, Gray?'

He lights his fag and breathes in, stares at her, furrows between his brows. 'What did he mean?' he says.

She looks away. 'About what?'

'About you taking an interest –'

'I dunno. He's mad.' *Was*, she thinks. She brushes crumbs from the table on to her hand then drops them on the floor.

Yella clatters out through the flyscreen and nudges his bowl about with his nose. Cassie goes out on to the veranda to feed him. The moon sails high in a cloudless sky, the hens roost, an owl cries, the night proceeds as if nothing's happened. Something has to happen. Could they sit here for ever like this? Stuttering in the moment like a stuck film.

'I guess we should go to bed,' she says when she goes back in. But they don't. And eventually something does happen. They hear the sound of Fred's ute. Almost a relief. Neither speaks. They go out on to the veranda to watch the approaching ball of dusty light. They stand close but not touching, the whisky bottle dangling from Graham's hand. It seems like hours before the ute appears through the dust, stops and Fred emerges.

'Hey,' he says, slamming the door. Cassie winces at the reverberation picked up by the iron roof and her fillings. He lifts out an eskie and a couple of bags. Puts them down on the step and rubs his arms. 'I could murder a coffee, love.' He comes up the steps. 'What's up? Got held up, didn't I? Told Larry I'd be here hours ago.'

'Come into the kitchen,' Cassie says.

Fred follows her in and sits down, stretches his legs, spreads out his dusty toes. 'Got some of them custard creams,' he says, 'and steaks for a barbie – too late for you folks? We can have them tomorrow.'

'Listen,' Cassie takes a breath ready to speak but Fred is doing a double take at Graham. His face is the colour of ash.

'Christ, mate, you look rough. Where's Laz?' He catches sight of the pile of bloody washing.

'We –' Cassie begins but Graham overrides her.

'We had a fight,' he says, his voice dry. 'Me and Larry, it was – we were drunk.'

'Larry, fight? Don't make me laugh.' He looks around. 'Where is he?'

'He's dead,' Cassie says, calmly.

Fred pulls a face, as if it's a joke. But, seeing their expressions, stops.

A long silence.

'Stone the flaming crows.' Fred gapes at them. He gets up from his chair, goes over to poke the bundle of darkly stained washing with his foot. 'Let's get this straight. Larry's *dead*. Where is he?'

'Study.'

'Where's Mara?'

'She's fine.'

'It was a fight,' Graham says, at the same moment Cassie says, 'An accident.'

305

'Get your story straight.' Fred looks from one to the other, almost a smile on his face.

'I killed him,' Graham says.

Fred pads round the kitchen, stops by the window. The kettle starts to whistle.

'Why?'

'Told you, a fight,' Cassie says. 'Then an accident. See –'

'Don't explain.' Fred says.

Cassie moves the kettle off the heat. The whistle falls to a sigh. Fred blows, shakes his head. 'You *sure* he's a goner? Wouldn't put it past Larry to come right through that door.'

They all look up at the door.

'We've *killed* someone.' Graham sounds as if he's just waking from a dream.

'Snap out of it, mate,' Fred says. 'Maybe I should take a look?' Nobody speaks. 'Right.' He stands bracing himself for a moment, goes out, a door opens and shuts and he returns. Goes to the sink and presses a hand over his mouth. 'Christ,' he says. 'You have and all.'

Cassie makes coffee for the two of them, avoiding with her eyes the charry black flakes on the hot plate. Fred stands with his back to them, staring at the window.

'Did you know,' she says, 'that he was spying on us? That he was *drugging* us? Doing some so-called *experiment*.' Fred turns, his face expressionless. 'You *did* know! I thought you were –' *straight*, she wants to say, *thought I could trust you*.

Fred opens his mouth as if to speak but shuts it again. He sits down, pulls the mug of coffee towards him.

'What happened to Lucy and Ben? All their letters are there! All our letters! We thought you were posting them.'

The sugar trickles from Fred's spoon and dissolves into the black. He takes a breath as if to speak and stops.

'What happened to them?'

'Calm down a bit, love.' Fred speaks quietly, face bleak in the tired light. He sighs. 'Lucy was an overdose, accidental, got carried away with his flaming experiment. Ben – well, he had to go too.'

'Go?' Cassie's voice quavers.

'Took 'em to Wagammara.'

'To Ziggy,' Graham says.

'Nah. He keeps his nose clean, lucky bastard.'

'Do you mean their *bodies*?'

'Bottomless pool, least that's what the Abos say.'

'But why –' Cassie starts, 'why didn't you go to the police?'

He grips his thumbless hand, like a wounded bird, in the other, looks at her a minute before answering. 'Told you about me missus and kids. Didn't tell you I was smashed, did I? Out of my skull. And it wasn't just them. Ended up inside, fair enough, but I couldn't hack it. Escaped – only a screw got hurt – accidental but he died later – so I was – reckon I still am, wanted. Four people dead. Four. Not one of them meant.'

He goes across and dabs at the pretty painted faces of his wife and daughters with a stubby finger. Struggles with his voice before he carries on.

'And Larry found that out. Got it out of me – maybe spiked me beer, I dunno, one night I got talking and couldn't flaming stop, could I? Then once he knew he paid me to do stuff. And if I didn't go along with him . . .' He spreads his dust-ingrained palms. Cassie looks at the tender dip where his thumb should be. She can feel the slow beat of her heart.

'After the others, I said to Larry: no more. He promised. No more. Would have topped him, if I'd had the nerve.' He throws his head back in a mirthless laugh. 'Four stiffs on me plate and I was too yellow to do Larry in. Deliberately,' he shudders, 'kill. Got the shock of me flaming life when I walked into the kitchen and saw you,' he nods at Cassie, 'looking so much like –' he hesitates, 'like the *other* it wasn't true.'

'You could have warned us,' Cassie says flatly. Tiredness is aching through her suddenly. No idea what the time is, her wrist too heavy to lift and look. Fred looks at the floor. His sweet bare feet on the filthy floorboards.

Graham mutters something.

'What?'

'Car keys,' he says. His lips look dry and flaky. 'He told me to get us out.'

'Not many tears'll be shed over Larry,' Fred says. 'I'll take him to Wagamarra.'

'But we have to call the police,' Cassie says.

'Listen,' Fred brings a hand down and the cups jump. 'You tell the cops and it'll go like this. I'll be banged up. Mara – Christ knows – and you – you might both end up inside yourselves.' He leans back. 'Or you keep your gobs shut. Go back home. Get on with your lives. Your choice.'

Cassie stares at him. It can't be that easy. 'But what about their – the others – their parents? They need to know –'

'Do you know how many people go missing in the outback, love? They was just another couple of idiots who got out of their depth. That's what their families'll think. But you tell the cops and we'll all be up shit creek.'

Cassie frowns, tries to think straight. 'So you mean just – *forget it*? Graham?'

But Graham doesn't answer. His injured hand lies on the table, puffy purple knuckles. He looks so pale.

'Have some sugar,' she says, 'sugar for shock.'

Graham shudders. 'Drink your coffee,' Cassie says. 'Go on.' But he takes another swig of whisky.

'Hey, mate.' Graham starts as Fred reaches for his arm. 'Look at me. Larry got what he deserved. With his sick games and his sick experiments. You got away with it, right?'

'If we just *went* – what would happen to Mara?' Cassie asks.

Fred gets up. 'I'll see if she's awake.'

'Wait,' Cassie says, 'if we hadn't – if the accident hadn't – then would *he* have,' she swallows, 'killed *us*?'

Fred goes out. The crash of the screen sends a shiver through the snarly column of flies. She could get the spray out and finish them off, the buzzing is driving her crazy. But somehow she can't. She can't kill a fly. An ugly smile stretches her mouth and she realises how stiff her face is, her jaw. She yawns her mouth open and it clicks. Graham swigs from the whisky bottle. 'Please don't get drunk,' Cassie says. 'Drink your coffee.'

'Will you shut up about the fucking coffee.'

She takes a sip of water. Even the smell of the coffee makes her belly buckle. She burps sourly. ''Scuse me. Need to pee.' She looks at the door through into the house. 'Suppose I might as well –' She thinks of the clean white bathroom. 'No one's going to mind now, are they?'

She stands in the hall and breathes in the still musty air. The door to Larry's study is shut. She is sick of this, doesn't want to be in it a moment longer. But there is no way out. She wants her home so badly she can hardly breathe. Her kitchen, her garden, her cat, her bird table, her sister, her friends. She doesn't care at this moment about anything, not what's happened, not even Graham. Just wants to be home *now*. Somewhere normal *now*. For all this never to have happened. She closes her eyes and wills, *prays* for this place to disappear, prays for her own view: gingham curtains, holly bush, blue-tits singing, the hill of trees. Snow? But when she opens them, there, of course, is the the study door, the high, dim, airless hall.

She unlocks the bathroom door, stands in the white space, the mirror reflecting her messiness back, never even washed her face or combed her hair this morning. She holds her breath against the sickly smell of sandalwood. Her teeth are dirty. She runs her tongue round them, eyes Larry's toothbrush, can't use that. *Could*. A shivery laugh.

She pees, washes her hands, splashes her face with water and buries it in a deep towel. Looks at herself in the mirror. It all makes sense, of course. She watches the reflection of her face as she makes sense of it. She is mortified to think of the things Larry must have seen, the things he must have heard, the things they said, the lovemaking – that feeling she had of being watched – that night she got wet and stripped off in the kitchen. He was probably *watching*. That night. He must have planned it. He must have watched her strip off, dropped something in her wine, watched as if took effect and then –

But now he's gone and it is over. And that is *right*. She won't feel bad about it. She looks boldly into her own eyes and takes a breath. He is gone and it is *right*.

She goes back into the kitchen, sits down by Graham. Looks up at the 'fire sensor' on the ceiling. They wait in silence till Fred comes in leading a bleary Mara, hair bushy over her breasts.

She looks round at them all with startled eyes, then gives a little moan, sits down, rests her forehead on the table. Graham stands up, he stares at Mara, at Fred, at the pile of bloody shirts. He looks so pale, bruised hollows under his eyes. He looks as if he's aged ten years. Cassie wants to get up and put her arms around him, but he goes out.

'What shall I do?' she asks Fred.

'Dunno.' Fred sits down heavily. 'Cup of tea, Mara?'

'A nice jam sandwich,' Mara says, suddenly sitting up.

'What?'

They all look at her. 'A sandwich. With jam.'

'OK.' Nobody else moves so Cassie gets up, watches herself get out a loaf, butter, a jar of jam and then, seeing the dark, clotted colour of it, push it back. 'No jam,' she says, 'honey?' As she slices and butters, her mouth begins to water. The bread is crumbly and textured with sunflower seeds, the butter is cool. 'I think I might,' she says, amazed at the sudden healthy hunger that rises in her. 'Anyone else?' She slices all the bread and makes a stack of sandwiches, oozing with honey and they eat, stolidly, wordlessly, chewing their way through them as if it is some kind of labour.

Thirty-four

F red gets up and stretches. The wads of khaki hair under his arms are sodden; his vest stained; he reeks of sweat. They all smell of staleness and fear, the flies snarl about in it, happy as – happy as – there *will* be flies on Larry now. Cassie bites her finger-ends, directs her mind away from him, from the flies, from everything, down to the spark inside her. The possible spark. Safe now. Home soon. *Home*. She forces her mind into order. Into what next.

Mara moans and puts her face on the table.

'Does she need anything, do you think?' Cassie asks, nodding at the pills.

'Nah,' Fred says. 'Let's see how she does without them.'

Mara sits up. 'But Larry says I need my medication.'

'We'll see how you do,' Fred says. 'What about a bath, eh? In the proper bath.'

Mara smiles, cautiously at first but then it spreads. 'I *could*, couldn't I?'

Cassie gets up. 'That would be good, if we could get clean, but –' She can't bear that soap, that sandalwood, the smell, even the thought of the smell. 'I'll get my own soap,' she says.

She goes out. It's dark. The moon hiding its face in a rag. She breathes the fresh air. It's very quiet. She walks round to the shearers' shed. Her legs don't feel like her own. The shearers' shed looks like a stage set, plonked there in the bush, moonlight flat on its roof. She goes to the sink. Two bars of soap: lily-of-the-valley and coal-tar; can't decide. She stands for a long time, a bar in each hand. If she can't decide between two bars of soap then how will she proceed? How will her life proceed? Coal-tar *soap*, what a strange idea. Whoever thought of making soap out of coal tar?

She looks at the door. Graham in there? Should go in and see how he is. She turns, suddenly fearful, to look back at the dark shape of the house. Where Larry is. She drops the lily-of-the-valley soap and goes to find Graham.

No candle. He's invisible but she can smell the fear on him and the whisky. He should have a bath too. Then he'll feel better. They must get clean. With the coal-tar soap. Once they're clean then they can proceed.

'Graham,' she says into the dark; she steps cautiously across the floor, sits on the bed, feels him tip towards her. He doesn't speak. She puts her hand out, touches something – his arm. She closes her fingers round it, warm, rubbery. She sits listening to the quiet, to his breath, to a faint creak from the pump.

'Can we do it?' she says, not entirely clear what she means. Can we keep our mouths shut. Our *minds* shut. She strokes her thumb along his arm, the soft hairs, her eyes becoming accustomed to the dark. She can see the dim shape of the white cardigan. This is something they can never tell another person. She can never even tell her *sister*. Is that possible? There's never been anything in her life she hasn't told her sister. Only Graham will know. She and Graham will be locked into this secret for the rest of their lives. Can they *do* that? 'Can we do it, Graham?' she says again.

He doesn't answer, maybe he's right, maybe now it's best to stay apart, stay separate, keep the knowing in their eyes inside their own eyes, let it all die down and focus on – on what comes next. Anyway he's probably too out of it to think: ill, knackered, drunk. He needs to sleep, like Larry said, sleep is nature's healer. That was one true thing he said.

She squeezes Graham's arm and gets up. There's something she really has to know.

She goes out and hurries back through the darkness with the soap in her hand, keeping her eyes away from the back of the house. When she gets in it seems so strange – so oddly normal – the door open to the hall, the sounds of voices and water running in the bathroom. She goes to the open bathroom door. In the steam, Fred stands behind Mara, brushing her hair. They don't see her at first. A lump rises in Cassie's throat, the tender way he brushes right from the root down to the ends, smoothing it after each stroke with his wingless hand. The water tumbles silvery and plentiful into the bath. Fred turns.

'I'll leave you to it. Got to –' he looks down, 'sort some stuff out.'

'After you,' Cassie says to Mara. 'Would you rather be alone?'

Mara shakes her head.

'You stay with her,' Fred says, 'she's had a shock.'

'We all have.' Cassie feels suddenly weak. She sits on the wide lip at the end of the bath, watches Fred pull Mara's hair into a ponytail and twist it up so it won't get wet. He does it so well, as if practised, but then – Cassie thinks of the wife, the two little daughters. 'I'll never trust myself with another person again,' he said once, but he will trust himself with Mara, she can tell, the way he touches her, as if with a kind of relief.

Fred tests the water with his hand, turns the taps off and goes out. Mara steps into the bath and slides down, wide hips wedged against the sides, backside squeaking against the bottom. She shuts her eyes with the pleasure of it. Cassie watches bubbles rise from her skin and fuzz the water. This may be the last time she has alone with Mara. And there are things she has to know. *Focus.* Mara seems blurred in the dim steaminess, her brown body gleaming, breasts lolling lazily down her sides.

'I need to ask you something,' Cassie says.

Mara's eyes snap open like a doll's. 'I'm sorry,' she says. 'Some of the things I've done – I don't know – just know I'm sorry.'

Cassie frowns. What has Mara done? She does almost nothing.

'Mara,' her voice comes out more sharply than she intends, 'I want to ask you something.'

'What will I do now?'

'Mara, please listen. *Concentrate.* I don't know how to say this. You might hate me but I have to know. Do you think it possible – do you think Larry might have,' she searches for another word but there really is only one word for it, 'do you think he might have raped me when I was drunk or drugged or –'

Mara's laugh is like the sudden shock of breaking glass. She sits up and the water surges up and splashes Cassie's thigh.

'What?' Cassie says, rubbing the wet with her hand. 'What's funny?'

Mara settles down again. Sighs. 'Course he would. He could never get it up type of thing with someone *conscious.*'

Cassie waves her hand as if to part the steam which seems to have invaded her head. If I am pregnant then, it could be Larry's, she thinks. A simple plinkety plink of a thought that changes everything.

'Oh.'

'And he likes his pictures.'

Cassie squeezes her eyes to shut out the waxy warp of Mara's wet body. It won't be Larry's. It is hundreds of times more likely to be Graham's. But it *could* be. There will always be that tiny chink of doubt. Fred comes in and Mara's face turns to him. Grey-faced, he goes to the basin and washes his hands, lets the water run over them for a while before he turns. 'Come on love, get washed up, let Cassie have her turn.'

Mara smiles up at him. 'Yes.' But she doesn't move.

He makes a fond, disgruntled sound in his throat, comes over and picks up Larry's soap, rubs it between his hands, ready to wash her.

*

Graham wakes and for a moment has no idea where he is. Feels like his head has been scooped out, his limbs turned into sand. And then a bird screeches and he recognises the heat of the baking room, the sun straining through the curtains. He opens his eyes. Cassie not there. He elbows himself up to sitting, feels so crap he can't believe it and then he remembers. He looks down at his bruised hand. Can hardly believe that it is true but it must be true.

They have killed Larry. Between them they killed him. *Killed*. His heart curls up inside him as if to hide its face. He lies down again, stunned, hardly even able to think until he's so thirsty he has to get up.

The sun already sizzles the ground, the distance wavers. The chickens crowd up to him. Cassie's not fed them. He finds her in the kitchen, on her hands and knees, emptying the fridge.

'What?' he says, looking at the jars and bottles, bowls half-full of stuff, old vegetables.

'Thought I'd sort it before we go. Look.' She waves some rubbery celery at him. 'Can't leave Fred and Mara to sort it.'

He swigs some water straight from the tap and sits down. 'The chickens,' he says.

'In a mo.'

He watches her bottom in its faded cut-off jeans move back and forth as she reaches in to wipe out the fridge. The floor, he notices, has been washed, a tang of disinfectant in the air, the mop airing by the door, its crazy head stained pinkish. He looks away, gets up, puts on the kettle. Top of the stove scrubbed clean too. She must have been up for hours. Or maybe she never came to bed.

'Where's Fred?' he says.

'He's gone –' She hesitates, sits back on her heels, but doesn't look at him. 'He's taken the – he's taken Larry to that place.'

'Wagamarra.'

She stands up and dumps a load of stuff into the compost bin. A cloud of flies rise and buzz. She goes out to do the chickens. He's being useless and he knows it. He sits, hands limp, listening to the slight rattle of the heating kettle; watching the flies settle down in the bin.

'Where's Mara?' he says when she comes back in.

'In the bathroom I think.'

'Cassie,' he starts.

'Right,' she says, rubbing her hands on her thighs, 'we haven't got long. When he gets back we're off. Airport. I reckon we've stuff to sort out, don't you?'

He stares at her but she doesn't look back at him. 'Have a bit of breakfast. You must be starved.' She puts a loaf on the table in front of him, butter and a knife. 'I thought we could have a fire.'

'What?'

'There's a lot of things we wouldn't want anyone to see, don't you think?'

He looks at her.

Mara comes in, her hair in wet snakes round her shoulders. She's wearing a towel tucked round her like a sarong. She half smiles and sits down at the table. She smells like Larry, his soap or something.

'Coffee?' he says. She nods. 'Cass?' Cassie sits down. Looks as if someone has suddenly pulled the plug on her energy. The dog comes in. He looks up at them and whines, puts his head on Mara's knee. Graham watches the dreamy way she strokes him.

'How are you feeling?' he asks.

She smiles at him, her eyes flinching off his. 'All right,' she says.

Graham makes the coffee, but Cassie pushes hers away.

'I'll just have water,' she says.

'Do you think he was putting it in the coffee?' Graham says, remembering the strong and bitter doses Larry brewed him before his mornings with Mara.

'All sorts I should think,' Cassie says. She stands by the sink and gulps a mug of water. 'Anyway, when you've finished, let's get the stuff out of the study.'

When he's chewed through a piece of bread, Mara takes the mugs and plates to the sink and runs the tap. He watches her for a moment. Strange to see her doing something.

'Come on,' Cassie says. He follows her down the hall to the study. She hesitates a moment before opening the door and then takes a deep breath and flings it wide. His eyes go straight to a dark stain on the floor. Otherwise it is just as it was when they went in – only last night? They stand for a moment. He tries not to breathe, probably only imagining a trace of sandalwood in the air. Cassie reaches over the desk, takes down the picture of them on the bed and rips it in half.

'We must destroy all the evidence,' she mutters. He has a sudden urge to laugh. Sounds like a line from some poxy movie, but he gets a hold of himself. Cassie picks up one of the files marked PHOTOGRAPHS. His heart lurches when she seems about to open it, but her fingers stop at the catch. She looks up at him, her irises flooded almost black. 'Let's not look at *anything*,' she says. Their eyes meet for a second and then skid quickly away.

They lug out all the files of photographs and correspondence; the notebooks; the audio tapes; the computer, scanner, printer, everything, and pile it all on the ground a safe distance from the house. Cassie brings out the blood-stained washing and, he notices, throws on top the white Egyptian cotton shirt. Fred arrives back, slams the door of his ute and does a thumbs-up. Graham feels a strange sensation inside him, like something snapping and falling away. So that's that then. Larry has *gone*.

Fred leads Mara out to watch. 'Go on, mate,' he says and Graham tips half a can of kerosene on the pile and flicks at it with his Zippo. They all stand back as the bonfire roars into a sudden whoosh of life: things exploding; glass splitting; plastic warping; stench of acrid smoke; soaring embers and flakes of ash. Like fireworks. In the face of all this vivid destruction some shred of Graham wants to cheer, or do a war dance, but Mara, standing with her hand in Fred's, looks sad and blank, and Cassie's expression, flickering in the flame, chills him to the bone.

Thirty-five

G raham wipes his brush on his sweater. Knee-length woollen thing, holey and paint-smeared, more paint than wool, Cassie says. On the canvas: red ridges, deep crimson tinged blue, thick; the delicious oily stink of linseed in his nose; fag pinched in his mouth; excitement unfurling in him as the colours work. The pebble in his pocket – he can feel it like a throb – as his hand, his eyes, his arm, build and thicken the land, feel of the land, the bush. The light is bad. Snow blotting the skylight but the light he needs is burnt into his brain. And though it's cold, the paraffin heater not doing more than taking the edge off the chill, he's as hot as he works as if toiling under the blazing sun.

He sucks in the last wet smoke from his dog-end and grinds it out. Stops himself immediately rolling another. But he does paint better with one in his mouth so he gives in, rolls it, lights it, breathes in the fresh hot smoke. Takes a swig of the cold coffee. Good sign when you forget to drink your coffee.

He squeezes out a worm of cobalt, dips in the edge of a palette knife to bruise the crimson lake before he wedges it on. Will take an age to dry. Satisfaction, this is. Coffee, fag, quiet, work. Nothing like it when work is a part of you. Without it a part of you missing. Which it has been. On the plane home he'd written to his parents, just a scribble on a card. Not said much, just Happy Christmas, let's be in touch. Given them his number and in a few days, whenever the phone rings he'll be on edge, he knows it. Hoping.

He can hear Cassie moving about downstairs, the toilet flushing. He feels wary of her, as if he doesn't quite know her any more. Always thought her soft. Softer than himself. An image keeps coming back to him unsettlingly: her face by that fire. And her face on the plane had been *steely* almost. Deep frets between her nose and lip, her sun-bleached eyebrows. 'We have to *forget*,' she'd said, 'and get on with our life.' *Our life.* He'd looked out of the window at the coast of Western Australia and his eye had snagged on a hook of land, a sand bar, dots on it tiny, too tiny to make out. Maybe people, maybe animals, maybe cars.

Cassie and Larry, did they, did they? He shakes the question from his head. He will never know and she will never know about Mara and what the hell should it matter now?

Brilliant red snaking through the blue. Colour practically hissing off the canvas. It's *something.* Can't wait to show it to his mates, to Jas. Last night, when Cassie had finally got off the phone from Patsy and her mum, he'd rung Jas. 'Did it work out then, Cassie's ultimatum?' she'd asked.

'Not sure.'

'Guess what!'

'What?'

'*Guess.*'

'*What?*'

'OK. I'll give you a clue. Think of the L-word.'

'Lampshade?' he'd guessed. 'Linguine?'

She'd laughed. 'No, you prat. *Love.*' And she'd told him about a guy she'd met at an exhibition and how they'd clicked just like that. Jas in love. A complicated feeling had spread through him, hearing that. She'd sounded quite unlike herself. But he is glad for her. He *is.* He needs to move a bit, come to

320

think of it, it's *freezing*. Not just the fag making his breath come out as smoke.

He goes downstairs, shoves his feet into the boots by the door and scrunches out into the snow, sending the birds from the feeder scattering.

*

Cassie pulls the last few things from the rucksack. Tomorrow Patsy's coming to stay and bringing Cat back. Then she'll feel properly at home. And she's got something to tell Patsy, something big. She hopes she's got the will power to keep it to herself for one more day. She wants to tell her face to face. She tips out the empty mirror frame – must get that fixed – and something else rattles in the bottom. She reaches in. A phial of pills. She frowns. A sensation like a big cold fingertip traces down her spine. She sits on the bed, turns the phial in her hand and watches the pills tumble. It's like something carried out of a dream and over into the real, solid, world.

She hears Graham running down the stairs, banging out of the door. Smell of smoke, well, he will smoke when he paints and he *is* painting. They've been home forty-eight hours and she's hardly seen him. She looks at the pills. Did she really consider –? No. No, that's all over. She takes them into the bathroom, unscrews the lid and watches them trickle out into the toilet. They do dissolve easily, just like Larry said, a brief fizzing and then nothing, nothing but clear water, but still she flushes the toilet just to know that they have really gone. That that is *over*.

She goes downstairs and puts another log in the stove. It's *so* cold. *You will acclimatise* floats to her from somewhere and she shivers. She makes a cup of peppermint tea and picks up her notebook. She's been planning a new layout for the garden, started it on the plane. And she's planning new sessions on composting and mulching. Work to do. She curls up on the window seat. No birds on the feeder – Graham's scared them off.

She looks through a frame of ivy leaves at the garden, at Graham, who is staring up at something. She looks but can see nothing. Oh, she is fat with news. Not told him yet, can't tell him till she's told Patsy. She likes the feeling of it, like a secret sweet hidden in her cheek. She wants to suck it a bit longer.

The phone rings and she gets up to answer it, carries it back to the window seat.

'Are you pregnant?' Patsy says and Cassie is stung with irritation. 'Only I woke up this morning with that feeling and it's certainly not me.'

Cassie can hear Katie babbling. Outside, Graham is kicking scuffs of snow away from a patch of lawn. What's he doing? She frowns.

'Say something then!' Patsy says.

'Sorry, I'm a bit dopey.'

'Jetlag.'

'Yeah. You OK?'

Graham has brought the ladder out of the shed. He carries it on to the green oval he's cleared.

'More to the point –?' Patsy waits a moment then sighs. '*Be like that then.*'

Cassie hugs her knees, the phone jammed into the crook of her neck. She watches Graham hold the ladder in both hands and tilt his head back. The streaks of paint, scarlet, orange, yellow, vivid blue on his sweater, sizzle against the snow. A streak of red in his hair. He's got a fag pinched in the corner of his mouth and his eyes squint against the smoke, squint in concentration as he steps up on to the bottom rung.

'You're right, of course,' Cassie says. 'Did a test this morning. I *am* pregnant. Wanted to tell you tomorrow.'

Patsy shrieks. 'I knew it. *Fantastic.* Oh that's fantastic. And I *knew.*'

'Well, you would!'

'What does Graham say?'

Cassie swallows. 'Haven't exactly told him yet. Look, got to go, Pats,' she says. 'See you tomorrow. Don't forget Cat.'

'Course not! Get that champagne in the fridge. Oh Cass, I'm *so* glad you're back. We were *so* worried. Spoken to Mum again? She was all for phoning the police you know – if you hadn't got in touch soon –'

'She told me. But we're OK. We're *fine*. See you tomorrow, Pats.'

Cassie puts down the phone. Now she's told Patsy she must tell Graham. She goes upstairs to the bathroom and retrieves the pregnancy-testing kit from the bin. She looks again at the white stick: in the little plastic window, a blue ring. Positive. For definite. Should go out and tell him. Shout it up the ladder at him. But there's a little shadow fluttering above her pleasure. Just a small cloud, smudge of doubt. 'No,' she says aloud. No *way* it could be anyone else's, no *way*. She will *not* think that, will never, ever entertain that thought again.

Ivy leaves are crammed up against the tiny bathroom window, each one cupping a tiny frill of snow. She peers out between them. Graham has reached the top of the ladder now. He looks so small from here, hair black against the snow, sweater brilliant: her man at the top of his ladder, swaying.

Afterwards

In the hospital lobby, Graham waits by the coffee machine for a fawn stream to fill a plastic cup. Bright out here after the subdued lighting of the birthing room. A buzzing neon tube. Green carpet stained with slops. He carries the cup outside, settles on a concrete wall, rolls himself a fag. Yeah, yeah, he will give up but if a guy can't have a fag after – he frowns at the hundreds of fag-ends on the ground.

Smoke hot, dirty in his lungs, great hit of nicotine. Coffee tastes like shit though. A car drives past, grey growl of engine. Ordinary. A pigeon with a withered scarlet stump pegs up to him but he has nothing to give. It pecks amongst the fag-ends, gives up and flings itself upwards. Graham puts his head back and blows a ring of smoke. The sky is like lemon sorbet, a pinkish weal where a plane has been.

Wishes he could get back to work. Soon as Patsy turns up he will. Cassie won't mind. Exhibition coming up. He runs his hand through his tangled hair, breathes in the sour whiff of fag-ends, exhaust fumes, his own sweat. Baby here now. Should he ring his dad and say, 'Hey Grandpa'? Can he say, his son? When she'd told him she was pregnant there was a question he should have asked but didn't. And it's too late now. But he'd seen the flinch of irises round inky pupils as she looked straight back. They'd held the gaze a moment and she had broken it.

Looked down. He'd noticed the fan of white creases where her squint lines had escaped the sun.

And now. Where are the feelings he should be feeling? They say your child's birth is the greatest thing you ever see. But he was – will never admit it to her or anyone – repulsed by the pain, the blood, the smell, the sound of tearing flesh. No. It's just that he's exhausted, shagged, knackered, wiped out and nothing much is happening where his heart is. Once *Larry* was born, he thinks. Once *I* was. He looks at the palms of his hand, each line ingrained with paint, deep red and umber, two maps of a burning land.

He takes a last deep suck and drops his dog-end on the ground among the others.

*

Cassie sits in a side ward eating rice crispies with cold milk and white sugar. Not something she would ever usually eat, a thick frosting of crunchy white sugar on the crispy hollow grains, but at that moment, a moment of stillness, leaning back against her pillows, listening to the snap, crackle and pop, it seems like the best thing, the most perfect food ever.

She shifts on the tight soreness of her stitches. It's getting light. Soon the rest of the ward will wake and start its day. Other babies will be born. And hers will not be the newest any more. And elsewhere in the hospital, probably, people will die. She swallows sweet milk, puts down her spoon, listens to the crackling of her cereal. She can't hear the breath of her baby in the plastic cot beside her but she can see the slight rise and fall of his chest. People will die, people do die and whether it is in hospital or whether it is somewhere else, it is all the same in the end. She frowns the thought away. She's good at frowning things away, two lines have grown between her eyes, she sees in the mirror every day, with the effort of the frown.

She looks at the tiny face, head the size of a grapefruit, the flutter of a delicate nostril. She searches the features for a look of Graham but he looks like nobody, just a newborn baby. Just himself. Her heart lifts. Because whatever happened happened in the past and this is *now*. The past is dead and this new person, this baby boy, he is *alive*.

*

The early morning traffic starts to thicken. An ambulance stops outside. Graham gets up, walks a little in the strange light. Cassie will be cleaned up and stitched by now. In the birthing-room, her need and pain had overwhelmed his own. That's all it was. Not that he can't feel. He turns back. Nothing open yet so he can't buy flowers. Doesn't matter, Patsy will be here soon enough with lorry-loads. He goes back into the hospital, back up the stairs.

Cassie is sitting up in bed with a bowl of cereal. Beside her a transparent plastic cot. She looks done in but kind of radiant, her hair brushed back from her damp face. He bends and kisses her.

'Where've you been?' she says.

'Just needed a, you know, moment.'

'Yeah.'

There is an aching pause. Obvious to both of them that he hasn't properly looked at the baby. Hasn't held him. She searches his face and opens her mouth as if she's got something big to say. His heart almost stops.

'Graham –'

'Let's have a shooftie then,' he says, fast.

He hears her trembly outbreath. They wait and listen to the moment pass. He bends over the cot.

'Why don't you pick him up?' she says.

'Can I?'

'Course you bloody can!'

He lifts the baby up. Afraid to look at the face. It, he, is a soft warm *minute* weight in his arms.

'He weighs – nothing.'

A tiny hand flails, baggy skin, fingers like bird claws. He lets it clutch his painty finger. Such a *grip*. Looks at the nails, ragged, papery sharp. He carries the baby over to the window, takes a breath and looks down into the red screwed-up secret of a face.

ACKNOWLEDGEMENTS

I would like to thank Bill Hamilton, Alexandra Pringle,
Liz Calder and Andrew Greig for their editorial advice.
This novel was completed while I was Writer in
Residence at the Cheltenham Festival of Literature
and the University of Gloucestershire.

A NOTE ON THE AUTHOR

Lesley Glaister teaches a Master's degree in Writing at Sheffield Hallam University. She is the author of nine novels which include *Honour Thy Father*, winner of the Somerset Maugham Prize and a Betty Trask award, *Easy Peasy, Sheer Blue Bliss* and most recently *Now You See Me*.

READING GROUP GUIDE

A free six-page guide to *As Far As You Can Go* for reading groups is available to UK readers. The guide contains discussion topics, background to the writing of the book and suggestions for further reading.

To order your guide, please send an email to:
readersgroups@bloomsbury.com
or log on to: www.lesleyglaister.com
or write to:
As Far As You Can Go Reading Group Guide
Bloomsbury Publishing Plc
38 Soho Square
London
W1D 3HB

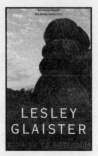

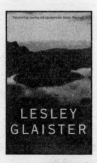
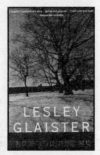
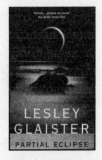
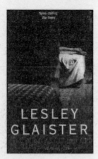